CW00351022

THE FIFTH SECRET

Also by Joanna Hines

Dora's Room
The Cornish Girl

THE FIFTH SECRET

Joanna Hines

Hodder & Stoughton

First published in Great Britain in 1995 by Hodder and Stoughton
A division of Hodder Headline PLC

10 9 8 7 6 5 4 3 2 1

British Library Cataloguing in Publication Data

Hines, Joanna
Fifth Secret
I. Title
823.914 [F]

ISBN 0-340-59650-3

Typeset by CBS, Felixstowe, Suffolk

Printed and bound in Great Britain by
Mackays of Chatham, Chatham, Kent

Hodder and Stoughton
A division of Hodder Headline PLC
338 Euston Road
London NW1 3BH

For
Diane, first reader, and
Valerie, companion from the early days.

With my usual misplaced optimism I was feeling almost cheerful [illegible] the day on which we heard the news [illegible]. [illegible]

[illegible] could have been better [illegible]

[illegible] had eleven thousand letters [illegible]

[illegible] But at breakfast [illegible]

[illegible]

[illegible]

As he glanced at each envelope and placed it on a pile [illegible] now permanent scowl of anxiety [illegible] deeper. Against my better judgement I peered across the table to watch. Today's jolly bundle consisted of four reminders of bills that should have been paid weeks ago, two circulars urging us to spend money we didn't have and had no likelihood of ever getting and yet another [illegible] letter from the bank implying that our present [illegible]

[illegible]

[illegible]

'Our accounts,' I said.

[illegible] surprise. [illegible]

[illegible]

1

With my usual misplaced optimism, I was feeling almost cheerful at the start of the day on which we heard the news about Esme. There was no indication, to begin with, of the changes and upheavals ahead. Okay, so the prospects could have been better: as this was the first day of half term, Laura and Billy would have unlimited time in which to perfect the art of sibling rivalry; outside the house the rain was coming down in torrents and, best of all, we had eleven thousand lettuce seedlings that had to be planted out in the main glasshouse. But at breakfast time I still felt able to rise above such petty inconveniences.

Owen was sorting through the post. Even in his frayed sweater and faded jeans he was startlingly attractive. You'd think that after knowing him since childhood and nearly seven years of marriage I'd be used to it by now, but watching him perform mundane tasks never ceases to fascinate me, like a stolen glimpse of one of Botticelli's angels carting out the rubbish.

As he glanced at each envelope and placed it on a pile in front of him, the now permanent squiggle of anxiety between his eyebrows grew a fraction deeper. Against my better judgment I peered across the table to watch. Today's jolly bundle consisted of four reminders of bills that should have been paid weeks ago, two circulars inviting us to spend money we didn't have and had no likelihood of ever getting and yet another petulant letter from the bank implying that our present financial doldrums were only the result of our own lack of consideration for them. I noticed that not one of the several firms who owed us money had seen fit to send us a cheque.

'The bastards,' I said.

To my surprise, Owen grinned, that sudden smile of his, like unexpected sunshine. 'So that's where he got it from,' he said.

'Who?'

'Billy called the postman a bastard yesterday. A clear case of blaming the messenger.' He turned to our son who, having finished his cereal, was gazing at his father with the slack-jawed stare of a four-year-old who has some trouble breathing through his nose. Owen explained, 'The postman only carries the letters, Billy. It's other people who send them. Besides, it's not a good idea to call people bastards. It tends to be counter-productive.'

Billy sniffed loudly, climbed down from his chair and went round the table to scramble on his father's knee.

I groaned. 'Can't you just tell him not to be so bloody rude?'

Owen's smile had vanished. 'Like smacking children to stop them hitting people, you mean?'

Whether he does it deliberately or not, Owen's knack of remaining reasonable at all times can be intensely irritating. I said, 'Don't be so damn logical. You're ruining my breakfast.'

'Sorry.'

'And for heaven's sake don't apologise. Can't you see that just makes it all worse?'

I caught a glimpse of his anger before the shutters came down. Laura had been observing us both intently. Now she leaned forward slightly towards her father and said, 'And bloody's bloody rude too, isn't it, Daddy?'

He patted her hand absent-mindedly before tipping Billy off his knee. Then he stood up without a word and began clearing away. His face had that rigid look which it got when he was being especially self-controlled – which recently had been a good deal of the time – at least in my company. I watched him as he ran water into the sink and washed out the mugs and bowls and set them upside down on the draining board. He worked with his customary calm deliberation. When he was a boy, he'd had the kind of appearance that makes old ladies grin and chatter like idiots. He still had the tow-coloured hair, the dark fringe of lashes around eyes that were somewhere between hazel and green, the delicately modelled features, but as he'd grown into adulthood the wide-eyed candour had given way to an expression that was reserved to the point of coldness. The combination of sensitivity and reserve was one which women of all ages seemed to find irresistible. Owen, of course, was always far too high-minded to notice the effect he produced, and probably considered his appearance to be quite ordinary.

Now, as I watched him, I no longer knew if I loved or hated him. I only knew that when I was with him I was always uneasy and often, as now, when he had failed to respond to my goading, there was a dull ache somewhere between my ribs. I was no longer entranced by his good looks; rather, I was exasperated by his immense stubbornness, his refusal to admit the error of his ways. Why else had he still not admitted that our marriage had been from the beginning a desperate mistake?

'I'll do that,' I said, as he began spooning food into a saucer for Drongo the cat.

'I've done it.'

My irritation cranked up another notch. I slouched a little lower in the chair and resisted the urge to flick a toast crust at Drongo's tabby head. I said, 'Why don't we leave the lettuces until tomorrow?'

'They're late already.'

'I know that.' The day's fate was sealed. 'God, I hate lettuces. In fact I loathe and despise them. Why any sane person would want to buy one I cannot imagine. I bet they're bad for you. I bet they're riddled with salmonella.'

Owen said merely, 'I'll make a start.'

'I think I'm developing an allergic reaction to lettuces.'

'Oh?'

'The skin on my hands keeps breaking into these terrible red blotches.'

'Wear rubber gloves.' Owen was already pulling on his overalls. 'Come on, Billy, you can help me set out the trays.'

Billy rammed his feet into his red boots and clumped out after his father, past the cement mixer and the concrete blocks and out into the driving rain. My good spirits were ebbing fast, driven into full retreat by the prospect of yet another day spent trailing in the wake of Owen's chronic perfection. I sighed. Fat Albert would still be snoring in bed at this hour of the morning. Fat Albert was a favourite creation of mine, an imaginary contrast to Owen the impossibly Good. I sketched him fondly on the back of the letter from the bank. Fat Albert was a selfish slob who lolled for hours in front of the television and who could never see anyone else's point of view except his own. He scratched his paunch through a dirty vest and belched frequently. He shouted a lot and had a loud laugh and dropped lighted cigarettes in the dregs of coffee mugs. In my Fat Albert fantasy I coped heroically and gained the sympathy and admiration of all my friends.

I thought what fun it would be to spend the morning painting a picture of Fat Albert (or Sweet F.A. as I called him privately) on the wall above the washing machine. A sunny picture, Fat Albert on his holidays in the Costa del Sol, all sunburnt beer gut spilling out over gaudy trunks.

Fat Albert would not be seen dead eating lettuce.

Nor would Fat Albert have fathered a child like Laura, who stood before me now. At the age of six she was in many ways the living spit of Owen, same bleached hair, same delicate features – and the same exquisitely reproachful face. Her fragile beauty tugged at my heart, but the moment she opened her mouth, her words jarred on my conscience.

'I've got nothing to wear,' she grumbled, '*again*. All my clothes are dirty.'

'What's wrong with those?'

She glanced down scornfully at her hand-me-down trousers and a sweater that had become matted with overwashing. 'But suppose we go out?'

'It's not very likely.'

'But still, we might.'

My failure as a laundress had been a constant grievance with Laura ever since her teacher, as part of a Mother's Day project, asked the class to say who made sure their drawers were always full of freshly washed clothes. Laura had been about to exclaim, 'But they never are!' when a chorus of voices shouting, 'Mummy does!' gave her the first hint that she might be missing out.

I was rummaging through a sea of dirty clothing on the bathroom floor when, above the drumming of the rain, I heard the unmistakable sound of glass breaking, followed, more ominously, by a child's high-pitched wail.

By the time I reached the glasshouse, Laura was explaining to a tearful Billy that being *nearly* hit by flying glass was no reason to make a fuss because it didn't actually hurt. Shards of broken glass were scattered over the freshly prepared soil.

I crouched down to comfort him.

'There, Billy, it's all right.'

'That's what I told him,' said Laura primly, 'but he wouldn't listen.'

'He's had a shock.'

'Well, I know that.' Laura had begun to pick up the icicles of glass.

'Don't!' I shouted. 'You might cut yourself.'

Laura was contemptuous. 'I'm not a baby.'

Owen was striding towards us down the length of the greenhouse and his face was white with anger.

'Did you catch them?' I asked.

He ignored the question. 'Laura, don't touch that glass, you could cut yourself. Christ, Jane, why didn't you stop her?'

Laura snatched back her hand as if it had been stung and eyed me smugly.

I said, 'You didn't catch them, did you?'

'Not this time.' He picked Billy up and hugged him protectively, before adding, 'But I will.'

When we had first seen the old walled kitchen garden with its neat paths and its old-fashioned sheds (and the former gardener's cottage which was to be our home), we had not speculated as to why every pane of glass in the place had been broken. The purchase price had been adjusted accordingly and the local glaziers called in. Only then did we discover that the lane beyond our high wall was a short cut used by people walking from the village to the new estate and, during the years that the property lay empty, local children had fallen into the habit of lobbing stones over the wall for the satisfaction, I suppose, of hearing the crash of broken glass. We heard their giggles and occasional cheers, but by the time we had sprinted all the way down to the front entrance and round, the lane was invariably deserted. It was the first indication that running a commercial nursery entailed a whole range of problems that had nothing whatsoever to do with the growing of plants.

And now it was more than just a nuisance, it was scary. Beyond the closed space of the OJ Nursery lay a hostile world which chucked danger at us over the walls. I was beginning to feel like a helpless member of a wagon train encircled by marauding Indians. But since the local police had shown little interest in our problem so far, where was the cavalry to come from?

'It's not safe for Laura and Billy out here,' I said.

'They'll be all right. The kids never come back twice on the same day.'

'It doesn't *feel* safe.'

Owen shrugged and began distributing polystyrene trays of lettuce seedlings down the length of the glasshouse. Rain was still drumming on the roof and sluicing against the windows. Nowhere is one so numbingly conscious of bad weather as in a commercial glasshouse. The rain streams over the roof, it gushes down the sides, water drops and leaks and splashes through every pane of cracked (and broken) glass, every ill-fitting joint. The cold makes the wet wetter and the wet makes it colder. Sometimes it's like trying to work under the onslaught of Niagara Falls. On a bleak November morning like this one, the din of the rain is loud enough to muffle the chatter of our teeth.

People who observe us at our work on balmy summer days imagine that we inhabit some enviable rural idyll. 'Oh, you are lucky,' they gush. They observe the children skipping around in the walled garden with their little spades and barrows, they see the fresh air and the healthy exercise and the proximity of nature. 'It's not all sunshine and flowers,' we protest, but they only smirk their disbelief. No one visits in winter – too snug in their 'boring' offices, I suppose – so they never see us with our numb fingers and chilblained feet, they never see the mountain of unpaid bills, our frantic and not always successful efforts to fend off damp and mildew and mould and rot.

I picked up the pieces of broken glass and noticed that the pain had come back in the joints of my left hand. Wonderful, I thought, not even thirty yet and already I'm arthritic. Just as I was convinced that no hidden shards remained to gash us as we worked, I heard the customer bell.

Against all reason, my spirits began to lift as I plunged out into the rain and ran down paths between rows of neatly ordered pots towards the lodge. A customer meant a potential sale, rare at this leanest of all times of year, a potential sale meant the prospect of money. Perhaps that gnomish-looking old man with the grey moustache and the tightly belted trenchcoat who was reading a leaflet from the Hardy Plant Society was about to request, cash with order of course, five thousand assorted primulas for the spring.

I greeted him warmly. He eyed me with suspicion.

'I'm looking for a Christmas tree,' he said.

My heart sank. 'We don't grow Christmas trees,' I told him, 'and anyway, it's far too early.'

'I especially wanted one now.'

'Sorry.'

'What do you have then?'

'Primulas,' I said firmly. 'This is a specialist primula nursery – primroses, polyanthus, cowslips, lots of interesting varieties for waterside plantings—'

He interrupted me. 'I suppose I could make do with a poinsettia.'

'Then I'm afraid we can't help you. However, if it is an unusual gift you're looking for, the obconicas will be ready in a month or so and they make wonderful house plants—'

'I told you,' he whined, 'I want something now. You're not being very helpful.'

'Maybe you'd have more luck at the garden centre on the other side of—'

'I imagined you'd be glad of the custom. I do live locally, you know.'

'How nice for you.' The words were out before I had a chance to censor them. And the tone of voice was all wrong.

His beady eyes swivelled furiously and he tugged at the belt of his trenchcoat. 'There's no call to be rude. I can see I'm wasting my time.'

I was overcome with remorse. 'Oh, no, please, I'm sure I can find something that—'

'And I shall definitely warn other people not to come here.'

I gave up. 'You do that.'

He huffed his outrage – if he had been a bird all his feathers would have become puffed up. He was probably working himself up for a major confrontation when he caught sight of Owen approaching and, believing (quite wrongly as it happened) that Owen would take my side, he turned up his collar against the rain and set off towards his shiny German car.

My brother Lucien's voice floated dreamily through my head:

> 'Hold off, unhand me, grey-beard loon!'
> Eftsoons his hand dropt he.

I must have said it out loud by mistake because I saw the man's shoulders flex involuntarily before he thought better of it and got into his car.

Owen arrived in time to see him drive off. He has long doubted my ability to deal amicably with customers.

'What was that about?'

'Just a grey-beard loon looking for Christmas trees.'

'What on earth for? We haven't had Guy Fawkes yet.'

'That's what I was trying to explain. Still, maybe we should see it as an omen. There's bound to be more like him. We ought to buy in some trees and sell them on. You never know, we might even make some money at it.'

Owen winced as if I'd suggested a devilish pact. 'We're trying to run a nursery, Jane. That means we grow what we sell. This isn't a shop. And besides, we don't have the space to grow Christmas trees.'

'Only because you've filled every inch of room with bloody primulas.'

'It's called specialising.'

We were poised on the brink of a familiar argument, familiar especially at this time of year. Late autumn is always the hardest. The primulas are still small green rosettes of leaves in their thousands of pots. By December the first ones begin to flower, the obconicas and the midwinter primroses with their magical, gloom-defeating range of colours, tangerine and lilac and fluttering nail-polish pink. By March, when the main sections are coming into flower, I am seduced anew: from the stolid-looking circle of leaves an Eastern bazaar of colours erupts: black-eyed Cowichans and purest whites; russets and ochres, flame and earth and sunset reds; indigo and aquamarine and clearest summer azure, tiny jewel-bright primroses and old-fashioned cowslips with their scent of long-forgotten pastures and wine-making abundance. But at this moment, that miracle of renewal lay far away. ‘

I was only prevented from making a detailed critique of Owen's philosophy of market gardening by the jangle of the telephone, its reinforced bell clanging loudly throughout the garden. My relief at being able to retreat to the house with a clear conscience lasted only until I heard my mother's voice. She was talking with the urgency that spoke of her full and interesting life, so could I please stick to the business in hand.

'Jane, dear,' she trumpeted, 'if anyone started acting suspiciously around the nursery, you would tell me, wouldn't you?'

'Not necessarily. Why?'

'Then you haven't seen anyone peculiar? Or had any odd phone calls?'

Only this one, I thought. I said, 'What sort of odd, Faith?'

'Surely it's perfectly obvious if someone is acting suspiciously. You'd know at once.'

'What made you think of this today in particular?'

'I was only speaking hypothetically. But as you've not had any trouble, there's no need to worry.'

'Another window was broken this morning.'

'Honestly, Jane, you should have got that sorted out by now.'

'How?'

'I mean, Laura or Billy might be injured.'

'Really? Do you know, I'd never thought of that.'

'Sarcasm, Jane. I'm only trying to help. And you must promise to tell me the moment you see or hear anyone suspicious.'

'Why? Why the sudden concern?'

'There doesn't always have to be a reason. Surely I can phone to see how my grandchildren are once in a while. How are Laura and Billy, by the way? You never bring them to visit.'

'You're welcome here whenever you like.'

'It's not easy, with Eric being so busy.'

'Oh, God, how disgusting.'

'What?'

Drongo, our exquisitely marked tabby cat, was sitting by the back door while, with a gourmet's fastidiousness, he crunched the skull of what had until recently been a small furry animal.

'It's only Drongo being loathsome.'

'Sometimes, Jane, it's hard to follow your train of thought,' said my mother as she hung up. Which was rich, I thought, coming from her.

Though I should have been hardened by now, I found my mother's veiled warning, coming so soon after the stone-throwing, to be distinctly unsettling. Danger was stalking through suburbia. Talking to Faith often made me feel as if the wires in my brain had become crossed and were sizzling furiously, but today there was the added bonus of an unspecified menace so that, at the sound of the back door banging, I started nervously.

A woman's voice called out, 'Hello-o! It's only me.'

No one was less threatening than Dinah. Her figure could have been described as stout, except for her air of compactness, like some neat and sturdy mountain pony. Her plump breasts and hips contrived to fit snugly inside her crisp Guernsey sweater and her pressed cord trousers. A decorative scarf was held in place at her throat with an amber brooch. She had well-behaved brown hair which grew back off her face and was held in place, as today, by a variety of bows and buckles in tortoiseshell and velvet. She had a face which signalled health and a good-natured personality, a much underestimated brand of attractiveness.

I saw in her arrival a temporary reprieve from ordeal by lettuce.

'Hello, Dinah. Hello, Duncan.'

'Hello, Jane.' Duncan's pale gaze roamed listlessly round our kitchen. There are few things quite so mortifying as a child's critical scrutiny. Adults could surely be relied upon to observe that our kitchen was 'full of potential' and that the mural I had begun above the vegetable rack would one day be a witty caricature of a Dutch still life. Duncan, I could tell, saw only that our kitchen units were on the verge of collapse and that the floor needed sweeping. Duncan had none of his mother's robust neatness. Rather, he resembled his father, Aidan, who was a solicitor with a City firm of accountants. One could almost imagine that those blue shadows under his eyes were the result of late hours spent wrestling over litigation files, rather than a preference for computer games over fresh air.

I said, 'Do you want some coffee?'

'Just a quick one or I'll be late.'

'Why the hurry?'

'I'm having my hair done in an hour. You said you'd have Duncan for the day so I've arranged to have lunch with a friend.'

'Oh, God, I forgot.'

'I can't change my plans now.'

Dinah looked piqued and I hastened to reassure her. Laura and Billy spent so much time enjoying the luxury of Duncan's home that the least I could do was have him for the day every now and then. The only problem was that the child quite sensibly loathed having to spend time at the nursery, which explained his depressed expression now. His home was the 'big house', one wing of it at least, and he avoided having to slum it in the gardener's quarters if he possibly could.

Dinah and Aidan had befriended us as soon as we moved in. At first Owen and I were so grateful for the occasional decent meal, bath and evening of comfort while we were struggling to start the nursery and renovate the cottage at the same time – even head gardeners, we soon discovered, were expected to endure spartan conditions that would have been the death of their tender plants – that we had not paused to consider what Dinah and Aidan were getting from the deal. Gradually it dawned on us that we were the token peasant friends who completed their picture of themselves as basically country dwellers. Aidan might commute to town every day, but his soul, or so he believed, was definitely rural. On fine weekends Aidan would don smart wellies with buckles on them and stride around the nursery with Owen, nodding thoughtfully while Owen talked of loams and acidity and late frosts. Once I even saw him surreptitiously snap off a blade of grass and chew on the stalk as an aid to meditation. It was probably a source of regret to him that we had failed to provide a five-barred gate to lean on. But although we might chafe at being cast in the role of honest rustics, we were endlessly in their debt for the amenities of life – and for babysitting, since our children were close enough in age for us conveniently to assume they were friends.

In my gloomier moments, and there was no shortage of those, I imagined that our friendship was based on Dinah's need to gloat and some masochistic flaw in my personality that compelled me always to be the gloatee. She was someone whose life appeared to run like clockwork, largely, I suspected, thanks to a heavy reliance on the advice dished out by magazines. She had a box file for handy cleaning tips and another for useful phone numbers and addresses (where to find the ultimate curtain tassel). Her freezer was stocked with neatly parcelled blocks labelled 'Chicken chasseur for one' or 'Spinach and goat's cheese filo for twenty-four'. Dinah was prepared for any contingency. By contrast, I found that even daily routine often took me by surprise.

Sitting opposite Dinah at our kitchen table, I was suddenly aware of how scruffy I must look. Chances were, I hadn't yet found time to brush my hair. Dinah occasionally claimed to envy my thinness, but beside her, it always felt like a scrawny, scarecrow kind of thinness, and I was under no illusions that I was someone who could look attractive in my shabby old trousers and sweatshirt. I have short dark hair and a narrow face which is quite without any particular merit. When I was about fifteen some kind soul told me I looked lovely when I smiled. I instantly interpreted this as meaning that I looked dreadful the rest of the time.

I said, 'Dinah, you haven't seen anyone acting suspiciously round here, have you?'

'No. Why?'

'I just had a weird phone call from my mother. All phone calls from Faith are pretty weird, but this one was worse than usual. She sounded worried, but wouldn't say why. Something about people hanging round the nursery. I thought maybe there'd been a news item about this area.'

'And has there been anyone hanging around?' Dinah glanced towards Duncan who, with drooping gait, was setting off to look for Laura and Billy.

'Only a grey-beard loon who was looking for Christmas trees.'

'A what?'

'You must know the lines:

> "Hold off, unhand me, grey-beard loon."
> Eftsoons, his hand dropt he.'

She looked at me blankly, so I explained, 'It's from *The Ancient Mariner.* It was one of Lucien's favourites – I suppose all children like it, that and the bit about the Lady of Shallot having the curse.'

Dinah had lost interest and was examining the envelope I had been sketching on. 'Who on earth is this?'

'It's an identikit sketch of the kind of suspicious character my mother mentioned.'

'I thought you said you hadn't seen anyone.'

'No, I haven't. Fat Albert is purely a figment of my imagination.'

'He's disgusting.'

Dinah pushed the envelope away and I felt quite unreasonably offended on Fat Albert's behalf. Nor was I mollified when she added, 'But he's very cleverly drawn, you know. I do think you're artistic.' I merely assumed she was trying to be kind.

She giggled. 'I thought for a moment he was a friend of yours. Oh, that's what I wanted to show you. There was a huge article about that friend of yours in a magazine I got yesterday.'

'Oh?'

But I knew who she meant at once. I had only one friend, one former friend, that people wrote articles about.

She unfolded the neatly scissored page and spread it on the table.

Rob's face, in artistically grainy black and white, smiled up at me. The image he projected was stylish but relaxed, as though he was far too absorbed in his work ever to spend time on his appearance but just happened to emerge looking terrific all the same. He was wearing a dark shirt, crisply ironed but open at the throat, and his brown hair (I knew it was brown though of course it looked black in the photograph) was expertly cut but ruffled and untidy. He appeared to be sharing an intimate joke with someone unseen; crow's feet were beginning to fan from the corners of his eyes. He succeeded in looking wise and funny and sympathetic and hugely attractive all at the same time. Quite a feat.

Rob Hallam, reluctant and unexpected media star.

I scanned the article. All the usual details had been included. His story was a good one and worth repeating, a contrast to the usual rags-to-riches saga.

He had been born in Australia just over thirty years ago, but from the age of eight he was sent to school in England. One result of these early upheavals was that to this day he could never be sure where he fitted in; he had resigned himself, in fact, to being the perennial outsider. (As I read, I realised that this had been confided to the female interviewer in a spirit of apparent intimacy, which was as beguiling as it was phoney since he 'confessed' as much to everyone.) Yet despite a continuing inner disquiet, he was outwardly successful: success at school, a respectable Oxford degree, post-graduate work and the beginning of his interest in the media.

And then – disaster.

He had been researching an item on homelessness and, with his customary care for authenticity, was sharing the conditions of the destitute, when he was arrested and charged with armed robbery. Though steadfastly protesting his innocence, he was convicted and served nearly four years of an eight-year sentence before a combination of fresh alibi evidence and a confession from the actual culprit led to his conviction being overturned. The years in prison changed his life. What had begun as a passing professional interest in society's rejects had turned into a personal crusade. He scripted and produced a highly influential 'docudrama' based on his experience and that of the people he had met in prison. He revealed such an aptitude for publicity that for several months no TV or radio panel was complete without him. One commentator said that he spoke for the outcast in a language the Establishment could understand.

Eighteen months ago, he had found a practical outlet for his beliefs by helping to set up Branden House, a new kind of hostel for homeless offenders. There had been rumours recently that he was being approached to enter politics. In the meantime he was to host his own television programme which would combine documentary, comment and topical interviews: 'A lighter look at serious issues.'

Rob Hallam, the article said, the man who put glamour into reform.

(Rob Hallam, I thought, the man who put betrayal into friendship.)

But it was not the article about Rob, nor the photograph, that I found so unsettling. It was the smaller picture, inset at the bottom right of the page. This showed Rob standing on the gravel driveway of Branden House with some of the staff and 'guests' as the residents of Branden House were called. Again he was smiling wisely (did he ever stop?) and managing to look simultaneously attractive and deeply caring.

But that woman who stood beside him, the one with the straight brown hair and the deadpan expression, surely that was Esme?

What was she doing there? She was hardly likely to be a redeemed mugger and I couldn't imagine her being much help at the hostel. She must therefore be in the picture because she and Rob were together again.

'There's more over the page,' said Dinah.

And there it was, a photograph of the two of them walking hand in hand under some autumnal-looking trees and a caption beneath it which read, 'In the past six months Rob Hallam claims to have discovered a new security and happiness with childhood sweetheart, Esme Drummond.'

I felt a stab of something I couldn't quite explain. Not jealousy exactly. More like that sinking, left-out feeling you get when you're a child and your two best friends run off together giggling and won't let you join in. I imagined them holding hands across the table of an exclusive restaurant, imagined them going to the theatre, taking expensive holidays, laughing at shared jokes and remembering old times.

Though why should I care? After all, I hadn't seen either of them for nearly ten years.

'Ironic, isn't it?' commented Dinah.

'Which bit?'

'Well, that he should end up with the daughter of a QC after all that happened to him. It says so there.' Dinah swivelled the article round for a closer look and read, '"Obviously Rob Hallam has no grudge against the legal profession, or maybe it is more a case of canny insurance, since the number one woman in his life these days is daughter of the former QC, John Drummond."'

'Former eminent QC,' I corrected her. 'All QCs are eminent, according to Lucien.' I could hear my brother's scornful voice, 'Did you ever hear of a QC who wasn't eminent? A second-rate QC, for instance? It's like all survivors are automatically plucky and children in hospital are always little. Haven't you ever noticed?'

But Dinah hadn't. Not for the first time, it occurred to me that my brother Lucien would have been wasted on Dinah.

She asked, 'How well did you know him?'

'Rob? It's hard to say.'

'Wasn't he a friend of your brother's?'

'Yes, his closest friend.' Then I remembered how Lucien used to torment him. 'Sort of closest, anyway.'

'You told me you always spent the holidays together.'

'Only some of them.'

'And that Esme girl was there too?'

'Yes. Her parents owned the cottage we stayed in.'

'And that was by the sea.'

'No.' I was shocked. 'It was by a river. By the river.'

Dinah did not notice the distinction. 'And Owen was there too?'

'Not in the beginning. He only came the last couple of times.'

Thoughtfully Dinah smoothed the pages of the magazine and her fingers slid over Rob's cheek. She said, 'I never realised Rob Hallam was so good-looking. Not like Owen is, but still . . .'

I made a noncommittal noise. The truth was that I hadn't either. The boy with the stolid face, the boy with the heavy jaw and the blunt nose and the restless, anxious eyes had been transformed. Social crusading brought a magic all its own apparently.

'Didn't you say you used to be in love with him?'

I hadn't, of course, but Dinah was adept at sleuthing and I guessed she was hot on the trail of Famous People gossip with which to entertain her friend over lunch.

'We were children,' I protested.

'How old?'

'Eight, nine, that sort of thing.'

'But later on. You told me he was at university with your brother, so you must have seen him then.'

'We bumped into each other a few times.'

Dinah's brown eyes were searching my face. 'And you were attracted then?'

I tried my best to look sincere. 'It's hard to explain,' I said – and that much at least was true. 'I'm not sure I understand it properly myself.' True again – 'Yes, you're right, there was an attraction between us, but there was always some kind of barrier there too, almost as if it was taboo. Like being brother and sister.'

My sincere expression was in danger of collapse. Take it or leave it, Miss Delving Dinah, I thought, that's the closest you get. I could tell from her slightly squinty expression that she was convinced I was hiding the fact that Rob and I had been lovers. It might have been easier, I thought ruefully, if we had been. I could remember all the men I'd had affairs with before Owen, names, dates and sexual preferences of each one. I could remember them clearly but without much emotion, even though I had believed myself in love with at least two of them. But Rob had been different.

Dinah said, 'And the last time you saw him was at the funeral?'

'He didn't come to the funeral.'

'But I thought he'd always been like one of the family.'

'That's what we thought, too.'

'And that was when you and Owen got together?'

'Sort of.'

I preferred not to remember those early days when Owen had seemed capable of picking up the pieces of my shattered life. It was too painful. He must have been regretting his misplaced generosity ever since. None of this was to be shared with Dinah.

'Odd, isn't it,' she commented, 'that you all four knew each other as children and now you're all still together. Well, she's with Rob Hallam and you're with Owen.'

I nodded. She was looking at the smiling photograph of Rob with an expression that said quite clearly: what a pity you had to end up with the loser.

And I was annoyed because a version of the same poison thought had just flitted through my own mind.

When Dinah had driven off in her sporty little car, I returned to the main glasshouse. Duncan was squatting on an upturned flowerpot and shivering inside his anorak. Owen had already made a start on the lettuces. Billy was driving a small car in and out of the mouth of a discarded Hallowe'en pumpkin and Laura was pretending to help her father so she could bend his ear about precisely what she wanted for Christmas.

The last shreds of my early morning good humour vanished completely. I felt guilty that Owen had started work while I was sitting drinking coffee in the kitchen, guiltier still that I hadn't remembered to bring him one. It struck me as grossly unfair that as usual everyone else was having a better time than I was: Dinah warm and pampered at the hairdresser; Rob and Esme revelling in their 'new-found security and happiness' as they strolled together under autumn trees. And now Duncan, his pale face staring out from under the hood of his anorak, a frail exile from central heating and fitted carpets, made me suddenly ashamed.

I walked down the path that ran through the centre of the glasshouse. On either side of me the soil had been carefully prepared, raked to a smoothness and then scored with hundreds of precise lines. An exquisite example of horticultural crosshatching. The lettuce seedlings had been grown in individual plugs of soil and it was these that Owen was dropping at regular intervals along the rows. They looked like a little army of sugar cubes with green bows on top. Not wanting to tread on the growing area, I was obliged to wait until Owen had worked his way into the centre.

Then I said, 'This is bloody ridiculous.'

'What's the matter now?'

'How can you waste all this time on stupid lettuces when you know perfectly well we'd make just as much money if we bought in a few dozen Christmas trees and sold those?'

'We've already discussed that.'

'So what? Why make everything harder than it is already? You're just afraid we might actually make some money for a change. You have to suffer all the time, God alone knows why.'

'I'm not suffering. I enjoy the work.'

'Then you must be mad.'

He merely shrugged and set off back down the next row. Take the seedling, drop it in position, move on a step, take another . . . the thought of spending the whole day on such a mind-bendingly boring task made me feel as if steel bands of frustration were being tightened around my skull. After a few moments he was obliged to return to the centre, where I was still waiting.

'Is that all?' he asked, glancing at me with an expression that could have been one of pure loathing – it was always so hard to tell with Owen.

'No, as a matter of fact it's not. Look at Duncan, not only is he miserable as sin, he's also in considerable danger of being injured by a stone or flying glass. Maybe you don't mind putting our own children at risk, but I draw the line at other people's. I'm taking them out for the day.'

'Where?'

'My mother's.' I hadn't actually considered this before, but where else could I go that was dry and would cost nothing?

Infuriatingly, Owen just kept on working.

Fat Albert would be foaming at the mouth by now. Fat Albert and I would probably have screamed at each other for ten minutes and then we'd have been able to indulge in a thoroughly enjoyable reconciliation. Oh, Fat Albert, why did I have to end up with England's leading marital pacifist?

Owen had completed the first section of planting and was busy fiddling with the overhead sprinkler system so the seedlings could be watered in. In order to continue our somewhat one-sided conversation I had to go round to the side and join him.

I said, 'Aren't you even going to protest? Don't you mind having to do the whole damn lot on your own? Don't you ever feel as if you're going mad in here?'

'Hold this a moment, can you? There, that's done it.'

The sprinkler system whirred into life, the patter of water on grateful plantlets. Oh, God, I thought, now it's raining inside as well as out.

'Well?' I prompted.

Owen turned to me briefly and said, 'My only problem right now, Jane, is that I don't know what the hell you want.'

'I'd have thought that was obvious.'

'Tell me then.'

When I didn't answer straight away, he began to sort out the next batch of seedlings. I thought: you've got to photosynthesise to get any attention round here. But still, there was no getting round the fact that eleven thousand was a great number of lettuces to cope with alone. I began to waver, lacking even the courage of my own selfishness.

'I suppose I could stay and help out for an hour or two.'

'I can manage.'

I felt vaguely disappointed. Had I been hoping all along that Owen would say he needed me, that he couldn't manage without my help? And was he now punishing me with his self-sufficiency? Even when I was doing what I thought I wanted to do, I had the uncomfortable feeling of being somehow outmanoeuvred.

I said, 'No need to be a martyr about it. I'll stay if you want.'

He paused in his work for a moment; he seemed to be staring intently at a patch of earth about six inches from the toe of his boot. Then he said, 'You decide what to do. The children would enjoy an outing,' and carried on with his work.

He had defeated me. Was he angry? I had no way of knowing. With other people there's usually some clue, but with Owen you had to hunt for the faintest signal – a muscle flickering beneath his eye, a hand clenching and relaxing again. Often I felt like some hapless archaeologist trying to conjure up a vanished civilisation from a fragment of broken pottery.

I took refuge in hostility and scowled at his back. To me it appeared rigid with sanctimonious outrage. I tried to stem the approaching gloom by imagining a painting of 'Owen The Blessed Martyr'. It would be done in the most gruesome style of the German medievalists. His face wore its most reproachful expression, hazel eyes rolling heavenward ('How long, oh Lord, how long?') and small wonder, since he was lashed to a stake while his wife, a skinny demon with spiky brown hair and a lethal expression, danced around him and showered him with tiny green plantlets.

It was not all that consoling. Imagining paintings I'd never have the time to complete was the nearest I'd got to any kind of creative endeavour in years.

The children, with typical perversity, were less than enthusiastic about this change in plans. Duncan had descended from his flowerpot and was constructing a multistorey car park for Billy's cars out of the empty polystyrene trays. Laura's eyes dilated with horror at the prospect of abandoning her father.

'Poor Daddy. All alone,' and she heaved a shuddering sigh, 'all day long. Never mind, poor Daddy, here's Wendy to keep you company.'

The doll had been kitted out for market gardening in a pale pink ballet dress; she had hair that sprang vertically from her pink plastic scalp and breasts that sprang horizontally from her pink plastic torso. Her vacant expression remained unaltered as she was rammed up to her knees in the soft earth between two tiny lettuces.

'Thank you, sweetheart.' To Laura's delight, Owen picked her up and hugged her. 'I hope Wendy doesn't mind being watered,' he added, and they both laughed together.

Not to be outdone, Billy clumped up in his too-big wellingtons. Unlike his dainty older sister, Billy was a child who seemed to be always on the verge of disintegration, mouth agape, shirt hanging out, nose running. Now he plunged a small Cortina, bonnet down into the earth. Owen set Laura down and hugged Billy in his turn and the child's face was radiant.

It wasn't that I was jealous or anything like that, but whenever I saw Owen with the children, I always felt crosser than ever. With them he was spontaneous and natural. They enjoyed each other's company and didn't seem to need me at all. Seeing Owen laughing with them and hugging them, seeing how even the dismal Duncan became animated in his company, seeing the way Owen's face became suddenly boyish with good humour and fun, only served to emphasise how stilted and awkward his manner was when he was with me. I should feel sorry for him, I thought morosely as I bundled the children out to the van, it must be wretched living with someone you can't stand any more and being too stubborn to admit it.

'Poor Daddy,' Laura's litany remained unaltered as she scrambled into the back of the OJ Nursery's van. 'All alone . . .'

'Poor Daddy, my foot,' I snapped. 'I offered to help him but he said he was happy to do it on his own.'

Laura did not deign to comment on this less than truth, since she was busy commandeering the best sacks and the only cushion to sit on.

Duncan said gloomily, 'We've got seat belts in the back of our cars.'

I said, 'Not much use without seats.'

The van refused to start.

The children began to squabble in the back while I became increasingly outraged. It's bad enough having to drive around in a rusting and geriatric van that smells permanently of potting compost and wet leaves, but not driving around in it is infinitely worse.

Briefly, I contemplated knocking myself senseless on the steering wheel, but then contented myself by snarling, 'Oh hell,' and thumping the dashboard. The children stopped arguing and fell silent – that anxious silence of children dependent on adults who are not coping very well with the outside world.

Now I'd have to ask Owen for help. Or worse, the van had died for ever and I was trapped within the four walls of the nursery with no possibility of escape. For a moment the claustrophobia was so intense I had to fight for breath.

Laura said severely, 'You'd better get Daddy.'

'He's as useless as I am,' I said, but went to get him all the same.

'The battery's flat,' Owen said, and with those three words he encapsulated the sum total of our combined mechanical expertise. 'I'll give you a push. Make sure you park on a hill. The jumper cables are in the back.'

'I know that.'

Since we still owed the garage an astronomical amount for the last make-do-and-mend job on the van, a new battery was not an option.

One day, I promised myself, as the car juddered to life on the road that led down from the nursery and the children cheered half-heartedly in the hope, I suppose, that from now on I'd be in a better mood, one day I'll be able to visit people who don't live on hills.

The rain had eased to a steady drizzle, the wipers grumbled and squeaked, the van rattled. Normally, as soon as I was driving away from the nursery with the children, I was able to relax and enjoy their company. Freed from whatever tangle of emotions Owen always seemed to inspire in me, there was usually nothing I liked more than to join in their games and their chatter. But today I was unable to shake off a deepening sense of gloom. That all-too-familiar feeling that I was only one step away from plunging headlong into a black hole.

I can remember the first time someone – it must have been Lucien – told me about black holes: those invisible spaces where all matter is swallowed up and the darkness is so intense that light disappears inside it. And I had thought: that describes it perfectly; I have spent my whole life on the brink of one of those. I have always felt myself to be surrounded by so much that was hidden, such unexplained darkness. It was the phone call from my mother that had triggered the feeling this time, that and the stone-throwing and the encounter with the grey-beard loon. I suppose the conversation with Faith had not been much on its own, but it resonated with the memory of a lifetime of incidents that didn't quite add up: phone calls and conversations that switched abruptly the moment I came into the room; ceaselessly moving house; inexplicable remarks and unanswered questions and heavy silences and the sidelong glances of strangers. For as long as I can remember I have felt like a pawn in an elaborate game where no one, ever, would stop and tell me the rules.

Always on the outside, never quite understanding – no, not quite always. There had been an interlude, four brief summers to be exact, when I knew what it was like to exist in the green and sunshiny heart of the world.

With a little sigh of surrender I allowed myself the luxury of slipping back into the past. And I wondered to myself, does everyone do it?

Does everyone gaze back through the narrowing lens of memory to re-enter a world that was never so precious until it vanished? Does everyone have a route down which to escape the anxiety and tedium of the present – rain and bills and misread messages and arguments that no one will ever win?

I had learned to be stingy with my memories, rationing them carefully in case the images faded from overuse.

Glory Cottage, its windows open to allow in the sweet-smelling air from the orchard. The unending song of the river. The smell of damp ground, earth and moss and fallen leaves. The smooth turf between the boathouse and the willow which, for four summers, was the living centre of our existence.

Five children sprawled in a rough circle on the grass. Four are waiting for the fifth one to speak: Lucien, my brother. Lucien, the magician.

Today he says, 'You must each think of a word. The most devastatingly tremendous and awe-inspiring word you've ever heard of in all of your whole life.'

Rob shifts anxiously. 'What sort of a word?'

'That's for you to say, dimwit.'

The rush and gurgle of the river only emphasises the silence, since no one wants to risk being first – and wrong.

Lucien says, 'You're the youngest, Esme. You go first.'

She frowns. Her brown hair falls across her face and she brushes river sand from between her toes.

'Go on then.'

'Um . . .'

Owen, stretched out on the turf, his arms folded behind his tow-coloured hair, is staring up through the willow leaves at the sky beyond. Already his expression is inscrutable.

'Harmonious,' he says, almost to himself.

'Wait. Esme first.'

'Um . . .' She screws up her face to show she is giving the task her full attention. Then she smiles. 'Chocolate,' she says.

Lucien groans. 'Try again. It's got to be a word with resonance, a powerful word, a word we can build the day on, a word to have adventures with.'

She gazes at him blankly.

'A word like cornucopia or alchemy or catastrophe—'

'Okay then, that one.'

'Which?'

'Cat – whatever it was.'

'Catastrophe?'

'That's it, that's the one. I'll have catastrophe as my word.' And Esme, satisfied, sits back on her heels and smiles.

And I smiled too at the memory of Lucien's addiction to long words. Inspired by his enthusiasm we trade them back and forth like sweets.

'Effervescent,' says Rob.

'Conundrum,' says Lucien.

'Arpeggio,' says Owen.

'Mulligatawny,' I say.

'Catastrophe,' Esme says again, and everyone groans, though she could never understand why, if the word had been good enough the first time, it no longer met with approval now.

2

Wherever she happened to be living, my mother always made her house easy to recognise by the For Sale sign at the front. Lucien used to say that she moved house so often in the hope that our stepfather Eric might one day get left behind by mistake. I thought she did it from a restless need to create new backdrops for herself. Each fresh home was decorated in a different style as if it were a stage on which she could perform daily. Owen, ever practical, said she probably supplemented their income that way, buying cheaply and selling for a good price once the transformation was complete. Whatever the reasons for her normally nomadic life style, she had been in her present home, a small terraced house in a Georgian town on the south coast, for about a year, which must have been some kind of record. Now, however, I noticed the familiar estate agent's placard signalled an imminent move.

Once upon a time my mother was an actress. She had been an actress briefly, before my brother was born, and a review in a provincial paper had apparently said (I'd never seen it) that she had a voice like the young Peggy Ashcroft. To my certain knowledge she had not set foot on a stage in more than thirty years, but in her heart and soul (and voice) she was an actress still, and would be always.

Owen said she must have been very good-looking, though I had never noticed it myself. It was probably the green eyes, together with the dark hair and the fine bone structure which caused people to call her attractive. My brother Lucien was said to resemble her. I, on the other hand, didn't look like either of them. Nor did I have the faintest idea from whom I had inherited my more sombre colouring, my far from fine bone structure. From my father, perhaps. Or at any rate, from his side of the family. But on that subject, as on so many others, I had no way of knowing.

In the past few years Faith had grown somewhat stout and her hair was beginning to go grey. But she still had a presence. Even I had to admit that.

'Darling Jane!' Despite the welcome apparent in her words, her expression plummeted towards gloom as she opened the door and recognised us. 'Have you left him?'

'Only for the day. Where's Eric?'

'He had to meet someone at the club this morning.'

Unlike most golf widows, Faith treated Eric's obsession with the utmost respect, as if his endless journeying from first to eighteenth hole was a highly responsible career which often, poor dear, meant he had to work weekends too. And Eric was flattered, being, as usual, too dim-witted to realise she was simply glad to have him out of the way.

She peered round me to look at the children. Billy was thrashing a puddle with his boot and showering Laura and Duncan with water. They squealed, but did not move out of his way.

'You have an extra child,' Faith told me accusingly.

'Surely you remember Duncan. Are you going to let us in?'

She pulled open the door with obvious reluctance and watched gloomily as three pairs of small but dirty feet trekked into her hall. 'I was just going out,' she said. 'Now I shall have to change all my plans. You might have phoned first.'

'I didn't think. Sorry.' And I was too.

It was only later, when her friend Deirdre arrived, that I realised my mother had lied about going out. A lie intended to make her appear busy and me feel a nuisance. Successful on both counts.

Deirdre turned up just in time since Faith and I were running out of safe topics of conversation. I had admired her present backdrop which seemed to have been inspired by the paintings of Douanier Rousseau: a green trellis of leaves and plants everywhere with walls and curtains in twining leafy patterns. The furniture was simple to the point of being primitive, a few wicker chairs, wooden tables and benches. I had admired the shelves and cupboards that looked as if they had been constructed out of random bits of driftwood and handed to the local playgroup for painting.

I had also made a half-hearted attempt to discover what had prompted Faith's anxious phone call that morning. But, as I had expected (which was why the attempt was half-hearted in the first place), she fobbed me off with platitudes about concern for her grandchildren. Two things were certain in my relationship with Faith: one was that she never did anything without a good reason; the second was that she generally kept her reasons to herself. She wore her air of mystery like a perfume. And she had a particular way of smiling at me if I was crass enough to confront her directly. It was a bright hard smile like a shiny metallic surface that my questions bounced off harmlessly. At times she seemed almost to be daring me to pester her, so confident was she of evading my enquiries. Her keep-off smile was bad enough; worse still were her occasional lapses into reproach – the mournful, how-can-you-persecute-me-this-way-after-all-I've-done-for-you? smile which could make me feel guilty for wanting answers to even the most basic of questions. So, although on this occasion I knew my mother had something on her mind which was worrying her a good deal and, although I was pretty sure that the something related to me and the children in some way, I did not waste much time trying to find out what it was.

We had reached the point where my mother traditionally felt obliged to ask about Owen and the nursery and I, knowing only too well her contempt for our endeavours, gave an account that was more loyal than honest. Though I might criticise the OJ Nursery endlessly at home, I had no intention of allowing Faith to do the same.

So we both turned to Deirdre with relief. 'Deirdre, darling,' exclaimed Faith, 'how heavenly to see you. I hope you don't mind but Jane has turned up without a word of warning and with hordes of children. We'll have to talk properly later.'

Deirdre merely fluttered and looked embarrassed.

She was my mother's current friend. Faith unearthed a new one each time she moved house: Deirdre, Annabel, May, Selina – the names changed but otherwise it could be difficult to tell them apart. My mother seemed to have access to an unending supply of devoted female admirers. Any normal human being would have been bored senseless by such time-servers – but then, Faith's capacity for absorbing admiration had always been anything but normal.

Deirdre was admiring the Amazonian green of the stairway and the light sconces which were disguised as clam shells. The children were absorbed with the ark.

The ark was the only possession that remained from our restless childhood. Faith had picked it up in a junk shop when Lucien was tiny and as children my brother and I had played with it endlessly, scorning the bright plastic toys endured by our less fortunate friends. The animals, which stood about three inches high, were carved from ash wood and smooth to the touch from long usage. Soon an ordered line, two by traditional two, was curving across the bare boards of Faith's jungly sitting room.

Duncan, a solitary zebra in his hand, was looking about him anxiously.

'What's the matter, Duncan?'

'The other zebra's missing.'

My mother, who had been telling Deirdre how to grow African violets properly, broke off and caught my eye. We smiled in a rare moment of complicity.

'That's right,' I told him.

Duncan frowned. He was an orderly child. In a couple of years' time he could probably have qualified as a filing clerk. He jigged the zebra up and down on the floor impatiently.

'There should be two,' he complained.

My brother Lucien was smiling down at us from half-a-dozen portraits and photographs displayed around the room. In the earlier pictures he resembled a dark-haired, dark-eyed elf with his heart-shaped face and a slippery intelligence shadowing his smile. In the older photographs his expression had become more complex but he never entirely lost that elfin, mercurial something that made him so utterly different from anyone else I had ever met. His moods had always shimmered between humour and a deadly seriousness, so that even now, as I sensed his laughter in the room, I was unable to rid myself of the notion that he was testing me.

I said, 'Duncan, didn't you know? Years and years ago, when I was younger than you are now, in an incident of terrible tragedy, the second zebra was eaten by a demented Jack Russell named Bimbo. We tried to save her, but her head had been reduced to splinters and it was hopeless. So poor Mr Zebra had to go into the ark all alone—'

'—And,' unable to restrain her impatience, my mother finished the story for me, 'that's why zebras have been extinct in Sussex ever since.'

Laura, who had been tipping her giraffe forward so he could graze on a ball of fluff under the sofa, smiled her satisfaction at hearing a familiar and much-loved piece of nonsense, but Duncan was not convinced.

His pale eyes were accusing. 'But zebras aren't extinct in Sussex,' he whined. 'I saw heaps at the zoo.'

'Duncan, you are a rotten pedant.'

'I am not.'

'You don't even know what a pedant is.'

'Yes I do.'

'Jane, darling heart,' my mother protested, 'don't squabble so. You're worse than the children.'

It seemed to me, as I stumped out to the kitchen to put the kettle on, that my brother's smile, reaching out from the frames, was gloating and tinged with triumph.

See, Jane, his smug smile was telling me, when you try to recreate my magic you just get hopelessly bogged down. I could have kept them entranced for hours. I would have made the wretched Duncan weep at the fate of the poor mangled zebra. I could have told him about the wild herds of zebra that roamed between Farnham and the sea in the aeons before the Flood. I would have made him quake at the picture of the crazed Bimbo, foaming at the mouth, fangs bared as he approached the helpless zebra. You may try, Jane, as much as you like. But you'll never have my magic.

And I felt again the familiar devastation of loss. The empty place where Lucien had been and which no one else could ever, possibly, fill. The awfulness of it prompted me to irritation.

'Oh, shut up,' I snapped at the kettle as it began its peevish whistling boil.

Through the half-open door I saw my mother roll her eyes at Deirdre in mock despair at my bad temper.

Just as I had given up hope of ever being given any lunch and was beginning to cut some bread and butter for the children, Eric arrived, which was the signal for my mother suddenly to swing into action and produce ham, cheese and salad to accompany the pile of bread and butter.

Eric gave me a jocular pat on the shoulder and rocked back and forward on the balls of his feet like an old-fashioned policeman. 'Hello, Jane. How are the little monsters?'

'Fine.'

'Good. Good.'

At which point our conversation ground to a halt. Eric was never a brilliant conversationalist at the best of times. He had all the mannerisms of a benign Victorian uncle but none of the substance. He would fix people with a knowing twinkle in his eye and they would think what a jolly character he was, until they discovered that he knew very little and twinkled even less. Lucien and I had never been able to fathom what Faith had ever seen in him. Aged about ten, Lucien had announced with great authority that she had only married him for sex, but as we grew older it dawned on us that Eric, with his little military moustache and his blazers and his ties that looked vaguely as if he'd been a member of some prestigious school or club, was an unlikely looking stud. Once I heard Lucien explaining solemnly to one of his friends that our mother suffered from a little known psychiatric disorder known as 'ennuiphilia' which he explained as an addiction to boredom. He went on to award Eric a first prize rosette, which Eric, in his innocence, interpreted as a touching token of his stepson's affection, never for a moment guessing he'd just been voted the most boring man in southern England.

But though the arrival of Eric did nothing to stimulate lively debate, it did mean we were able to have something to eat. Even Lucien had always recognised that Eric had his uses.

It was during lunch that Deirdre took the trouble to ask, 'Do you have any time to do your painting these days, Jane?'

'Not much.'

'What a pity. That portrait you did of Billy was so good.'

I glowed. 'I did one of Laura a couple of weeks ago,' foolishly I was unable to resist, 'I sent it to Faith as a late birthday present. Would you like to see it?'

My mother was putting salad on Eric's plate. 'Really, Jane, I don't suppose Deirdre wants . . .'

'But I'd love to see it.' Blindly, Deirdre hurtled towards disaster.

'Oh dear, what a catastrophe.' Faith beamed vaguely at the centre of the table. 'Oh dear, this is quite dreadful. I think it may have got muddled up in a pile of magazines . . .'

'Jesus, Mother, you haven't thrown it away.'

'There's no need to overreact, Jane.'

'But I gave it to you. For your birthday.'

'I know, it was very sweet of you. And of course I didn't throw it out. How could you even think such a thing? Sometimes I wonder about you, Jane, I really do. But it was just a piece of paper. You hadn't even taken the trouble to get it framed properly before you gave it to me. You know perfectly well I'd never have thrown it away.'

'But somehow it just sprang into the dustbin all on its own?'

'Don't be childish. No one has encouraged you as much as I have . . .' (I ground my teeth.) 'I think it's wonderful that you have a hobby, everyone should have a hobby and some of your drawings are really very nice.' Seeing that she was making little headway with me, she turned to the ever-obliging Deirdre, 'All my family are artistic, you know, Deirdre, that's where Lucien got it from. Did I ever tell you that when he was eleven, his schoolmasters said they had never seen a child of that age who was such a good draughtsman? And when he was in the sixth form his art teacher simply begged me to encourage Lucien towards art school.' She laughed. 'It was horrid to have to disappoint the poor man, but it had always been perfectly obvious that Lucien was Oxbridge material. I mean, art school!' (This was said with a scorn normally reserved for a career removing gold fillings from corpses.) 'Art school would have been a quite appalling waste of his abilities.'

And I, who would have given ten years of my life to go to art school instead of the mind-blistering boredom of the local secretarial college, but somehow had never been able to insist ('Art school? You, Jane? Whatever for?'), longed for an icy and crushing retort, but my mind was so boiling with rage that all I could manage as, a little later on, I gathered the children together for a speedy departure, was to accidentally knock a particularly smug-looking portrait of Lucien to the floor. The glass didn't even crack.

My mother scooped up the picture and clasped it to her bosom in triumph.

'Poor Jane,' she crowed. 'Always the clumsy one.'

Our less than fond farewells were cut short by the ringing of the phone.

Faith pounced on the receiver. 'Faith Piper, yes?'

So far it could have been some unfortunate trying to sell loft conversions, but then, 'Oh, dearest heart, it's been such an age, whatever have you—' And then, unusually for Faith with a telephone in her hand, total silence.

And in that silence I escaped.

'Your grandmother is an unmitigated cow,' I said as I turned the key in the ignition.

'Moo,' agreed Billy, delighted that the car had started without any problem. But Laura pursed her lips in imitation of her father's disapproval.

And then her expression turned to dismay. 'Stop, Mummy. Granny Faith is waving. She's trying to tell you something.'

'Then she's too bloody late,' I said, steering the van into the traffic with such uncharacteristic panache that a Mr Whippy was forced to brake suddenly.

'But she's waving at you to stop.'

I glanced in the mirror. Sure enough, my mother was indulging in a semaphore display to which her weight did not predispose her. I grinned.

'She's probably remembered another of my defects.'

'But . . .' Laura, her face pressed against the rear window as she tried to read her grandmother's lips, was almost in tears.

'What's a defect?' asked Duncan.

Something my brother didn't have, I muttered under my breath. And then, to help myself recover, I snapped at Laura, 'Oh, for heaven's sakes, stop moaning. You know how Granny Faith dramatises everything. If it's that important she can always ring me at home.'

Sick, that's what it is, I told myself furiously, it's sick. Call it sour grapes or jealousy or whatever you like, but I will always maintain that my mother's obsession with her only son, dead or alive, was definitely abnormal. Since his death, Faith and I had fought over Lucien's white bones like two highly strung vultures, each of us determined to preserve our own version of him for posterity. And every time she extolled his perfections, every time she bashed on about Lucien the paragon, Lucien the boy genius, the infant prodigy, the wonder child, I felt my own grip on him slacken. He was brilliant, yes, I was the last person to deny that. But the Lucien whose memory I treasured had also had a gentler, a more tender side. My Lucien was the older brother who had shepherded me through the early years, the only person who had bothered to read me stories and teach me things and explain. When I started school he alone bothered to make sure I had clean clothes and brushed hair and a properly equipped pencil case. Faith had never seemed to notice such details. Only with Lucien did I feel as if I mattered.

And now, damn Lucien, damn him. The only person I had ever dared to rely on and he had died. The perfect specimen of manhood preserved for ever at his twenty-three-year-old prime. I might have missed him more if I hadn't been so angry at the terrible legacy he had left me: a lifetime of being nothing more than second best.

And what about our father? Didn't the adoring Deirdres and the rapturous Annabels ever think it just a teeny bit odd that there were no photos of our father dotted about the place? Not a single one? Not a trace?

Rex Turner, it said on my birth certificate, which I had not seen until I needed it to get married. (A virgin birth – or AI, its modern secular equivalent – had been an intriguing possibility until then, but Rex Turner was an altogether earthy name.) And they were married, too, my parents, married well before Lucien was conceived, so she must have cared for him once. And since then she had eradicated all trace of him. Not a photograph, not a whisper, not a ring or a book or a letter: my father, the invisible man. I imagined him sometimes coming to my school carol concert or sports day: he wears a suit, shirt, tie and shoes, even a homburg hat like the man in the film – but no face, no flesh. 'Hello, Jane,' the air under the hat speaks, 'I'm your father.'

Whatever he was like, this invisible Rex Turner whom I never knew and who vanished without leaving a single footprint, he seems to have set a pattern of disappearing men. First him, then Lucien, then Rob.

Owen next?

Sometimes I have to laugh about it.

By the time I had reached the OJ Nursery, my bad mood had so rubbed off on the children that they were tired and cranky. Owen must have been listening out for the sound of the van as he came in from the glasshouse almost at once. His expression was serious. I wondered briefly what it would be like if those dark-lashed eyes were to light up with a smile at my homecoming, then suppressed the thought at once. It was too painful. He looked tired, drained even. I fought down a twinge of lettuce guilt and readied myself for defence.

'Have you heard the news?' he asked.

Laura flung her coat down on the bottom stair and in so doing she contrived to swipe Billy on the nose. He roared his protest while Duncan watched with resignation.

'How the hell can I hear the news? I can't even hear myself think.'

Owen said firmly, 'That's enough, Billy. You're not hurt.'

Billy opened his mouth to contradict, then saw the expression on Owen's face and closed it again.

'Your mother phoned.'

'Already? What have I done wrong now?'

'It's not you. It's Esme.'

'Esme?' I stared at him stupidly.

Laura swooped into the momentary silence with some detailed complaint concerning her misspent day, but Owen interrupted her brusquely and told her to go and watch television with Duncan and Billy so he could talk to her mother. His peremptory manner was beginning to make me feel uneasy.

'What's all this about, Owen?'

He pushed the door of the sitting room shut after the children. 'There's been an accident,' he said, then frowned. 'No, not an accident. She was attacked. They don't know yet who did it.'

'She's not . . . ?'

'She's in a coma. She was hit on the head. They're hoping she'll pull through but . . .' Owen went on speaking. Or at least, I suppose he did.

There's been an accident.

An accident.

Those words belonged in another time, they were an old echo from the days of Lucien's fall, they had no business recurring now. Like an old tune that doesn't know when to stop. An accident.

No.

I said, 'You must have got it wrong, Owen. I saw a picture of Esme this morning in a magazine. She looked fine, better than ever. They must have confused her with someone else. Who would want to attack Esme, for God's sake? Why would anyone . . . ?'

'I know, Jane. It's hard to take it in. But it was Esme, I'm afraid. Her father telephoned Faith from the hospital. It happened earlier this afternoon. Apparently Esme had been living in that hostel of Rob's for the past few months – or in his flat, which is attached to the hostel. Of course, suspicion is bound to centre on the inmates—'

Automatically, I corrected him. 'Guests, Rob calls them.'

'They're trying to get hold of him now.'

'Rob? Who is?'

'The police. They need information on the people she might have been in contact with. Poor Rob. If it is one of his inmates – guests, I mean – then this will do a lot of damage to his hostel.'

'To hell with his damned hostel. I can't believe that Esme is lying in a coma in some hospital bed, perhaps even . . . and all you can think about is Rob's wretched hostel.'

Owen took a step towards me, then hesitated. 'Jane, I know you're upset. So am I. But it's not going to help Esme if you're just angry about it. Here—'

He raised his hands slightly, offering comfort. I wavered. Part of me ached to find refuge in the circle of his arms. But I was desperately afraid that if once I gave in to weakness I would have no protection left against the horror of what had happened.

So I backed away. 'Why shouldn't I be angry? Everyone can't be cool, calm and collected all the time. Thank God—'

'For Christ's sake, Jane – oh, what's the point.' He turned away with a shrug and said, 'I'll go and finish the lettuces.'

Now I was shaking. 'How can you even think of lettuces at a time like this? And if you tell me life must go on, I shall scream.'

'You might feel better if you did.'

'How dare you patronise me. Just tell me what happened. Where was she? What sort of attack? And what are the police doing about it? Why don't they hurry up and find the bastard who did it?'

'I expect they're trying.'

'Stop being so damned reasonable.'

'Look, Jane, you're not the only person who's upset.'

'Oh? You're upset are you? That's news. How am I supposed to know? Why can't you—'

Just as I thought Owen might be on the verge of actually betraying some emotion for once, there was a loud knock on the back door and Aidan let himself in. He had come to collect Duncan.

'Hello, you two. Don't let me interrupt if you're having a row. I can always referee.'

But the moment had passed. Owen had jammed his fists into the pockets of his overalls. He did not look at me. He seemed to be trying to collect himself. But in the gap caused by Aidan's interruption, I had caught a glimpse of the hurt and realised that he had only been saying the truth when he said he was upset about Esme. I wanted to reach out to him, but of course, I'd been such a cow just now that he would only have rejected me. Now he was safely walled up in his solitude again and explaining to Aidan what had occurred. From time to time Aidan nodded professionally and slid a glance at me to see how I was taking it.

As so often in Aidan's company, I was beginning to feel uncomfortable without quite knowing why. He was not an attractive man, certainly not a handsome one. He was as peaky-looking as his son Duncan and when we had first met I had wondered what on earth Dinah saw in him. He had wispy, lifeless hair and a face that seemed to have had all the colour sucked out of it. But his manner was at variance with his looks. He had a deep, rather seductive voice and the self-confidence of a man who believes himself to be irresistible to women. Most of the time he seemed to carry the illusion off. Once or twice I had even wondered if he was testing the waters prior to making a pass at me, but I had always dismissed the idea. I wasn't the kind of alluring female that men usually made passes at, not even grey-faced solicitors. And he and Dinah had always appeared perfectly contented in their marriage.

This evening Aidan did no more than gaze at me with intense sympathy and squeeze my hand. And his friendship was comforting. He asked if we wanted to have supper with him and Dinah, to help distract us. We both said no, we needed to stay close to the phone in case of further news.

'Drop by for a drink later on if you change your minds,' said Aidan as he collected Duncan from the sitting room. 'You're always welcome.'

'Thanks.'

It occurred to me that he was probably trying to protect Owen from having to spend an evening arguing with me. But he needn't have bothered. As soon as Aidan had gone, Owen returned to the glasshouse, without so much as a glance towards me.

Briefly, I pressed my fingertips to my forehead. The black hole was suddenly closer than ever, too close for comfort. That dark vortex into which Lucien had been swept, and which perhaps hid my father, was now threatening Esme too. I did not know how to withstand it a second time.

I began to prepare the children's supper, but my hands were shaking and my heart was bucking around under my ribcage as though it wanted to leap out and escape. What was going on? How had the attack happened? Who was it? Why was there always mystery and confusion and terrible, terrible not knowing? Stupid, stupid Esme. There's been an accident. An accident. Esme was always so careless. If there's one thing that made me really angry it was carelessness. Lucien had been careless when he tried to climb that cliff in Dorset, and now it was Esme . . . Don't these careless people ever bother to think how their carelessness affects other people? We're the ones who have to carry on and make supper for a pair of tired children while the world shudders and collapses all around us.

My mother phoned.

'Oh, my darling, have you heard?'

Her voice was at its most throaty, vibrant with emotion. There was a catch in it to show that she was deeply moved, had probably been crying. It was a voice designed, presumably, to reduce its audience to floods of tears. On me it had the opposite effect.

'Of course I've heard. Owen told me.'

'I simply can't take it in. To think of darling Esme being set upon by some maniac. The poor child is in a coma.'

'Yes. I know.'

'Her father phoned me at once. We were always so close, John and I, just like you and Esme. Oh, to think of that dear child . . . I'm going to the hospital tonight. I don't suppose there's anything that anyone can do, but I feel I must be there . . .'

My hand was gripping the phone so hard that my knuckles had gone an odd greeny white colour. I looked at them with some surprise. During the three weeks that my brother was in hospital before he died my mother hardly left his side, except to go to the Ladies to freshen up her make-up. And at his funeral she looked stunning in black. And now she was preparing to do a modified repeat performance. I wondered what she would chose to wear for her hospital visit. I knew I did not want to be there to form part of the audience. It wasn't that I doubted the sincerity of her feelings. I'm sure she was quite fond of Esme in her way. No, it was the way her emotions were tarted up for public display that I had always found so repugnant. Perhaps that was why I tended to go to the opposite extreme and totally refused to rhapsodise over Laura and Billy. Occasionally I did wonder if I'd gone a bit far in the direction of taciturnity. But it was precisely because my feelings for the children were so strong – the only part of my life that I was sure of – that I could never cheapen them with theatricals.

'Jane, are you there?'

'Yes.'

'What are you going to do?'

'Right now I'm trying to cook some fish fingers for the children.'

'Oh, Jane, always so practical. I don't know how you do it. I feel as though I could never eat again, just the thought of food makes me nauseated . . .' She broke off and I could hear her snuffling at the other end of the phone.

I imagined her devouring a huge sandwich so she could turn down all offers of food later on.

'Is that all, Faith? I am rather busy.'

'So cool, Jane,' her voice had gained a familiar vicious edge, 'I almost envy you sometimes. It must be wonderful to be so thick-skinned. Nothing ever affects you, does it? You don't know how lucky you are not to be as sensitive as I am. I feel everything so intensely and sometimes it's hard not to—'

I hung up the phone.

'Bitch,' I hissed. 'Bloody hypocritical sanctimonious theatrical lying bitch.'

Owen came in and shook off his boots.

'Your mother?'

'How did you know?'

He shrugged. 'I must have the gift of second sight.'

'Damn know-all.' I felt trapped by his omniscience.

The phone rang again and Owen lunged to pick it up before I could. 'Yes, Faith,' his voice was soothing, 'I know – must have been cut off. I think there's something wrong with the phone. Yes, I will report it – I know, we're devastated too – no, I don't suppose it has sunk in yet – no, the hospital said there wasn't any point in visiting until tomorrow – no, I haven't said anything to the children. They've never met her, remember. We've neither of us seen Esme in years.'

Nearly ten years.

Not since the funeral.

The evening brought a volley of phone calls but little further information beyond the fact that she had been struck across the back of the head with an alabaster bowl and that everyone, predictably, was devastated. The vagueness of it all was maddening, and the sense that our life could be so affected by an apparently random 'accident' only increased my feelings of darkness and muddle. The panic and despair which ever since Lucien's death had always been only a step away. My sense of foreboding was increased by the fact that on three occasions, when Owen picked up the phone and spoke, the line went dead at once. I was reminded, uncomfortably, of my mother's unspecified fears when she had rung earlier in the day. I drew the curtains against the November dark and wished that our nearest neighbours were a little closer.

Owen, as always at moments of crisis, gave no indication of what his own feelings might be, and coped admirably. Laura and Billy, perhaps sensing my own edginess, were difficult and whiny until Owen sat them both down at the piano and made up nonsense songs with them about two little notes called Crotchet and Minim. Watching the three of them squeezed together on the piano stool, Owen and Laura both so fair and beautiful, Billy round and rosy and overexcited, I could almost imagine that the darkness of the world was not so threatening after all. That we might still be a happy family.

Later, when Owen and I were lying in bed, unable to sleep, unable to comfort each other, he said, 'It's nine years, isn't it?'

'Nine years what?' Though of course I knew.

'Since we last saw Esme.'

'I suppose so.'

The memory of Esme at the funeral was somewhat blurred which was odd, because I remember all the rest of that day quite clearly: what people were wearing, what everyone looked like. But there was something fuzzy about Esme, as if she was out of focus. 'Enigmatic' would have been the charitable word to use. 'Out of it' was perhaps blunter and more accurate. But then Esme and I hadn't had any real contact since we were children.

Esme, the child, I could remember with perfect clarity.

I remembered the first time I ever saw her. Lucien and Rob and I had just arrived at Glory Cottage. All the way down in the car, my mother had been droning on about how her friends the Drummonds had a daughter just my age so she and I could play together and I wouldn't have to tag along behind Rob and Lucien all the time. I had spent the journey sunk in misery. Esther (my mother had of course got the name wrong) was sure to be a bossy, horsy sort of girl and would resent having me dumped on her just as much as I resented this blatant attempt to stop me joining in with Rob and Lucien. She was an only child, I knew that much, so she was bound to be horribly spoiled. The holidays were going to be a disaster.

Glory Cottage had been the first shock. It wasn't particularly grand or beautiful, just an ordinary little house at the end of an orchard behind a much larger house. But it had an air of completeness about it, a sufficiency with itself. 'Unpretentious' is the word adults used to describe it, but I didn't know that word then so I just thought of it as perfect. Maybe not right away, but soon. And even at the beginning I could see that it had something special. All the doors and windows were wide open as if to welcome us and the rooms were full of birdsong and great heaps of sunlight. Everything about the place seemed to have existed there for ever: the sofa in front of the open hearth, the faded pieces of carpet, the cupboards at the kitchen end of the ground floor which were green-painted, streaked and chipped and lovely; the bedrooms with their bare boards and sloping ceilings and fluttering white curtains.

My mother had already gone up to the main house to say hello to the Drummonds. The two boys and I wandered down to the river. Lucien, who was neither practical nor physically very strong, was eyeing the boat that was tied there with some suspicion.

'Rob and I will launch it without you,' he said, 'it might be dangerous.'

'I don't care.'

Lucien grinned at Rob. 'I suppose she might be useful as ballast.'

'What's that?' Instantly my suspicions were aroused. I had seen myself as the figurehead, being noble at the prow.

'Of course,' Lucien went on, 'we'd have to chuck you overboard if we began taking in too much water. Then you'd drown. Still, if you insist . . .'

'Drown yourself,' I retorted, my usual level of sparkling repartee at that age when confronted by Lucien's all-embracing superiority.

'Jane-the-Pain,' taunted Lucien, while Rob smirked. I was about to hurl myself headlong into the boat to make sure I didn't get left behind. It was then that we noticed we were being watched. A girl of about my own age was standing among the drooping branches of an enormous willow. She was dressed in boy's shorts that were far too large and held up with a plastic belt. Her faded T-shirt was far too small. She had straight brown hair cut in an old-fashioned pudding-basin style and a face that, even then, was solemnly beautiful. In her arms lay a huge white rabbit. It had grey ears and grey markings around its lovely black eyes. The girl was nuzzling the fur behind its ears with her chin. She shifted her weight from one foot to the other.

'Hello,' said Lucien, 'you must be Esther.'

'Who?' She looked puzzled. 'I'm Esme. And this,' she hoisted the rabbit up against her shoulder, 'this is Snowy-two. Do you want me to show you the Rams?'

Owen shifted his position in the bed beside me.

He said, 'I keep thinking of how Esme was when we first knew her. I keep thinking it's a child that's been hurt, that she's lying there in a children's ward with big cartoon pictures all over the walls and—'

'Stop it, Owen, that's just nonsense.'

'Still . . .'

It was disturbing that we could feel so hopelessly separate and yet react in such similar ways. After a while, I ventured, 'She was always useless at Lucien's games, do you remember? But she never got upset when she made mistakes.'

'I think she was so pleased to have people her own age to play with that she would have put up with almost anything.'

That was true. Unlike me, she never minded being teased, and in consequence no one bothered to tease her very much. And when the joke was against her, she laughed as much as anyone. Like the time when . . .

But Owen's memories had been running along a parallel track. 'Do you remember when she shut herself away in her father's study so she could find a word for Lucien's game? And she was so certain we'd be impressed.'

'And we were.'

'She enunciated the word perfectly. "Cunnilingus". And when Lucien had stopped laughing long enough to ask her if she knew what it meant, she was most indignant.' Owen mimicked Esme's voice. '"Extremely cunning, of course. It's obvious. Like very clever grown-ups." Heaven knows what book she found it in.'

'Some boring law book probably. We were furious that no one would explain the joke.'

'I wasn't altogether sure myself. Lucien told me that when he did tell Esme about it a couple of years later, she accused him of making it up.'

It ought to have been funny but we were neither of us laughing. We lapsed into silence. More than anything else, at that moment, I felt frightened. The day had brought a catalogue of random incidents – the stone-throwing, my mother's phone call, the aching distance between me and Owen. And now this utterly meaningless and terrifying attack on Esme. Had it been a burglary that went wrong? A case of mistaken identity? In our civilised modern world there are so many ways for the innocent to suffer.

My body felt spiky with tension. Owen lay beside me in the darkness, separated by inches, separated by an impossible gulf. His body, which I knew so well, was lean and muscular from physical work, his hands were marked and callused.

'Oh, God,' I said, not wanting Owen to fall asleep and leave me all alone. 'Poor Esme.' But at that moment I was thinking only of myself.

Owen rolled over to face me. His fingertips began to brush against my upper arm, then slid down to touch my breast. My body responded with an involuntary flicker of desire. I felt myself slipping into his power.

I stiffened. Our lovemaking had begun under the shadow of loss. In the weeks following Lucien's death I had been numbed by grief and at the same time more fiercely alive than ever before. The nearness of disaster made every present moment intense and precious. And when, in that dark and terrible time, Owen and I had first embraced, I had hungered for him, not so much for pleasure as for survival. And afterwards there was always the guilt that our lives continued and we could try for our blundered glimpses of happiness, while Lucien's had been wiped out. Now a new shadow had fallen across our lives, and it was as if it had been there always. Once again I was healthy and miserable and did not dare to reach out for comfort.

I said, 'How can you, Owen? I keep thinking of Esme.'

'I thought it might help.'

'Well, you're wrong.'

Obscurely, I was disappointed when he rolled away. I was on the point of accusing him of sulking when I realised from the steady rhythm of his breathing that he had fallen almost instantly asleep. I was filled with a great sense of emptiness and longing, though what it was for I could not have said.

Almost as soon as I fell asleep, I slid into the snarled net of the familiar dream. The details might vary, but I knew I had been here before. I was standing in the wings of a theatre. Dressed in my ordinary clothes I watched with interest while people scurried around me. All were wearing elaborate costumes. I had a copy of the script in my hands and was following the play, which was one I had never seen before, with a mixture of curiosity and mounting alarm. Then the script was pulled from my hands. 'It's your cue,' someone next to me hissed, 'you're on.' I was about to protest when a violent push from behind sent me stumbling on to the stage. The lights were very bright. In the darkness of the auditorium a full house was waiting for me to speak. There was silence. I was frantically trying to remember what I had so far seen of the script. What on earth was I supposed to be doing? The other actors became aware of the waiting silence. They smiled at me encouragingly – presumably they thought I was suffering from an attack of nerves. Then, one by one, their smiles faded, they began to frown and shift uneasily from foot to foot. There was a rustle of impatience rising from the audience. 'Get on with it,' a voice came from the wings, 'we can't carry on without you. Everyone is waiting.' I tried to speak some word, any word, but my throat was numb, my jaw paralysed. Sweat was pouring from me. A bell was ringing.

It was the telephone. Owen, no doubt enjoying the deep sleep of an easy conscience and hard work (eleven thousand contented lettuces), merely grunted and moved a little deeper in the bed. I tried prodding him surreptitiously and pretending to be asleep, but without success. I switched on the light, but even that didn't seem to bother him.

'Your turn,' I said hopefully.

He sighed happily.

Still the phone rang. Cursing, I stumbled down the stairs.

'Hel-LO,' with the emphasis firmly on the second syllable, in case the caller was too witless to know it was now nearly one o'clock in the morning.

'Jane?'

'Who's that?' But the knowledge of who it was made me suddenly very wide-awake indeed. I began to say his name but . . .

'No, don't speak. Don't say anything. Just listen,' he cleared his throat, laughed nervously. 'Urgently Derby. That was it, wasn't it?'

'Yes, but what—'

'As soon as you can. Urgently Derby. And not a word to anyone. Not even Owen.'

'But—'

'You heard me. You've not forgotten. Derby, it's urgent. Oh, Christ, you mustn't let me down.'

There must have been something wrong with the line. His voice sounded crackly – not like Rob at all. Not how I remembered him, anyway.

'But . . .' I said again.

It was too late. The phone had gone dead.

Urgently Derby.

I sat on the stairs and looked at the phone. Perhaps it would ring again. The house was very quiet. There could be no doubt that I was wide-awake. Boots were tumbled in one corner of the hall. Drongo stalked towards me from the kitchen and rubbed her flanks against my leg. Urgently Derby. Words from another time. Words from a green place between the boathouse and the willow.

I could hear Lucien speaking, that rather precise, schoolmasterly way of talking he slipped into whenever he was particularly excited about something.

'We need a code,' he was saying, 'something no one but us will ever know, and on pain of death most horrible you must never, ever, ever breathe a word of this to anyone at all.'

That was the summer of the Murder Games and Lucien was especially keen on the threat of death most horrible. Sometimes I thought of boiling oil, the sort used by the defenders of medieval castles, and sometimes I thought of falling from a high window on to spiked railings like the ones around the last house but one. Sometimes I thought that Lucien must know of ways that were even worse. The glint in his eyes when he said the words was chilling and to this day, though he had been dead for nearly ten years, I'd never have dared to break the secret.

'We won't,' we all murmured our agreement.

'From now on, for ever and ever, until we are all dead and buried and food for horrible worms, if one of us is in trouble – but it has to be real trouble, bad trouble, something life or death – they can call upon any one of the others by using the special words.'

'What words?'

'Wait. I'm coming to that. And when you hear the words, no matter what you're doing, you have to drop everything and go to help them. Do you promise?'

We promised.

'And now the words: Derby. Urgently.'

'What?'

'Why?'

'Because of the Derbyshire Ram, stupid. You know the song. It's a way of saying where without anyone else knowing. Because that's where you'd go. That's the secret place where the person in trouble would be hiding. In the Rams.'

But that had been years and years ago and we'd all grown up and gone our separate ways and forgotten all that foolishness.

Hadn't we?

I mean, I thought as I stroked Drongo's arched back, no one still believes in all that stuff. Do they?

I hadn't seen Rob in nine years. More than nine years. He hadn't even bothered to come to the funeral. Probably he had phoned because he was drunk or stoned and it was all a silly joke.

But then I remembered that crackly edge to his voice. He hadn't sounded as if he was drunk, or joking. He had sounded terrified. Desperate. Could the person who had attacked Esme now be hunting Rob as well? I remembered too what Owen had said about the police looking for him. Was he the vital witness who must be silenced? Why?

The Rams. I was sure I must have dreamt that conversation just now. I had forgotten all about the Rams. They probably didn't even exist any more.

It was way past one o'clock. I was quite sure I wasn't going to set off now. Besides, there was no petrol in the van, it probably wouldn't start and I had no desire to break down somewhere between here and Glory Cottage at three in the morning.

I decided to wait. In the morning I'd be able to think more clearly. Most likely Rob would phone again and tell me it had all been a hoax.

A door creaked on the landing. I turned round and saw Laura standing in her long nightdress at the top of the stairs. Her blue eyes were staring so fixedly that for a moment I thought she must be sleepwalking, but then she said, 'I dreamed I was at school and the fire bell was ringing and it rang and rang and wouldn't stop.' She was looking at me accusingly, but even so I felt a surge of tenderness towards her. During the day she might work hard at being an apprentice tyrant, but now, woken from a deep sleep, she was simply a beautiful and very fragile child, barely more than a baby.

I said, 'It was only the phone. Come along, I'll tuck you back into bed.'

When she was settled and I returned to my own bed and moved close to Owen to seek out his warmth, he murmured, 'Who on earth was that?'

I hesitated.

Then, 'Just a wrong number,' I told him.

It was the first lie.

3

Perhaps it was the ease of my escape that was so disturbing.

After that bizarre conversation with Rob, I hardly slept. I kept waiting for the phone to ring again; it seemed vitally important that I should be the one to answer it, not Owen, so that I could hear Rob's voice saying, 'Sorry about that call, Jane. Just a stupid joke. I must have been stoned.' But the night remained resolutely silent. By the time the alarm clock went off and Owen rolled out of bed, I was feeling both wide-awake and horribly jaded.

I said, 'Did the phone ring last night?'

'Yes.' He stretched, then rubbed the small of his back. 'A wrong number, you said.'

I moved further down into the warmth of the bed and tried to think clearly. Maybe it had been a wrong number after all. Maybe the phone had rung and I had answered it but I had dreamed the bit about Rob because of the magazine article and the anxiety over Esme. So what was I going to do about it? I had been struggling with this decision all night, and decision-making has never been my strongest suit. I thought: if it's raining, I'll do something; if it's dry I'll just wait and see.

'What's the weather like?'

Owen pulled back the curtains. I could see his face in profile, the straight nose, the perfectly formed lips – a pre-Raphaelite face outlined against the grey dawn. He spoiled the painterly effect by scratching and pulling on an old T-shirt.

'Drizzle,' he said as his fair head emerged through the neck of his work shirt. 'Drizzle and mist.'

As omens go, that one was unclear.

Owen put on his socks, one brown, one green. 'I'll bring you a cup of tea.'

'I'm not bloody ill,' I said, sitting up at once.

Owen's face clouded with annoyance. 'How on earth can you find a way to be angry at the offer of tea?'

'I only said—'

'You're impossible.'

Now, I thought, now we're going to hear some truths. But at that moment Billy pushed open the bedroom door.

'Muncle had a bad dream,' he said, trailing his knitted monkey behind him by his tail.

Owen switched off his annoyance with me as easily as flicking a light switch. He stooped down and took the little boy by the hand. 'Poor old Muncle,' he said gently, 'you can tell me all about it while I start breakfast.' They padded down the stairs together and I could hear the murmur of their voices rising from the kitchen. I gazed out at the drizzle beyond the windowpane and wondered, not for the first time, what it would have been like to have had a father who listened to the saga of my bad dreams. I might have turned out a nicer person.

The phone rang again while I was brushing my teeth and its shrill call startled me so much that I jabbed my gums with the end of my toothbrush.

I rinsed out my mouth. 'Who was that?' I yelled. The bathroom is on the ground floor next to the kitchen. Laura, who was eating cereal from her frog bowl, rather pointedly put her hands over her ears.

I shouted again, 'Owen, who is it?'

He came into the kitchen. 'Your mother. I didn't think you'd want to talk to her. She said she's been in touch with the hospital and the news is that Esme is stable—'

'Stable? How can she be stable when some maniac has just hit her over the head?'

'It's what hospitals always say. Apparently she hasn't regained consciousness yet. I told Faith we'd try to get over there this afternoon.'

'Oh.' I looked out of the window and the drizzle suddenly looked extremely rain-like.

'Not me,' I said, 'I'm not going. Well, I am going, but not to the hospital. Not today at any rate. But I am going away today.'

Owen had been spooning cat food into a saucer. He paused, his hand in midair. 'Going?'

'Just for the day. I expect. Probably.' It dawned on me that some kind of theme was needed for my sudden departure, so I rambled on. 'All this Esme business has knocked me for six. I can't just hang around here doing nothing and waiting for news, and I'm sure as hell not going to endure another of my mother's faultless hospital bedside cameos—'

'That's cheap—'

'You don't know Faith like I do. You just get taken in by her glamour and her—'

'No. I only see a rather sad and lonely woman who—'

'Lonely? Sad? That woman is evil . . .' Laura and Billy had both stopped eating and were watching me with interest. Even Muncle's woolly eyes seemed to be following the debate. '. . . the way she exaggerates. She overdramatises everything.'

Owen almost smiled. 'You aren't doing too badly yourself,' he murmured.

That did silence me, but only for a moment. 'Anyway,' I went on, 'I've done enough hospital watching to last a lifetime and I have no intention of starting up all over again.'

'Very well. We don't have to go today.'

'You go. I know you want to. I just need to get out of here. Spend a bit of time on my own . . .'

A little more on the theme of 'needing space' (always a good one, that, I don't know why I never tried it before) and being upset about Esme (which was true enough, God knows) and my departure entered the realm of established fact.

There remained a few practical problems. To be precise, one practical problem: lack of funds. Unless we were prepared to burst in with Balaclavas over our faces and sub-machine guns in our hands I saw no way of withdrawing any further money from the bank. The kitty in the tobacco tin on the shelf by the back door contained £17.40 from the sale of some wallflower plants but that was needed for food and petrol. I persuaded Owen to stop off at Dinah's on the way to the station and borrowed £50 from her. She was busy ironing Aidan's socks but was full of compassion, having heard from Aidan about Esme's injury. Sensing a drama, she was only too willing to help in my getaway.

'And we were only talking about her yesterday,' she said, following me out to the van. She had had her hair cut into a rather vampish wedge shape and she was wearing make-up even though it was only nine-thirty in the morning. She looked as though she was Making An Effort and I wondered what she had read in the magazine. She once told me that she had read an article recommending candlelit dinners and saucy underwear to put the pep back into marriage and had followed the instructions to the letter. The thought of Dinah wearing a lacy teddy and solemnly serving candlelit salmon *en croûte* had made me giggle so much that she had been offended and wouldn't tell me if her efforts had been successful in terms of pep, or not.

She told Owen she thought he was wonderful to be so considerate and then offered to look after the children for the morning if that was any help. Warming to her good neighbour theme, she said she'd bring them some lunch from the freezer at midday. Owen brightened visibly at the prospect of a neat little foil-wrapped lunch and everyone seemed thoroughly content as the children scrambled out of the back of the van and raced into her house for a few hours of educational games played on warm carpets. They barely even bothered to say goodbye. Of course, I didn't want anyone to be upset, but I began to get the familiar message that my presence was surplus to requirements. My departure ought to have caused rather more of a stir.

Owen drove me to the station. It struck me as odd that he hadn't asked me where I was going. I certainly would not have told him, but still, his omission piqued me for some reason.

The main morning rush was over, but the station car park was still quite busy. Our corroding green van with OJ Nursery written on the side in dark red lettering came to a halt between a shiny Rover and an equally shiny Peugeot estate. I felt a surge of protectiveness towards the van, like the smelly little boy in the classroom that none of the other children will sit next to. Owen began climbing out.

'Don't bother to see me off.'

'I wasn't going to. Give me a ring later on and let me know what you're doing. I know things haven't been easy the last couple of months. You should have had a break ages ago. Just relax and enjoy yourself.'

I stared at him. The drizzle (it still wasn't proper rain) was fuzzing his halo of blond hair and glistening on the shoulders of his navy sweater. His handsome face was wearing the wonderfully considerate look that had so impressed Dinah. And I thought: you bastard, you're glad I'm going away, you're only too relieved to get rid of me. You might at least have pretended to care about where I might be going.

I said stonily, 'It's no use asking me what my plans are because I haven't made any yet, and even if I had—'

Exasperated, he interrupted, 'I wasn't asking. All I said was to enjoy yourself.'

His generosity was depriving me even of the pleasure of escape. Fat Albert would have made a terrible fuss but at least I'd have known he liked having me around.

'A bit eager to get rid of me, aren't you?'

'Oh, for heaven's—' he turned away and thumped the bonnet of the van. 'This is ridiculous.' He got into the driver's seat and slammed the door shut.

'That's what I've been trying to tell you!' I threw the words at his furious profile behind the car window, but there was no knowing if he had heard or not, since, crashing the car into first gear he drove away with a roar of noise.

It was the most powerful reaction I'd had from him in ages, and I should have been pleased, but for a moment, standing all alone in the misting rain of the car park, I merely felt bereft. After all, maybe he had just wanted to be kind, and now I'd alienated him more than ever. But then, as I began walking towards the booking office, all that doubt was replaced by a massive and totally exhilarating sensation of release – of breathtaking, wonderful, soar-to-the-skies-and-don't-look-down freedom.

London, briefly, flummoxed me. I hadn't been to the place since before Laura was born. So much noise and activity, so many purposeful, hurrying citizens, made me feel very much the country mouse. I bought a ticket from one of the machines and caught a Circle Line train without having to wait at all. Just as I was beginning to relax and enjoy the anonymity of London crowds, I realised I had boarded a train travelling in the wrong direction. I was blushing with embarrassment as I left the train at St James's Park and crossed to the opposite platform. No one mocked me.

Paddington was relatively straightforward. A shiver trickled down my spine as I said the name of the station at the ticket office. I had never really expected to go there again. The ticket man looked down his extremely long nose and I half expected him to say, 'Funny time of year for your holidays, isn't it?' but all he asked was, 'Are you coming back today?'

I glared at him. What business was it of his? If I hadn't told Owen, then I sure as hell wasn't going to . . .

He tried again. 'Single or return?'

'Um . . .'

He told me the price of a normal return and I instantly decided in favour of a cheap day. Of course I'd be back the same evening. Rob wasn't even likely to be there.

Once I was safely on the train and gazing out of the window at the drizzle-shrouded suburbs, this thought began to haunt me. Rob wasn't even likely to be there. Or maybe he had just set this all up as an elaborate practical joke, proof once again that Jane was the most gullible person on earth. I tried not to think what an idiot I'd feel to have galloped halfway across southern England and all because someone I hadn't seen in nearly ten years said 'Urgently Derby' down the phone.

And anyway, even if Rob was in trouble, why should that concern me? Why should I bother to help him? What had he ever done for me apart from abandoning me when I had needed him most? At the thought of his betrayal I felt a familiar knot of anger and hurt tighten in my stomach. A vague scheme came into my mind. I could find out what his problem was and then leave him to stew in his own juice. Let him discover what it feels like when friends let you down. Why not?

But then, as the soft greens of the Berkshire countryside told me I was approaching my destination, I answered my own question. Curiosity. That was the morsel with which the hook was baited. What on earth, if it had been genuine, had prompted that extraordinary call?

I had never thought of Glory Cottage as a location on a map. During those four holidays that we spent there it always felt like a place that existed outside the normal everyday world. Like those other realities that children in books reach when the clock strikes thirteen or they find the secret doorway in the panelling of an old house.

Also, I realised, as I got off the train, it had always been a summer place. A place that existed for our pleasure in the long summer holidays; to think that it continued to be there once children returned to their schools and leaves fell from the trees, was somehow disconcerting.

Glory Cottage was, as far as I could remember, about two miles from the station. I decided against taking a taxi because that was quite out of keeping with the whole cloak-and-dagger mood of this venture. If Rob's message had been sincere and if he was in some kind of trouble, then the last thing he would want was for me to announce my arrival.

So I followed the road that led towards the towpath. Down by the river everything was dripping and cold in the mist. A couple of ducks were drifting moodily between the high walls of the houses. The river looked sombre, almost sulky, and quite unlike the vibrant rush of water which was the chief glory of Glory Cottage.

Red brick buildings gave way to suburban houses and the towpath changed from pavement to mud and weeds and then petered out altogether. Then came a stretch of half-a-dozen fields where the farmers had apparently gone out of their way to make life difficult for walkers. But at least scrambling through hedges and brambles helped to take my mind off Esme; as I drew closer to Glory Cottage I had found myself thinking of her more and more.

Then the river twisted and spread out between two lines of willows and Martin's Court was in full view.

Martin's Court was a large house, blue-painted, with a simplicity and squareness which made it resemble an enormous doll's house. It was all that remained of a much larger house, built in an era when Martin's Court was the centre of a vast estate with farms and tenancies and cottages for the workers. The house had been destroyed by fire sometime in the twenties and the blue-painted square box that stood there now was all that remained of the original building. Most of the cottages, the stable block and the workshops had been sold off and converted; all that now was left, apart from the house, was Glory Cottage, the orchard in which it stood and a couple of fields that edged the river.

Still hidden by the hedge that separated the garden from the neighbouring fields, I realised that I had a problem. To reach the cottage and the Rams, I must either cross the lower stretch of lawn, in full view of the house, or else go round by the road and enter along the driveway in full view of anyone who happened to be passing.

I considered. A few rooks flapped overhead and cawed at my indecision. I plumped for the lawn which was quicker. If apprehended I could always pretend to be a hiker who had got lost. As I remembered, Mrs Wicks the housekeeper had waged perpetual warfare against 'lost' walkers, but she was surely dead by now. Clare Drummond, Esme's mother, had been dead for some years. Most probably her father had sold the house after that.

I walked purposefully across the lawn, keeping as close to the river as possible. There was a curdling apprehension in my stomach that was only partly to do with my fear that an irate Mrs Wicks might erupt from the house in her most furious hiker-attack mode at any moment, and only partly because I couldn't imagine what I was expecting to find, but more, much more, because I suddenly heard the faint but utterly distinct and unmistakable thump of the Rams.

Esme had shown them to us that first day of our arrival.

'Do you want to see the Rams?' she had asked, standing in a fringe of willow and gazing at us as we mooched about in the uncertain way of newly deposited children who had yet to find their bearings.

Rob and I said nothing; we knew better than to venture any opinion which might result in our being left out of the day's activities.

'We might do,' said Lucien at length. It would have been against his principles to admit that he didn't know what the Rams were. Then casually he asked, 'Are there many round here?'

She stared at him. Even then I was struck by her calm, brown-eyed stare. I've never known anyone whose face could look quite so blank as Esme's. For some reason, perhaps because it was a beautiful face, people always assumed that the most feverish amount of thinking activity must be masked by such sphinxlike impassivity, though occasionally, in the years that followed, I had my doubts.

When she had stared at Lucien for a bit she walked, the huge white rabbit still lying as placid as a pyjama bag in her arms, down to the edge of the river and nudged the punt with her pink plastic sandal in a proprietorial sort of way.

'The boat's no good,' she announced. 'It leaks. My mother keeps saying she'll get it fixed but . . .' she lapsed into silence.

'I expect we'll get it mended while we're here,' said Lucien. I was impressed by the speed with which he laid claim to the punt, though I did wonder who 'we' was. None of us knew the first thing about boats. Lucien might know a fores'l from a mizzen from his reading, but had no practical experience. Depending on his current employment status, Eric might be able to provide insurance for a boat. And as for our mother, the only kind of craft Faith had ever been in was one of those two-dimensional cutouts that creak up and down at the back of a stage.

Esme heaved the rabbit a bit higher on her shoulder and it half closed its eyes as if already bored by our company. She sighed. I had the impression that she was more awkward than shy. She said, 'They're over this way.'

As she began to lead us from the garden to the orchard, the rabbit suddenly bucketed out of her arms.

'Quick,' yelled Rob, 'before it escapes.'

Esme shrugged, but continued walking. 'He always comes back at night,' she said.

The rabbit was lolloping in the general direction of the main house, pausing only to decapitate a few flowerheads on the way.

'Holy shit!' (Rob's favourite phrase, age eleven.) 'Free-range rabbits.'

'And rams,' said Lucien, quickly catching up with Esme.

Rob and I followed.

We became aware of a steady thumping noise.

'What's that?' asked Lucien.

'The Rams, of course.'

It was enough. Lucien was away. 'Do you hear that, you two?' He turned back to us and his face was glowing, most elflike when excited. 'It's the Berkshire Minotaur! In Crete it's a bull but here it's a ram, the Ramotaur, can you hear it? That's its heart beating, the frightful drum that compels sacrifice – did you realise that we were going to spend our summer holidays practically cohabiting with a mythical beast? Does this one demand human sacrifice, Esme? That could explain why we passed *hardly any* young men and maidens as we came through the village. Holy shit!' (Rob had only been copying Lucien, in this as in everything else.) 'No wonder your mother was so keen for us to come and stay this summer, Esme. I expect she thought Jane could be sacrificed in your place. How about that, Jane? You'd better start practising your leaps and somersaults; bull dancing is pretty difficult stuff and I should think ram dancing is just as hard even though they're a bit smaller. Of course, you die in the end, it only postpones the evil hour, some dancers just stand there and wait for the ram's horn to pierce their stomach; they prefer to get it over with quickly, you see—'

'Shut up, Luce.' Even though I was pretty sure he was making it up, prickles of anxiety began to creep across the back of my neck.

Esme, who seemed to be withstanding her first exposure to Lucien's rhetoric with remarkable calm, merely said, 'They're for the water.'

Lucien was undaunted. 'Well-disguised, obviously. I have heard it said that the Minotaur in Crete now hides under cover of an electricity generating station and it's only when his hunger and blood lust become absolutely unendurable that he emerges and snatches unsuspecting villagers as they toil in the fields, or some feeble tourist who has strayed too far from the safety of his air-conditioned de luxe, loo-in-the-back charabanc. That's why local people generally prefer to pick the victims themselves – it makes the whole thing much less uncertain—'

He would undoubtedly have gone on for some time longer but Esme was pushing open a little gate that led from the orchard into a field.

'They're here,' she interrupted.

It was a field quite definitely without any livestock, mythical or otherwise. A stretch of buttercuppy grass and, in a far corner, a couple of heaps of what looked like corrugated iron.

'Over there,' she explained. 'They pump the water from the stream up to the sheds above the house. It goes through all sorts of sand and filter stuff. Then we drink it. No one is ever, ever allowed to go inside except Mr Wicks.'

It was by way of being her welcoming gift to us, the children who had invaded her lonely life. The secret of a forbidden place.

The drizzle was binding together and forming quite sizable trickles of water down the back of my neck as I squelched across the field towards the ever louder pulse of the Rams. The barbed wire that fenced them from the rest of the field looked new and efficient, but the corrugated iron covering the pits was as colourfully rusted as ever.

I by-passed the first one. Then squeezed through the wire that fenced off the second. I looked around me and prayed that there were no witnesses to this ultimate act of folly of attempting to talk to an empty pumping station. I crouched down and prised back a loose sheet of corrugated iron and squinted down into the clammy dark

'Is anyone there?'

Silence, then a brief rustling sound that could – oh God, please not – have been the scurrying of rats. One more try and then I could return to the station and sanity with a clear conscience.

'Hello,' I hissed to the rat-rustle. 'Urgently Derby – I'm here.'

And then a voice emerged from the darkness. 'Thank Christ, Jane. I thought you'd never come.'

'Rob!' I lurched back in astonishment and snagged my jacket on the barbed wire.

'Ssh. Has anyone seen you?'

'There's no one around.'

'Come on down then.'

'Can't you come out? It's almost stopped raining.' I had always hated the Ram pits, not because they were forbidden, but because they were cold, dark and eerie.

But his irritated, 'God, Jane, do you think I'm down here for the view?' decided me. I squeezed through the gap in the corrugated iron and clambered down into the pit.

Rob was crouched in the far corner. I couldn't see him very clearly. His face was in deep shadow and it was impossible to make out his expression. He didn't move.

I said, 'Hello, Rob.'

'Hi.' Although he had been anglicised for so long, his voice still held the trace of an Australian accent, making even a greeting sound tentative and interrogatory.

For a few moments neither of us spoke. I had been angry with him for years, yet now all that had vanished and I was only curious. There was so much to say and no way of knowing where to begin.

He was absolutely still. Then, 'What about – Esme?'

'No change.'

'No change from what, for God's sake?'

'She was hit on the back of the head.'

'I know that. But is she—'

'She's in hospital. She hasn't regained consciousness. Apart from that no one seems to be saying anything much.'

He groaned and, slumping down, he covered his face with his hands. After a moment he looked up and asked, 'You didn't bring any food, did you?'

'I didn't really think you'd be here.'

'It doesn't matter.' The way he said it made me certain he was famished.

I said, 'I thought your phone call was a hoax.'

'Jesus, I wish it was.'

'So what happened?'

'Where do you want me to begin?'

I considered. 'Well, for a start, you can tell me what the hell you're doing down here and what I'm supposed to do to help.' (And then, I thought, you can add in a few hundred other things, like why you abandoned us all for nearly ten years.)

'Sure.'

Now that I could see more clearly in the semidarkness of the Ram pits, I was able to make out his expression. His face was haggard. He looked thinner and altogether less substantial than the man whose photograph Dinah and I had pored over the previous morning. And his eyes, which had glowed with understanding and humour in the photograph, were guarded, blank screens to repel all sympathy. I suppressed a twinge of satisfaction at seeing the media star in such an uncharacteristically vulnerable state. I noted also that, unshaven and dishevelled as he was, Rob was even more attractive than in the photographs.

He began to shiver. I waited. At length he said, 'The police are going to think I'm a suspect.'

'What? That's crazy.'

'Of course it is. But it looks . . . everything is stacked against me. It's too complicated to explain it all now but—'

'That has to be the stupidest thing I've ever heard.'

'I know, but—'

'No. I mean you're stupid, skulking down here like a criminal. Even if no one suspected you to begin with, they're bound to if you hide yourself away like this.'

In the first show of emotion so far, he rounded on me in a fury. 'That's right, Jane, state the obvious as you always did. Go ahead and tell me I'm digging my own grave. Tell me truth always prevails in the end, go on, tell me. But you see, I've already done time once for a crime I didn't commit, I know what it's like in those sewers they dump people in, I know how long it takes for mistakes to be put right. I couldn't stand it again, not even for a single night. I'd sooner kill myself first.'

There was no denying his passionate sincerity, yet I couldn't help being struck by a certain theatricality in his manner. As though he meant the words, yet was acting a role all the same. I dismissed this thought, put it down to the cynicism that went with being Faith's daughter.

'Okay, okay, I get the message. But I still fail to see the sense in hiding away down here. You surely don't think I can keep smuggling food to you until they find the real culprit. It might take months.'

'I had thought of that, as it happens. I'll explain. About six weeks ago Esme came back to Martin's Court. She's been in therapy for a while; it was my suggestion – she was in quite a state when we first got together – and her therapist thought she had reached the point where she ought to come back here and confront her past.'

'Her father still lives here?'

'Yes. He's been living here since Clare died. So she came back, and while she was here she wrote some kind of diary: her testament, she called it.'

'What's that got to do with—?'

'Just listen, will you? I'd forgotten you were always so bloody impatient. I want you to get hold of the diary – testament – for me. I'm sure there'll be a clue about who attacked her.'

'But it could have been anyone.'

'No. She was in the flat – our flat. There was no sign of a forced entry. Either the person had a key or Esme knew them well enough to let them in.'

'Maybe they said they'd come to read the meter.'

'Don't be flippant. Besides, Esme was cautious. She had to be. She'd been heavily into drugs for some time, and she'd been hinting that someone was putting pressure on her, though she wouldn't say why. She'd been acting strangely for a couple of days, but she swore blind she was clean so she'd hardly tell me if she was still involved.'

I tried to imagine Esme, cool and sophisticated Esme, being associated with homicidal drug dealers and found it impossible. In fact Rob's declaration had a distinctly melodramatic flavour.

He said earnestly, 'I just pray to God the diary will provide some clues.'

'How do you know it's here?'

'She told me.'

I pondered. 'So you want me to march up to the front door and say: Mr Drummond, I'm frightfully sorry about your daughter but if you don't mind I'll just ransack your house on the off chance that she left her diary somewhere because that might, just might, contain some information about the dubious characters she was mixing with so that the police won't suspect Rob Hallam, who, as it happens, is lurking in your Rams and—'

'You can skip the bit about me lurking in the Rams but otherwise, yes.'

'And in the meantime you stay here and flirt with pneumonia?'

He pulled his jacket more tightly around him. 'Probably, yes.'

I said, 'I think your plan stinks.'

'Can you come up with a better one?'

'Not yet, let me think.'

It didn't take all that long to find one. Perhaps it was the sight of Rob looking so vulnerable and forlorn that made me resourceful by comparison.

I said, 'My plan may not be exactly brilliant but it's about a thousand times better than yours.' (My plan's better than your plan: for a moment it was as if we were both nine years old again.) 'The only real difficulty I can see is lack of cash.'

'Oh, that,' said Rob, with the wonderful insouciance of someone who is not up to their overdraft limit at the bank and haunted by unpaid bills. 'Cash is the least of my worries.'

It was only when I scrambled back up into the drizzle-misty field that I thought what an odd first conversation that had been. Did he know that I'd had two children since we last saw each other? He must have known that I'd married because at the end he managed a polite, 'And how is Owen, by the way?' to which I replied with the obligatory and not quite accurate, 'Oh, he's fine.'

And that seemed to take care of all the intervening years.

4

As the afternoon progressed, I began to realise, with a twinge of guilty horror, that I was thoroughly enjoying myself. My pleasure struck me as mildly obscene. There was Esme still struggling to emerge from unconsciousness (at some stage I phoned the hospital and they reported 'no change'), Rob mouldering damply in the Rams, Owen and the children abandoned and with no idea where I was or when I would return, and here was I revelling in the drama and my own part in it.

I walked back to the station. By now it was way past lunch time and my hunger could be gauged by the fact that the normally loathsome sandwiches on sale in the buffet looked mouth-watering. I bought two.

Having checked the time of the next London train I went to the phone box and dialled the number of Martin's Court.

The ringing was interrupted at once. A man's voice: 'Hello?'

'Mr Drummond?'

'Yes.'

'It's Jane Baer here. I—'

'Who?'

'Jane Baer.'

'Is that the hospital?'

I cursed myself. He sounded so desperately anxious. Of course, he had been standing by the phone, waiting for news.

I began again. 'Mr Drummond, I just heard about Esme. I'm so sorry . . .' Such a useless phrase, I always think. But about a hundred times better than my mother's customary dirge.

'Oh, well. Yes . . .' His voice became quieter once he knew I had no information for him. Suddenly I tensed, anticipating his next phrase, 'These things happen, you know.'

It's the understatement of grief that is so painful.

When I could speak again, I said, 'I'm Faith Piper's daughter.'

'Oh, yes, of course. Esme's friend. I spoke to Faith yesterday. Stupid of me not to recognise you just now. Sorry . . .'

Don't apologise to me, I begged silently, not when I'm about to launch into deception. I tried not to imagine him, white-haired and anxious, waiting by the telephone table in the hallway at Martin's Court.

I said, 'Mr Drummond, I know this sounds odd but . . . I've been so devastated by this news about Esme and I can't . . . well, the truth is that things haven't been too good between me and Owen recently,' (the first rule of lying is to tell the truth whenever possible), 'and I wondered if . . . I'd be awfully grateful if you'd let me stay at Glory Cottage for a day or two. Or maybe it already has tenants?'

'No.' He sounded vague, remote from a conversation that did not concern Esme. 'There's no one there. I don't see any problem. It's probably a bit damp, that's all. We did have a gardener chappie living there but he turned out to be a dud.'

'Oh, Mr Drummond, that's wonderful.' Did my voice sound as insincere to him as it did to me? 'I'm in London now, but if it's all right with you I'll come down later on. Some time early evening.'

'As you wish. I probably won't be here. Just popped back to pick up a few things. One wants to be at the hospital as much as possible. Mrs Wicks will let you in.'

In my mind Mrs Wicks sprang from the grave to which I had so prematurely consigned her and reasserted her former dominion at Martin's Court.

'I hope that's not a nuisance.'

'No. She lives in now.'

'Great. And, Mr Drummond, I'd be really grateful if you didn't mention this to anyone. Especially not to Owen or my mother. Just for today.'

'As you wish.'

I burbled some more gratitude until he pointed out gently that if there wasn't anything urgent I wished to add, he'd like to keep the phone lines clear, just in case . . .

I put down the phone. The first and most potentially hazardous part of my plan had gone brilliantly. A living-in Mrs Wicks was a nuisance but one I could deal with later. Feeling quite smug I went to the platform and munched a sandwich while waiting for the Paddington train.

Owen and I had occasionally conjectured that we were likely to be the last people in Britain to possess a cash-point card. Perhaps there might remain some illiterate Gaelic-speaking pensioner in a turf croft somewhere in the remoter Hebrides who would be even slower than us to catch up with modern technology and, more important, solvency – but it was sure to be a close-run thing. Our finances had always been precarious but at the beginning of that year our major customer had gone bankrupt owing us a large amount of money. Since then our own situation had been increasingly desperate, forcing us to juggle our debts and rely on the cash from sales to the public. The idea of using a piece of plastic as an Open Sesame to untold wealth was quite intoxicating.

And now here I was, standing among the crowds in Piccadilly with not one, but two cash-point cards in my pocket, and Rob's PIN numbers written in biro on the back of each hand. We had decided on Piccadilly because a central location merely indicated that Rob was still in London. I had been anxious that if the police were searching for him they would have frozen his bank account, but Rob reasoned that they were more likely to use withdrawals as a means of tracing his movements.

Little realising, I thought, that he was being aided by an unknown accomplice.

As I stood in the queue for the first cash-point machine, I began to feel nervous. Not only because I was expecting the heavy hand of the law to fall on my shoulder at any moment, but also because everyone else appeared so very nonchalant about the whole procedure. I was sure to display some shocking ignorance and would be unmasked as an imposter, or a cash-point thief. I began to sweat.

When my turn came I was startled by how obliging the machine was. (Unlike the cashiers in our local bank who always made me feel like the worst kind of poor white trash as they scurried off to check our balance before handing out the pittance that was all I ever dared to request.) The friendly wall was positively effusive in its pleases and thank-yous. And then, 'How much do you want?' Giddily I pressed the arrow pointing to the figure £200, half expecting the machine to flash, 'You must be joking.' Instead it purred contentedly to itself for a few moments before disgorging ten crisp £20 notes into my hand. I was grinning like an idiot. Far from applauding my brilliance, those behind me in the queue remained impassive.

I could hardly wait to find the second of the two banks Rob used and repeat my conjuring trick.

Later, when I had retreated into the secrecy of a public lavatory and was counting out £380 and hiding the notes in the soles of my shoes, inside my bra, at the bottom of my bag, a sudden wild vision sprang into my mind: with £400 I could disappear and have the spree of a lifetime – but curiosity about Rob and Esme, combined, of course, with my inherent honesty, dissuaded me. And by now the shops were closing anyway.

Returning to Paddington, I remained alert for muggers. It seemed impossible that I should have such a frenzy of money strewn about my person without it showing in my appearance.

At Paddington, I discovered I had hidden too much money and was obliged to slink off to the Ladies again and take a couple more notes out of the bottom of my bag in order to purchase a ticket.

This time I did not hesitate. 'A single please.'

My voice rang with new-found assurance.

It was rush hour and the train was crowded. Wedged between several surly commuters, I suddenly realised how tired I was. The day seemed to have stretched to accommodate the endless toing and froing on various forms of public transport. At the O J Nursery, Owen must now be juggling the children's supper and bedtime with the evening chores. I couldn't remember when I had last been away from the children for a night, then realised this was the first time. Like testing a tooth with a hole in it, I checked to see if I missed them or not, and found that my main feeling was a kind of unfocused anxiety. My mother's veiled warning, broken glass in the greenhouse and the news about Esme, worst of all that ragged parting from Owen – all these things contributed to my unease. I tried to distract myself, but my mind kept returning to the last picture I had of the children disappearing into Dinah's house and I ached to think of them both so precious and so vulnerable. Like Owen, they seemed always to be in need of something I was unable to provide for them. I wondered if perhaps it was exhaustion that caused my thoughts to follow such a morbid course. Yet my present tiredness was quite different from the routine exhaustion I was used to which was made up of a lethal compound of boredom and overwork. And, of course, worry. Worry is surely the most tiring emotion of them all. This fatigue, by contrast, felt almost like a kind of exhilaration.

I took a taxi from the station and at my request the driver, who had one of those very narrow heads that make people resemble clothes-peg dolls, especially when seen from the rear, waited while I went into a little '8 til late' supermarket. The sensation that everyone was watching me was growing stronger, and I agonised over how much to purchase. It seemed essential that any casual observer would assume I was shopping for myself alone, yet by now Rob must be ravenous. Besides, it was fun to buy all those delicacies we always had to deny ourselves at home – olives and exotic cheeses and real coffee and a bottle of wine that was not the absolutely rock-bottom cheapest of the range. But when the check-out operator was passing the items over the electronic eye, I felt obliged to explain, 'I always eat like a horse on holiday.'

She looked puzzled, but said nothing.

The taxi driver helped me with my bags and I repeated my explanation about holidays and horses. Clothes Peg said that for his part he always drank like a fish on holiday, so between us we'd make the beginnings of a zoo. Then he said, 'Where to now?'

'Martin's Court. Do you know it?'

'The big blue house?'

'That's right.'

I slumped into the back seat. It occurred to me then that I ought to ask him to stop at a call box so that I could phone Owen, but my mind had gone strangely blank on the subject of what I could tell him. It seemed altogether simpler not to bother. 'He won't be expecting a call until tomorrow,' I told myself. This turned out to be a depressing thought.

And then, as the car headlights shone through the mist and illuminated the square plain façade of Martin's Court, so many conflicting emotions – memories of childhood arrivals with Rob and Lucien and my mother, a sudden stab of grief for Lucien and a moment's panic at what I was doing (what was I doing?) – surged through me, that my brief moment of gloom was quite eclipsed.

It was immediately apparent that Mrs Wicks had not only failed to die, she had failed to change in any way. It was nearly twenty years since I had seen her last; twenty years during which I had grown up, seen my brother die, got married, borne two children and started a not very successful business, while in all those years Mrs Wicks didn't look as if she had changed out of the bosomy navy cardigan and buttocky brown skirt she had been wearing throughout the summer of our last visit. Her face still had that buttoned-up and pale look which Lucien, with more accuracy than kindness, had said made her look like a constipated cauliflower. In the past I had always assumed she was unfriendly towards us because she was one of those people who don't like children. Within five minutes of my arrival at Martin's Court, I had learned that she didn't like adults either.

She told me that it was a funny sort of time to turn up and that I didn't seem to have brought a suitcase, both facts I was well aware of. She made them sound like a crime.

'Spur of the moment,' I said.

She scowled and told me that Glory Cottage would be damp, hadn't been aired, wasn't really suitable for winter habitation and had I thought to bring a torch because she didn't see why she should be expected to have to trek across the orchard at this time on a November night, thank you very much. This last remark caused her to breathe rather more heavily.

Of course, I had not brought a torch, which was more of a problem for me than she realised, since I also had to find my way across the field to the Rams.

I said humbly – or as humbly as I could manage – 'Oh, I'd never dream of asking you to show me at this time of night. Do you have a torch I might borrow? I promise I'll get one of my own first thing in the morning.'

She glared at me. 'And what am I supposed to do if there's a power cut?' she demanded.

Several activities occurred to me, but I didn't mention any of them, tried hard not even to look as if I was imagining them.

Some more grumbling negotiations had to be endured before she finally yielded up the wretched torch. Also the key to Glory Cottage. It was huge, altogether a proper key.

Just as I had gathered all my carrier bags, torch and key and was preparing to leave by the back door, I remembered and asked, 'What's the latest news of Esme?'

She sniffed. 'I wondered if you'd bother to ask,' she said. 'No change. That's all I know.'

'Poor Mr Drummond. He must be so worried.'

An even louder sniff. 'If he's suffering, then it's only what he deserves,' she said.

I choked back a volley of abuse. Somehow I managed to gurgle a reasonable 'Good night', before the back door was slammed shut behind me and I was free to snarl my outrage into the muffling mist as I set off across the lawn.

Either I had forgotten the path round the edge of the garden and through the orchard, or else some interfering swine had moved it. I twisted my ankle, stumbled through a couple of puddles and ripped one carrier bag on some brambles before finally reaching the threshold of Glory Cottage where I promptly whacked my shin on the boot scraper. In the morning I would no doubt be grateful for the cottage's hideaway position, but right now it was quite literally a pain.

I set down my carrier bags and turned the key in the lock. The door opened without a sound. The torchlight picked out random objects in the darkness. For the first time I felt a shiver of fear. I fumbled for the light switch. A single hanging bulb shone out in the centre of the room and the moment of apprehension passed.

Nothing had changed. The large room which took up the whole of the ground floor of the cottage was still furnished with the same few shabby items. There were the two bulging sofas, the wooden table, the massive open fireplace, the 'kitchenette' with its green-painted units, the few cheap rugs scattered across the linoleum. And yet everything had been altered. The sounds and scents of the summer holidays – voices murmuring in upstairs rooms, the clatter of crockery being cleared away, the bustle and the busyness and the life – all that had been snuffed out. Silence and emptiness had settled here with the damp and the veil of dust.

Pausing only to rub my smarting shin, I turned to go and fetch Rob from the Rams, but as I pulled open the door a shadow detached itself from the surrounding dark.

'Christ,' said Rob, 'you took long enough.'

I was aggrieved. 'It's good to be appreciated.'

He pushed the door shut behind him and, without even a glance in my direction, he began hunting through the carrier bags. He found the loaf of French bread and tore off a large piece. His hands were filthy, and the gesture of tearing the food was so desperate that for a moment or two I simply stared.

In all the times I had dreamed of seeing Rob again, I had never imagined this.

I said, 'I'll cook up some pasta. It won't take long.'

'Great.' He had pulled out one of the bottles of wine and, pausing only to glance disparagingly at the label, he asked, 'Where's the corkscrew?'

'How should I know?'

He found it in a green-painted drawer at the kitchen end. But as I watched him push the spike into the cork, I realised that his hands were shaking too much, or else they simply lacked sufficient strength to open it.

'Oh, hell,' he said. His arms and shoulders went limp and he turned his head away. He was on the verge of breaking down.

It was hard to imagine a greater contrast to the various images of Rob Hallam that I'd seen on television and in newspapers and magazines over the past few years. No trace of the buoyant smile, the assurance and energy of a man with ambition and the confidence to achieve it. His face was haggard, his eyes darkly shadowed. His jacket was rumpled and hung damply from his broad shoulders making him appear frailer than he should, for though he was not especially tall, Rob was strongly built. His brown hair looked manky and unbrushed. And he was shaking. Not just shivering with the cold. But shaking.

At length he turned to face me. His dark eyes shifted nervously. He attempted a smile. 'God, Jane, I've really fucked up this time.' His voice wavered. 'If you hadn't turned up I don't know what . . .'

He couldn't finish. I hesitated. For a moment I felt let down, betrayed by his vulnerability. But only for a moment.

I crossed the room, took the bottle and then the corkscrew from his hands and set them down on the draining board. Then I wrapped my arms round him and held him tightly. After a few moments he raised his hands and placed them against my back. He was still shaking. His coldness was overpowering. His cheek pressed against the side of my face was like a slab of ice.

'That bloody hole in the ground . . .'

'It's all okay,' I soothed. 'Soon you'll be warm and fed and you'll feel much better.' I must have sounded like somebody's mother. 'I'll open the wine.'

As I released him, there was a papery crackling in the region of my bosom.

'What on earth is that?'

'Oh, yes . . .' I pressed my hand against my breast and it obligingly crackled again.

'I thought only dossers wore newspaper under their clothes.'

'Things aren't quite that bad. Not yet, anyway.' I opened the bottle, poured him a glass and handed it to him. 'Cheers,' I said.

He drank it at once and poured himself some more.

I explained, 'I thought I'd better hide most of the money for safekeeping.' I hitched up my sweater and extracted the no longer crisp notes from my bra. With some regret, it must be said. I had enjoyed the brief proximity of wealth. Rob watched with growing bewilderment as I sat down, pulled off my shoes and liberated several more notes.

'These are all yours.' I handed them to him.

'You don't have a bag? A purse even?'

'I did put some in my bag. Here—' I fished out the remaining notes and added them to the pile. 'I've never had so much cash before and I didn't want to be mugged.'

'Of course not.'

For a moment I thought he might burst out laughing, but he was sunk too deep in anguish for that. Still, a faint ray of lightness had penetrated his despair.

I felt brisk and competent. As I busied myself in the cottage I discovered that Mrs Wicks had earlier qualified herself as a probationary member of the human race by putting on the immersion heater, so I ran Rob a deep bath. He took the remains of the French loaf and the bottle of wine with him to the bathroom while I set to work downstairs. I lit a fire and put his clothes to air in front of it, unpacked my shopping and cooked us a meal. The sauce had lashings of garlic and olives and anchovies in it and I set it on the table with a flourish of pride. I need not have bothered. Rob was so ravenous he would cheerfully have devoured raw horseflesh if there had been any hanging around. He didn't pause to talk much, but I had broached the second bottle while I was cooking and was consequently garrulous. I told him of my happy introduction to cash-point machines and of my less than happy reacquaintance with Mrs Wicks. Rob murmured from time to time, as a sign that he was attending. I had even found a couple of old candles and placed them on saucers between us on the pine table. The combination of the candlelight and the bath had improved Rob's appearance considerably. He had lost the vagabond air and his dark hair clung damply to his forehead. While he was absorbed in eating, I was able to study the changes that ten years had brought. On the whole, I thought, age had improved him. His face had thinned and grown more characterful. His jaw, which had always seemed too large, now looked purposeful and strong. Lucien's lieutenant had grown accustomed to command. It suited him, I thought, as the old wriggle of attraction curled through me. I poured myself another glass of wine.

When he had finished he leaned back in his chair and let out a long sigh.

'Now it's your turn,' I announced. 'Tell me exactly what happened.'

He frowned. Then, pushing back his chair, he stood up and crossed the room to the sofa where he slumped down, utterly exhausted. 'Do I have to?' He gazed hopelessly into the fire. 'Christ, but I'm tired.'

I stoked up the fire and settled on the rug near the sofa. I remembered reading somewhere that people find it easier to talk about difficult matters if they don't have to make eye contact. And I was determined that Rob was going to talk.

'I can't help you unless I know what's going on,' I said.

'All you have to do is find the journal.'

'Why?'

'I told you.'

'But I still don't see . . .'

He shifted irritably. 'I'd have thought it was obvious. Her therapist had suggested she use the journal to write down everything that was troubling her. I assume she wasn't any better at talking to him than she was to me.'

'Why the therapist?'

'That was my idea. I thought it might help.'

'Obviously.'

'Esme and I ran into each other again about a year ago. I suppose we were both wary about getting close – after what happened before. But we did all the same. She's been living with me for about six months.'

'I know. I saw that article in the magazine.'

'She never talks much about herself, but I knew she'd been through one hell of a bad time – for years and years. I hoped the therapy would help to build up her confidence.'

'And did it?'

He didn't answer.

I said, 'None of this explains how you fetched up hiding in the Rams.'

'Can't this wait until the morning?'

I was beginning to feel about as sympathetic as Torquemada, but I insisted, 'You phone me with a ridiculous message in the middle of the night and then drag me halfway across England to help you – the least you can do is explain.'

'Hm. I guess I must have panicked, that's all.'

'Why?'

He sighed. 'Yesterday afternoon I had to go to a meeting at the Home Office, something to do with the hostel. Esme and I had had a row at lunch time—'

'What about?'

'What? Oh, I can't even remember now. But I was thinking about her all through the meeting. Having to sit in that office for hours while pompous men droned on about things they'll never understand. I couldn't get away from them fast enough. On the way home I bought a bunch of flowers – chrysanthemums – I was desperate to see her. Maybe in some instinctive way I knew she was hurt. Then I got to the flat. I opened the door. And there she was. Lying on the floor, all twisted around. And there was blood. I didn't even know if she was breathing. I found the alabaster bowl. I – I—'

'So you called an ambulance? The police?'

'I – maybe – I don't remember.'

'What?'

'I know it sounds crazy, but I simply don't remember what happened after that. Not until it was nearly dark and I found myself walking beside the Thames. I couldn't think clearly at all. I began to see how bad I'd made it for myself by running away. The flowers were there on the floor. I'd handled the alabaster bowl. I'd run away. I walked up and down by the river for hours. I thought of throwing myself in, just ending it all right there. The idea of being cross-examined by the police all over again for something I didn't do, seeing the disbelief on their faces, hearing myself stammer – I knew I couldn't face going through that again. I nearly jumped. And then I heard Lucien's voice. I suppose it must have been inside my head, but it sounded . . . maybe it was being by the river that put the idea there . . . I heard his voice saying the code. So I came down here. And tried to get in touch with you.'

'Did you phone earlier last night and hang up when you heard Owen's voice?'

'Yes. I couldn't trust him. After I'd spoken to you, I hid in the Rams. That's all.'

I had believed him until then, but his final 'that's all' jarred on my ears. Quite clearly that was anything but all. But at least it was a start.

His hand brushed the top of my head. I leaned towards the touch. He said, 'I meant to explain everything to you properly, but when I heard your voice, it was as if I'd suddenly flipped back ten years. I couldn't handle it . . . all I could say was the code. Afterwards, I was afraid you'd think I was mad.'

'I did wonder. And then I thought that maybe I was the mad one and I'd imagined it all.'

'You came, anyway. That's the important thing.'

'Yes.'

Now, at last, I allowed myself to twist round and look up into his face. For the first time that day he seemed almost relaxed. The beginnings of a smile were softening his features. His brown eyes were losing their haunted look, were almost warm . . . but as he returned my gaze, a change took place. Not slowly, but all at once, as if he had recognised something in my face that terrified him. Shock – worse than shock, sheer panic – flared up in his eyes. He snatched his hand away.

'What is it? What's the matter?'

'Lucien . . . You looked . . .'

I turned back towards the fire and said, 'It's happened before.'

Lucien and I had not looked much alike. He was all quicksilver charm where I was ungainly. If we were both feeling serious about something, he managed to look thoughtful while I was in danger of being accused of sulking. And yet, for all our differences, we were unmistakably brother and sister. I had heard people say it was something to do with the set of our mouths, the rapidly changing expression of our eyes.

I hugged my knees to my chest. 'I know, it's grim. After all this time and still the pain hits you when you expect it least.'

'You don't understand.'

But I was convinced that I did. 'Every now and then I think I've caught sight of Luce in the street. Maybe it's just someone who looks like him from the back. Or who has his way of walking. Do you remember how he used to do those funny little crab skips when he'd been struck by what seemed to him an outstandingly brilliant, earth-shattering idea. Some brain-scorchingly wonderful insight or—'

'You even talk like him.'

That wasn't true, not really. I only began to talk like Lucien when I talked about him, and I did that less and less.

I went on, 'Only yesterday I was trying to tell a friend's child about zebras and how zebras became extinct in Sussex. Do you remember that ridiculous long rambling story of his? Of course, the wretched child didn't have the first idea what I was talking about, because I'm not Lucien and so I don't have his magic.' As I spoke, I realised the strength of my longing to talk to Rob about Lucien. The words flowed like pent-up tears. Only Rob could recognise the Lucien who had meant so much to me, the brother who was not only clever and amusing, but infinitely tender and loving too.

'I feel so angry with him sometimes, isn't that awful? The way he dominated my life for so long, totally dominated my life. All my earliest memories are of Lucien. Faith never seemed all that important. It was Lucien who told me stories, Lucien who calmed me down when there was thunder, Lucien who made sure I had a pencil case with all the right things in it when I started school. Maybe if I'd had a proper father, maybe if Faith and I had got on better, then Lucien wouldn't have been quite so important. But he was everything in my life. And then he just finished. Like someone taking away the sky. And do you know what the worst part of it all is, the bit that really sticks in my throat?' Rob didn't answer so I blundered on, 'Do you remember that summer when Lucien plagued us all with secrets? Everyone had to think of a secret and tell him, but he absolutely refused to tell us his. The fifth secret he called it. He kept dropping hints about how amazed we'd all be if he ever condescended to tell us, but of course he never did. And then I half forgot about it – but never completely. And whenever I thought about it I'd say to myself, he's sure to explain one day. And now he won't, not ever. I'll never know. The bastard, how could he die without telling anyone? Why didn't he tell me?' I paused. 'Did he ever tell you, Rob?'

There was silence.

'Rob?'

I nudged his knee with my elbow. With a sound a bit like a tyre going flat, he keeled over behind me.

I twisted round. He was fast asleep.

'Damn you,' I said.

I went and refilled my wine glass and curled up in an armchair which was covered with fading chintz roses, and contemplated Rob's sleeping form. I felt drunk and weary and not in the least bit ready for sleep. I had waited a long time to talk to Rob – ten years, in fact – and if he was asleep when I finally managed it, well then that was a shame, but I supposed it was better than nothing. Beggars can't be choosers, as Mrs Wicks used to tell us with such relish. Lucien had altered her phrase to 'buggers can't be choosers', which used to upset Esme for some reason.

Rob looked as though he didn't intend waking up for at least two days. It would probably take that long for me to sort out how I felt about him now. Or even longer.

I realised then that there never had been a time when I had known how I felt about Rob.

I was eight when he first came into our lives. He was my brother's closest friend and three years older than me, and we quickly established an almost brother-and-sister closeness. Almost. It was easiest when he and Lucien treated me like an honorary boy. I was content to abdicate my girlie status in return for being included in their world. I cheerfully betrayed my girlfriends – blurting out their secret hopes and fears and heartaches without any remorse – simply to win their approval. Rob and I were united in our devotion to Lucien. It was the only tie that bound us.

Or so we pretended. The fiction proved harder to maintain as we struggled through adolescence. Once or twice I caught Rob watching me, when he thought himself unobserved, with a less than brotherly expression in his eyes. Our rough and tumble sometimes became vindictive; we affected surprise at the marks and bruises that resulted.

Lucien encouraged the pretence. Though he was friendly enough when we were alone together, his public opinion was that 'sisters' were a subspecies of human life form. I might protest, but deep down I agreed with him. By the time Lucien and Rob began to show an interest in girls – which was rather later than most of their contemporaries – I must have been about twelve and as awkward and lacking in confidence as possible. I could barely bring myself to look in the mirror long enough to pull a brush through my hair. The dark eyes that stared back from my reflection had a starved and haunted look. Once, in an effort to cheer me up, Lucien said my kind of thin face was what artists called 'gamine' but even I could tell that the dividing line between gamine and peaky was a thin one, and that I generally fell down on the wrong side of it. My mother's increasingly frequent 'poor Janes' were little consolation.

And then, when I was about seventeen and beginning to emerge from these ugly duckling horrors and discover that, though I would never be a swan I could perhaps be a tolerable duck, Esme swam back into our lives. And Esme was stunning. She had been working in a London art gallery when she happened to visit Oxford in the company of her current admirer. I have lost count of the number of times Rob must have told me how he practically fell out of his college window in his efforts to catch her attention. He fell for her on the spot. Endlessly long legs, flawless skin, velvet brown eyes and an air of quiet assurance that left me gaping. And she was the first girlfriend to drive a wedge between Rob and Lucien, though I am sure she never intended to. Anyway, since there was no hope of ever competing in the goodness or beauty stakes, I set out to make myself as foul as possible – but even that is more difficult than most people realise. I shaved my head, had a small raven tattooed on my shoulder and avoided the sickeningly gilded threesome as much as possible.

By then Rob and Lucien were in their final year. Since I saw very little of them, I never knew how Rob and Esme paired off. Nor, a year later when Rob was a post-graduate student in London and Lucien was trying to find a suitable outlet for his restless talents, did I ever really know how Esme stopped being Rob's girlfriend and became my brother's. All I knew was that suddenly Rob craved my company. At first I was flattered, imagining that the old unspoken attraction between us was finally coming into the open, but my disillusion was swift. I soon discovered that he only wanted to be with me in order to indulge his desire to talk about Esme.

It was the oddest sensation.

'Hi,' his voice was always friendly enough on the phone. 'How about supper this evening?' – and like a fool I'd accept. We'd meet at a restaurant. He'd ask me how I was, show an interest in what I was doing. I'd begin to relax. And then, after a couple of glasses of wine, he'd move on to the real business of the evening. Esme. 'I wonder how Esme . . .' 'Did I ever tell you about the time Esme and I . . . ?' However hard I tried to reroute the conversation, Rob always managed to veer back, stubborn as a compass needle, to Esme. I began to feel that it was my body only that was present at the meal, while the spirit of Esme loomed over all. I tried to make a joke of it, pulled up an extra chair and referred to her as Banquo, but Rob merely looked puzzled. I soon began to fear that I was losing focus, becoming blurred around the edges, that if I wasn't careful I was in real danger of sliding out of the picture altogether. The change was so gradual that it was only afterwards that I could give vent to anger.

'What about me?' I'd wail to my empty room, 'Look over here, can't you see me?' But by then Rob had gone and it was too late.

Too late until the afternoon, one hot Sunday towards midsummer, when we were walking across Hyde Park together. Suddenly Rob stopped, the all-too-familiar expression of wistfulness shadowed his face and he said, 'Esme and I came here every day when it snowed last winter. We had snowball fights and I made a sledge and—'

'That's it,' I announced. All at once the London heat was overpowering, like a steaming cloth pressed against my face. 'I've had enough.'

'What?'

'If you want to witter on about Esme until you're blue in the face, that's fine, go ahead, feel free. Just get yourself a therapist or a dictaphone or something. Don't use me for your boring jaunts down memory lane.'

He stiffened. 'I just happened to mention—'

'I know, I know. I've heard it all before, remember. Esme in the snow, Esme at the beach, Esme gets stoned, Esme buys antiques. I'm sick to death of hearing you drivel on about bloody Esme. I don't care if she wins the Nobel Peace Prize or marries the Pope, I simply don't want to hear about it.'

Now his face was grim. He said he hadn't realised that certain topics were off limits, that he clearly should have asked my permission before being thoughtless enough to mention an old and mutual friend, that he couldn't understand why I was suddenly being so unreasonable. And then he said that since it was obvious I found his company boring, he'd burden me with it no longer.

'Good,' I snapped. (What else could I say?) But as I watched him stride away across the park, I understood exactly why I had put up with all those evenings spent being a phantom witness to his heartbreak. Being with Rob, even if he was talking about Esme, was infinitely better than the prospect of not seeing him at all.

To my amazement he telephoned me at work the next day. He said he realised how selfish he'd been in using me as a way of getting over his affair with Esme. But he said my outburst had shown him he was cured of the past. He wanted to apologise properly and to celebrate. Would I consider supper that evening?

Of course I agreed. The day had been hot, and as daylight faded the heat lingered on in the warm pavements and the stuffy London air. I wore a slip of a dress with shoestring straps and, as I looked in the mirror before going out, the face that gazed back at me was somehow fuller, more confident. I could almost believe I might be attractive. And then, just when I would have endured any amount of chatter about the peerless Esme, Rob never mentioned her once. His attention was all on me. What was more, I gradually realised that he was wooing me. The effect was like champagne.

But when it came to the end of the evening and Rob asked, 'Do you want to come back to my flat?' I found myself saying, 'Next time.' His transformation had been too abrupt and I shrank from the idea that he might make love to me and all the time be wishing it was Esme in his bed.

He kissed me gently on the mouth. I almost changed my mind.

'Promise?' he asked.

He was looking at me as if he had only just noticed that I was beautiful.

'I promise.' After all, what difference could a day or two make?

He told me then that he was going away for the weekend and we arranged to meet on Sunday evening. I spent the next two days in a torpor of delicious anticipation. The heat continued. London was shimmering and unreal, warm dirty air rising in the streets, hot nights that banished sleep. Like a love-struck adolescent I lounged in baths that turned from scalding hot to tepid before I even noticed; I wandered alone through the crowded city and was entranced by everything I saw; I sprawled on my bed, too energetic for sleep, too languorous for activity.

It was into this state of blissful anticipation that the message came that my brother had been in an accident. He had fallen from a cliff, had been rushed into intensive care and no one would say what the prognosis might be.

In those first stunned moments, before the real horror of Lucien's accident had sunk in, I can remember feeling furious that my brother had once again managed to scupper my plans. But I was still confident, as the train carried me across the parched countryside to the Dorset hospital where he lay, that my rendezvous with Rob had been delayed only.

I had no way of knowing that Rob would vanish altogether, would from that moment onwards be erased from my life as surely as if it had been he, and not Lucien, who had fallen from that Dorset cliff.

The fire was going out. Rob was wheezing gently in his sleep. Strange how a face remains the same, yet alters as it ages. The lines were deeper around his mouth; his skin was coarser and already lined; his cheeks were hollowed, leaner than I remembered, but all in all he looked so achingly familiar lying there, that for a brief while I thought all I had to do was reach out and touch him and we would both be children once again.

My whole family, even Eric, had been so flattered by his devotion. Which only made his defection the harder to endure. For once I even had sympathy for my mother's 'But Rob was always like a second—' and she'd break off, unable to form the word 'son', and carry on, 'like a nephew. He was one of the family. How can he simply vanish?'

But that was exactly what he had done.

I said, 'Rob, we understood when you didn't show up at the hospital. When you didn't come to the funeral, we tried to understand. But afterwards, Rob, you could have picked up the phone once to tell us how you were. You might have sent a Christmas card, to show you hadn't forgotten us completely. People don't just cease to exist, you know. You can't try to wipe them away like that. It isn't fair.' Even to my own ears my voice had a whining tone.

'It wasn't fair, Rob,' I insisted.

He snored a contented reply.

'For God's sake, tell me what happened to you?'

No answer.

I stood up. The fire had died down and it was growing cold again, but I no longer had the energy to find where the logs were kept. Suddenly I didn't feel as if I had the energy for anything any more. My legs were rubbery and my head throbbed.

I crossed the hearth and gazed down on him. Sleep had washed all the tension from his face. While he was awake, something haunted in his expression had kept me aware of the years that had separated us, but now the familiarity of those features was all that I could see. I crouched down beside him. His clothes smelled of woodsmoke from their drying by the fire and his hair still had a soapy smell, like a child's after a bath. A huge tenderness washed through me. Tenderness and a vast relief that an essential part of my life had been restored to me – by whatever mystery or accident, I did not care. Only Rob had loved Lucien as unquestioningly as I did. Only Rob could have understood how much his death had robbed me. Only with Rob could I have shared my grief.

I picked up his hand and pressed it against my cheek. He pulled it away without waking and rolled over. A glimmer of anger tempted me to force him awake. The frustration of years. How dare he abandon me when I had needed him most! For a moment I considered spending the night beside him on the sofa, cramped and uncomfortable as it was, just to make sure he didn't have a chance to vanish again. At least not until he knew how he had made us suffer all these years. But I knew I was much too tired.

I straightened up. 'You bastard, Rob,' I said. But now my anger was draining away and the epithet sounded almost amicable.

Even in my fuddled state, it dawned on me that the little explaining he had done so far hardly painted a convincing picture. For a split second the possibility flashed through my mind that Rob had been Esme's attacker. I was sure I had read somewhere that husbands and boyfriends are always the most likely suspects in these kinds of cases. That would account for his terror of being questioned by the police. If that was so then I was busy helping a potential murderer. The thought evaporated as soon as it was formed. I had known Rob far too long ever to suspect him of attempted homicide.

I went upstairs and pulled an eiderdown off one of the beds and carried it down the stairs. Rob stirred slightly as I covered him with the eiderdown and pulled off his shoes, but it would have taken more than that to wake him now.

I was planning to leave the disordered table just as it was, but then I reflected that someone might notice it had been laid for two, so I scooped the plates and glasses and shovelled them into the sink. I locked the door and checked that all the curtains were pulled close.

I knew I ought to be making plans, evaluating the situation, deciding how to act for the best in the morning. But a shutter of fatigue was coming down inside my head.

I crawled into a bed, the one that had always been mine, and pulled the blankets around my ears. I really should find some sheets, I thought briefly, just as the familiar lullaby of the river was soothing me into sleep.

5

Rob was perched on the edge of my bed. Weak daylight was filtering through the clouded windows.

'Wake up, Jane.'

I must have heard him about the tenth time he spoke.

I twisted my wrist round to catch the light and peered at my watch. 'Why so early? It's not eight yet.'

'I've been up for hours. Come on, get going, Jane, you've got a lot to do today.'

'I thought I did a lot yesterday.'

'Now it's today.'

I pulled the blankets over my head and groaned. 'You sound just like Owen.'

He bounced to his feet and began pacing round the room, peering through the low windows, touching the few items of furniture with his fingertips as though checking for dust. Sleep appeared not merely to have refreshed him but to have endowed him with huge quantities of surplus energy. Since my head was clogged with the after-effects of wine, his alertness was galling.

I said, 'Keep away from the window, you idiot. I can't imagine why you opened the curtain, someone could easily see in.'

'Jane, we're on the first floor and there's an apple tree right outside. Breakfast is ready.'

'I don't want any.'

'You've got five minutes.'

I closed my eyes firmly only to discover I was far too curious about the coming day to go back to sleep. When I went downstairs I saw that he had cleared away all signs of the previous evening's meal, the kitchen area sparkled and the table was laid with toast and juice and scrambled eggs. He had even unearthed a chequered tablecloth. The curtains were still drawn and the dim light suited my throbbing head; but the radio, voicing strident opinions of the day's events, most certainly did not. I switched it off. Rob sprang to his feet and snapped it back on. When I opened my mouth to protest he said, 'It's to drown the sound of our voices.'

He watched with impatience while I ate. Either he had breakfasted earlier or he wasn't hungry. This was an altogether different Rob from the shaken and exhausted character of the previous day. The nervous energy he was generating would have done a string of racehorses proud. Yesterday I had been competent in contrast to his frailty; this morning I said meekly, 'What do you want me to do?'

'Find Esme's journal, of course.'

I surveyed his crumpled clothes, his unshaven jaw. 'I thought I might go into town and buy you a shaving kit and some fresh clothes.'

'It's hardly a priority. First the journal.'

I sighed. This morning's Rob was incapable of remaining still for more than about thirty seconds. Already he had leapt to his feet and was sweeping away the dirty plates.

'What will you do meanwhile?' I asked.

'God knows. Prowl around upstairs and try not to go mad with impatience.'

I followed him to the sink. 'What makes you so sure her diary will help? It might not even mention anyone, and even if it does—'

'That's my problem. You just find it.'

'But I don't understand. If this diary is the key to the whole situation, as you say, why not simply tell the police about it, so they can do a proper search and—'

His face turned pale beneath the stubble. 'That's the stupidest idea I've ever heard.'

'But why?'

'For Christ's sake, Jane, stop arguing and find the bloody thing!'

He slammed the last of the dishes down on the draining board and strode over to reach my jacket from the peg by the door. He jammed it down on my shoulders. I was on the point of telling him that he could bully all he liked but he'd have to find the journal himself, when suddenly he gripped me by the arms and insisted, 'Whatever you do, Jane, you must not look at her journal. Do you understand?'

I jerked free. 'No, I most certainly do not. How am I to know what it is unless I take a look? Besides, I thought the whole point was to find out what she said about—'

Rob drew in a huge breath. Clearly he was making epic attempts to remain calm as he said, 'Listen. Sorry. But just listen. We're talking about Esme's private journal, the kind of intimate stuff she couldn't even share with me, had barely begun talking about with her therapist. You must know what a private person Esme always was. Is. She'd be devastated if she knew people had been peering into her private thoughts. Even though she's in hospital, she still has a right to some privacy.'

'But still—'

'Maybe you've forgotten what she's like, but I've been living with her for six months and believe me, if Esme thought that you or a whole troop of unknown policemen had been reading her journal, she'd be appalled. You must promise not to look. For her sake, not mine.'

I was annoyed at being lumped together with all those anonymous policemen, but I could see the argument was getting us nowhere.

Rob added, 'Imagine it was you lying there.'

'All right.' I pulled my coat on properly. 'I'll be as quick as I can.'

'And you won't look, will you?'

'Not unless—'

'Promise, Jane.'

'I promise.'

Only then did his expression begin to relax and he attempted a smile. 'Good hunting,' he said.

I didn't answer. There could be no doubting his sincerity, so why, as I pulled my jacket tightly around me and stepped out into the brisk morning air, was I left with an aftertaste of melodrama and deceit?

It was a cold morning. The drizzle had stopped, and though the mist remained, it had grown more benign, thinning in places to let shafts of watery sunlight through. As soon as I was sure I was out of Rob's line of vision, I paused. His urgency had transmitted itself to me and my heart was racing. For a few moments I stood quite still in the midst of the apple trees and drew in several deep breaths of air. Though the reasons might be bizarre, the fact was that I was enjoying my first break in years from the rut in which my life had become stuck. I intended to enjoy myself. Besides, I needed to plan how to circumvent Mrs Wicks.

I imagined her sitting on a tablecloth by the door to Esme's room, her eyes as big as teacups like the dog in the fairy story, but I couldn't remember what the character had done to vanquish the dog.

Taking care to remain out of sight, I wandered down towards the river. Soon I was pushing aside the fringe of willow and standing in the green space beside the boathouse. It was smaller than I remembered and, disappointingly, an altogether unremarkable spot to adult eyes. I crouched down and half closed my eyes and tried to recapture the magic, but without success. Just a patch of mossy grass where children had once played.

And then I caught sight of the punt; it must have been hauled from the water years since and now it was slowly capsizing back into the earth – the timbers were rotting and grass grew between the seats. Poor punt, no one had ever taken proper care of it, though it had served us well. We had ventured upstream and down, but never very far. More than a couple of miles in either direction would have brought us to a built-up area and that would have spoiled the illusion that our stretch of water was merely a part of a wild and untamed journey. We preferred to go only as far as some open fields or the little patch of woodland where the river became wide and shallow with frequent shingly banks. We did not want to follow it into urban captivity.

It had been a versatile punt. I smiled. We had turned it into a Roman galley, the *Marie Celeste*, the Ancient Mariner's ship. For a while Lucien had been quite keen on *The Ancient Mariner*, having learned most of it in school, but the rest of us were less enthusiastic since the poem offered few decent roles. Lucien, of course, was the Ancient Mariner, and Snowy-two was roped in to play the albatross, which he did with his usual nonchalance, but the rest of us . . . ? I heard Lucien's precise voice:

> The many men so beautiful!
> And they all dead did lie:
> And a thousand thousand slimy things
> Lived on; and so did I.

Rob and Owen had grudgingly agreed to be the many men so beautiful, even though they claimed it was really boring to have to lie around being dead all the time, and they weren't too happy about being beautiful either. Esme and

I, needless to say, had to be the thousand thousand slimy things, which I resented bitterly.

We had been thankful when Lucien announced he was sick of *The Ancient Mariner* and had thought of a new diversion: the Murder Game. Rob had followed him in this, as in everything else, but Owen, to everyone's surprise, had said that thinking of ways to murder people was a stupid waste of time and he had better things to do. I can remember being flabbergasted: no one had ever dared to criticise Luce before. We had been sitting in our usual wavy circle and we had all looked at Owen as if seeing him for the first time. Until now we had noticed only his sensitivity, his delicate features and his long gentle hands. Now we saw the stubbornness that was the heart of him. Lucien's eyes had narrowed and I watched anxiously to see how he would deal with this threat to his authority. 'Why not?' he asked at length.

Owen considered for a moment before answering, 'It's so easy to destroy things. Much better surely to create them.'

'Christ, what a boring prig!' Lucien had exclaimed, but his accusation was so wide of the mark that for once it fell flat and fizzled out harmlessly. Looking back I could see Owen had won Lucien's respect in that moment, though neither he nor any of the rest of us had realised it then. And he hadn't been trying to, that was the point. His opposition would have been meaningless had he been hoping to gain anything by it.

So Owen simply shrugged his shoulders and left us to play the Murder Game without him. After a couple of days, something obsessive in Lucien's fascination with this latest game made me look back with nostalgia for the relative simplicity of life as a slimy thing. But that was later.

While I was riffling through my memories, the sun came out and glittered on the wet grass and sparkled on the strands of willow. In the branches above my head a blackbird began to sing, his bubbling music a counterpoint to the rush of the river and the unceasing beat of the Rams.

Birdsong, the river and the Rams – for the first time it almost felt like the Glory Cottage of my childhood.

Mrs Wicks was not sitting on a tablecloth but she was ironing one. I took this to be a good omen, though her expression did not augur well. I hitched up the corners of my mouth and tried hard to look like the sort of person who would be interested in arthritis or bad feet or whatever it was that made her so grim.

'Hello, Mrs Wicks, how are you this morning?'

'Well enough.'

I looked serious. 'And what's the news? Of Esme, I mean.'

She glared. Her eyes were not as big as teacups, but they were round and hard like old-fashioned boiled sweets. She tugged at the buttons of her navy cardigan with a fleshy hand. 'She's still in a coma, won't respond to anything. Didn't even respond when I spoke to her last night. Her father says he's trying.'

She sounded highly sceptical of Mr Drummond's efforts. I swallowed my anger and tried to think how Owen – the only child Mrs Wicks had ever had any time for, I now remembered – would have proceeded.

In an Owen-sort of concerned voice I said, 'And how is Mr Drummond coping?'

For the briefest moment an almost human expression softened her marble-hard eyes, then she glared at me again, 'He copes.'

'Is he here?'

'At the hospital.'

'Poor Mr Drummond. Such a terrible shock.'

She continued ironing furiously. 'Did you remember the torch?'

Oh, hell.

'Goodness, I completely forgot. Shall I go back for it now?'

'That' s up to you.'

My efforts to woo her were having the opposite effect. I said, 'Do you suppose Mr Drummond would mind if I borrowed something to read? I thought I might look in Esme's room.'

'You might.'

I realised this was all the encouragement I would receive. 'Thanks. I won't be long.'

'I'm going out in half an hour.'

'Don't worry.' (My spirits soared.) 'I can always let myself out.'

'I'll lock up after you,' she said firmly. 'I wouldn't want to have to answer to Mr Drummond if I let strangers roam around his empty house. There's been a deal of burglaries around here recently.'

Not trusting myself to answer at once, I walked towards the door. Then I said, 'She always used to have the room next to the bathroom.'

'Still does.'

I left the kitchen and went into the hall. There was a new striped rug on the floor. The newness of it made me aware of how little else had changed in the house in twenty years. I couldn't imagine Martin's Court ever changing – the same few items of furniture, the same cold austerity. The only cheerful note was struck by the coloured light shining through the stained-glass window above the main staircase. Esme's mother, Clare, had always been notoriously stingy, and since her death her husband had apparently not been inclined to alter anything.

I glanced through the half-open doors that led off the hallway: a large sitting room with polished wooden floors and a few items of sagging furniture, a couple of drab prints on the walls and another room that was Mr Drummond's study. This contained a smattering of books and a large desk, but little else besides. Each room was only saved from chronic bleakness by tall French windows which overlooked the long lawn leading down to the willow-fringed river.

About two-thirds of the way up the stairs there was a small landing where the stairway made two right-angled turns. A chill bathroom and Esme's bedroom were both on this intermediate level. I pushed open the door of Esme's room.

It was nearly, but not quite, as sparse as the rest of the house. A narrow metal bed – probably picked up by Clare Drummond from a scrapyard – stood in one corner. There was a white-painted dressing table, a wooden chair, a bookcase and a small bureau. During her teens, during the time that we lost touch with each other, Esme must have struggled to make her room more personal: there were a couple of posters on the walls, a cheap durrie beside the bed, a scarf draped over the chair.

I sat down on the edge of the bed and a couple of metal springs scraped against each other noisily. Somehow I felt I had been caught off balance by coming here and now needed the chance to gather my thoughts. If I had feared that seeing her room would evoke her personality and so make me feel her present danger more keenly, I need not have worried.

As I sat on her bed and looked round her cold room with its half-hearted attempts at decoration, it dawned on me that I knew almost nothing of Esme. She was a part of all my most intense childhood memories and yet I could not say we had ever been friends. She had, or so I believed, been in love with my brother at the time of his death, but even then I had learned almost nothing about her. And since then, she had simply slipped from view. Not dramatically, like Rob. She had sent the occasional card; I think she and my mother may have met for lunch a few times in London, but she and I had not seen each other at all.

Rob had said she had 'been through one hell of a bad time – for years and years'. He said they had been living together for six months. But when he spoke of her, he didn't sound like a man whose lover is in a critical condition in hospital. More than ever I had the sense of information withheld.

And now, if she did not recover from her injury, I would never have the chance to know her. Once again I was reminded of how easy it was for people to slip out of my life without revealing themselves. Faith never shared her true concerns with me, Owen was in many ways a stranger still and Lucien had died taking his famous fifth secret with him. Years ago Esme had woven herself into the fabric of my life without once sharing herself with me. And now she might die and then I'd never have the chance to discover who she was. It was vexing in the way that a magician's sleight of hand can be annoying; as though she had deliberately obscured herself from view.

The sound of tyres crunching to a halt on the driveway at the side of the house reminded me of my purpose. I knelt down and examined the contents of the bookcase. A pile of well-thumbed books – well-thumbed, I soon discovered, because almost the entire collection had been bought for a few pence at charity shops – indicated a somewhat desultory interest in reading. But no journal.

I looked through the bureau: one drawer had a few pairs of socks and a half-used writing pad; the next had a photograph album with only three pages of photographs glued in (mostly Snowy, none of me) and some foreign stamps; the bottom drawer contained a few comics. Without much hope I turned my attention to the dressing table, and there I found the journal almost at once. It was in the bottom drawer, under a couple of old hand-knitted jerseys. It didn't take great powers of detection to recognise it: quite apart from the secret location, the large, hard-backed pale blue notebook had 'Private Testament' written on the front.

I was just wondering how to smuggle such an awkward object past the theft-wary Mrs Wicks, when I heard footsteps on the stairs.

In the grip of sudden panic, I shoved the diary back in the drawer and closed it noisily, then spun round and seized a couple of random paperbacks from the pile, just as the door creaked open and a man whom I recognised at once as John Drummond came into the room.

* * *

Even though I had spent four summers living on their doorstep, I had never got to know Esme's parents. Her mother was generally agreed to be odd, but in a secretive, unobtrusive sort of way. Faith had told us that John and Clare Drummond were friends of hers, but though she was friendly enough with John, she seemed to regard Esme's mother with a sort of baffled curiosity, as if she were an exhibit in a museum. My chief memory of Clare was of a tall, stately woman who walked with stiff dignity across the lawns and did not always answer when spoken to. Once or twice I saw Mrs Wicks leading her gently back to the house. Hardly surprising, given the oddness of his home, John Drummond spent his weeks in London, only returning briefly at the weekend so that his wife could wear herself out doing all his washing by hand. None of us had ever seen his London flat. Lucien constructed an elaborate fantasy which had the eminent QC inhabiting baroque rooms that were richly furnished in red and purple brocades and velvets, his dining table buckling under the weight of lavish meals, champagne and oysters in abundance. Later Lucien added exotic mistresses to the picture.

Now, as Mr Drummond and I stood facing each other in Esme's little bedroom while he caught his breath and I tried not to look as guilty as I felt, I realised that this shadowy and eminent QC (retired) must have once been a very handsome man. He had those regular, clean-cut features, now grown a little blotched and whiskery, that fighter pilots have in old Second World War films.

He had been looking at me with some surprise, but then his expression showed recognition and he stepped forward. 'Of course, Faith's daughter. Jane. For a moment I couldn't think who you were. All a bit of a muddle since . . . since the accident.'

'How is Esme?'

He hunched up his thin shoulders, let them fall again hopelessly. Then he sat down on the edge of the bed, which creaked again, and put his hands on his knees and his expression was so anguished I could have wept.

'Wish to God I knew. No straight answers at the hospital. Ward sister said it was "up to her now". Said she'd seen worse cases make a full recovery. She seemed to think it was a question of whether Esme was prepared to put up a fight. Wish I could understand how she can fight – the poor child can barely breathe unaided. What do they mean by fight?'

'Oh.' I sat down on the little chair and tried to think of something – anything – encouraging. 'It's all so—'

He hadn't heard me. 'They keep asking questions about her. What sort of music did she like? Apparently a favourite piece of music can sometimes break through the coma better than voices. How should I know what pop music she likes? Do you?'

'No.'

He skipped his hand on his knee in a gesture of irritation. 'My God, but I wish Rob was here. What a damn hopeless time for him to go walkabout. If only I could reach him, tell him about Esme . . . he'd be sure to know about the music. The police say they're looking for him, but heavens above, he might be gone for weeks.' He appealed to me, 'You can't think where he's gone, can you?'

I stared at him. 'Sorry. No.'

'Hm. The twins will be back in a day or so. I only got hold of them last night. But I don't suppose they'll be much help. They saw even less of Esme than I did.'

Mr Drummond's casual mention of his twin sons astonished me, and I realised that they had played so small a part in my time at Glory Cottage that I had somehow erased them from my memory of the place. Amazing to think that those two bawling bundles of energy and mess must now have left school.

I asked, 'What are the twins doing now?' I couldn't remember their names, even. Perhaps I had never known what they were.

'Travelling,' said their father absently. 'Before university next year.'

Since my main memory of the twins during our last summer at Glory Cottage, when they had been all motion and no sense, was that they had at all costs to be kept from tumbling into the river, I felt a twinge of anxiety at the thought of them travelling unsupervised. But Mr Drummond was looking round the room. 'Hospital wanted to know if she had a teddy bear, but I'm damned if I can think . . .'

Like me, he was becoming painfully aware of how little he had known her. And it was worse for him, the not knowing, being her father.

'Can't see anything here,' he sighed. 'Maybe in London . . . Damn Rob, where the hell is he? He's the only one who can help us.' He stood up. 'Let's find ourselves a drink. What were you doing up here anyway?'

'Looking for something to read.'

Simultaneously we glanced down at the two books I had snatched in such a hurry from the shelf: *A Palomino for Pauline* and a manual on the care of pet rabbits.

He looked puzzled. Then, for the first time, there was the hint of a smile on his face as he said, 'Like you, I think light reading is best on holiday.'

I followed him as he led the way down the stairs.

Esme's journal remained hidden beneath the old jerseys in the dressing-table drawer.

6

Fortified by an after-breakfast glass of sherry (John Drummond had had two) I walked back across the lawn and the orchard to Glory Cottage. The last of the mist had cleared and the sunshine was almost warm against my face. A few leaves were still clinging to the apple trees and the brambles that had snared me the previous evening yielded a couple of late blackberries. By the time I pushed open the cottage door, I had reached my decision: since I had lied to everyone else during the past twenty-four hours, it seemed churlish not to lie to Rob as well. Besides, I was sure he was only telling me half of the truth and I felt the need for a secret of my own.

'I couldn't find it,' I told him.

'What?'

He must have been pacing up and down on the landing because he rocketed down the stairs as soon as I entered. The strain of waiting was evident in his taut mouth, his piercing eyes, and his disappointment when I spoke was so tangible I half regretted my lie.

'It's all right,' I said, 'I can go back later and have a proper look. It's bound to be there somewhere.'

'What the hell have you been doing all this time?'

'Talking to John Drummond mostly. Listen, you can't keep hiding like this.'

'That's my business.'

'Not any more. Mr Drummond is frantic to get hold of you. The people at the hospital have been asking him about Esme – what sort of music she liked, that sort of thing – and he doesn't have a clue what to tell them. He needs you.'

'Music? Why?'

'Apparently they use it sometimes to get through a coma.'

'Oh.' He began to move restlessly around the room, picking objects up and setting them down again without looking at them, before saying, 'You know, it sounds mad, but I really don't know much about Esme's likes and dislikes.'

'Not even after six months?'

'No. And it isn't just music either. Food and films, books, people, what to do, it was always me who did the choosing. Esme never seemed to mind much one way or another. After the battles I'd had with the woman I was with before, I must say I found it rather soothing. To begin with, at least. Recently it was sometimes . . . annoying.' He frowned and straightened the corner of the hearthrug with his toe.

I said, 'There must be something that was special. Maybe it was a piece of music you liked which might remind her of the happy times you spent together.'

If they were happy times, I thought. I was beginning to have my doubts. Suddenly I noticed that he was gripping the back of the armchair so ferociously that his knuckles were white as bone.

'What's the matter?'

'They might try—'

'Yes?'

He turned to me with an embarrassed smile, then glanced away quickly, but not quickly enough to hide his expression of black despair. 'Tell them to try playing the theme music to *Match of the Day*.'

'Is this a joke?'

'No. Just tell them. If they want to reach her, they can try that.'

'I didn't know Esme liked football.'

'Don't be dense, Jane.'

'Anyway, you'll have to tell them yourself. I can hardly march in and say that actually I haven't seen Esme since she was a child but I do know that the one piece of music that really means a lot to her is the theme tune to *Match of the Day*. I'd have to be bloody clairvoyant. You'll have to tell them yourself.'

'I can't.'

'You mean you won't.'

'Okay, won't. It may look selfish, but you just have to trust me for a bit. And I promise I'll reappear the minute you hand over her journal. Surely you can see that by disappearing at the very moment of her attack I've made the situation impossible for myself. Can't you understand?'

I did. And then again, I didn't.

What I did see, for the first time since all this began, was that his feelings for Esme were genuine and strong.

He was still standing near the fireplace, his hands gripping the back of the armchair, his face averted. I walked across the room and put my arms around him.

'She'll be all right,' I said uselessly, 'I know she will.'

'Just find the diary.'

'I will.'

Only then did he begin to relax. He folded his arms round me and rested his cheek against mine. I had believed my gesture was intended to comfort merely, and was startled by the way the surface of my skin shivered into life at his closeness. I made the tiny adjustments necessary for our bodies to fit snugly together and brushed my cheek against his stubble. And then I felt an answering change in him, that subtle but monumental shift from solace to desire, as though the attraction we had felt for each other all those years before had never ceased to exist, but had simply gone underground to wait for this moment, like those seeds that lie dormant for years under the desert sands waiting for the coming of the rain.

My throat was dry. I thought: this is all wrong. I disentangled myself slowly. Rob was looking at me and he was smiling.

'Jane—' he began.

I said, 'Hand over some money, Mr Rich Man. John Drummond has offered me a lift into town and I told him there were a few things I needed.'

He rubbed his palm across his jaw. 'Like a razor?'

'If he asks, I'll tell him I shave my legs daily. And I'll get you some fresh clothes. I can always pretend they're presents for Owen.'

'What about the journal?'

'Mrs Wicks would smell a rat if I went straight back now. I'll try again later.'

'I could just break in.'

'Don't even consider it. The whole place is sure to be bristling with alarms, and the last thing you need right now is a burglary charge.'

'Okay.' But I could tell he was less than charmed by my good advice. He pulled a wad of money from his trouser pocket and peeled off ten £20 notes. 'Will that do?'

'Probably.' My voice emerged squeaky with suppressed greed.

Rob said, 'And get something for yourself.'

Cheered by this instruction, I was sorry I had not asked for more.

'Don't be long,' he told me as I buttoned up my jacket to leave, 'I go crazy here on my own.'

We embraced briefly and his kiss grazed the edge of my mouth.

Being with John Drummond again after such a long time made me feel as if I had reverted to childhood. I quickly realised that his offer to drive me into town had not been entirely altruistic. Having spent the whole night at Esme's bedside, he couldn't face returning there at once, although he phoned the hospital every twenty minutes or so in case there was some change, and shopping with me was as good a way of filling the time as any other.

To my embarrassment he insisted on accompanying me to the shops which somewhat damped my enjoyment. He expressed no surprise that I was devotedly buying an entire set of clothes for the husband I had come to Berkshire to escape from. I remembered Rob's instructions to get something for myself and bought a loose wool top in a flattering shade of red and some stripy leggings.

Over coffee at the local hotel, which John had gone into in order to make another call to the hospital, he politely asked me about myself. I launched into an honest description of the precarious fortunes of the OJ Nursery, but then, seeing his confusion, I had to dilute the truth to accommodate the fact that I'd been showering £20 notes in all the shops. Besides, given his present traumas, our financial flounderings were insignificant. One way and another I was having a hard time being honest with anyone.

Hoping to compensate somehow for the necessary lies, I offered, 'We always had such good holidays at Glory Cottage. The best. They were magic times for all of us.'

He brightened. 'Really? I'm glad to hear it. I used to worry that Esme was alone too much. It wasn't easy to know what was best. One tried not to interfere, but still . . .'

It was odd, I thought, he talked about Esme more as if he was a distant uncle, not her father. He must have been thinking along the same lines because he added suddenly, 'Esme and I have never been as close as I would have liked. Shame, but there it is. Spent most of her time with her mother, of course, and Mrs Wicks. One never quite knew what to say to her. Your brother, now – Lucien – he was a remarkable child. Never at a loss for words.'

'Yes,' my response was automatic, 'very clever.'

'But it was more than that. He had such a zest for life, such vitality.' I was waiting for John Drummond to add the usual gloss about the tragedy of Lucien's early death, but instead he looked at me sideways and said, 'He always cut through the humbug, didn't he? Saw right through to the heart of things. I suppose Faith must have told you . . .'

He broke off.

I just stared at him blankly. Afterwards I could have skewered myself with frustration at having let the opportunity slip. If I'd had the wit to respond casually, 'Oh, yes, of course, Faith told me all about that ages ago,' John Drummond could have been tricked into revealing something I didn't know, something, perhaps, that might have affected me directly. But I didn't, and by the time I had realised my error, John Drummond had deftly sidestepped his potential blunder and was talking of other things.

An old curiosity stirred. My childish attempts to make sense of the adult relationships around me had been occasionally disastrous, more often comical. I remembered the time I had commented to Lucien that Faith seemed to be different when in the company of Mr Drummond. At the time I had not been able to put my finger on the exact nature of the difference, and had merely said that they seemed to be really good friends. But I saw now it was more than that. There had been an ease between them, as of two people who can let down their guard with each other, who no longer have to act out a pretence.

I had stumbled on them together one afternoon when they had been walking along the towpath. My mother's face had been bare of all artifice as she said with heartfelt sincerity, 'Even nightmares have to end, thank God. I don't think I could have stood it much longer,' and Mr Drummond, younger then, and handsome, had just looked down at her with real admiration and squeezed her hand. It was too late for me to hide and my mother's annoyance at the sight of me was galling. Later, when I reported all this back to Lucien, he said, 'He's probably an ex-lover,' in his most world-weary twelve-year-old way, 'Faith cast him off like an old glove and now their relationship is entirely platonic.' A concept that meant little to me then. Later that summer, in a rare moment of intimacy, I said to John, 'Faith finds you a real tonic.' His pleased expression added weight to an idea that was forming in my mind that the eminent QC was in fact our mislaid father, an idea not finally buried until the discovery of Rex Turner on my birth certificate. I had wondered if it was perhaps some complication concerning Clare and Esme that had forced Faith to settle for the unpromising Eric. Luckily, for the time being at least, I kept these thoughts to myself.

I said now, 'Do you remember when I said Faith found you a tonic?'

He smiled, though it could have been politeness. 'Funny little child you were,' he said. 'Face like thunder most of the time, but when you smiled . . . and the best friend Esme ever had.'

'Really?'

He nodded. 'Did she ever talk to you?'

'Not much.'

'She never talked to me,' he confessed, 'never has done. My fault, I suppose, should have spent more time with the family. And then I think she blamed me for the whole boarding school episode. I thought it was for the best, but she saw it differently. Did she ever mention it to you?'

'Never.'

'Bit of a dark horse all round then. Never seemed to have many friends. I tried to get to know her when she moved to London, but a bit late in the day then. It was easiest when she was with Lucien. I don't think she has ever approved of me much.'

'Why not? Because of the boarding school?'

He thought for a moment, glanced at me quickly as though tempted to yield up a confidence, then thought better of it and said briskly, 'Among other things. Shall we go?'

After another phone call to the hospital (no change), we began to walk back towards the car park. On the way I went into a large stationer's and bought an A4 notebook, as nearly as possible like the one in which Esme had written her 'Private Testament'.

To the ever-attentive John Drummond I explained, 'I need something to jot my thoughts down in while I'm here. A kind of journal.'

'Funny thing,' he muttered hoarsely. 'That's just what Esme did, last time she was home.'

On the way back to Martin's Court, John (I couldn't carry on calling him Mr Drummond after our shopping spree) said, 'Why don't you come to London with me? Esme might recognise your voice.'

'I doubt it. We haven't seen each other in years.'

'Come along anyway. I'd be glad of the company.' Through the careful nonchalance of his invitation I could see his dread of visiting the hospital alone.

'Maybe tomorrow,' I said stonily.

'As you wish.' But he sounded hurt.

I sat in silence, hating myself. I couldn't leave Rob alone and besides, I was terrified of bumping into Owen or my mother at the hospital. I really ought to phone Owen. Anxiety for him and the children mingled uncomfortably with my guilt. I tried to put them all out of my mind.

I turned to John and said, 'I know it's cowardly, but ever since Lucien's accident I've had a phobia about hospitals. That smell and all the waiting around and that awful cheerfulness and not being able to do anything.'

'I do understand,' he interrupted my rambling.

His tact only increased my sense of being, as Lucien would have said in his days of reading old-fashioned adventure books for boys, a rotten cad and a stinker.

'You rotten cad,' I said to myself over and over again as we turned in before the pale blue façade of Martin's Court. 'You utter utter stinker.'

Deep-dyed in caddishness I might be, but I was still able to congratulate myself on having solved the problem of how to extract Esme's testament. There was, however, a new difficulty.

'I'll carry your bags down to the cottage,' said John.

I protested as forcefully as I could, but without effect, and I could see no way of stopping him, so I was reduced to sending telepathic messages to Rob instead.

John was fidgeting. 'I'll just put a quick call through to the hospital first.'

I seized my chance. 'I thought I'd pick out another of Esme's books. I did err rather on the side of lightness.'

But he must have forgotten *A Palomino for Pauline* and the rabbit book, because he said only, 'Of course, go ahead. You might find something in the drawing room.' Already he was dialling the hospital.

I was careful to keep the bag from the stationer's with me as I went up the stairs. It was a simple enough procedure to remove Esme's journal from the dressing-table drawer and replace it with the one I had just bought. I even remembered to pick a battered thriller from the shelf before returning down the stairs and putting the stationer's bag into the one which held my newly purchased clothes.

John Drummond was replacing the receiver.

'Any news?' My question was obligatory, even though his expression was painfully easy to read.

'No change. But I'll go up anyway. You never know.'

I hesitated, then, 'I've been thinking about Esme and music and . . . I know it's a long shot but . . . you might try . . .' I cleared my throat, but it had to be said, 'You might suggest they try the theme music to *Match of the Day*.'

'I'm sorry?'

'The football programme. It has a jolly sort of tune to introduce it. Esme was rather taken with it.' I was floundering, not surprisingly. 'Apparently. At least, I think I remember . . .'

My explanation had only confused him further. But John Drummond was nothing if not courteous. 'Yes, I see. Well, thank you. I'll certainly tell them at the hospital. I'm sure they'll be . . .' He couldn't quite complete his sentence.

'Baffled,' I wanted to say for him.

It was lucky for me that he was too distracted to concern himself with my increasingly odd behaviour. In my efforts to warn Rob of danger, I began to tell John, as we crossed the lawn, some of my most poignant memories of Glory Cottage. By the time we were halfway across the orchard my voice had risen to a socialite shriek. Just to be on the safe side, I fumbled with the key and tried turning it the wrong way several times before John, with commendable patience, said, 'Here, let me.'

'Oh, heavens!' my exclamation notched up several more decibels. 'I'm always hopeless with keys. Either I lose them or I can't make them work or—'

'There. It wasn't locked.'

I scuttled ahead of him into the downstairs room and scanned it swiftly for signs of dual occupation, but, as I should have known, Rob was not so easily caught out.

I allowed my voice to return to normal. 'Would you like some tea? It's very kind of you to let me stay here.'

'I'd best be off to the hospital.' He was about to leave when he suggested, almost shyly, 'But I might look in later on this evening, if you don't mind. Or you could pop up to the house for a nightcap? Then I could tell you . . . how things are . . .'

I shielded myself against his desolation. 'I'm planning an early night. I'll come up to the house in the morning and you can tell me then.'

'As you wish.'

'Oh, and John, you won't tell anyone I'm here, will you?'

'You can trust me,' he smiled.

Which is more than you can do with me, I thought bitterly as I watched his frail straight body disappearing between the apple trees.

I found Rob in one of the back bedrooms. To my surprise, he had been stripping the wallpaper from one of the walls. He was standing in a pile of discarded paper, a sponge in one hand and a table knife in the other. His face was haggard, as though he had aged several years in the few hours since I had seen him.

'What on earth are you doing?'

He advanced towards me, his face taut with rage. 'What the hell do you think you're trying to do? Tea? What did you invite him in here for? Are you completely mad or just practising?'

'This happens to be his house, or had you forgotten?'

'What took you so long? Have you any idea what it's like for me being cooped up in here all day with nothing to do but worry?'

'No need to blame me. I'm the one who's helping you, remember?'

'Are you? I don't suppose you've even bothered to look for the journal yet, have you?'

'No.'

I honestly believe it had been my intention to hand it over to him straight away but his ungrateful outburst made me so angry that I decided to let him sweat it out for a little longer.

'Damn you, Jane. I should have done it myself.'

I flung the carrier bag containing his clothes down on the heap of wallpaper scraps. 'You do that!'

I retreated to the bedroom I had slept in the previous night and shoved the carrier bag containing my clothes and the journal into a drawer.

For a few minutes all I could hear was the sound of a knife scraping against the wall, paper being peeled away, the river's music in the background. Then, as I had anticipated, footsteps crossed the landing.

'Jane, I'm sorry.'

I said nothing.

'I shouldn't have been so angry just now. You don't know what it's like being caged up all day like this. Worrying myself sick. Nothing to do.'

'Except tear the place apart.'

He came into the room and stood smiling at me. 'That same wallpaper's been there for twenty-five years at least. I always hated it. Besides, it was falling off anyway. And a man must have some occupation or there's a real risk of madness. Prison taught me that.'

'Mrs Wicks will have a fit.'

He shrugged. 'And thanks for getting the clothes, Jane. I know you're doing your best to help.'

He was still smiling. A warm, coaxing smile. And I felt myself begin to blur at the edges, as I had done ten years before when he had talked to me about Esme. And I thought: he doesn't see me here at all. Only what he needs from me.

I said, 'Therapy, is it? In that case, I'll give you a hand.'

By mid-afternoon the second wall had been stripped bare.

It was while I was unpacking the wine and the few items of food I had bought with John that morning, that I noticed Mrs Wicks's torch. I cursed silently. Pulling back the curtain slightly, I saw that the early dusk was being hastened by dark clouds and the approach of rain. Suddenly the interior of Glory Cottage looked remarkably cosy.

'Damn torch,' I said. Rob and I had worked amicably together throughout the afternoon, and I planned to hand over the journal over a convivial glass of wine.

When I told Rob I had to return to the main house, I also anticipated his inevitable response. 'Yes, yes,' I assured him, 'I promise I'll think of some excuse to hunt for the journal.'

Mrs Wicks was crestfallen by this evidence of my reliability. 'I said I'd return it before dark,' I said smugly.

Since she was incapable of thanking me, she maintained a rigid silence while regaining possession of the torch. She stood in the kitchen doorway, her solid bulk forbidding entrance, which only goaded me to insist.

'Do you mind if I come in?' I cast around for an excuse, 'I want to phone my husband and Mr Drummond told me to use the phone at any time.'

'He said nothing to me about that.'

'I expect he forgot. He does have rather a lot on his mind right now.'

I edged past her and went through the kitchen to the hall. I could hear her disapproving wheezes as she hovered, just out of sight. No doubt she was peering through a crack in the door to make sure I didn't walk off with the light fittings or the telephone directory – there wasn't much else worth stealing.

I dialled the OJ Nursery number.

'Hello, Owen.'

'Jane! Where on earth are you?'

'Oh, well . . . how are the children?'

'All right. I thought you said you'd phone last night.'

'Did I? I meant to but . . . it was awkward.'

'Awkward? Why? What's the matter? Are you safe?'

'Of course I'm safe. Why shouldn't I be?'

'I just wondered . . . your mother phoned . . . she sounded anxious, wanted to know where you were. She seemed to think someone might be trying to make contact with you, God knows who, she wouldn't say. But I got the impression she thought there was some kind of—'

'Danger?'

'Something like that.'

I stifled a twinge of unease. 'Oh, that's just Faith being melodramatic as usual.'

'Just so long as you haven't been kidnapped or anything.'

'Why the hell should anyone want to kidnap me?'

There was a muffled sound at the end of the phone, a sort of choking, perhaps, and a muttered phrase that might have been, 'Your sunny personality, perhaps,' but which was too indistinct for me to be sure. Come to think of it, Owen's voice had been distinctly blurry throughout.

'Owen, are you all right?'

There was a shifting noise, as if he was standing to attention. 'A-one okay,' he said briskly. Not a phrase I had ever heard Owen use before. My uneasiness was growing.

'What about the children?'

'Nnhh. They're fine. In fact they're busy making popcorn at the moment.'

'Popcorn? Whatever for?'

'We thought it might be fun.'

Right on cue came the distant sounds of children having fun. I was just beginning to relax again and smile with maternal fondness at the chirrups of innocent pleasure when I realised there was a more mature note being struck among the noises off.

'Owen, who's there?'

'Here?'

'Yes.'

'Well, Laura and Billy . . .'

'I know that. Who else?'

'Oh, no one in particular. Someone just dropped by. They'll be going in a minute. Jane, when are you coming home?'

'No one – someone – *who*, for God's sake?'

'Actually, Dinah's here. I don't expect she'll stay much longer. She said she'd have to go home soon. She's only been here a few minutes, haven't you, Dinah?'

'Dinah?'

I sat down on the bottom stair and the phone nearly jerked off the table. The black hole I had spent a lifetime trying to avoid had suddenly moved very close to me indeed.

'Dinah?'

'Yes. She was just dropping Laura and Billy back. I expect she'll go in a minute.'

'That's the third time you've said it.'

'Ah well. Must be true then. Good of you to take an interest, I must say.'

I didn't speak. Couldn't speak in case my words took me to the very edge of the black hole and forced me to look in.

After a moment's silence, Owen said, 'Thought I might have a bit of fun before the ship goes down.'

'What's that supposed to mean?'

'I'd have thought it was obvious. Anyway, I blame the gin sling. Or maybe it was the sidecar.'

'What?'

'We've found all these cocktail mixes in a magazine. I'd never realised there were so many. You should try them, Jane. Learn to relax a bit. Enjoy yourself. Don't worry about me. I'm fine. Never been better. Having a wonderful time. Maybe I should send you a postcard.'

'Owen, you're drunk.'

'Am I now? You're well out of it then.'

My head was filled with coloured lights and I felt as if I was going to be sick. Owen didn't want me there. No one had ever wanted me there. Not really. Only Lucien, sometimes . . .

'Jane, I've been worried about you—'

'Give up, Owen. You've always been a hopeless liar. I'll ring you again tomorrow.'

'When are you coming back?'

'Give my regards to Dinah.'

I put down the phone. I was shaking. I clenched my fists and almost choked. 'Bitch. You bloody bitch.'

It was still only a guess, of course. Maybe it was simply my guilty conscience creating dramas out of nothing. After all, there wasn't anything remotely unusual about Dinah dropping by for a while when she brought the children back. And if she and Owen decided to relax over a few drinks together, that didn't mean . . .

I tried to work up some anger. How dare he be so irresponsible when he was supposed to be in charge of the children? But it didn't get me very far. Owen couldn't be irresponsible if he tried, not really. The children were fine with him, always had been and always would be. It wasn't concern for Laura and Billy that was making me feel as if I was trying to stand on the deck of a ship heaving through a Force Nine gale. It was the fact that he actually sounded as if he was enjoying himself. With Dinah, he was having fun. Something he hadn't done in my company since – when? The misery of it was that I simply couldn't remember.

I could imagine him now, as he set down the receiver and returned to Dinah and the children and the popcorn and the experimental cocktails. He was smiling, his hair was tousled, his manner relaxed. When all the restraint and coldness had drained away, there was no one so giddyingly handsome, no one I would rather be with. I imagined him making some idiotic joke that reduced Laura to peals of giggles; I imagined him taking Billy on his knee and kissing the boy's fat rosy cheek. I imagined him smiling across the room at Dinah and saying, 'That's okay then. The coast is clear at least until tomorrow. We're in luck.'

'Bitch. BITCH!'

Mrs Wicks waddled in from the kitchen and switched on the hall light the better to observe my stricken face.

'Trouble at home, dear?' For the first time since my arrival, the miserable old goblin was smiling.

'Of course not. Everything is fine,' I announced.

But she was still grinning as I left the house.

7

Instead of going back to the cottage, I began to walk along the road towards the town. All thoughts of Rob had vanished from my mind and I wanted only to get home again as quickly as I could so as to blaze out my anger against Owen. How dare he push me into second place! How dare he try to lie to me about Dinah! Hadn't I been lied to all my life, patronised and kept in the dark? Even today John Drummond had been about to mention some past secret of Faith's and then had held back when he realised I was still being kept in ignorance.Faith had never told me anything unless she had to. And now Owen thought he could deceive me and fob me off with lies. No more lies. I'd had enough. My rage would blow the whole situation sky high, but at least I'd be told the truth. Besides, I didn't need Owen. I didn't need anyone. So long as I knew the truth.

It was only when I had tramped the road for about a mile that I realised I had no way of getting home: no ticket, no money, no credit card. I felt obscurely that this too was Owen's fault, but after stumping up and down the deserted road for a few minutes, I was forced to admit defeat and turn back towards Martin's Court. Rob could lend me the money; after all, he owed me. I'd give him his wretched journal and take his money and then he'd be on his own. I'd done my part. The only alternative was to hitchhike home, not really my idea of a fun activity on a gloomy November evening.

But by the time I reached the garden of Martin's Court, my anger was beginning to fade. It's always been an odd fact of my nature that I was able to work myself up to a white-hot fury over relative trifles, whereas major injustices somehow disarmed me. Now I was almost overwhelmed by that sick resignation that comes sometimes when your worst fears are realised. After all, hadn't I been expecting this all along? Not Dinah, particularly – in fact, never for a moment had I suspected Dinah – but I had been waiting for Owen to give up on me for years. Almost from the beginning. There was even a certain grim satisfaction to be derived from being proved right in my pessimism. There you are, a voice inside my head squeaked in triumph. I told you so. I knew all along that you and Owen would never last.

I couldn't face Rob just yet. Couldn't face anybody. I went down the path that bordered the house and the lawn and reached the river. The sky was not yet dark. I began to walk along by the familiar trees and kicked at the occasional dying nettle. Owen, you bastard, you promised so much. But in the end you're no better than all the others.

And he had promised much to begin with. We hadn't seen him for years but he must have heard about Lucien's accident somehow. I had been at the hospital for only three days but it seemed much much longer. I went through each day like a zombie, quite unable to take in what had happened. I sat by Luce's bedside, talked to the nurses, bickered with Faith, ate meals punctually three times a day and made endless, futile, unanswered telephone calls to Rob's flat. And then, suddenly, Owen was there. Fair-haired, tanned and healthy from working outside in his uncles' nursery. And unbelievably attractive. He sat down on the other side of the bed and took Lucien's hand.

'Lucien,' he said, 'I love you. You gave me so much.'

I was about to say something banal – 'Did you have a good journey?' probably – when I noticed that his face was streaming with tears. His eyes were brimming with them, tears glistened on his dark lashes and he made no attempt to check them. It was in that moment I began to grieve for my brother.

Faith said many times that she didn't know how we'd have managed without Owen, and for once this platitude was only the truth. He was comforting without ever once offering false hopes. He knew when to be cheering and when to let grief flow. He coped with the doctors, the relatives, the newspapers and the undertakers. He coped with my mother and he coped with me. (Eric, thank heavens, took himself off to the golf club and virtually lived there for weeks.) And afterwards, when Lucien's ashes had been consigned to the earth, and I found I could no longer go back to my life in London, nor could I go 'home' with Faith and Eric, nor did I have any idea where else I might turn, I returned to his uncles' market garden with Owen. No one was surprised. It was by then generally accepted that we were a couple. Just how this arrangement had come about, I was never quite sure. But it had always seemed to me like Owen's final act of coping: now he could take care of Lucien's little sister for ever. And when I became pregnant, we married.

Except that it didn't work out like that. Maybe one day I would understand how the gradual souring of our relationship had come about, the gradual decline into disillusion. Had we talked to each other once, in the beginning? Or was it just that we had both been so pole-axed by Lucien's death that we had never noticed the chasms that gaped between us? I know that in those first tentative months it had felt like a crime to laugh and to enjoy ourselves, a crime to find pleasure in lovemaking with such a tragedy so fresh in our lives. Had we been unsuited from the very beginning or might we have stood a better chance if it hadn't been for Laura's swift arrival, the Chinese torture of sleepless nights and financial pressure by day?

I had reached the stile that led into the field with the Rams. Their steady thumping provided an echo of less complicated times. I sat down and pulled my jacket closely around me to keep out the cold. A few spots of rain were beginning to fall, but that didn't seem to matter much.

My mind kept searching out the solace of the remembered summer days when we had been a group of four children, and then five.

The first two summers that we spent at Glory Cottage there were only four of us, Lucien, Rob, me and Esme. When, bursting with anticipation, we tumbled out of the car for the third time, Esme greeted us with the news that not only had her mother recently given birth to twin boys (which we knew), but that she was now busy having a nervous breakdown. We were all extremely intrigued by the nervous breakdown, never having witnessed one in the flesh before, and spent a good deal of time hunting for excuses to go up to the house so that we could spy on her. But after a while, since none of us witnessed anything more exciting than Clare Drummond asleep on the sofa (me), Clare Drummond puffy-eyed and smoking cigarettes (Rob), and Clare Drummond crying quietly in a chair (which is what Esme said she did most of the time), we were forced to the conclusion that hers was a particularly boring form of breakdown. Lucien returned from his recce with tales of wild violence and hysteria, but for once we did not believe him. The twins were left to Mrs Wicks's care and were of no interest to us whatsoever.

John Drummond was summoned from his London retreat by my mother and told firmly that something must be done. John Drummond agreed in principle but showed no inclination to be the one to do it. More than ever he was anxious to return to his mysterious London flat. Lucien explained privately that Mr Drummond had to return to his paramour. Concubine was another favourite word of his that summer. He later told us that Clare Drummond had found out about her husband's harem and that had caused her breakdown. Before he left, John Drummond must have given Faith some kind of carte blanche to do whatever she thought best, because, since she had absolutely no intention of ruining her summer holidays with the care of an invalid friend, let alone twin babies, she spent the next two days phoning around every agency in the book.

The result was Angela Baer.

She arrived with a typewriter, two suitcases full of books and manuscripts and a couple of carrier bags stuffed with clothes. And a fair-haired son named Owen.

Angela Baer was one of the most beautiful women I had ever seen. She had a cloud of yellow hair, huge brown eyes and the kind of gossamer femininity that advertisers adore. She did her utmost to undermine her natural advantages. She wore the most hideous clothes and seemed to go out of her way to neglect her appearance. Her movements were clumsy and she smoked roll-ups. Later, I grew to understand that for Angela, a clever woman from a background without any academic pretensions at all, her beauty was a desperate embarrassment, a handicap. No one interviewing her for a job or a post-graduate grant could ever quite reconcile her earnest dedication to minor Latin poets with the radiant young woman who made even the most desiccated old professor feel chivalrous and lusty in just about equal proportions.

Her son had inherited her stunning dark-lashed eyes and her cloud of yellow hair. Old ladies loved him. But even as a child he had a harshness about him, something unyielding and stern, that was nothing whatsoever to do with Angela. There was no mention, then, of any father. If we thought about it at all – which I don't think we did – we probably assumed his parents were divorced. Increasingly, divorcing seemed to be what parents did best.

We were furious at the invasion and ostracised the newcomer totally. Faith made half-hearted attempts to integrate us. 'He's such a nice child, I don't know why you have to be so beastly to him' – to which we responded with appropriately withering silence. Lucien trained us to squeak 'Oh for the wings of a dove' each time we saw him as a penalty for his choirboy appearance.

Once or twice I caught sight of the 'nice child' walking alone by the river, or else belly down on the lawn, reading a book. I felt sorry for him and thought secretly that my mother had a point. He did look rather nice. But I'd never have had the courage to break Lucien's embargo and run the risk of being ostracised by him too, so I was as haughty and cruel as the rest.

Occasionally during that first week, apart from the noise of babies howling and raised female voices, the sound of piano music floated out across the lawn from the main house. We ignored it.

Then, one evening after rain, Rob and I were idling about by the river and wondering what had happened to the other two. After a while we became anxious; to be left out, even for a short time, was always an ominous sign. We began to bicker. It never even occurred to us that we might initiate some activity of our own. Lucien was ruthless in ridiculing any show of independence.

We wandered back to the green space beside the willow. Lucien and Esme were there, sprawled on the huge canvas cushions from the boathouse. And with them was Owen.

Lucien barely bothered to look up. 'Hello, you two. This is Owen. He's probably going to be a world-famous musician when he grows up.'

In some ways that was the best summer of them all. The adults were too absorbed in the crises thrown up by the twins and by Clare's collapse to take us on boring outings or visits to other families. We were left to ourselves. Lucien concocted an elaborate fantasy about the elderly couple who lived in a modern house about half a mile upriver towards the town. He convinced us that the rather benign-looking old man who could be seen disbudding his chrysanthemums, an excitable grey poodle at his heels, was in fact a former Nazi concentration camp commander and responsible for terrible suffering and thousands of deaths. Our task was to spy on him so that we could compile a dossier of suspicious behaviour, and especially to note down any lapses into his native tongue such as *Gott in Himmel* or *Achtung* which was all the German any of us then knew. Apart from that we did all the usual things: turned the punt into a man-of-war, made dams, stole food from Mrs Wicks and tried making willow baskets to sell by the roadside. Our efforts resembled a series of nests made by remedial crows and not surprisingly they remained unsold until Faith bought Lucien's. For several years she displayed it in a series of sitting rooms and even convinced a few people that it was the work of a leading contemporary sculptor. We continued to practise our survival skills and made pits for hedgehogs to tumble into so we could bake them in clay in the ashes of a wood fire. This prospect briefly reduced Esme to tears, until she realised that the local hedgehogs were far too cunning to be taken in by our traps. And we tried teaching Snowy-two to cooperate in magic tricks. Snowy-two obligingly learned to sit for long periods in an old top hat. As he was a particularly lazy rabbit, this was no hardship. The problem was that none of us ever became very proficient at the conjuring, though Lucien could do the patter very well, so this was only a partial success.

Owen's presence in the group changed it more than any of us would ever have admitted. Rob and I were both completely under Lucien's spell and Esme had always been content to trail along behind us, questioning nothing. Owen, though clearly pleased to be part of the circle, never followed Lucien with quite the same unthinking loyalty. He applauded the good ideas but, unlike us, he queried the bad ones. This challenge only spurred Lucien on to think up more ambitious projects: also, Lucien made skilful use of Owen to keep the rest of us in our places.

Also, that was the summer of the secrets.

Lucien gave us our orders one cloudy morning. 'Think of a secret,' he told us, 'something absolutely private. Something you've never told anyone in all your whole life. You've got twenty-four hours and it had better be good. And no cheating.'

'What about you?'

'I've already got my secret. My secret is absolutely brilliant.'

I was thrown into instant panic. Lucien had a mania for secrets. 'Tell me, you must tell me!' he would insist if he ever thought I was keeping anything from him. But he had high standards. I knew I would never get away with anything as tame as, 'I want a pair of roller boots for Christmas.' In desperation I concluded that I would have to invent a secret, but even that would not be easy. It had to be interesting and it had to be convincing. I lay awake half the night worrying.

It poured with rain the next morning, driving us to seek shelter in the boathouse. Even now, if I ever hear talk of 'secrets', a smell of canvas cushions and damp wood and cobwebs comes back to me, and I can hear the patter of summer rain.

Lucien was excited as we gathered round in the usual bendy circle; his cheeks were flushed and his eyes had their most Merlin-like sparkle. I wondered what he was expecting to hear – or perhaps it was the prospect of telling his own secret?

He said, 'You first, Esme. You're the youngest.'

'That's not fair,' she hugged Snowy-two protectively, 'I always have to go first.'

Lucien considered this judiciously. 'All right then,' he turned to Rob, 'you can start then. We'll go round in a circle ending up with me.'

Rob looked uncomfortable.

Owen said, 'I'll be first if you want. I don't mind.' His expression was taut.

'No, Rob first.'

'Right then.' Rob had clearly decided to make the best of a bad job. He glanced at Lucien nervously, then he said, 'It's about the old man down the way. The one you said was a Nazi. Well, I've checked him out and it's not true. He's never even been across the Channel because his wife is frightened of travelling. He wasn't even in the war because he was too young. I've seen the photographs. He was born in Yorkshire, some place called Beverley. His name's Holborough.'

Lucien said nonchalantly, 'I knew that all along, stupid. I was only waiting to see how quickly you lot twigged.' And then, the giveaway, 'How did you find out?'

'I asked him. I told him I had to do a holiday project for school about the war and he was only too keen to be helpful. In fact he went on about it for hours and it was really boring.'

Lucien said nothing, but I knew he was annoyed. Rob was sure to pay later for having burst the bubble of that particular fantasy. It was the nearest Rob ever came to an act of rebellion.

'You're next, Owen.'

Owen nodded. His expression was more intense than I had ever seen it. He said, 'I'm not going to be a musician.'

'Why not?'

'I'm just not.'

'But I thought you loved playing the piano and all that stuff.'

'It's all right, I suppose. But musicians have to move around all the time. Travelling is part of their job. When I grow up I'm going to have a proper house and a proper job where I don't have to keep moving around.'

'Is that it? That's your secret?'

'Yes.'

'A bit boring,' was Lucien's only comment. But I could tell from the expression on Owen's face that it wasn't boring to him at all.

It was Esme's turn. She smiled. 'Mine's better.'

'Go on then.'

Her brown eyes were unusually animated. She said, 'Mrs Wicks has got webbed feet.'

'What?'

'It's true, I've seen them. There's these sort of disgusting skinny bits between the toes.'

'Like a duck?'

'Uh-huh. Only they don't fan out like a duck's.'

'How do you know?'

'I saw them once when I was little and she thought I wasn't looking.'

Lucien was impressed. 'Well done, Esme.' She smiled obliquely into Snowy-two's fur.

Suddenly realising that it was my turn next, my insides began to bubble with excitement and nerves. Surely my secret would outdo even Esme's.

But Lucien said in a patronising voice, 'You don't have to go, Jane. Yours is bound to be really pathetic.'

'It's not.'

'Surprise me, then.'

And I did.

'Mum told me about it once when you were at school. We talk together quite a lot, you know, when you're not there. We're more like sisters than friends, actually. Sometimes we just sit together and talk for hours and hours.' (This fantasy was so appealing that I could feel myself beginning to flush with happiness.) 'She said it was time I knew the truth. She said she wanted to tell me about Dad—'

Lucien had gone white. 'Jane, stop it!'

'She told me all about him, actually. She said he was a really kind man and he loved children, and had been really pleased to have a little girl. And a son too, of course. He was a racing driver and he was killed in a crash when—'

'Shut up!' Lucien shrieked.

'I only said—'

'Shut up, shut up, SHUT UP! How dare you make up stories about our father, how dare you!' He had leapt to his feet and began to pummel me with his fists. I was so astonished that it was a moment or two before I even tried to protect myself. Lucien's attacks, vicious though they were, were always verbal. For him to resort to physical violence was unheard of. I screamed at the top of my voice.

Lucien stopped.

'Now you've done it,' he panted. 'How dare you make up a secret. How dare you!'

'How do you know I made it up?' I wailed.

'I just know, that's all. You're stupid and pathetic and I loathe and despise you. I'll never speak to you again as long as I live.'

It felt like the end of the world.

Owen stood up and said firmly, 'She didn't mean to upset you, Luce. Forget about it and tell us your secret.'

Lucien turned on him a look of bitter contempt. 'I wouldn't tell you my secret now if I was under pain of death. Not for the worst, most horrible tortures. And mine was the best of all. Mine was the fifth secret. You would have all been aghast, dumbfounded, absolutely obliterated with amazement. But now you'll never know. I'll never tell you and it's all because of that vile moron.'

And with that he swept out into the rain.

He hardly spoke to anyone for the rest of the day. He refused even to look at me. I contemplated running away and joining a circus or throwing myself into the river and drowning, but was persuaded against this by Owen who went out of his way to be kind. Dimly in my misery, I felt a pang of guilt that I had not befriended him when he had been suffering Lucien's rejection.

The next day a kind of uneasy harmony was restored, though it was several days more before he relented completely towards me, when Lucien announced that we had to uncover the secret of Mrs Wicks's webbed feet. We devised strategies. We begged her to take us to the local swimming baths. We found a pair of shoes in a charity shop and brought them home for her to try on. Owen spilled soup over her feet when we were having lunch at the Court one day and, in his consternation, fell to his knees and began undoing the laces of her shoes, only to receive a swat across the head with a tea towel. We never did discover the truth about her toes.

And I had been so appalled by Lucien's reaction to my make-believe that I never again dared mention my father to him at all.

And he had never told us the fifth secret either.

* * *

The following year it seemed entirely natural that Owen should be there again. An au pair had been employed to help with the twins through the winter, but now she had gone back to Basle, or Hamburg, or wherever she came from, and Angela returned to Martin's Court with her manuscripts and her optimism, though Clare and the twins allowed little space for anything, let alone for contemplation of minor Latin poets, and once again she grew more harassed and desperate as the summer progressed.

And for us too, some of the magic was beginning to wear thin. Lucien was restless and moody and soon tired of our games. To amuse himself he grew increasingly skilled at playing Rob and Owen off against each other; once or twice I was afraid they might be driven to kill each other. I began to have frequent nightmares, and only some of them were caused by Lucien's delight in the Murder Game.

The only event that united us was when Snowy-two, who had accompanied us on a raid of the former Nazi commandant's fruit cage, was killed by his hysterical grey poodle. Lucien masterminded the funeral rites. It was intended as a Viking extravaganza until Esme understood that Lucien really did plan to set fire to the wooden boat on which the shoe-box coffin had been placed. Her sobs became frantic. Then, as Owen waded out into the river to retrieve the smouldering boat, the coffin fell in the water and was nearly swept away before the dripping corpse could be recovered. Eventually Lucien relented and agreed to a more conventional ceremony. Esme had spent the whole afternoon drying Snowy-two's sodden coat with a hair dryer which made his white fur stand up stiffly from his rigid body. Lucien made up a poem in praise of Snowy-two's many virtues, which made Esme cry again, but as he chucked the first handful of earth on the coffin lid, he said cheerfully, 'Eaten, burned, drowned and buried. A fairly comprehensive death, don't you think? For a rabbit, anyway.'

By now it was pitch dark and I was frozen. And miserable. Far from cheering me up, my memories had only served to make me more wretched. If only Owen and I had stayed friends, had never become lovers, then something that had once been magical would never have been destroyed. Owen had wanted to be kind, that was the trouble, but he had tried too hard. He had felt sorry for me in the months after Lucien died, but you can't build a marriage on pity, however hard you try.

I began to walk back towards the cottage. By now it was pitch dark and I had to find my way carefully. I had quite enough problems without falling into the river as well.

As I pushed open the door of Glory Cottage, Rob sprang down the stairs and burst out, 'Where in God's name have you been? You look like a drowned rat. Have you found the diary?'

'Damn the bloody diary,' I told him. 'I think Owen's having an affair. I think my marriage is probably over.'

Rob did his best. He stopped going on about the journal and listened with a patient expression while I ranted on about Dinah. Twice I announced my intention of returning to the OJ Nursery that same evening and twice I allowed Rob to persuade me to stay at Glory Cottage for the night and not to do anything rash. Of course, he only wanted me to stay because of the wretched diary, but it felt nice to be persuaded. It made it easier for me to pretend that Dinah and Owen meant nothing to me and that I was quite unmoved by their infidelity. Rob poured me a drink, ran a bath, lit the fire – all the actions I had so enjoyed doing for him the previous evening. It occurred to me, as I lay in the bath, that I should hand over the diary now. But then he would no longer need me. He would find the information he wanted and make his dramatic reappearance at Esme's bedside. Rob would be with Esme, Owen with Dinah, and I would be the only one left alone. Right now, that aloneness was an altogether unbearable prospect. What difference does one night make? I asked myself. I'll show him in the morning.

Our supper together was a good deal more elegant than that of the previous evening. For one thing Rob was no longer famished, so the consumption of food proceeded at a leisurely pace. For another, we were both wearing the new clothes I had bought earlier in the day. If John had not been with me, I'd probably have agonised for hours over what to buy for Rob; in the life of high sophistication which I imagined him leading he wore only exquisite clothes with designer labels. In the end I had purchased a cream shirt, a sweater in a rather fetching shade of mulberry, as well as trousers, socks and underwear. To my relief Rob's only comment was that it was all a bit smarter than he was used to – I assumed this was false modesty. Now that he was shaved and scrubbed and wearing new clothes, Rob began to lose his vagabond air and resemble more closely the media hero whose photograph had made such an impact on Dinah. (Damn Dinah, bloody Dinah. I had no intention of thinking about her. What on earth were she and Owen doing now?)

My announcement had at least jolted Rob out of his total preoccupation with his own woes; for the first time in over twenty-four hours it dawned on him that I too must have had some kind of existence during the previous ten years.

'Your turn,' he smiled, filling our glasses with wine. 'What's this nursery you keep mentioning? I always thought Owen was going to be a musician.'

I was torn. My pride urged me to paint a rosy picture of events; my longing for sympathy prompted me to exaggerate our woes. As a result, I veered back and forth between the two, which would have been confusing for Rob, had he been listening with more than half an ear.

'That's what Angela thought too.'

'Angela?'

'Angela Baer. Owen's mother.'

'Oh, yes, the beauty with the manuscripts.'

'That's right. When Owen left school he announced that he was going to work for his uncles in their market garden. Poor Angela couldn't understand it. She'd spent her whole life trying to escape her background and Owen went right back to base.'

'Why did he do it?'

'Bloody-mindedness, probably. I don't know. He says he enjoys it. He says he'd never have been more than a passable musician. Then, after we got married, his father made over a small sum of capital—'

'His father? I never knew he had one.'

'Everybody's got one. Except me. Professor Armand Baer was the man who supervised Angela's PhD. He seems to have known more about minor Latin poets than about contraception. For years Angela thought he'd leave his wife, she even had their names changed by deed poll, but of course he never did. Anyway, Owen never saw much of him, and when he offered us the money Owen was all for refusing it, but I managed in the end to persuade him not to be totally daft. Then Faith stumped up some kind of insurance policy she'd been hiding away for me and so we were able to scrape up enough money to buy a derelict Victorian walled kitchen garden with a semiderelict gardener's cottage thrown in.'

'Sounds idyllic.'

'Does it? You should try the reality sometime: customers who won't pay and cars that break down and buildings that leak and banks who give you hassle. Not to mention the cold and the hard work and the sheer boringness of it all. If that's an idyll, you can keep it.'

I've noticed before that people often resent having their fantasies about country life tampered with. Rob was looking sceptical. He was obviously determined to think I spent my days skipping through sunny meadows in a white dress with my arms full of wild flowers.

I said, 'Heaven alone knows how we'll cope if we split up. We'd have to sell, of course.'

'Christ, Jane, you don't even know for sure if he's having an affair yet, and even if he is, it doesn't mean the end. Most couples run into trouble sooner or later.'

'But this is Owen. You know how serious Owen always is. He's hardly the one for a casual affair.'

Rob yawned. 'I expect it will work out.'

I was annoyed. He had expended as much sympathy as was necessary to keep me at Glory Cottage for one more night, but now that was accomplished he was unable to hide his boredom for more than about ten minutes.

I said, 'And partly it was your fault.'

Rob reacted angrily. 'Me? But I never even met this Dinah woman.'

'I didn't mean that.'

'Well, if you think it's my fault because you've been here for a couple of nights then you must be mad. You can hardly keep watch over Owen every day of your life.'

'No, not that. But years ago, when Lucien died . . .'

Rob's eyes dilated with sudden shock and he said in a trembling voice, 'That was nothing to do with me.'

'But what about us? You never came to the hospital. You just abandoned us. We needed you, Rob. But you weren't there. And Owen was. And that's why I ended up with him. I think I believed that if we were married then at least there'd be one person in my life who couldn't just disappear off the face of the earth without any warning.'

'Jesus, Jane, you can't lay that one at my door too.'

'Where did you go, Rob?'

'Listen, you married Owen because you wanted to. Maybe it was a mistake, and if so I'm sorry, but no way was it my fault. Not that.'

'Okay, forget about Owen. What about you? Why did you disappear? I tried to ask you last night but you were asleep. Why, Rob?'

'If this is how you nag Owen then I'm not surprised he's having an affair.'

'That's cheap. I've got a right to know. We were your family.' My voice had risen to a wail and I lowered it carefully, 'You've got to tell me, Rob.'

He was fiddling with his knife and fork. Without looking up, he said, 'If I told you that for a year, two years, I forgot I ever had a friend called Lucien, would you believe me?'

I stared at him.

An icicle of fear slivered into my brain. His dark eyes were fixed on some unseen landmark and his expression was definitely unhinged. Of course. He's mad. Why didn't I realise that before? It would explain everything – the phone call, hiding in the Rams, his paranoia about the police. Everything. Maybe even what happened to Esme . . .

He rose to his feet and began to clear away the plates, but he was shaking so much the crockery danced around in his hands. He was panting.

'If I told you that for two years I forgot I ever knew a family called the Pipers, would you believe that? Would you believe that I forgot this place, forgot it ever existed, forgot those summers, forgot . . . everything.'

I didn't move a muscle. 'I don't understand, Rob. How could you?'

He turned on me with sudden triumph and contempt. 'Of course you don't understand. How could you? You weren't there, were you?'

Just as I was about to protest again, the glass that he had been holding shattered into a hundred fragments and a bright caterpillar of blood sprang out on to his palm.

'Where, Rob?'

'It doesn't matter. I'm going out.'

'You can't do that! What about your hand? Someone might see you—'

But he was gone, leaving the door swinging wide open. A blast of cold night air rushed into the cottage.

8

The face that stared back at me from the mirror offered scant comfort. My dark hair had been cut short a little while before; the effect was intended to be sophisticated, but in fact it just looked short and dark and nondescript. My features are of the kind that need to be animated to look attractive. How often had I longed for the heart-shaped delicacy that made Lucien and my mother so bewitching to look at. I tried smiling at my reflection, but the eyes remained dead. A scowling expression seemed far more natural somehow.

So I sat upstairs in the empty house and listened to the rain falling and the fan heater in the corner puffing dust around over the surface of the floorboards, and contemplated my morose reflection in the mirror and told myself it was hardly surprising that Owen had grown tired of me. Dinah, in contrast, had blossomed into a woman of Amazonian beauty and accomplishments. Why had I never realised before how glamorous she was? Darkly attractive, talented, witty, entertaining and sexually assured.

My own confidence, never great, had now vanished entirely. It had only been a matter of time, after all. Hadn't I always joked that Owen deserved a better partner than me? Now it seemed he had reached the same conclusion. Jealousy was fizzing at the pit of my stomach. Terrific, I thought, I'll probably get an ulcer as well. But who would care? I began to glide into a slightly wine-induced mood of renunciation. Dinah would not have been my first choice for his course of self-improvement, but who was I to say? Owen would soon learn that I could be generous in defeat.

Overwhelmed by my uncharacteristic magnanimity, I watched in the mirror as a couple of tears rolled down my cheeks. Perhaps Owen would be so amazed by my self-sacrifice that he would understand at last – but too late – what a paragon he had thrown away. I was actually on the brink of feeling sorry for him, when I heard the front door of the cottage bang shut, footsteps on the stairs.

The room in which I was sitting was furnished with Clare Drummond's habitual parsimony and was lit only by a weak-bulbed bedside light. Without turning round I could see the doorway in my mirror. The footsteps had stopped just beyond the door. It swung open slowly. Rob stood on the threshold, a shadowy figure.

'Jane?'

'Yes?'

He stepped into the room. I did not need to turn round, but examined his reflection. I had known Rob, off and on, for a long time, for most of my life, in fact. I had seen him laughing often, occasionally I had seen him close to tears. I had seen him triumphant, angry or depressed. In photographs and on television, as his career progressed, I had seen him successful and seductive. Last night I had seen him as a fugitive. Now, for the first time, I felt I was seeing him naked.

Rob's face had always fallen short of the classically handsome because of a heaviness around the jaw; his short nose and well-formed mouth were offset by the bulldog weight of his lower face. No one could look more determined than Rob when his mind was made up. It shocked me now to see all that stripped away. His eyes were clouded with some emotion that went beyond despair and the air of dogged certainty had vanished utterly. As he hesitated in the doorway, his vulnerability, so close to my own present mood, moved me in a way his assurance had never done.

'Rob?'

His gaze met mine on the dusty surface of the mirror as he crossed the room to stand behind me. He stooped slightly to wrap his arms around my shoulders.

He said in a low voice, 'Believe me, Jane, no one wishes they could change the past more than I do.'

I nodded, but still I did not turn, merely watched in the mirror as my head tilted to brush against his cheek. He closed his eyes and turned his face so that his lips grazed the corner of my mouth. Small explosions of desire were suddenly being detonated up and down my spine as his hands slid down to caress my breasts. I watched with curiosity to see how the dark-haired woman in the mirror would respond. I saw her give a small gasp of pleasure and anticipation. As I watched our reflections go slowly through the motions,

I became a voyeur in our joint seduction, both distanced and at the same time doubly involved.

Rob placed his lips on the inside of my neck. Then he opened his eyes, looked up, and our gaze met once more. My expression was oddly wooden, considering the firework display that I was experiencing within. His thumb brushed one of the tears from my cheek.

He said, 'Forget about Owen.'

I shifted forward to lean my elbows on the dressing table and sighed, 'But I can't forget about him any more,' and I thought, damn you, Owen, you've spoiled everything. 'If this had happened last night . . . but now it's not the same.'

'I know.' He kissed the side of my face.

'It's all been ruined, Rob. As if I'm just trying to even up the score.'

He was still kissing me. 'You worry too much,' he said.

'No.' I stood up, turned away from the mirror and faced him at a little distance.

He said, 'So what's the problem?'

I shrugged hopelessly.

Rob went to the window and peered out into the rainy darkness before pulling the flimsy curtains across. They were so old that they were rotting in the folds. 'Do you remember that time when there was a thunderstorm and Esme was sleeping up at the house and you were frightened to be on your own?'

'Yes.'

'And you came into our room and Lucien wouldn't let you get into his bed because he said you were as bony as an armadillo so you came in with me instead?'

'What innocents we were.'

'Speak for yourself. For me that night was a revelation, but I was hardly going to embark on any early explorations with Lucien just a couple of feet away. Imagine how he would have ridiculed us.'

'So you suffered in silence?' But his talk of our shared childhood had diffused some of the tension that had been growing up between us.

'Jane, I don't think I want to be alone tonight. Can't we just pretend everything is how it used to be, just for one night?'

Later, when we had pulled the eiderdown and blankets around us, I said, 'I ought to find some sheets, I suppose.'

'There aren't any. I already looked.'

'That's all right then. I wouldn't have bothered anyway.'

Protected by the darkness, I said, 'Talk to me, Rob. Keep my mind off Owen and that stupid bitch.'

'What about?'

'Anything. You.'

'Me?'

'Yes. Where did you come from? What about your family? You never talked about your parents.'

We were lying side by side, more companionable than comfortable. Rob was silent for a little while before saying, 'Bedtime stories, eh? All right then. My parents went out to Australia when I was about six months old. It was intended as a last attempt to save their marriage but failed completely. They both had busy lives, my father travelled a good deal and they soon drifted even further apart. My mother had her career and plenty of lovers. I was just in the way. All my earliest memories are of closed doors and empty rooms. Silence and waiting.'

'If you're trying to make me feel sorry for you . . . Anyway, I always thought Australians were a jolly bunch and had barbecues all the time.'

'Barbecues? I only remember one. At someone's beachhouse, I think. Mostly I was struck by how at ease the other children were with their parents, the way they were able to take them for granted. And then, when everyone else had left, it turned out that my mother had vanished with some man she'd just met and had forgotten all about me. The host family had to keep me for the night and they tried to be kind but you could tell they thought it was pretty odd. And I felt guilty about it, as though it was my fault somehow. When they got hold of my mother the next morning she treated it like a joke, and I was so desperate to please her that I pretended I thought it was funny too.'

'Rob, this is not my idea of a soothing bedtime story.'

'You asked.'

'I wish I hadn't. No, I take that back. Go on. There has to be a happy bit.'

'There is. When I was eight my parents suddenly decided the Australian schools were crap and I needed an English education. That meant they could pack me off for months at a time and with any luck the grandparents could be persuaded to deal with some of the holidays. When my father put me on the plane it was like being sent into outer space. Even now I always get ill in airports just at the thought of flying.'

'Hurry up and get to the happy part.'

'I'll skip the grandparents, then. The scene moves to a fairly ordinary boys' prep school. The linen room, in fact, where a row of new boys are lining up to hand over their sheets and towels. Enter Lucien. He took me under his wing then and there, God knows why. I did ask him once, years later, but he was just evasive. I still wonder sometimes.'

I pondered this for a while. Perhaps Lucien had realised that in Rob he had at last found the person who, without being an out-and-out loser, was still vulnerable enough to offer him the absolute devotion he had always wanted from his friends. Rob was reasonably clever, attractive and athletic, and once he had fallen under Lucien's spell, he would probably have died for him.

Rob went on. 'I couldn't believe such luck would last. Lucien was hugely popular, he could have picked any friend he wanted. I kept waiting for him to find a friend as quick and brilliant as he was. But he never did. And then, after I had known him for about a year, he invited me to spend the summer with his family and I thought life was never going to be so perfect again. I was desperately afraid my father would withhold permission and I tried to intercept the headmaster's post just in case – I was almost expelled.'

'That was the first summer we came down here.'

'You all seemed such a normal family.'

'Normal? Us?'

'Lucien must have told me that Eric wasn't his real father, but at least he was around most of the time. It was his total dependability that was so impressive about Eric. For the first time in my life I felt as if I belonged somewhere, and yet I knew that was an illusion, that I could be banished to my grandparents' house at any moment.'

'No wonder you were always so polite. My mother adored you.'

'It was mutual. And I was happy here, those four summers we had.'

Outside, the wind was beginning to stir through the trees. A handful of raindrops rattled against the pane. Simultaneously we shifted our positions to be more comfortable. I rubbed my foot along the ridge of his shin and felt him drop a kiss on the bridge of my nose. The sexual tension that had flared up between us as we watched each other in the mirror had almost all subsided, and it occurred to me that this present closeness was in some strange way a deeper intimacy than sex.

Rob seemed to have finished his story. I rather thought he must be asleep and was beginning to drift towards sleep myself when I heard him say, 'I always watched a lot of television when I stayed with my grandparents. One time, I saw a programme about the sea, the coral reef. And among all the wonderful underwater life, there was one creature in particular that caught my imagination. I can't remember what it was called; all I remember is that they spent the whole of their existence attached to the same piece of rock. So long as they were glued to their rock they were fine, but the moment they became dislodged then they were doomed, couldn't function at all. They drifted helplessly about until they were eaten up or died or simply disintegrated. And I can remember thinking: that was what it was like before I met Lucien. Just drifting. Quite lost. But I had survived it then because that was all I knew. You see, Lucien was more, much more than a friend. He gave me a place on this planet, a sense of who I was and what I was doing here. So that when he died . . .' he broke off and didn't speak for a while and I could hear the wind moaning in the trees. 'When he died, I had lost not only my closest friend, I felt as if I had lost a whole chunk of myself as well. For months I felt as if I was disintegrating. I suppose it was what they call a breakdown, but the word doesn't really describe the experience.'

I didn't answer. I knew only too well what he meant. Others had admired Lucien for his brilliance, his energy and his courage. But perhaps only Rob and I had known his wonderful ability to make those he loved feel cherished and important. A sense of belonging, Rob had called it. To me it simply felt like coming home.

I could have wept for those sea creatures, wrenched from their protecting rocks. I knew what it felt like to be free floating and helpless. I moved a little deeper into the bed. The rain and wind were whooshing all around the cottage now. It was a cold and hostile world out there and I was afraid of tomorrow.

Owen had already begun his journey into some unreachable part of the ocean.

Lucien was long vanished.

And now Esme . . .

Imprisoned in our separate loneliness, and yet closer than we had ever been before, Rob and I spent the night together while outside it rained without ceasing.

In the morning the rain had stopped and I was alone in the bed. It reminded me of one of those wake-up scenes in films where the naive heroine wonders if the hero acted the gentleman while she was drunk or drugged or asleep the previous evening. Was he? Or – gleam in the eye – wasn't he? I smiled to think that Rob had most definitely remained a gentleman throughout, but then remembered with a jolt of pain like an electric shock, that Owen, in the company of the unspeakable Dinah, almost certainly had not.

I lay there for a few minutes hating everyone and dreading what the day ahead would bring. First I must hand over the journal to Rob, whereupon he would cease to have any interest in me at all; and then I must return to the nursery and confront whatever situation existed between Owen and Dinah. The prospect of planting eleven thousand lettuces, which had depressed me so much a couple of days before, would have been welcome by comparison.

Convinced that I was an innocent victim of the selfishness and perversity of others, I went downstairs to make myself a cup of tea.

It was all Rob's fault for having been so insistent that I must not read the journal. He should have known his prohibition would only whip up my curiosity. I'd lay odds any day that if the Lord hadn't made such a song and dance to Lot and Co. about looking behind them, Lot's wife would never have bothered and the world would have been minus one pillar of salt.

I took my cup of tea back to the bedroom with the vague idea that I was only going to glance at the notebook to make sure it was in fact the journal that Rob was so desperate to lay his hands on, and not one Esme had written years and years before. After all, it would be cruel to raise his hopes for nothing. Of course, the truth was that I was curious to see if the journal contained any references to me. Esme had, so Rob said, written it when she came back to Martin's Court, which was the place where we had spent the most time together, but I had never had any idea how she regarded me. Had she even liked me? I reassured myself that if I read anything I thought Esme wouldn't want me to read, then I wouldn't read it. And Rob, who was just running himself a bath and so was safely out of the way for the next ten minutes, would get the journal the moment he emerged from the bathroom.

I wrapped the eiderdown around my shoulders and began to flip casually through the notebook. Less than half the pages had been covered in Esme's large, backward-sloping and distinctly childlike handwriting. I glanced at the last line: 'Oh well, I suppose I'd better go back to London and face reality again,' and then, at the top of the first page, 'Here I am back at Martin's

Court after all this time and it feels as if I'd never been away.' Clearly the reader of this diary was not about to embark on a feast of original prose. It reminded me suddenly of the one I had been obliged to write for a school holiday project. 'Monday, got up, had breakfast, mucked about outside till lunch, had lunch, mucked about outside till tea, had tea, mucked about . . .' The soothing mantra of endless summer days. The prize had gone to a snotty girl who had apparently wasted her summer rescuing kittens from trees and having boring conversations with old ladies; mine had been singled out as a clear example of how not to write a diary, but I had been happy to know that the secrets of my summer had remained safe from interfering adult eyes.

I continued to flip through the pages, idly looking for my name. I spotted it on the top left-hand corner. 'Jane was in a cross mood as usual.' I was taken aback. Me? Cross? As usual? Perish the thought. The surrounding paragraph seemed to be about Snowy-two's Viking funeral. Esme's choice of adjectives as she recalled the event was touchingly childish, like her handwriting. Lucien had been 'beastly' (but not 'as usual', I noted sourly) in even considering the incineration of 'poor' Snowy-two, and Owen had been 'absolutely sweet' (how times change) when he waded in and fished the corpse from the river. What Rob had been she did not divulge, and I, of course, had been 'cross as usual'.

I resented the 'as usual' more than the 'cross' and began to feel less mean about reading her secret journal. I could hear Rob's bath water roaring down the waste pipe in true Glory Cottage operatic style. He could have the journal and I wished him joy of it, though it didn't look as if it was going to be any help at all in finding her attacker. Just a jumble of fairly pedestrian memories about childhood and school and . . . secrets.

I looked again more closely. 'The fifth secret.' She too remembered the summer when Lucien had tantalised us all with his secret, the fifth secret, the one he would never divulge. Esme wrote: 'How I hate secrets. I've always hated them. Ever since Lucien kept going on about the amazing secret he had and how it would change all our lives if we ever found out what it was. Everyone kept pestering him to tell, and I pretended to want to know too—' (Get on with it Esme, I thought. Did he ever tell you? What was it then?) 'But I never wanted to know. Secrets have always frightened me. I suppose because I half knew and yet didn't know about Mummy's and Daddy's. Maybe it's cowardly, but I've never wanted to know anyone's horrible secret. Especially not this one of Rob's. And now he's made me promise promise

promise not to tell anyone, not even a therapist, and it feels like the most ghastly weight on top of me and I simply cannot think how to shift it. And I never wanted to know in the first place. I never asked him about Lucien's death. But now he's told me, I can't forget about it, no matter how hard I try, and it just keeps preying on my mind that I ought to do something or tell someone, but I mustn't even do that. Oh, I wish—'

The bathroom door flew open with a small explosive noise and I was so startled that some of my tea sloshed on to the eiderdown.

'Jane? How about breakfast?'

His tone was so eerily normal that I thought at first he was trying to put me off my guard by acting as though nothing had happened.

There was a brief pause of blind panic before I shoved the journal back into its hiding place and called out, 'I'm on my way down!'

Rob came into the bedroom, his face smiling and serene.

9

I was beginning to feel as jaded as any regular commuter as I slogged back across London and caught the train south to our local station. Rob had been disbelieving when I told him I was going home and, although I promised to return the same day and continue the search for the journal, he was still fuming when I left.

I had promised . . .

The journal was in a carrier bag, wrapped in a sweater. I held it on my lap as I travelled, but gingerly, as if at any moment it might explode like some verbal jack-in-a-box and shower Esme's suspicions around the carriage. The words of Esme's journal were snow-storming in my head: the secret . . . Rob's secret . . . something to do with Lucien's death. A whole mass of information was there, tucked away among the childish platitudes, but my brain kept seizing up every time I tried to piece the information together. It doesn't make sense, I kept saying to myself, it just doesn't make sense at all. The trouble was, though, that it did make sense, but of a terrible, unimaginable kind, and just now I was unable to face up to the sense that it did make.

Perhaps the truth was that Esme was a bit unhinged and liked to make up dramas. Maybe she took after her mother. People had always said that Clare Drummond was eccentric, but looking back I could see that she had really been pretty mad. Maybe, like her mother, Esme inhabited a private world where people did strange things, and that was the reason she was seeing a therapist. Although this interpretation was hard on Esme, it was a lot easier to believe than that Rob was a . . . that Lucien had been . . . that Rob had actually . . .

Third refusal. Eliminated from the competition.

I still couldn't accept what the journal was saying.

I tried, with spectacular lack of success, to think about something – anything – else.

Owen was waiting for me at the station. He was wearing the tweed jacket that he kept for visits to bank managers and accountants and his best pale blue shirt. This only accentuated the pale blue shadows of exhaustion that ringed his eyes. At the thought of who had caused his lack of sleep and precisely what he had been doing through the night, I became almost demented with rage. It didn't help in the least that he was looking, despite his obvious fatigue, about as handsome as I had ever seen him.

'Hello, Jane,' he eyed me warily, reached forward to take the carrier bag, then backed off again quickly as I rammed it possessively under my arm.

'So good of you to bother to meet me,' I hissed. 'I'm amazed you could spare the time.'

He sighed, turned round and walked with hunched shoulders into the car park. Don't you play the martyr with me, I thought, as I followed him to the van.

Owen made for the passenger door. At first I thought that an excess of guilty courtesy had inspired him to hold it open for me, or that perhaps he didn't feel like driving, but then he crawled over the left-hand seat and settled on the driver's side.

'The right-hand door fell off last night,' he explained. 'It's tied on for now. I haven't had a chance to fix it yet.'

'Oh, brilliant.'

The smell of potting compost and motor oil and sacking was infinitely depressing; it was the smell of working for month after month and getting deeper into debt, like a car with its wheels stuck in the mud – the more they spin to escape, the deeper they sink. For a moment it was as though the past forty-eight hours had not existed.

Owen pulled out of the station car park, but instead of taking the road that led back to the nursery, he was heading for the motorway.

'Where the hell are you going?'

'I've got some plants to deliver.'

'Can't they wait?'

'And then I thought we'd go on and visit Esme.'

'Hang on a moment. How about asking me first? Don't I have a say in all this? You could at least have consulted me.'

'How? I didn't even know where you were.'

'I phoned to tell you which train I was catching. It wasn't impossibly difficult just to mention this little jaunt.'

That stumped him. He drove without speaking for a little while, then he said in a low voice, 'I thought we needed a chance to talk.'

I wondered then if it was the motion of the van after the endless travelling, the horticultural odours all around us, that made me feel suddenly nauseated. Owen wanted to talk. I knew exactly what he wanted to say. He was going to tell me that he'd fallen for Dinah, that our marriage was over, he wanted a divorce, there would be a hundred and one things to sort out. Knowing Owen he would be calm and practical and civilised about the whole thing and in doing so would probably drive me clean out of my mind.

I said, 'There is absolutely nothing to discuss. What have you done with the children?'

He glanced at me quickly, then looked away. 'Dinah's taking care of them,' he said.

'Dinah! I don't want that woman near my children.'

'It's not for long.'

Owen had not challenged my sudden hostility to Dinah. In spite of all my fears and fury, I had still been hoping my suspicions were unjustified. With four words, Owen had confirmed them all. For a moment all I could see was blackness and I thought, oh good, I'm going to faint, that'll create a diversion, but then the blackness passed. My brain seemed to have filled with lead weights meanwhile and a pulse was beating painfully behind my left eye. And the nausea was getting worse. I said, 'Dinah, of all people. The bloody freezer queen. I just can't believe it.'

Owen didn't answer. We must have driven along for nearly ten minutes in aching silence before I couldn't bear it any longer and burst out, 'For someone who has practically kidnapped me and all on the pretext of wanting to talk, you don't have much to say.'

But all he said was, 'I didn't kidnap you, Jane. Why do you always have to exaggerate?'

I hugged the carrier bag holding Esme's journal to my chest and stared out of the window at grey streets and houses and dingy shops and petrol stations and grey people hunched up against the cold. On a piece of waste ground some boys were throwing rubbish on a bonfire. A wave of misery swept over me. Who would take Laura and Billy to watch the fireworks this year?

I said, 'All right. We'll see Esme. But only a short visit. I want to get back to my children.'

Owen nodded his assent and drove on in silence. I no longer goaded him about his supposed need to talk. All the hateful hurtful things I wanted to say to him I kept locked away inside me. I told myself we might as well get this first ordeal over before unleashing all that bitterness. Besides, I was frightened, frightened of the moment when Owen would drop his mask and say all those terrible things he had left unsaid for years.

We pulled up outside a rather tatty garden centre we often did business with, and I helped Owen to unload the plants from the back of the van.

'Don't these people owe us money?' I asked.

'They promised to pay for the last order when we delivered this one,' he said, and when he emerged from the manager's office, once the plants were unloaded, I could tell by the smiling goodbyes that the cheque was in his pocket.

'That should cover a couple of bills,' he said, as he climbed over the passenger seat and settled behind the wheel.

'Just so long as it doesn't bounce.' I climbed in after him.

A little further on he pulled to a stop on a double yellow line outside an electrical shop in a busy south London high street.

'Now what?'

'I need to get out.'

'If a traffic warden comes along—'

'You'll just have to persuade him not to give us a ticket.' Still rigid with rage, I climbed out of the van and stepped neatly into the path of an oncoming juggernaut. Owen grabbed my arm and pulled me back just as the massive wheels pounded past and a horn like that of a steamship blasted in my ear.

'Jesus!' Owen exclaimed. 'We nearly lost the other door!'

'What about me?'

'Oh, you're more than a match for a lorry.' The thought seemed to amuse him as we performed a more circumspect version of the van evacuation procedure. Owen didn't look as if he would have minded in the least if I'd been flattened by the lorry. Leaving me on guard for traffic wardens, he went into, not the electrical shop, but a smaller one next door to it whose window sported a bizarre display of dog beds, birdcages and things that looked like transparent cake tins. He came out a few minutes later carrying a cardboard box which, when we were once more settled in our respective positions in the van, he placed on my lap.

The box lurched towards the door.

'Bloody hell, Owen, it's alive.'

'Yes.' He turned the key in the ignition.

'What is it?'

'A rabbit.' He pulled out into the traffic.

'A rabbit! We've just planted eleven thousand lettuces and now you're buying rabbits! Why not pour weedkiller over the whole lot and have done with it? How about a swarm of locusts or—'

'I planted those lettuces, so less of the "we". And anyway, the rabbit is for Esme.'

'Oh, good one, Owen. Just the thing for someone in a coma, they'll just love you in intensive care.'

He frowned. 'It's a white one,' he said, as if that was any kind of explanation. 'How many did she have? The last one I remember was Snowy-four, but that was ages ago. Maybe we should call this one Snowy-ten or -eleven just to be on the safe side.'

I stared at him. Two nights of passion with Dinah had apparently corroded his common sense. My train of thought was interrupted by the discovery that the box was beginning to leak warmly on to my knee.

'Ugh.' I reached into the back for some polythene and, too late by far, placed it under the box.

'You might have warned me. Now I shall stink of pee.'

'Sorry.'

I prised open the lid a half inch and a single raspberry pink eye glared up at me. I shut it again hastily.

'Owen, you idiot, it has pink eyes. You know the Snowies always had black ones. Esme hated pink-eyed rabbits, you'll have to take it back.'

Owen said, 'I promise you, Jane, that if Esme sits up and complains about the colour of his eyes, then he'll have more than earned his keep.'

'They'll never let you take it into the hospital. It's probably riddled with disease, you can't disinfect a rabbit; I never heard of anything so impractical. They'll probably have a myxomatosis epidemic at the hospital and we'll be blamed.'

'Humans don't get it.'

'How do you know? Since when did you become an expert on the illnesses of animals, you're not a damn vet . . .'

And so on, through the London suburbs. It was safer to unleash my Dinah-anger in the cause of a rabbit.

'This is insane,' I said as Owen took the box from my arms and strode towards the hospital entrance.

He didn't even bother to answer.

The nurses on Esme's ward had the slightly glazed expressions of people who have been subjected to the *Match of the Day* theme tune since their shift began. To my disappointment, they made no comment on the cardboard box, but I had reckoned without the Owen-effect.

'Can we sit with Esme for a little while?' he asked. 'We've known her since we were children.'

The staff nurse, a horsy-looking Irishwoman, looked as though Owen could stay for ever as far as she was concerned, but she said merely, 'If she shows any sign of coming round, please let WPC Ferris know; the police are waiting to question her.'

'Of course.'

Owen remained oblivious to the impact he had made on the nurse, who watched him greedily as he crossed the ward to Esme's bed. He must go through life assuming that the human race is generally helpful and friendly, not realising that the response he evokes is highly unusual and that a mere plain female like me has to cope with routine suspicion and hostility.

The policewoman was seated on a metal chair a little distance away and reading a doctor-nurse romance while reaching from time to time into a bag of peppermints with a determination that indicated a recent giving-up of cigarettes. I wondered briefly if the nurses all amused themselves with detective stories.

I had been so busy berating Owen about the rabbit that I had forgotten to prepare myself for the shock of seeing Esme. All the usual barrage of tubes and machines was there, but Esme herself looked both older and yet younger than when I had seen her last, somehow combining the vulnerability of a child with the weariness of an old woman. Her eyes were closed, and as those enormous velvet brown eyes had always been her most arresting feature, her full beauty remained hidden. Her skin was taut and shadowed and there was a large gauze patch on the back of her head, but in spite of everything, her serenity was untouched.

Owen, ever the accomplished sick-bed watcher, sat down on the edge of the bed. I pulled out a chair and placed it near her feet, putting myself as far away as was possible while still remaining technically a visitor.

'Esme,' he placed his hand over hers. 'It's Owen. And Jane is here too.'

He spoke in a normal voice rather than the hushed tones people usually adopt in these situations, and he managed to say things like being happy to see her and where they had last met without it sounding trite the way it usually does.

After a bit he glanced behind him and frowned. 'Why do they keep playing that hideous music?'

'*Match of the Day*? They thought it might get through to her.' And then, remembering, I tried to look vague and added, 'At least, I suppose that must be the reason.'

'God knows why,' he said, turning the cassette player off briskly. 'More likely to dig her deeper in. That's better.' He turned his attention back to Esme and touched her cheek lightly with one hand. 'Can you hear me, Esme? Now that the music's gone. If you can hear me, just nod or try to open your eyes. You don't have to say anything, I shall know that you can hear.'

He squeezed Esme's hand. She remained impassive as marble. I wondered vaguely if she might give some response if I walked over and shook her. He leaned forward slightly and brushed a strand of brown hair from her forehead. A sudden vivid image bannered across my mind: Owen's gentle hands were brushing the hair from Dinah's forehead as she lay naked in the crook of his arm. My insides churned violently and it felt as if my stomach was tying itself into a knot any master mariner would have been proud of.

I said, 'Why Dinah, of all people, that's what I can't understand; why that bloody bitch?'

The Irish staff nurse with the long horse-like face had come to join us and she looked startled by my question. She said to Owen, 'Nothing seems to get through to her but we keep trying. Her father suggested the football music. Luckily my sister-in-law's uncle has a TV favourites CD and we were able to tape that.'

Owen said, 'You must have moved very fast,' and the staff nurse beamed. She never noticed that the cardboard box was quivering between his feet. She paused only to dart an acid glance in my direction before heading off towards a side ward.

Owen glanced at WPC Ferris who was reading her novel still, a pink tinge of excitement colouring her cheekbones. Barely altering his position, he reached into the box and pulled out the rabbit and settled it alongside Esme's ribs. It flattened its ears and its pink eyes swivelled around frantically, alert for danger. Still holding the rabbit in place with one hand, Owen lifted one of Esme's – the one that was unencumbered by tubes and wires – and placed her fingers on the soft fur at the back of its neck.

'This is Snowy-ten,' he explained. 'Do you remember all the Snowies? Snowy-two was the first that I knew, though I suppose there must have been an original Snowy once upon a time . . .'

The rabbit was quivering with terror. You'd have thought the ward was a haven for killer hawks.

I said, 'This is ridiculous, Owen. You're going to get us thrown out, and for what? That stupid rabbit does nothing but crap and pee. We should have brought a piece of old fur, something we could leave behind when we go. You must remember how the Snowies used to love electrical wires, it'll probably cut off the machines, given half a chance. This is just a waste of time. If she doesn't respond to her own father, or to us or anyone, why the hell should she perk up for a bunny?'

Owen ignored me, as usual, and carried on chatting about the Snowies, and guiding Esme's finger over the wretched animal's ears, back, its soft underbelly . . . And Esme might have been dead for all the response she gave. That was when it hit me that Esme had almost died, might never properly recover.

I said sharply, 'You know your trouble, Owen? You just won't admit when you're wrong. She's never going to—' I stopped. Blinked.

Owen's face was taut. 'Look, Jane, she's smiling!'

'Don't be ridiculous. She's still unconscious.'

'No, look, I'm sure she smiled.'

His determination to believe the impossible wrung my heart. 'You're just deceiving yourself, Owen.'

'But she did, I know she did.'

'No, she . . .' And then I fell silent, watching and suddenly I heard Owen give a whoop of joy as Esme's eyelids fluttered and the trace of a smile hovered around her lips.

In his excitement Owen must have relaxed his hold on the rabbit, because just at that moment it took off vertically from the bed and shot off across the ward with the speed of an electric hare. WPC Ferris glanced up from her book to see a white blob of fur skimming over her lace-up shoes and she inhaled sharply and almost choked on her peppermint.

Hearing the commotion the staff nurse advanced in my direction, glaring at me – of course the assumption was that I was sure to be the culprit. Not wishing to shoulder unfair responsibility for the introduction of wildlife into the ward, I set off in pursuit and soon had Snowy-ten cornered between a bedside locker and the cardiograph machine. WPC Ferris watched with round eyes and glanced into her bag, obviously fearing one of her colleagues had slipped in a confiscated hallucinogen as a joke.

Owen, meanwhile, was soothing the outraged staff nurse. For one blissful moment I thought she'd really give him a hard time, but I was disappointed. Within minutes she was commending him for his wisdom and enterprise and saying she didn't know why animals weren't encouraged on wards as studies showed that patients often made a speedier recovery in the presence of some dear little four-legged friend. Owen took the rabbit from me, but before he put it back in its box, all the nurses, as well as the policewoman, came over and made a fuss of it. Any fool could see that it was really Owen they were taken by, not the rabbit.

10

By the time I had succeeded in prising Owen away from the nurses, I was beginning to panic. We'd been lucky to visit at a moment when Esme was alone, but I did not want to risk bumping into my mother. Nor did I relish the idea of coping with John Drummond. It was too much to expect him to pretend he hadn't seen me just the previous day and Owen would have been certain to work out what was going on. If relations between us had been easier, I might have been glad, since Rob's secrets were weighing heavily, to say the least. But there were enough complications with Owen already.

Whichever way I turned, there was turmoil. Seeing Esme so helpless and pale had at last rammed home the full horror of her attack. As we left, the staff nurse had commented to Owen that Esme was 'lucky to be alive'. If the blow had been struck a little harder, or a fraction to one side . . . the sentence was left ominously unfinished and, despite the suffocating warmth of the ward, I found that I was shivering. Look another way and I was confronted by the gut-wrenching horror of the Owen-Dinah sideshow. Turn away from that one, and I came face to face with Esme's words about Rob and Lucien's death. Those thoughts I couldn't handle at all.

I didn't even try. In order to survive the next few hours, I was acquiring some kind of mental filing system. For the time being the problems of Owen and Dinah, and the riddle of Esme's journal had been slotted into the 'pending' section of my brain. The system broke down every now and then, as filing systems always do; I would catch sight of Owen and toy with the notion of tearing Dinah limb from chubby limb, or I remembered the journal and thought, 'No, not that, anything but that,' but on the whole I seemed to be managing remarkably well. Just as long as nothing else unexpected took place during the next two years I might even survive without a total nervous collapse.

And then, just as Owen and I were leaving the lift in the main entrance and the doors to the outside world were already in sight, a woman's voice called out, 'Hello, you two.'

I swore under my breath. Then consoled myself with the thought that at least this was Owen's mother, not mine.

Angela Baer had changed surprisingly little since the summer afternoon when she had turned up at Martin's Court with her manuscripts and her piano-playing son to help Clare Drummond after her breakdown. It was still easy to see that she had once been beautiful, but heads no longer turned as she came into a room. Her fair hair had faded to a more discreet shade of blonde and there were anxious lines fanning out from her mouth and eyes. Now that her appearance was no longer an impediment to being taken seriously, I noticed that she had begun to take more trouble with her clothes. Instead of dungarees and battered trainers, she was wearing proper trousers and shoes. But she still carried the enormous bag which could hold a manuscript, several books and anything else she chose to throw in at the last moment, and which seemed to have made her left shoulder permanently lower than her right.

My surprise at seeing Angela at the hospital was short-lived. After all, she had stayed at Martin's Court for two long summers and had grown to know Esme well. Angela regularly quarrelled with her friends but she never dropped them altogether.

Mother and son eyed each other cautiously. Ever since Owen had given up his musical career, there had been a distinct tension in their relationship. Angela insisted on seeing market gardening as a temporary aberration and was waiting for him to 'grow out of it'; though knowing Owen as she did she must have realised that any opposition would only strengthen his resolve.

'Hello, Mother.'

'Are you all right, Owen? You don't look all that well.'

Owen mumbled something about a late night. If Angela had been sympathetic I think I might have screamed but all she said was, 'That's all right then. I was hoping I'd bump into you. Let's go and have a coffee.'

There was a rather scruffy little canteen area running along one side of the hospital foyer, next to the 'guilt corner' where flowers and chocolates and magazines were on sale.

'Have you seen Esme yet?' asked Owen as we shuffled along in the queue.

'Steeling myself,' said Angela. 'And you?'

'We've just been.'

'How is she?'

'It's hard to say,' Owen admitted. 'We thought she might be showing some improvement.'

Owen and Angela each took a polystyrene mug of coffee and seemed not to notice there was food on sale as well. But it was past lunch time and I was hungry. Nothing that was happening seemed to diminish my appetite in the least, quite the contrary. I helped myself to a sandwich and a cake and a cup of tea. We sat down next to a dying rubber plant.

I said, perhaps to distract their attention since both Owen and his mother were gazing with some surprise at my laden tray, 'Owen conjured a white rabbit out of a hat. The nurses want him to do it again tomorrow.'

Angela looked anxious, unsure whether to believe me or not. There had always existed a coolness between us. For my part I found her anger too unpredictable and destructive and had never felt easy in her company. I assumed that mothers of only sons disapproved of their daughters-in-law on principle. Though in fact she always reserved her main criticisms for Owen, so that I had frequently found myself defending him. On this occasion I decided he could fend for himself. But for once Angela was restrained, merely watching while Owen poured water into a plate and slipped it into the cardboard box.

'So it *is* a rabbit,' she conceded.

Owen nodded. 'You remember the Snowies. All those rabbits Esme had. The doctors had been asking about things that were important to her.'

'Poor Esme. She was such a sweet child. How are Laura and Billy?'

Owen was avoiding my eye. 'They're fine.'

There was a long silence. Angela picked up her coffee mug then set it down again without a taste. She put a pale hand on Owen's arm. 'I've been thinking and thinking about those holidays by the river. It's so terrible, it's hard to take it in properly. I've been remembering those summers the five of you had together. Just playing by the river, God knows what you were up to half the time, but it never seemed to matter. You all had such a lot going for you, all your future ahead. And now Lucien's dead and poor Esme is practically . . . and I can't . . .' She broke off suddenly and I realised that her eyes were swimming with tears.

Owen said gruffly, 'They think Esme may make a full recovery.'

'God, I hope so. But still, that's not the point.'

'Oh.'

She sniffed, then rubbed her eyes with bony fingers. 'The point is,' she insisted, 'that people are the only things that matter. Really matter. Don't you see, they're all we've got? It's as if we had a huge pile of money in the bank but we never noticed it until it was too late.'

Owen was frowning. Perhaps because his mother had never had even a small sum of money in the bank so her analogy was not based on experience. He looked as though he was developing a severe headache and I tried to tell myself that it served him right.

'Yes,' he said uneasily, 'I see what you mean.'

She was not to be put off. 'Owen, I've been critical of you in the past and I want to say now that I'm sorry. I had my heart set on you becoming a first-rate pianist and it took me a long time to let go of that dream. I should have done it years ago. I'm sorry. I've been meaning to talk to you about this for ages, but I just kept putting it off. Then, when I heard the news about Esme, my first thought was, supposing it had been you? Then you'd never have known how I felt.'

'Yes,' said Owen, 'I see.'

He was not reacting as I would have expected. Perhaps it was the hangover, but he seemed distinctly unenthusiastic about his mother's olive branch.

'So now I'm telling you both. Whatever you decide to do, I wish you every success. I hope your nursery flourishes and brings you all the satisfaction you could wish.'

I thought Angela's speech, if a little stilted, was truly generous, so it seemed grudging of Owen merely to smile weakly and say, 'Thanks, I appreciate that,' while all the time looking as though her words had only added to his burden.

He stood up. 'It's stifling in here. I'm going out for some fresh air before the drive back.'

I scowled at him to show what I thought of such churlish behaviour and said, 'I'll follow in a minute.' I still had a mammoth slice of cake to get through and besides, I felt sorry for Angela.

As she watched him disappear with the Snowy box under his arm she said thoughtfully, 'Are you sure he's all right? He looks distinctly off colour.'

I thought of Dinah and said acidly, 'He's just a glutton for punishment.'

'Hmm. I suppose that's my fault. Mothers are usually to blame, aren't they? I think that's why I tried to be as little like other mothers as possible, but that never seemed to work much either.'

She tipped her cheek on to her hand and her brown eyes gazed at me meaningfully. Since I was confused by the direction our conversation was taking, I mumbled something vague into my mouthful of cake.

She said, 'Time is so precious, Jane. You mustn't squander it. I should know. I've wasted plenty.'

I was beginning to feel a twinge of anxiety. Angela was talking with the seize-the-moment intensity of someone who's just been told they've got six months to live. 'How?' I asked.

She leaned back in her chair and smiled at me suddenly. She was still extraordinarily beautiful when she smiled. 'Did you know that Armand Baer's wife died earlier this year?'

'He wrote and told Owen.'

'I've known Owen's father most of my adult life. I was twenty-five the first time I set eyes on him. He was giving a lecture on Statius and his place in the late Latin world – I can still remember every word of it – and I think I must have fallen in love with him before the lecture ended. I've certainly believed myself in love with him ever since. For over thirty years I thought the only obstacle to utter bliss was his poor benighted wife. In the early days he used to talk about leaving her but, stupid though I was in lots of other ways, I wasn't so completely daft as to believe that. I changed my name to Baer. I pined for him. I was often lonely. But I coped.'

'Yes.'

'Last week Armand wrote to me. He's been travelling in the States since she died and he said he'd done a lot of thinking. He suggested that we meet sometime. Though he's too proud to spell it out, it's pretty obvious that he's lonely and wants us to get together at last.'

'Oh, Angela, how romantic.'

'Isn't it?' She smiled at me oddly. 'And do you know what I felt when I read his letter?'

'No.'

'Complete panic. As if someone had just suggested, ever so kindly, that I spend the rest of my life trussed up in a straitjacket. I was being offered the future I had always wanted and I turned it down at once. Closed the door for ever and ever. I wrote back by return of post and told him that since we had last met I had developed a severe drug dependency problem and was going to live in a radical lesbian commune in the north of England and grow cabbages.'

'Ah.' (I was wondering how to break this latest development to Owen.)

'All lies, of course. But I thought that combination would be enough to prove that I was a hopeless case. He'll have no problem finding a kindly female to shield him from loneliness and I wish them every happiness. But domestic bliss is not for me. There's nothing like having your dreams handed to you on a plate to make you learn the kind of person you are.'

'I wouldn't know about that.'

Either Angela didn't notice, or she chose to ignore the bitterness in my voice. 'Take it from me,' she said. 'I've thought about it a lot these last few days. Probably Armand's main attraction was the fact that deep down I knew he'd never leave his wife. I've been a gypsy since I was a child, Jane, and it's far too late to change now. I wouldn't want to if I could.'

Now if Faith had suddenly announced, in her most vibrant thespian tones, that she had been a gypsy all her life, I have no doubt I'd have been quietly sick, but Angela wasn't striking a pose, merely stating a lesson that had been hard to learn. Since Angela had never confided anything to me before, I assumed I was supposed to relay all this to Owen.

She said, 'It's such a relief not to have to pretend to myself any more. I always had this idea that settling down was what adults were supposed to do. Well, maybe it is, but in that case I never intend to grow up.' She grinned. 'I'm only sorry I had to wait until now to see the light. You two are lucky. That's what I've been trying to say. I'm so glad that you've found what's important.'

'We have?'

'With the nursery. In spite of all the opposition, you've both stuck to your guns and I'm sure you'll make it a huge success. You deserve it anyway. Both of you.'

I began fumbling in my pocket for a handkerchief. The gulf between Angela's fond vision of our lives and the desperate reality was painful. Still, I was touched by her sincerity and it was a moment or two before I could trust myself to speak.

'You ought to be telling Owen this,' I said, 'not me.'

'Another time. When he's not under so much pressure. And anyway, how about you? How's the painting going?'

Angela's ability to reroute conversations had always been disconcerting. I said, 'I don't get any time.'

'Tosh. You must make time. That's the whole point of what I've been trying to say. Besides, that's just an excuse and deep down you know it, like Armand's poor wife was always my excuse. Your only trouble, Jane, dear, is that you have no self-confidence. Hardly surprising, given the ridiculous way Faith doted on that brother of yours. I was always critical of the way she pushed that boy. I suppose I was nearly as bad with Owen, but at least I had some excuse. He was all I had.'

I was beginning to think I ought to join Owen in the car park when Angela sighed loudly and said, 'It was always hardest on Owen, of course.'

The conversation had been derailed again. 'What was?' I asked.

'All that endless moving around. I pretended to hate it but really I thrived on the whole business. I suppose that's why I always managed to spark off rows. Like that dreadful one between Faith and Clare. It was never deliberate, not consciously at any rate. But I can remember when I had to pack my bags in disgrace thinking: Hurrah, no more dreadful twins and ghastly Mrs Wicks to put up with. Time to move on. That's when I've always been happiest, moving on, even if I had to upset everything in order to fight my way out. But poor Owen longed for a real home. I remember him saying once he wanted to stay somewhere long enough to lose things. And find them again, I suppose. I can see now that's why the nursery must be so important to him. Up to his elbows in potting compost all day. You can't get much more grounded than that.'

This concentrated dose of insight and honesty was now making me genuinely anxious. 'Are you sure you're all right, Angela? You're talking as if we're never going to see each other again.'

She stared at me uncomprehendingly for a minute before bursting into giggles. 'Oh, I see. No, it was hearing the news about Esme that triggered all this; I'm not about to pop off.'

'Good.' That settled, I decided it was definitely time to go. 'You must come and visit us very soon. Before the spare room gets too impossibly cold, anyway.' I marvelled at the insouciant way the invitation slipped off the tongue. 'Us' at that moment was a wistfully old-fashioned notion and there was comfort in the pretence. 'Laura and Billy are wonderful these days.'

She smiled at me gratefully as I stood up. 'I'll do that.'

I hesitated, then stooped and gave her a swift and unprecedented kiss. It was cruel and ironic that Angela and I should be having our first real conversation just as relations between Owen and me were hurtling towards disaster. I realised that I had never really trusted her. Not since that last summer when she had sparked off the row that brought our Glory Cottage days to an end. And for which I had, most unfairly, got the blame.

Owen was in the car park, leaning against the side of the van, his hands deep in his pockets, his shoulders slightly hunched. He was so lost in thought that he did not notice my arrival until I spoke.

'Your mother has mellowed,' I said.

'Yes.'

'You don't sound very enthusiastic.'

He shrugged. 'A bit late in the day,' was his only comment.

It was only as I climbed into the van that the message behind his words sank in. Late in the day – that could only mean her support was now an irrelevance. Our enterprise had already failed because we were no longer partners. I could feel the blackness of despair begin to wrap itself around me like a suffocating cloak and there was to be no return to the fragile hope I had once had.

Deciding to attack before he did, I said, 'Aren't you even going to try and explain? Or apologise?'

He frowned, but kept staring straight ahead, as though concentrating on his driving. 'I don't know that there's necessarily anything to apologise for.'

'What? You just about wreck our marriage and then you have the gall to ask—'

His mouth curled into a cruel smile. 'What marriage?'

The question was so lethally quiet, so terrifyingly stripped of emotion that once again I had the feeling that we were teetering on the brink of saying those huge and deadly words that can never be retracted. I drew back. Owen was still smiling as if at some private, bitter joke. Perhaps now that he had reached some kind of decision he was looking forward to the coming break. Perhaps he had only thought he wanted to settle down but had found family life to be after all the straitjacket his mother had always feared. Knowing Owen, he would have persevered for as long as he possibly could, but now that release was fast approaching he must be impatient to break all ties. Perhaps, after all, he had inherited his mother's restless, gypsy nature along with her pale hair and good looks.

Unlike me, he was sure to cope admirably. He had shown no emotion, I remembered, when the final break had come at Glory Cottage.

I had been the catalyst. I had always assumed it was my fault and was relieved to learn that Angela held herself responsible.

It had been raining for days. Faith had taken the others to the local swimming pool for the afternoon but because I had toothache I had been left behind to keep Angela company and help her with the twins. Clare Drummond and Mrs Wicks were busy with one of those mysterious activities – sewing threadbare sheets sides to middle or unravelling piles of old sweaters gleaned from jumble sales – with which they filled their afternoons. Angela was trying to read a book while the year-old twins staggered around through a sea of broken toys and gleefully smeared soggy biscuit on the walls. I didn't mind her ignoring the twins, but I was piqued at not being shown any attention myself. Besides, I needed some entertainment to keep my mind off the toothache. My efforts to engage her in conversation failed utterly until, in some desperation, I said boldly, 'It is entirely possible that Esme and I are sisters.'

Her brown eyes flashed at me over the top of her book.

'You're fond of each other?'

'I suppose we're bound to be.' I had gained her attention at last and intended to keep it. 'Because of Faith and Mr Drummond.'

'Really?' One twin was ramming biscuit in his brother's ear but Angela paid not the slightest notice.

'They have an understanding,' I mumbled. I had just remembered, with a wobble of panic, what had happened the last time I had allowed my imagination to wander on the subject of fatherhood. Lucien had been angrier than I had ever seen him before or since and hadn't spoken to me for days. I reassured myself with the thought that as Lucien was not here, he'd never know what I was saying. Besides, it was so pleasant to have Angela's lovely eyes watching me with approval.

'Really?' she said again, and her voice was most encouraging.

I imitated Lucien's worldly tone of voice. 'Of course, they haven't been lovers for ages and ages but he still finds her the most terrific tonic.'

I was saved from further indiscretions by the biscuit-eared twin's determined attempt to decapitate his brother with a spoon. Angela watched the resulting mayhem for a moment, threw her book into a corner and promptly burst into tears. 'I can't stand this any longer!' she sobbed. I decided to help out and swiftly removed the spoon from the aggressor and tapped his bald head with it, a bit like a boiled egg. He roared. By the time the others had returned from the swimming pool I had forgotten our conversation entirely. Angela, sadly, had not.

Four days later Angela, Faith and Clare spent a wet morning yelling at each other and by four o'clock in the afternoon Angela and Faith had decamped with their respective children and the Glory Cottage days were over. The row had begun, we later discovered, because Clare had broken her teapot into so many fragments that even she had to admit it was beyond repairing and, shaking with horror at the waste, she had allowed Mrs Wicks to throw it away. She had found a replacement in one of the storerooms behind the kitchen and then spent the next two days hunting for the milk jug which matched.

On the morning of the final bust-up Faith, losing patience with Clare's unceasing lament for the missing milk jug had said, 'Why not ask John? I'm sure there's one like that in his London flat.' When she was describing the scene later to Eric she said it was only when she saw the stricken look on Clare's face that she remembered Clare had never set foot in John's mysterious London flat.

'How do you know?' Clare asked.

Faith began to backtrack rapidly and disaster might possibly have been avoided had not Angela staggered in at that moment carrying a huge pile of laundry. She had been kept awake all night by a teething twin and was probably a lethal weapon looking for a target. She summed up the situation swiftly and, I saw now, must have opted to make it worse. She accused Clare of wilful ignorance and Faith of double-dealing and, for good measure, she accused John of smuggling his lover into his home under the cloak of friendship. Cue in hysterics and fury. At one point, apparently, Mrs Wicks could barely be restrained from attacking Angela with a flat iron.

The rain had eased and we were preparing to launch the punt when Angela swept across the lawn and shrieked at Owen to pack up at once as they were leaving. Owen had been handing Snowy-three, who was young and still skittish, to Esme who was already in the punt. He turned very pale. The rest of us assumed this was merely a brief hiccup since we had no inkling of the battle that had raged all morning in the kitchen. 'See you later,' we said and, 'Come back soon,' but Owen just said, 'Goodbye, everyone,' and followed his mother towards the house. Even then, I noticed, he walked in that stiff-shouldered, slightly jerky way that he sometimes has now.

Twenty minutes later Faith came down to find us and by teatime Esme was once more alone at Martin's Court. By that time Faith had uncovered Angela's sources and was ready to direct her formidable rage on me. Mercifully I remember almost nothing about her ensuing diatribe. What I do remember with perfect clarity is that Lucien made Rob have the front seat so that he could sit beside me in the back as we drove home. He held my hand as I cried and whispered, 'Don't be upset, Janey-oh. It was always an accident waiting to happen.' And he had continued to stand by me in the days ahead.

But now I was driving home with Owen and there was no Lucien any more to hold my hand and offer words of comfort to shield me from the coming storm. The somewhat maudlin mood of renunciation that had coddled me while I sat in front of the mirror the previous evening had vanished utterly. Impossible now to imagine that I had ever considered such drivel. Wish them both well? Ha! If they were going to make me miserable, then I'd make damn sure they were miserable too. The only problem was that right now Owen and Dinah were holding all the trump cards. Especially as I had to return to Glory Cottage that evening, thus leaving them alone together once more. And what was Aidan doing all this while? Why wasn't he around to restrain his marauding wife?

'What marriage?' Owen's question kept repeating itself in my head but I dared not try to answer it. I longed to lash out at Owen, but was terrified that if I did so he would have the power to hurt me far more than I could ever hurt him. I was forced to hold my fury back. But as we neared the house I said, 'You go on home. I'll drive on and pick the children up.'

Owen frowned slightly. His face was in profile and he has always looked his most steely from the side. His nose and chin were very sharply defined and his lips were pale and compressed. I thought bitterly that the coming upheaval would have been much easier if he had not been so sickeningly good-looking.

All he said was, 'Okay. If that's what you want.'

'Of course it's not what I want!' I snapped. 'What the hell do you care about what I want?'

'That wasn't—'

'This is a fine time to start pretending you care about what I want!'

'Leave it, Jane. You're blowing all this out of proportion.'

'Oh, that's—'

But he had timed his remark perfectly since it was delivered as he slowed the van to a halt in front of the main glasshouse. I suppose I could have forced him to continue the conversation by remaining glued to my seat, but there didn't seem much point.

I climbed out of the car and he followed. He attempted a smile.

'It looks as though Esme may pull through.'

'Yes.'

'Don't be long.'

He turned and walked round the side of the house to the back door. As he disappeared from sight I felt a sudden and almost unbearable sense of loss. I had always promised myself that one day I would do a proper portrait of Owen, one that did justice to his peculiar combination of delicacy and strength. I had done sketches before, but they were brief and hurried. Some of them had caught his slightly hunched way of standing. I had never yet drawn his hands.

I raged for the opportunities that had been missed.

Dinah, when I arrived at her house to collect the children, did not conform in any detail to my image of the 'other woman'. Her hair was swept back under a spotted headscarf and she was wearing a pair of bib-overalls covered in red giraffes. And she greeted me with her usual friendly smile.

'Hello, Jane. Come in. It's all chaos here. We've been having such a busy day.'

As I passed through her artificially lemon-and-pine-scented hallway, I was suddenly acutely aware of the rabbit stain reek of my clothes. Bits of horticultural debris, which must have clung to me while I was in the OJ Nursery van, chose this moment to detach themselves and drift gently on to her café au lait carpet. Even in our friendly days, entering Dinah's spotless home had always made me feel a degree grubbier and less kempt than I did before.

The three children were seated round her kitchen table cutting up old magazines and wrapping paper and gluing them on to cardboard boxes. Laura was working with the fierce concentration she brought to any task, her lovely face intent and determined. Billy, flushed with the effort of having to keep up with older children all day, looked as if he would rather be watching television.

'Hello,' I said, 'how are things?'

Laura, who was snipping expertly round a picture of a tin of cat food, barely glanced in my direction. Billy leaned his head on a dimpled hand and gave me a watery smile. I fought down sudden and inexplicable tears. Why did everything always have to be so complicated? Why could I not whisk them both away to some safe place where we could just be happy together?

Duncan said politely, 'Hello, Jane.'

Not content with the children's creativity, Dinah had clearly been busy with some 'show and tell' stuff of her own. Half-a-dozen oranges with bright ribbons quartering them stood in a row at the far end of the table. Two of them were already studded with cloves.

'Pomanders,' she explained superfluously, 'there was an article about them in a magazine I was reading at the hairdresser's.'

I stared at her in disbelief.

Laura had finished cutting out the cat food with a dramatic flourish and she set down the scissors for a moment while she reached forward for the glue pot. Billy's arm snaked out and grabbed the scissors she had been using. Laura jammed the glue pot down on his hand. 'Those are *mine*.' Billy threw his own scissors down on the floor and began to sob snuffily.

I moved to comfort him, but Dinah was there before me. 'Oh, Billy,' she said, whisking a slice of home-made apple cake off a tray as she pounced. 'You've been so wonderfully good all day. Don't spoil it now.'

Billy allowed himself to be mollified by the cake and even said sweetly, 'Thank you, Dinah.' I knew then how a commander must feel when his troops defect to the enemy in the heat of the battle. I decided to make a move before I lost yet more ground.

'We need to talk. Privately.'

'Yes. Of course.' Dinah threw me a glance which seemed to be one of saintly compassion and began tidying up the kitchen table. 'That's enough for now, children. Poor Jane has just been to see Aunty Esme' (*Aunty* Esme? Whose idea was that? And how did she know anyway?) 'and I expect she needs a nice cup of tea and some peace and quiet. And you've all been so good and busy all day, now it's time for that new cartoon video I promised you earlier.'

Perhaps it was because she spoke to them in the precise and confident tones of an old-fashioned guide leader that the children allowed themselves to be shepherded into the television room without protest. I wondered if that same bright-toned bossiness was the secret to her success with Owen. 'Owen, dear, you've been such a hero with the lettuces and primulas all day, now how about some invigorating sex?'

I picked up one of the grenade-shaped pomanders. My hand itched to throw it. I set it down carefully. Dinah came back into the room.

'Tea, Jane? You look as if you could do with something a bit stronger. Shall we stretch a point and have some sherry?'

I clutched at my hair. 'Stop going on as if nothing's happened. As if I didn't know . . .'

She plugged the stopper back in the sherry bottle and said blandly, 'About Owen, you mean?'

'Yes, of course about bloody Owen.'

'You must have realised I found him attractive.'

'Maybe, but that doesn't mean you have to go to bed with him.'

'I don't see why not. Aidan and I have never subscribed to all that old-fashioned possessive nonsense. We've always believed that if you really love another person, that means you respect their right to freedom and variety.'

'Funny you never mentioned that before.'

She looked vague for the first time. 'I suppose it just never cropped up.'

'No, because you knew I'd never let you near Owen if I guessed what you were up to.'

'Really, Jane, I'm surprised to hear you still clinging to all those dead notions of love as some kind of ownership. I wouldn't be all het up if you and Aidan—'

'What?' The idea of the anaemic and unappetising Aidan as some kind of trade-off for Owen was so appalling that for a moment I was almost speechless, 'I wouldn't touch your creep of a husband with a bargepole.'

'That's just spite.'

It was her air of surprise that got me. 'You pretended to be a friend, Dinah. And now you're trying to wreck everything.'

'Don't exaggerate so. All I did was have sex with Owen a couple of times.' She sipped her sherry thoughtfully. 'Well, four or five times actually.'

My stomach heaved with sudden nausea. 'You bitch!' I hissed.

Her eyes narrowed. She took a large swig of sherry and said, 'Anyway, you've only yourself to blame.'

'Meaning?'

'I'd have thought it was obvious. You treat Owen as if he hasn't any feelings and then you pretend to be surprised when he turns to someone else. It would bloody well serve you right if we stayed together.'

The thought that Owen, always the most loyal and restrained of friends, had been complaining about me to someone else was more than I could bear.

'You got him drunk deliberately,' I said. 'People say all sorts of stuff when they're drunk.'

'*In vino veritas*,' she said smugly. Two spots of colour had appeared on her cheeks but she maintained her stolid tone of voice. 'It might actually be helpful for you to know, Jane, that we came to the conclusion that you're probably incapable of maintaining a long-term relationship with anyone. It's probably not your fault. You've always had such an idealised picture of your brother Lucien. No living person will ever be able to match up to him so you'll always be dissatisfied. We both thought it was terribly sad . . .'

How I managed to get both the children out of her house without killing, or at the very least, severely maiming Dinah, I shall never know. But as I drove the short distance back to the nursery, my disbelief was almost stronger than my rage. How could I have been so wrong about Dinah for so long? I had always assumed that she was utterly conventional, the kind of woman whose genes programme her to be in charge of the church flower rota by the age of fifty. And now here she was, proselytising sexual freedom and open marriage like a founder member of a hippy commune. And I had always thought I was the Bohemian one. Which only shows how utterly naive and blind you can be. Compared to that vamp in play-group clothing, I had always been a paragon of all the domestic virtues. It occurred to me briefly that Dinah might have derived her views on marriage, as she had so much else, from the magazines she was always reading: Page 10, pomanders, the ideal Christmas gift. Page 64, do you love your partner enough to set him free?

Absolutely *no*, I thought. From now on I didn't intend letting Owen out of my sight.

Then I remembered I had to return to Glory Cottage that night.

Then I remembered what Esme's diary had said – or not said – about Lucien's death.

Then I became utterly confused.

And the van rattled to a halt on the concrete outside our back door.

* * *

Owen was closing the vents in the main glasshouse. It was a job we had often shared in the past, but right now, sharing anything at all seemed quite impossible. As I watched him, an early firework traced an arc in the sky beyond the glass and exploded noisily.

'Guy Fawkes tomorrow,' he said.

Not trusting myself to speak straightaway, I said nothing. I had a sudden understanding of fireworks. So many emotions were boiling around inside me that I felt at any moment the top of my head might burst open and a storm of brightly coloured emotions would shower upwards from my brain. Emotions are traditionally represented by different colours and I could surely come up with a fairly comprehensive rainbow: red for anger, green for envy, yellow for cowardice, black for despair. Though, of course, black wouldn't be much use in a firework. My train of thought alarmed me, with its indication of approaching madness.

I drew in a deep breath. 'How dare you discuss me with Dinah. That was cheap. That was worse than . . .' I broke off. My fury was no protection against the hurt that was swelling inside me and which any moment threatened to burst out in bitter and hopeless tears. I said stonily, 'Anyway, I'm going away again. Just for tonight.'

He turned round slowly. 'Must you?'

'Yes, as a matter of fact, I must. And don't pretend you give a damn what I do.'

He did not answer, merely carried on with his task as if he was hardly even aware of my presence. One of the panes of glass had jammed and his only concern seemed to be to get it shunted home.

I said icily, 'I don't suppose there's much I can do about you two, but I don't want that witch near my children, not ever again. Is that clear?'

'Clear, yes, but also irrelevant, I'd have thought,' he condescended to answer. 'Damn!' he exclaimed. But his anger was for the piece of glass, not for me, as it snapped in two against the metal upright. 'I'll have to put in a new piece tomorrow.'

He was so calm that I could hardly believe it. Just like Dinah. I had a premonition that before long Owen too would be lecturing me on my moral failings, pointing out my selfishness and my outdated concepts of fidelity.

He set down the two pieces of broken glass and took a step towards me for the first time. His face remained without expression.

'Where are you going?'

I shook my head. 'I'll be back tomorrow.' Though for what reason I could not, just at that moment, remember.

'Don't you think you should stay?'

'I can't.'

He turned and began tidying some empty seed trays. 'A couple of policemen were here earlier. They wanted to talk to you.'

'Why me?'

'They said it was just routine. They're talking to everyone who knew Esme. Mostly they want to talk to Rob.'

'Oh.'

'They thought it was a bit odd that I didn't know where you were. They implied that I did know, but was hiding you for some reason.'

'Why would you do that?'

'Hide you?' (Was he smiling?) 'I can't think.' No, he wasn't smiling. 'But as I said, it's Rob they really want to interview.'

'Why keep telling me? I don't know where he is.'

'I never said you did. The weird thing is that Rob seems to be the main suspect for the attack on Esme. Unbelievable, isn't it?'

I turned away. I could feel a nerve beating just behind my left eye. 'Ridiculous.' My voice sounded flat and unconvincing.

Owen continued his meticulous tidying. His calm movements were somehow soothing, and yet at the same time so inappropriate that I wanted to scream at him to stop. As I waited for his next words, I hardly dared move.

He said, 'Apparently one of the people in the hostel overheard them arguing a few hours before the alarm was raised. They heard a man's voice, they were sure it was Rob's, threatening that he would kill her if she didn't . . .'

'Didn't what?'

'They weren't altogether sure. They said it sounded like "keep quiet".'

'The police told you this?'

'They told John Drummond who told your mother.'

'Who then told you? Chinese whispers are notoriously inaccurate.'

'Yes, and anyway, the whole thing's ridiculous. Rob may have had his faults, but he was hardly homicidal.'

'No.'

'Did you know he and Esme had been living together for the last six months?'

I nodded. 'There was a photograph of her in an article about him recently.'

'I always thought they were well suited. I never could understand why she left him for Lucien.'

'My brother always got what he wanted.'

All the venom had drained from our conversation, leaving us with the stilted politeness of the recently introduced. Suddenly I had an image of how it might have been had we still been friends only, not husband and wife on the brink of disaster.

Owen added, 'By the way, I should have told you earlier. A man's been phoning, asking to speak to you. But he wouldn't leave a name or contact number.'

'Who was it?'

'I didn't recognise his voice. Well-spoken, though. And he said you'd be wanting to hear from him.'

I assumed it must have been Rob. Presumably he had wanted to contact me about something and had managed to disguise his voice. 'When did he call?'

'This morning.'

Rob.

'And a couple of times last night.'

So it couldn't have been Rob after all. Suddenly I was reminded of my mother's concern about strange phone calls, unknown people hanging around the nursery. The glasshouse suddenly felt like a very vulnerable place to be.

The children, who had been introducing the rabbit to the delights of television, were outraged at being torn away from their new companion for yet another draughty ride in the van. Especially when Owen insisted that Snowy-ten remain behind.

'He's had a busy day. Rabbits need a bit of peace and quiet every now and then.'

'But he'll miss us!' bellowed Billy.

'Anyway, Snowy-ten is a stupid name for a rabbit,' asserted Laura. 'Snowflake is all right. Snowflake is a much better name.'

Listening to their irrelevant chatter, I was amazed that they were so totally unaware of the dramas that were being played out around them. And I was swamped with love, and envied the simplicity of their lives.

But as we drove past the entrance to Dinah's house, the tension between

Owen and me was crackling like a badly tuned radio. My anger began to revive. I couldn't imagine how I had been lulled into letting down my guard while we spoke in the glasshouse. I tried desperately to think of something crucifying to say to Owen as we parted, something that would leave him feeling as raw and lacerated as I did now.

The van stopped in the station car park. 'Don't bother to see me off,' I told Owen, once I had said my goodbyes to the children.

'I won't,' he said. But then he spoiled it all by saying, in a voice that reminded me unbearably of the times when we had seemed to care for each other, 'Jane, promise you'll be careful.'

I wrenched myself away and clutched the precious carrier bag to my chest. 'Fat lot you care!' I snapped, then stood in the rain feeling stupid and miserable as the van drove away. My anger had made me sound all of nine years old.

11

Once I was on the train I almost broke down. In front of Dinah, even in front of Owen, I had been able to keep up the pretence that I was tough and self-sufficient but as soon as I was alone, I felt suddenly vulnerable and very afraid.

To stop myself from going demented with misery, I decided that now was as good a time as any to explore Esme's journal. It was certainly a diversion. If you should ever find yourself in danger of becoming bored with public transport, let me recommend the reading of someone else's private diaries. I considered that I was fully absolved from my promise to Rob by the fact that he had obviously lied to me about them in the first place. And anyway, I was curious. With good reason, as it turned out. Esme's journal was riveting; the only drawback was its brevity, and by the time I had travelled to Victoria, round to Paddington on the Circle Line and out into Berkshire, I had read it several times over. I think I was trying to learn it by heart.

> Here I am back at Martin's Court after all this time and it feels as if I'd never been away. I'm not sure that I see the point of all this really. Peter suggested it first, he likes it when I talk about what happened when I was a child. And Rob says I ought to follow through any suggestion Peter makes or else I won't be giving the therapy a proper chance.
>
> It's really odd being back here. After Mummy's funeral I was so angry with Daddy for bringing that man here – and at a time like that! I really hated him! – and I swore I'd never come here again. I hated everything about the place, all those horrid secrets. But Peter said I should come back here so that I can start the process of forgiveness.

The trouble is, I'm not sure that I want to forgive anyone, certainly not yet, but I suppose I will do in the end. The funny thing is that Peter is always telling me I shouldn't do things just because people tell me to do them. That I should learn to decide things for myself. But then when he goes and tells me to come back here and learn to forgive everyone, I do it.

That's the strangest thing about secrets. A part of you knows that it's there, but because it's a secret the main part of you doesn't know at all. Peter says it was all the secrets that affected me so much when I was little: the one big secret and all the other deceptions that followed from it.

Later. How I hate secrets. I've always hated them. Ever since Lucien kept going on about the amazing secret he had and how it would change all our lives if we ever found out what it was. I absolutely never wanted to know. Secrets have always terrified me. I suppose because I half knew and yet didn't know about Mummy's and Daddy's. Maybe I'm the most dreadful coward but I've never wanted to know anyone's horrible secret. Especially not this one of Rob's. And now he's made me promise promise promise not to tell anyone, not even my therapist, and it feels like the most ghastly weight on top of me and I simply cannot think how to shift it. I never wanted to know in the first place. I never asked him to tell me about Lucien's death. But now he's told me I can't forget about it, no matter how hard I try, and it just keeps preying on my mind that I ought to do something or tell someone, but I can't even do that. Oh, I wish he'd kept his beastly secret to himself.

Rob says that when he told me it was a sort of pledge, to show me I was the most special person he had ever known. I didn't know what to make of that because it seems a silly way to me, putting that kind of burden on someone. He says there are lots of different ways of killing people and I remember Lucien used to go on about it all the time too. He says we are all of us killing people all the time. He explained it over and over, but I still don't really understand.

I do remember Lucien's Murder Game though. We all had to think of as many different ways of killing someone as we could. As usual, Lucien was absolutely brilliant at it. The rest of us could only think of boring things like guns and brake cables, but Lucien got

> really serious. He learned up all the different poisons and he was really upset that the laburnum pods were all gone and it was too early for deadly nightshade. I wasn't sorry though. I was afraid he might try out some of his wretched poisons on dear little Snowy. It gives me the shivers now, when I think about it. Like a kind of premonition of his own death.

Shivers was the word. Esme's words were opening the door onto possibilities that were so dark and frightening that I began to understand her horror of secrets. Like her, I was tempted to shut my eyes and not want to know the secrets that had surrounded Rob and Lucien. Safer, perhaps, to wonder what secret of John and Clare's she was hinting at. I had never realised, until now, that she too had felt her childhood to be shadowed by the secrets her parents had chosen not to share with her. Perhaps that was what had given us a sense of kinship with each other, because I had always felt close to Esme, even though I never felt I knew her very well. Perhaps, because we had both grown up with secrets, we had never learned the openness that makes real friendship possible.

I read on; now I was hoping to discover Esme herself, as much as for any insights she might offer.

> Later. The sun came out this afternoon and I walked down by the river. It all looked just the same, except that the boathouse has got a bit more tacky and the poor old punt is a complete wreck. I had forgotten how green the light is by the river, especially in the evenings. I always liked it best down by the river.
>
> I used to spend hours and hours down by the river, just watching the water moving, always moving. I used to watch how the bits of twig and leaf and stuff used to flow down so peacefully, towards the sea, I suppose. I always thought that was the best way to be, just flow with the current and then you won't get hurt. Now I'm beginning to think that that was my big mistake. Next time someone wants me to do something I don't like, I won't do it, no matter what.
>
> The best times were when the others were here – Rob and Lucien and Jane. And then Owen. I suppose really they were the only friends I ever had. The village children always hated me for some reason. They said I was stuck up – but they were the ones who refused to

play. Then they said I was rude, and I didn't understand that at all because I tried to be friendly but they were the ones who threw mud and stones at me after school. I always hated school. Most days I didn't go. Mummy never noticed anyway, and when the man came from the school she always managed to fob him off somehow. The village children said we were rich and posh, but they all had washing machines and computers and all sorts of things. We never even had a proper television at Martin's Court.

With the summer friends it was different. They were magic. We never cared two hoots about anyone else. We were too busy with Lucien's games. You could never be bored for a moment when Lucien was around. He'd just have to say, 'I think I've just had an amazing idea—' and that look would come into his eyes and I'd get all goose-bumpy with excitement. In Lucien's games even the sad things became dramatic and memorable somehow. Like after Snowy-two was killed by that horrid little dog. Lucien was absolutely beastly about it and was going to burn poor Snowy-two as if he was just rubbish, and you can't have Viking rabbits, everyone knows that, so I didn't see the point of that. But when Owen saw how upset I was he was absolutely sweet about it and waded in and got Snowy-two back and he was able to have a decent Christian burial after all. Jane was in a cross mood as usual. Probably because of something Lucien said. But it never seemed to matter then. I wish those summers had never had to stop, but something to do with a stupid old milk jug set all the grown-ups quarrelling and that was that.

Funnily enough, because we were never particular friends or anything, it was Jane I missed the most. I suppose I'd always wanted a sister and she was the closest I ever got. By the time the twins came along it was too late really and I never got to know them as proper people, which is a shame, I can see that now. When Daddy made me go to that frightful boarding school I thought I would find someone like Jane there, someone who'd be my friend, but then all the other girls treated me like a freak. Just because we didn't have television and I'd never heard of any pop stars much and the only boys I had known were Rob and Lucien and Owen and they'd always been friends, not boyfriends, the other girls made me feel as if I'd just landed from Mars. I don't think Jane ever saw me as a freak. I'd love

> to ask her about it one day. I thought I had a good excuse to get in touch with her because of that man who keeps pestering me about her, but Faith says I absolutely mustn't. And she told me not to say a word to Rob either. Even Faith has secrets. Not that I would have told Rob anyway, because he makes such a fuss over things like that.

That man who keeps pestering me about her . . . There he was again. First Faith, then Owen, and now Esme . . . For an icy moment I could feel a stranger's eyes following me. Someone was trying to get hold of me, perhaps they were choosing their moment right now. I examined the few other occupants of the carriage. They all looked ordinary enough. The man sitting opposite me was grey-haired, nothing remarkable about him at all, but when he glanced at me over the top of his *Financial Times* I felt suddenly naked and afraid. I glared at him and went back to my reading.

> Later. Then when I left school I discovered that boys didn't seem to think I was a freak at all. They acted as though they liked me and that was a surprise. At any rate, they wanted to have sex with me and I can't remember ever saying no. I liked the closeness of it all, even though it never lasted very long. That empty feeling always came back again. Until Rob. Rob was different. I didn't realise to begin with. I still like to remember the day we met again after all those years. He was leaning out of his window at the college talking to someone on a sunny March afternoon when he saw me strolling across the quad with Sam Pearson. He says he was so excited to see me that he nearly fell out of the window. Lucky he didn't, because we got together at once and that was the start of the best times of all. He had his exams to work for, of course, and often I'd sit for hours in his room, just watching him while he worked. To begin with he got a bit embarrassed and thought I must be bored, but after a while he got used to it. Then he came to London and everything carried on being lovely until that dreadful evening when we planned to go out with Lucien and then at the last minute Rob had too much work to do. So Lucien and I spent the evening together and then, oh, I don't know how it happened, but we ended up making love.

No. That won't do. I have to work out the reasons and it's no good just saying I'd had too much to drink (though of course I had) or anything feeble like that. Well then:

a) I'd never learned how to say 'No' to anyone and that's what Peter says I have to do now. Something to do with Self-Worth, though I can't really see what that's got to do with anything and

b) I still regarded Lucien as such a hero. He'd always been the leader in absolutely everything and just so brilliant and clever and funny that I couldn't imagine him having much interest in me. So I suppose I was amazingly flattered, and

c) I suppose I've always been a bit feeble about things like that. And anyway, I *was* horribly drunk.

Anyway, we did it, and it really wasn't all that wonderful, not like with Rob, but when Rob realised what had happened he was frightfully upset. I think maybe that was the worst evening of my life. Rob kept saying: 'You've got to decide, Esme, don't you see, you've got to make up your mind.' It all seemed so silly because I didn't see what there was to decide about, but I couldn't say anything because Rob was so angry I just assumed I'd lost him anyway. So I just cried. And he went away. Then Lucien was killed and I knew I'd lost them both.

Things went a bit fuzzy after that. I worked at different jobs and there were different men but in a funny sort of way they all seemed the same because they weren't Rob.

Then he started appearing on TV and I just used to sit and watch him and cry to think of what I had lost. I could hardly believe my luck when he got in touch last year. He had changed, though. He was much more cautious. I thought it was wonderfully romantic the way he said he'd waited but never given up hope and then come hunting for me. But he wouldn't make love for absolutely ages. I thought maybe he was testing me in some way, but he just said it had to be different this time. It certainly was. I finally broke down his defences when we were watching some unutterably boring football game on TV. After that football and sex at the same time became something of a ritual and a joke between us. Once at some absolutely crucial moment in a match someone scored a goal and we both came at once and all the crowd cheered madly. It was terrific. We tried it with cricket and tennis a couple of times, but it wasn't the same.

The trouble with Rob now is that he always seems to be wanting something, I don't know what it is so I never seem able to give it to him. Once I told him he wanted too much but he just turned round and told me I didn't want enough and that was worse, so we didn't get anywhere much on that one. Still, perhaps he's right. What do I want? Rob says I ought to know what I want, but I don't. And it's not because I'm always happy. Far from it.

Later. Yes, I do. It came to me this afternoon while I was out in the garden. I was sitting in the place where we always met when we were children. I could hear the river and the Rams beating same as ever. I want everything to be just as it was then. I want Lucien to be still alive and us all to be children and together. That's what I want most of all – just the five of us together in our own little world.

Sometimes I dream it is that way still. Those are the good dreams. But sometimes the dream turns into a nightmare. Last time I dreamt that Lucien was drowning in the river – he'd fallen out of the punt – and Rob was watching him and laughing and wouldn't try to save him even though I begged and begged. And when I woke up from that nightmare, there was Rob in the bed beside me, and even though he was fast asleep, I felt frightened.

I can't talk to Rob about those nightmares. He says he still has nightmares because of what happened and I don't want to make them even worse. He says he's always been haunted by what happened and what he did. He says that the Ancient Mariner's albatross was guilt and he'll never be free of it as long as he lives. I tried reading *The Ancient Mariner* the other day, but I couldn't see the point of it and gave up after a bit. I told Rob I thought it was great but I think he suspected a lie.

Oh dear, if I try to understand, everything just seems more of a muddle. I suppose that's why most of the time I don't bother. And, to tell the truth, why I don't really see the point of this journal. And why I certainly don't want to know who the man is who keeps phoning about Jane. And why I never wanted to know Lucien's beastly fifth secret.

Later. Rob said he only told me his secret because he loved me. He said he knew I'd never tell anyone because I love him too much for that. Then he asks me if I love him. Of course, I always say yes. But how am I supposed to tell? I really think I must do. Which is odd, really, because Owen was always my favourite. Maybe because the other three all had each other but Owen and I were both loners. I sometimes think it's odd that he's the only one I never got together with. I would have been quite glad to, but I suppose he never wanted it. I think he only ever cared about Jane, but she was always too angry and stupid to notice.

Sometimes I don't think I like Jane at all. And that's odd too, in a way, because I've already said she was the only friend I ever had. Perhaps it's because she was always such a cow about Owen.

Later. Rob tells me I should get myself together. I don't think he realises how hard I've been trying, but it is far from easy. If there was something I was good at it might make it a bit clearer. That's why I always envied Jane her painting. At least she always knew what she wanted, even if she did get angry and upset about it. The wanting seemed to give her a kind of passion. I've never been much good at anything. People often seem disappointed when they get to know me. They say that when they first met me they thought I looked interesting.

Later. It scares me being back here. Actually, to tell the truth, I don't like it at all. Mrs Wicks still treats me as if I was about four years old. She absolutely hates Daddy and I suppose it's not all that surprising. I always thought she'd leave when Mummy died, but now I think she feels she has to stay just to keep Mummy's end up. Sort of like protecting someone even after they're dead, which is pretty spooky when you think about it. Last night I thought I could hear Mummy crying. This morning I half believed that if I walked down to the river, the others would all be waiting for me beside the boathouse.

You could go mad here, all alone.

Later. Oh, well, I suppose I'd better go back to London and face the music.

It was only when the grey-haired man sitting opposite me threw a large cotton handkerchief at me from behind the safety of his *Financial Times* that I realised I was crying.

'Thank you,' I said, mopping my eyes and wondering if his offer included nose-blowing as well.

'Don't mention it,' he said amicably. 'City reports often have the same effect on me.'

When he stood up to get off at the next station, he told me I could keep the handkerchief if I wanted. The effect of such unexpected kindness from a stranger was to reduce me to fresh tears.

My first impulse on reading the diary as I travelled west into Berkshire, was to hurtle straight back to the hospital and take Esme in my arms and tell her I would always be her friend. Poor dear Esme (to borrow a couple of her favourite adjectives), I'd never had the first idea what was going on behind her calm and beautiful face. Like everyone else, I'd never even bothered to find out. But what I had mistaken for security had all the time been a desperate naiveté, a kind of endless sleepwalking through life. Maybe she would have been the sort of person who is easily influenced anyway, maybe she had never been very bright, but her isolated and strange childhood had left her hopelessly ill-equipped to deal with the world that existed beyond Martin's Court. I grappled briefly with the conundrum of John and Clare Drummond's secret, then dropped it thankfully. Like Esme, I had had my share of secrets.

But most of all, it was her innocence that struck me. The innocence that sometimes made her appear infuriatingly childish, even deliberately stupid, but which at other times seemed like a rare and precious gift. Something that I and others like me had lost – or never even had – and that I wanted to be able to honour.

How much of what she had said about Rob was true? There was no way of knowing. Like all innocents, she could often be hopelessly wrong, but she could also produce startling insights. Whether I liked it or not – and of course I did not – pennies were beginning to drop into place so fast I could almost hear them clinking.

Rob had good reason for wanting to get hold of Esme's journal before anyone else did. In a moment of weakness he had told Esme his darkest secret, and he had no way of knowing if she had stuck to her promise not to tell anyone. Something to do with Lucien's death . . . Perhaps also it was something to do with Lucien's secret. The obvious explanation was so fantastical that I pushed it firmly to the back of my mind.

If I had hoped that Esme's journal would answer all my questions, then I was far from satisfied. But at least now I knew some of the questions that needed asking.

But that wasn't what had made the tears pour down my cheeks:

> Owen was always my favourite . . . I think he only ever cared about Jane, but she was always too angry and stupid to notice.

And I remembered Owen's bitter question, 'What marriage?' Regret was too weak to describe how I felt. Like someone who discovers too late that they have thrown away a diamond necklace in a pile of rubbish. Owen's love was a treasure I never knew I had until I lost it.

I took a taxi from the station, then walked across the dusky lawn and the straggly wet orchard grass towards Glory Cottage with no clear idea of what I was supposed to say to Rob. How should I act with this oldest of friends who for ten years had nursed some terrible secret about my brother's death? Phrases floated through my mind, each one less helpful than the last as my overworked brain fell back on a couple of useless platitudes. 'Bitten off more than you can chew, eh?' said a voice. While another, 'I expect it will all come out in the wash.' Whatever that was supposed to mean.

Looking back, I can see that the strangest part of all was that I didn't feel the least bit afraid of Rob; yet the police suspected him of trying to murder Esme; Esme thought he had had a part in Lucien's death.

All I was sure of, as I pushed open the door into Glory Cottage, was that Rob was using me as a bit-part player in his own private drama without even bothering to share the story with me. All my life I'd been kept in the dark by those who should have been closest to me – Faith with her endless evasions and silences, Lucien and his fifth secret, Dinah and Owen forging deceptions the moment my back was turned – and I was damned if I was going to let Rob get away with the same old shabby trick. The more I thought about it, the angrier I became. And this was a different kind of anger from my usual chronic irritation. This anger was a cool knife that could slice through to the truth, and never mind the cost.

The cottage was in darkness. At the thought that Rob might have slipped away while I was gone I was filled with conflicting feelings of disappointment and relief.

I switched on the light. The downstairs room was spotless and all the curtains were drawn across the windows.

'Rob?'

Silence.

Then again, more loudly, 'Rob? It's me, Jane. I'm alone.'

A figure appeared at the top of the stairs.

'Jane, thank Christ. I thought you weren't coming back.'

And his face, as he came down the stairs and into the light, was so haggard and hopeless and so achingly familiar that I faltered. I'm going mad, I thought. I've known Rob since we were both children. How can I suspect him?

As if to compensate for my treacherous thoughts, I said at once, 'I've found Esme's journal. Here—'

He made an odd sound, but did not speak. He snatched the journal from me and I noticed that his hands were shaking violently. He skimmed through it, turning the pages without giving himself a chance to read it properly, as if he was looking for something. His name perhaps? Then he paused, grunted in apparent satisfaction at having found what he was looking for, read for a moment or two and then snapped the book shut. It was only when he crossed the room to the fireplace that I noticed the hearth had been carefully laid with firelighters and kindling.

'Rob, what are you doing?'

I reached out to grab the journal from him, but he pushed me away with a force so unexpected that I lost my balance and fell among the soft cushions of the sofa.

'Damn you, Rob. Stop that.'

'Keep back.'

He struck a match. Then, as the first blue flame curled upwards towards the chimney, he placed the journal in the fire. He remained there for some time, squatting down with his back to me, occasionally adjusting the pages or adding fresh sticks, until every last scrap had burned and there was only a pile of ash remaining.

I was still sprawled on the sofa when Rob stood up and brushed the dust from the knees of his trousers.

I looked up at him. 'Why did you have to burn it?'

He turned away, avoiding my eye. 'It's what Esme would have wanted,' he said in a low voice.

'Liar.'

He flinched, paused for a moment, then shrugged slightly as if deciding against a particular course of action. My anger began to rise again as I saw him go to the kitchenette and pull a bottle of wine from a cupboard.

He attempted a smile. 'Well, you've found the journal at last. This calls for a celebration, don't you think?'

I stood up and followed him across the room. 'You said there'd be information about Esme's attacker,' I persisted.

'Well, I was wrong, that's all.'

'How do you know? You didn't even read it properly.'

He paused. His fingers tightened round the neck of the bottle.

'Jane, stop interfering. You don't understand.'

'I do. Some of it anyway. You made up all that stuff about Esme and drugs and knowing the wrong people. You only wanted the journal to protect yourself. Not for Esme's sake at all.'

For the first time since he had taken the journal from me, he raised his eyes and his gaze met my own. In that moment his expression was that of a man who could happily do murder. And have no regrets. I felt as if I was beginning to see into the secret heart of him for the very first time.

He was barely able to phrase the question. 'You read it?'

I nodded.

'Damn you. I told you not to. You promised.'

I said nothing.

'Jane, I trusted you.'

That did it. 'Trust? What are you talking about, Rob? I'm the poor fool who did the trusting. I'm the gormless idiot who abandoned my family to help you when you sent that SOS. I'm the one who's lied to everyone on your behalf and stolen someone else's property just so you could burn it. For all I know I could be had up for helping a criminal. Serve me right too. And what do I get from you? A pack of lies about Esme and the journal. Well, I'm sick to death of everyone lying to me and using me. I've had enough of it. You destroyed that journal because you were afraid of people reading what it said about you.'

As my voice rose out of control, Rob had gone pale as chalk. His eyes were narrowed. 'Why, Jane? What did she say?'

'About you—' I was gasping. 'About you and Lucien when he died – she said—'

'No, don't say it.' He sprang forward and cupped his hand over my mouth. I twisted my head away.

'She said that you—'

'I know, I know. And that's what I was afraid of, that's why I had to destroy the journal. Listen to me, Jane, you've got to listen to me. I'll tell you the truth, I'll tell you what happened.' He caught hold of my wrists. 'But you must let me explain. Please, Jane.'

His hands were very tight round my wrists and his eyes were only inches away from my own. I could see the flecks of gold in the darker brown of his irises, the texture of the skin around his eyes. We were both breathing heavily. A bead of sweat appeared on his forehead. A tremor of something that was not fear but which felt almost like an electric shock raced up my arm at the pressure of his hands. My heart was beating rapidly.

'Why should I listen to you now? You've done nothing but lie to me.'

'No, that's not right. Okay, so I haven't always told you the truth, but I haven't lied. Not really. Trust me, Jane.'

His voice had become coaxing. He relaxed his hold on my wrists. His expression mellowed. I did not trust him, not for a moment, but I was curious to learn what explanation he was going to come up with.

'Tell me then.'

'Sure.'

He turned away and picked up the bottle of wine. 'Let's do this properly,' he said. 'I need a drink, don't you?'

He opened the bottle and poured us each a drink. 'Here—' He handed me a glass and smiled at me encouragingly. He was being nice in the way that double-glazing salesmen are nice – because he was trying to sell me something. But he was still agitated. He was trying to look calm and trustworthy but he couldn't help making constant little nervous gestures, adjusting the position of the wine bottle, moving restlessly from one corner of the kitchenette to another, flexing and relaxing the muscles of his hands.

'So,' he began, 'Esme said in her journal that I blamed myself for Lucien's death. Right?'

'How do you know?'

'I read that much.' So he had just been looking for his own name.

'And now you want to know how. Well, I suppose I owe you that much at least.' He reached over to the tap which was dripping occasionally and turned it off more tightly. 'It's hard to talk about, that's all.' He drank the glass of wine and poured another. 'More?' I shook my head. 'I think it was the guilt that made me crack up afterwards. I just couldn't handle it. That's why I didn't come to the funeral and do all the normal things that were expected of me. I just couldn't do it. I felt the whole ghastly tragedy was my fault.'

'But why?'

He refolded a tea towel and placed it carefully on the draining board, then glanced towards me with a strange smile.

'It was my idea, you see. I suggested that walking holiday. It was the middle of June. We hadn't seen each other for months. Not since he and Esme got together. I was still angry. Angry and hurt. Then, out of the blue, he phoned me up. Said he needed to talk to me. He said it was urgent. I said forget it. I think I hung up on him. The next day he phoned again. He was acting as if nothing had happened. I couldn't understand it. I was still furious with him, but he wore me down. The moment I started talking to him it was as if I was ten years old again. I seemed to lose my will. I wasn't in control any more.' Rob had thrust his hands into his armpits and was staring at the colourless linoleum between his feet. 'He said he'd come to my flat. That we could spend the weekend together and it would be just like old times. I panicked. I said: no, don't come here. I knew it had to be on neutral ground. I couldn't bear to have him invade my space and take over everything I had all over again. So I said: let's meet in Dorset. There was a pub near the sea I'd heard of. Some friends had stayed there at Easter and they said it was cheap and fairly decent. I knew Lucien must be hard up. I'll meet you there on Friday evening, I told him. We can spend the weekend walking. I thought I could cope with that. I knew I couldn't have him in my flat all that time, I'd go mad. But I thought, in the open, outside, I could manage that.'

'So you were there when it happened—'

'No!' His head jerked upwards in denial and he banged his fist down on the counter. 'No, that's not true. I wasn't there. I didn't go. I chickened out.'

'What?'

'On the Friday evening I found I couldn't face it. Him. I thought: I'll go down tomorrow. I phoned the pub and left a message. I told him I'd catch an early train and join him. I thought about it all night long. Then in the morning I phoned the pub and left a message to say I wouldn't be down after all. I took my phone off the hook and went out. I stayed with friends. And then, when

I got home, I heard what had happened and I thought: it's all my fault. I killed him. It was too much. I couldn't take it in, not all at once. I felt like his murderer.'

'But that's crazy.'

'You think so? But if he'd come to my flat like he wanted to, then the accident would never have happened. If I hadn't suggested that particular place then the accident would never have happened. Even if I'd been with him, then I might have been able to stop him. I was the single most important link in the chain of events that ended up with him lying at the bottom of the cliff. Can't you even try to understand how that has made me feel?'

I was on the verge of telling him: nonsense, how can you possibly blame yourself? when I remembered having experienced a similar kind of guilt myself. That same week Lucien had phoned me and suggested that we spend the weekend with Faith and Eric. If possible we always went to see them together; it lessened the awfulness of family life. I had put him off because I was already contemplating the days ahead with Rob. When Lucien died, I too had felt guilt, but over the years I had forgotten. For Rob, apparently, the guilt had not faded so easily. It had remained to haunt him. His albatross.

'I suppose so. But then, what was the panic over Esme's journal? Surely all you had to do was explain that to the police.'

'You're saying I overreacted? Maybe I did, but that's hardly surprising. Don't forget, I *know* what it's like to be accused of something you haven't done. To sit there protesting your innocence and all the time see the look in their eyes. See them thinking, you lying bastard, we've got you now. Those smug faces of the jury and all the time you're twisting and turning like some godforsaken worm on a hook. When you've been through that once in a lifetime, believe me, panicking is easy.'

His last words burst out with bitter sincerity – and why not? After all, he had spent four precious years in prison for a crime he did not commit; small wonder if the fear of a second miscarriage of justice made him act wildly. His hand was shaking as he raised his glass and drained it.

'It'll be okay,' I said, refilling it for him.

He looked at me doubtfully. 'Maybe.'

I was trying to piece together what he had told me of that midsummer weekend of Lucien's accident with what I already knew. We both remained silent for a moment, then I said, 'Do you remember the last evening we spent together? It must have been the Thursday before Lucien fell.'

His expression did not change. 'Yes.'

'You told me then that you had to go away for a couple of days. Why didn't you tell me you were meeting my brother?'

He shrugged. 'Maybe it just seemed easier to keep you and Luce in separate compartments. My feelings for Lucien were muddled enough.'

And what about his feelings for me? The question, unspoken but understood by both of us, lay heavy in the air between us.

He shifted slightly. He was watching me intently. For the first time since I had found him in the Rams two days earlier, I knew that he was remembering the attraction that had existed between us during those brief days of midsummer before everything changed for ever. I discovered that I was not yet ready to respond to the expression that was shadowing his eyes. I moved away.

'Who did you go and see?'

'What?'

'You said that when you couldn't face joining Luce in Dorset, you went to visit friends. Which friends?'

'Oh, that . . . I can't remember now. Does it matter? I suppose I should have come to see you.'

'It's not important.'

Rob was still staring at me. 'What did you think?' he asked gently. 'That I pushed your brother over the cliff?'

I finished my glass of wine and poured another. The bottle was empty. This was no longer a conversation I wished to pursue sober. I said, 'I didn't know what to think.'

He smiled, as if the very idea was fantastic. 'I had the motive, I suppose, if you can call it that. Lucien had pinched my girlfriend. The love of my life. I had every reason to hate him. Because of Esme.'

'Esme, yes.' There was a constriction in my chest at the thought of her. It was something to do with the way Rob was looking at me, all that I had learned from the journal, an awareness of imminent betrayal. Casting around for some way to diffuse the tension, I said, 'Owen and I smuggled in a white rabbit. He thought it might remind her of the Snowies. She did seem to make some kind of response. Almost as if she was trying to open her eyes, or smile. But then I was afraid that maybe we imagined it because we were hoping so hard. The nurse said we should regard it as a good sign.'

'Excellent.'

'But that we shouldn't raise our hopes.' I hesitated. 'So now that you've burned the journal, there's nothing to keep you here any longer, is there? Will you go and see her tonight?' (And if you do, I wondered, what will I do next?)

He was still watching me. In contrast to my growing confusion, he was suddenly very calm. In a voice so faint I could barely make out the words, he said, 'Is that what you want?'

'I don't know. There have been too many shocks and I'm not thinking straight any more. Owen's been having an affair, I was right about that. They didn't deny it, just accused me of overreacting. I don't understand . . .'

'Poor Jane. You've been through hell. And I don't know what I'd have done without you.'

I was just thinking how phoney his words sounded, as if he was reading from cue cards, when he took a step towards me and brushed the hair back from my forehead in a gesture of infinite tenderness. 'You know, all day I've had nothing to do except sit here and wait for you to come back. And I realised how self-obsessed I must have seemed the last couple of days. I'm sorry for that. But I also realised that it was you I wanted to see, Jane. You, and not just because of the journal but—'

There was a loud thump at the door and almost simultaneously it was flung open. I just had time to catch sight of Rob's horrified expression as he dived behind the doubtful protection of the kitchen units. I was wondering why he should continue to hide now that the journal had been found, when John Drummond came into the room.

One glance at John's face was enough to tell me I could have been entertaining half the village and he'd never have noticed.

'I can't be more than a minute,' he said, talking rapidly between gasps of breath. 'I'm just off to the hospital. Thought you'd want to know. The police have arrested the chap who attacked Esme. One of the lads at Rob's Branden House place. Exactly what we always guessed.' I could hear the chink of Rob's wine glass toppling over on the floor, but John noticed nothing. 'The fellow's done this sort of thing before. Famous for it, in fact. Fingerprints all over the place. And then the hospital phoned to say Esme's on the mend. They think she's coming round. Police are standing by to talk to her. Just to confirm the man's confession.'

His mouth fell into a grin of pure delight and his eyes were brimming.

All I could manage through my own tears of relief was, 'Oh, John, I'm so . . .'

He patted my shoulder. 'I know, my dear. I know. So am I.'

And he was gone.

12

Rob was mopping at his trousers with a tea towel as he stood up. 'Damn,' he said, 'now there's wine on the clothes you bought me.'

'Did you hear what John said?'

He nodded. 'It must be Hamish. I thought he was over his bad habits by now, but apparently not. Poor bastard, I suppose he must have made a confession. The fingerprints don't mean a thing. He was in and out of the flat the whole time, they all were. Jesus, I hope they've picked up the right one.'

'Of course they have. They wouldn't have arrested him otherwise.'

'Don't be naive, Jane. The police do make mistakes. I'm the living proof of that.'

As the evening wore on, I realised that more than one interpretation could be put on that remark. But, as the evening wore on, I had other things on my mind.

'So what happens now?' I wondered.

'A celebration, don't you think? Can you track down some more wine?'

'Of course.'

When we went into town together the previous day, John had told me to help myself to his wines rather than buy second-rate stuff at the supermarket, and I decided that this was an occasion to take him up on his offer. My own problems were as tangled as ever, but in view of Esme's improvement and John's happiness, it seemed selfish to think about my own worries. When I made my way up to Martin's Court, I found that even Mrs Wicks had mellowed on that evening – she must have been more upset about Esme than I had realised – and she watched me almost maternally while I copied out the names of the two bottles of wine I was taking.

Rob's mood, as we broached a new bottle, was impossible to gauge. His relief at the discovery of Esme's attacker and the news of her expected recovery had only increased his agitation. He was more exasperated than angry that one of his 'guests' had gone for Esme. I was impressed by his lack of bitterness. Rob spent a little while trying to imagine what could have motivated such a vicious attack, but without success. Skilled as he was in manipulating the media to his own ends, he knew only too well what damage the inevitable publicity would do.

'I should be there now,' he said. But without much conviction as we were well into the second bottle of wine.

'Leave it till morning,' I counselled selfishly. 'You'd be no use to them like this anyway.'

'You're right.' He slumped down beside me on the sofa and draped an arm across my shoulders. In the grate the fire wheezed laboriously and occasionally made a loud spitting noise while outside a gentle wind was cruising through the apple trees.

After a little while Rob said, 'Now that it's nearly over, I'm glad I've had these two days here. When I was in prison I used to think about this place a lot. I told myself I'd come back, but somehow never got round to it. Now I feel I've touched base. I should have done it years ago.'

'Me too. I'm glad you Urgently Derbied me.'

'I don't know what I'd have done otherwise. Gone into the river probably.'

'Don't say that.'

His fingers were fiddling with the hair above my ears. I told myself this was our last chance to recapture the magic and innocence we had known as children, that Rob had always been like a brother to me. Gradually, the silence and strangeness of Glory Cottage began to weave its half-remembered spell. It was as though for one last night Rob and I had made an unspoken pact to keep the outside world at bay. All the problems that were waiting for us on the other side of the orchard – hospitals and partners and decisions and responsibilities – all that could be forgotten until the morning. At this moment our world was only what could be reflected in the shining curve of a wine glass, half tilted to catch the orange glow of the fire.

After a little while, wanting to talk about the past, I said, 'Do you remember the secrets?'

'Vaguely.'

'Lucien said everyone had to think of a secret. You unmasked the poor old Nazi commandant. Lucien was furious, though he wouldn't admit it.'

'Now I remember. And we never did find out if Esme made up that stuff about Mrs Wicks's webbed feet.'

'I invented mine.'

'What about Luce?'

'He wouldn't say. He was so angry with me for making up a secret about our father that he refused to tell us his. The fifth secret – he said it was the best one of all. And he never did tell me what it was.' I hesitated. 'Did he tell you?'

'Never.'

'I'd give anything to know what it was.'

Rob turned to face me. 'Maybe there wasn't one,' he said.

'What?'

'He probably didn't have a secret of his own. He just wanted to hear ours. Or maybe he realised that his was nothing special. Getting angry with you would have been a typical Lucien way of wriggling out of something: pile the blame on someone else. Maintain superiority at all costs.'

'That's not fair.'

'Isn't it? Think about it.'

I turned away. I didn't want to think about it. Long ago I had resigned myself to never finding out what the fifth secret was. But the mere fact that it existed somewhere, that once someone had known what it was, had always been a bastion against the muddle and the dark. Take away even the possibility of its existence and there wasn't much left.

I shifted my weight so that I was leaning against Rob's shoulder. 'Hold me, Rob,' I said. He put his arm around me and pulled me companionably close. 'I'm sure he must have had a secret,' I went on when I was comfortable. 'Lucien always came up trumps in the end. He was the most amazing person that ever lived.'

'That's crap, Jane.'

'Why? You always thought so too.'

'Once. Once upon a time. But I learned to see through him at the end.'

'What do you mean?' I twisted angrily away from him. There was a kind of triumph on his face, as if he was daring me to contradict him.

He said, 'Sometimes I think your brother was nothing but a brilliant con man.'

'What?'

'No, con man is too generous. Lucien was a shit and we were all his willing dupes.'

'You're just drunk.'

'You're damn right I am.' He thrust his face close to mine and his eyes were full of loathing. 'And I plan to get drunker yet. Just don't give me all that bullshit about Lucien the hero. I couldn't stand it. Not tonight. I've had enough lies in the last couple of days. Can't we just be honest with each other for once? Just for once?'

'Lies?'

'You do know, Jane. You must have always known. You've got your faults but you've never been stupid. So when did you start to realise the truth about Lucien, eh? I expect you were just like me, didn't want to see, pretended for years that it wasn't happening. Did you have to wait until he'd damn near destroyed you before you admitted the truth?'

'Shut up. You're mad. Luce was everything.'

'Oh, don't I know it. Believe me, Jane, I don't hold it against you. I fell for it too, God knows. When I tried to tell someone how I used to feel about Lucien, they thought it was just a homosexual crush, but it never was, not even when we were still at school. Actually, I don't think he was particularly interested sexually in males or females. From what Esme has told me about their affair, sex was the least of it. My guess is that he was too much in love with himself to be able to make any real contact with another human being.'

'Don't be sick. I'm not listening to this.'

But when I attempted to rise, Rob pressed me back against the corner of the sofa. I could have freed myself, I know I could, but I did not even struggle.

'You will listen, Jane, because you're the only person in this whole bloody mess who'll ever understand. Just as I understand you. For years I was blind to his faults. Just like you were. In my eyes he was a high-flying comet, one of those extraordinary people who are thrown up perhaps once or twice in each generation. All I wanted was to be close to him. To be a part of that greatness.'

'But you were right, Rob,' I was almost pleading with him. 'Luce was the most extraordinary—'

He cut in, ignoring me completely. 'Do you know, I've never been sure if he deceived us on purpose or if he actually believed the myth himself. I know damn well I should have seen through the deception years before, but of course I didn't. In fact I helped keep the illusion going. I didn't want to see the truth. I've often asked myself why. Anything rather than admit I'd spent my life believing in a charlatan.'

I pushed his shoulders back with my fists. 'Jealousy, Rob, that's your problem. It always was. Lucien was ten times the man you'd ever be. You've been eaten up with jealousy right from the start. It's pathetic.'

'Don't tempt me. You know nothing about him.'

'He was my brother.'

His laugh was contemptuous. 'Christ, the trouble he went to, to keep his family in the dark. Where do you want me to begin? He never won a scholarship to Oxford, he barely scraped in. The whole thing was a lie from the beginning. He cracked up before finals. No great shame in that. It could have happened to anyone. But, of course, Lucien didn't see it that way. He had to keep it secret. He insisted on sitting the exams, even though he was a wreck. He was lucky to get a third. That was a secret too. It always amazed me, the way you and Faith just believed everything he dished out to you, never bothered to check anything. And so it continued. The more he failed, the more he had to pretend. He couldn't cope with being less than perfect. As far as he was concerned, if he wasn't seen to be the best, he wasn't anything.'

'But he'd always been brilliant.'

'In school maybe. In that little artificial world. But in the real world he was just another bumptious prat who thought he was God's gift to the universe. He couldn't hack the competition. He didn't have the first idea what to do with himself after university. He tried one or two things but he loathed having to start at the bottom like the rest of mankind.'

I saw a chink of light. Surely Rob must remember that Lucien's faults and shortcomings were all part of what made him so special. I said, 'He told Faith and me once that he planned to start at the top and work up from there.'

'I bet she lapped that up. She never guessed, did she, that he was working in a pizza place at the time of the accident?'

'That's not true. He was doing research.'

'Is that what he told you? The only research Lucien was doing then was into the eating habits of London's teenagers.'

'I never knew.'

'No. You never knew the half of it.' Suddenly his voice became gentle, and there was pity in his eyes. 'Poor Jane,' he said. 'You were even more his dupe than I was.'

'That's ridiculous.' But all the fire had gone out of my protest, and still I could not move. Not because of Rob's physical bulk pressing me into the corner of the sofa, but because of the weight of what he was saying. I would not have bothered to protest unless deep down I had recognised the grain of truth that lay buried in the heart of his words. Only Rob, whose love for Lucien had come near to equalling my own, could have even begun to say these terrible things.

In all the turmoil of my feelings at that time, I was totally unprepared for what happened next. Very slowly, he lowered his face towards mine and pressed his lips against my mouth. For a moment I opened myself to his kiss, and when I turned away, my eyes were suddenly overflowing with tears.

I said, 'I miss him, Rob. I've missed him every day for ten years.'

'I know. I have too. He was a bastard though.'

'Don't say that. Please.'

He was remorseless. 'Do you know why he screwed Esme? Why he stayed with her after that first night even though he thought she was boring and silly? His words. Because he couldn't bear to see us happy together, that's why. He couldn't bear to be shut out. No one was allowed to have any pleasures unless he dished them out. That's the kind of man your precious brother was.'

It was too much. 'That's not true!' I yelled, and with my full strength I rammed my hands against his chest to push him off and at the same time wrenched myself away from the corner of the sofa. He grunted slightly with the impact of the double blow, then caught me round the waist as though to stop me from falling to the floor.

'Why not?' he hissed. 'Don't you want to hear the truth? I'm not making this up, Jane. He never really cared for Esme.'

I stared at him in horror. He was almost smiling. I could feel myself slipping, could feel the rough texture of the carpet against my back.

'How do you know?' I asked.

His face was hanging above my own. I had never seen that expression in anyone's eyes before. He was supporting himself on his hands. He adjusted his height a little so he could kiss me again, then drew back.

'He told me so himself,' he said, as I reached up and twined my arms around his neck to pull him down to me again. 'He told me in Dorset on the day he fell.'

It would be easier now if I could report that as soon as Rob had said those words I turned away from him in disgust. That I stood up there and then and insisted he tell me what he meant. But I didn't. He was returning my kisses gently, tenderly, as if his lovemaking could shield us both from the stark horror of his words. We fumbled for each other and dragged at our constricting clothes. I surrendered myself to sensation in the hope perhaps that the energy that flooded through my body, the energy that flowed between us both, would blot out all thought and consciousness.

He drew back while I pulled my sweater over my head. He was now so close to me that he had become blurred, an eye or nose or mouth disconnected from the familiar face. I realised then, as I absorbed at close range the separate items that made up the well-known whole, that Rob had become a familiar stranger. The inflexions of his voice, his unchanging features, so many little mannerisms, were as much part of my life as if he were family; a gap of a mere ten years made no difference to that. And yet I knew, in the rawness of our journey towards each other, that the person he was offering me now was nothing at all like the Rob who had always existed in my mind.

Dorset on the day he fell . . .

In the breathing space that occurred while he removed shoes and trousers, I tried to clear my thoughts.

'What are you saying?'

He began running his hands lightly over my body. He stopped abruptly. 'What do you think?'

But before I had a chance to think of an answer, his tender mood had vanished. He pushed me down against the floor and began to kiss me with a harshness that was almost a kind of anger, and his hands were no longer gentle but urgent and demanding.

A tremor of fear threaded down my spine as a sudden image of Esme, his lover for six months, lying still as death in her hospital bed came into my mind.

'Rob—' I began, but he forced my silence with his mouth pressed against mine as he thrust himself inside me, and my body answered with a passion that had nothing whatever to do with the doubts and suspicions that were crowding my mind.

Or everything. In some distant part of myself I was horrified to think that the pleasure I was enjoying was perhaps fuelled by that very frisson of danger, that it might be Rob the stranger rather than Rob the friend I had known since childhood to whom I responded with an intensity that was near to madness. And then there was no thought.

Our lovemaking was quickly over. Given the time we had waited and the wine we had drunk, it was hardly surprising that our pleasure was short-lived. If pleasure it was.

Afterwards we lay together side by side on the cheap carpet where we had spread our games and books when we were children. We did not talk. Rob may have slept, I don't know. I did not, but I wasn't properly awake either. I seem to have been in a state of suspended trance, aware of the flickering firelight and the position of my body on the floor, yet drained of all thought or feeling. Time was no longer a factor. I could have lain like that for ten minutes or ten hours, either was insignificant. Images formed and dissolved in my mind but I had no control over them. Welcome to life in the black hole, said a voice. But I found I wasn't afraid.

When at last I stood up and looked at my watch it was well past midnight, so I must have been there for some hours. I did not even look at Rob. Instinctively I went upstairs and ran myself a bath. I lay there for a long time and soaped myself all over several times, but I was still feeling dirty as I dried myself on the threadbare towel.

I went downstairs. I half considered leaving right there and then. I could walk to the station and wait for the early morning train and leave this whole sordid mess behind. It was tempting, but also quite impossible. I had come too far to quit just as I was on the threshold of understanding.

So I cut myself a piece of bread and butter and made a pot of coffee. Rob, as I knew with the instinct that from now on would bind us for ever with ties closer than friendship or liking, was only pretending to be asleep. I nudged him with my foot and held out a mug of coffee.

'Time to talk.'

He groaned and rolled over. I persisted.

'Jesus, Jane, it's the middle of the night. Can't this wait?'

'I've already waited ten years.'

'Don't be melodramatic.'

I pushed the coffee mug towards his hand and he sat up crossly. He grumbled some more about the time and his aching head.

I cut across his complaints. 'You were there, weren't you? You were with him when he died.'

'Leave it alone, Jane, can't you. It's all such a long time ago. It doesn't matter now.'

'Why not? You were all fired up about the truth when it was just a matter of slagging off Lucien. Now it's time for you.'

'I thought you deserved the truth about your brother.'

'Thanks. But to get the full picture I need to know about you too. About your albatross.'

He winced, and darted me a glance of pure hatred. 'That was in Esme's journal?'

'Yes. Was that why you had to destroy it? In case she had spelled out exactly what the albatross was?'

'I couldn't remember how much I'd told her. We were both stoned when we talked about it and . . . I was furious when she said she'd mentioned it in her journal.'

'How furious?'

Rob's eyes darkened slowly. 'Christ, Jane,' he said, 'you don't think I tried to kill her, do you?'

'Of course not,' I lied briskly, since at that moment I was far from sure about anything. 'Besides, they know who did it.'

'That's right.'

'So now tell me what happened.' Still he didn't speak. I said, 'You want me to know really. That's why you've been dropping all those hints.'

'Since when did you become an expert on the subconscious?'

'I think I must be doing a crash course.'

He seemed to be considering. 'Okay,' he shuffled to his feet. 'First, I'm going to the bathroom. I can't think straight like this.'

I was on the verge of protesting, half afraid he might still try to wriggle out of telling me at the last minute – climb out through the window and hare across the orchard in his socks or try to finish himself off with the newly purchased razor blades, nothing seemed too fantastic in the eerie dead-of-night stillness of Glory Cottage – but even I could see that stopping someone from using the bathroom was somewhat extreme.

But when he emerged a few minutes later, I saw with dismay that he had recovered much of his composure. His hair was damp and clinging to his forehead. He went to the kitchen area and topped up his mug of coffee. 'Another time you should get the other sort,' he commented amiably. 'This kind is for filters.'

I was becoming so frustrated I could feel my ears turning red. With heroic self-control I said, 'Are you going to tell me about you and Lucien?'

'Don't make up dramas, Jane. There's nothing to tell.'

'Liar.'

He didn't answer, and I could feel the little ascendancy I had achieved when he woke up all evaporate. I cast around for some way to break him down.

Then I smiled.

It was years since I'd bothered to try, but I found I could still do a fair imitation of Lucien's schoolboy treble. In my normal voice I said, 'You have to tell me. You won't be free of it until you do.' And then in my high-pitched Lucien voice I began to recite:

> Since then, at an uncertain hour,
> That agony returns:
> And till my ghastly tale is told,
> This heart within me burns.

The trick is to stress the important words like 'agony' and 'ghastly'. Anyway, I could tell it was working because Rob started to shake and the spoon he had been using for the coffee fell to the floor.

'Shut up, Jane, for God's sake. You're being ghoulish.'

'Then tell me.'

When he did not reply I returned to my Lucien voice:

> An orphan's curse would drag to hell
> A spirit from on high;
> But oh! more horrible than that
> Is the curse in a dead man's eye!

'Damn you, Jane!' He was gripping at the edge of the sink as if afraid he might fall over. 'Damn you!'

'Tell me.'

But already he was regaining control of himself. He stood up straighter and glanced at his watch.

'Hell. It's practically morning. I should be at the hospital.'

I abandoned subtlety. Besides, I couldn't remember any more of the poem. 'You murdered my brother,' I said flatly.

Now at last I had his absolute attention. He stared at me for a long time, his face washed clean of all expression. I stood my ground and forced myself to return his stare. Then, to my amazement, he half smiled and, pulling out one of the wooden chairs, sat down at the little table.

'Okay then. If that's how you want it. Do you remember Lucien's Murder Games?' he asked almost casually. 'Do you remember his obsession with everything to do with murder during that last summer we spent here?'

'You're changing the subject.'

He ignored me. 'He used to go on about it all the time. I could never understand why. He made endless lists of all the different ways you could murder someone. Accidental or deliberate. And all the grey areas in between. He asked questions, endless questions, but never waited to hear the answers. If a drunk driver ran over a pedestrian, was that worse than putting a knife into someone in self-defence? What about neglect? Was that worse than rage or not so bad? And then what about the generals who send soldiers into battle when they know the odds are hopeless, isn't that murder too? Yet they are given medals. Why? On and on he went with his questions, night after night, until I was sick of it. But still he kept nagging me, "Which is worse, Rob, tell me." '

'So? I don't understand—'

'Nor did I. I never knew how to answer him. He seemed to be hunting for something but I could never figure out what it was. Even after that last summer, he came back to the same subject from time to time. Supposing someone dies because there aren't enough medicines, isn't that a kind of murder? Or if a child starves in a far-off country because you didn't bother to put money in a collecting box? Maybe the truth is that everyone on this earth is a murderer in some way or other. Once when he said that I thought he seemed to be almost hoping it was true. Hoping we were all murderers. It didn't make sense.'

'I don't see this has anything to do with Lucien's death.'

'Ah, but it does, you see. It has everything to do with it.'

There was a long silence. 'Why?' I prompted.

Still he did not speak. His eyes seemed to be looking at his hands which were spread on the table in front of him, but I knew that he was seeing a scene far removed in time and place from this still night at Glory Cottage.

I asked, 'Did Lucien phone you that last week?'

'Yes,' his answer was barely audible. 'He said he wanted to go to Dorset at the weekend. I said no.'

'Why?'

'I was angry with him, of course.'

'Because of Esme?'

'Yes. But it was more than that.'

'What—'

'Because of him. Because the whole business with Esme finally forced me to admit that I'd been wrong about him from the beginning. He had failed me. I couldn't forgive him for that.'

He paused. I was about to prompt him to go on when I realised there was no need. He was talking now to justify himself, to try to convince me of the inevitability of what had occurred.

'I didn't want to see him. Not then. The wounds were still too raw and painful. I think I might have told him I was planning to spend the weekend with you. But you remember what Lucien was like, he'd never take no for an answer. He phoned again with a slightly different scheme. I said yes. I think deep down I was hoping he would do or say something that would make it possible for me to love him again. Anyway, I agreed. The plan was that he would drive down to Dorset on the Friday night and I would join him on the Saturday morning. That's what happened. He picked me up from the station and we drove to a village on the coast.

'Lucien was acting as though it was some kind of damn celebration. He'd always been keen on the idea of "walking tours". He said it made him feel Wordsworthian or like one of those eccentric Victorians. Apparently Dickens walked leagues every day. Of course, he utterly despised all the other walkers. "Ramblers" was a term of particular abuse. He made a point of always dressing in the most impractical clothes. That day he was wearing co-respondent shoes and that blue stripy jacket which made him look like a deck chair.'

'I remember the one. He used to say "Mistrust any exercise that requires special clothes." He never even wore swimming trunks, only shorts or underpants.'

Rob barely noticed my interruption. 'We started off along the cliff path. Right from the start I had the feeling that he'd brought me down there for a purpose. Before long I realised he wanted to check out what my feelings were for Esme. I gained the impression that he was desperately bored with her, but he didn't plan to end it until he could be certain we'd never get back together again. He needed to know he'd killed our affair stone dead. At first I couldn't believe what I was hearing. Then I was furious.'

'Did you show it?'

'What do you think? Surely you remember how quickly Lucien moved in for the kill the moment you lost your temper.'

'And?'

'We were walking along a sandy beach. The cliff path ran above it. At the beginning of the beach there was only a shallow slope between the two, but as it went further along, the land was higher. After a while I realised we'd either have to go back the way we had come or else we could scramble up the cliff and join the path that way. Lucien was all in favour of retracing our steps.'

'He loathed climbing.'

'So I remembered. He made all sorts of Lucien-type sneering remarks about mountaineers being people with their brains in their crampons. He wanted to know if I'd seduced Esme in the first place with my goat-like propensities. For once, I didn't even bother to argue with him. I started to climb up the cliff. At that moment all I wanted was to get away from his hideous, taunting, bloody superior voice. I thought he was sure to go back along the beach. At least that would give me half an hour's respite. I needed the chance to calm down and decide how to handle the situation. The prospect of a whole weekend with him was intolerable and I had half a mind to cut across to the road and hitch a ride back to the station. I hated him so much I couldn't bear having him close to me for an instant.

'But then, when I was almost at the top, I realised the stupid bastard was following me. I told him not to be such a bloody idiot. He just said, "Two can play at Spiderman," but I could see he was terrified, right from the start.'

'Why did he do it?'

'He couldn't let me get the better of him, not even over a trivial thing like climbing over a few wretched rocks. He'd grown worse in that way since the breakdown. When I had reached the top I looked back, and he seemed to be doing okay. Sweat was pouring off his face. When he only had a few feet to go, I started to walk away from the edge of the cliff. Then I heard him shout, "Rob, wait, come back. Don't leave me here!" I ignored him. After all, he was practically at the top. He shouted again, "Damn it, man, I'm stuck!" I went back. He was trying to make a joke of it because in a way it *was* a joke. He was only about six feet from where I stood and the last part was the easiest bit. But he was frozen with panic and couldn't move an inch.

'I crouched down on the edge of the cliff. Lucien's face was turned up towards me. I'll never forget his expression; it was like seeing him, really seeing *him* for the first time. Before that moment I had always seen what he wanted me to see, now I was seeing what he really was. He was afraid. It was as though the fear had made his face cave in on itself. I can't explain. The terror had stripped his soul bare.' Rob was silent for a few moments, remembering every detail, and when he continued, it was to say, with cruel satisfaction, 'And I thought to myself, you bastard, Lucien, for the first time in my whole life I'm the one who has the power over you. And if you think I'm going to hand it back so easily, then you're bloody wrong. I was enjoying myself. I was strong.'

He broke off. He seemed, for a moment, to have forgotten that there was anyone in the room. Then he glanced at me. The gloating expression faded from his face and was replaced by a look of utter anguish and remorse. He covered his eyes with his hands and said in a low voice, 'God help me, I enjoyed seeing him suffer and afraid. And all the while he was gibbering about why didn't I help him. I could have reached him easily, you see. All I had to do was reach out my hand.'

A terrible numbness was spreading through me. Rob's hand was clenched in a fist and pressed against his forehead. He did not speak. At length I said, 'And did you?'

After a long pause, he shook his head slowly. 'Worse. I told him that the edge of the cliff was in danger of giving way. I said it wasn't safe for me to try to reach him. He was whimpering. I told him not to worry, said there was a farm nearby and I'd go for help. I'd get a rope. I said I'd be back in five minutes but in the meantime he must stay exactly where he was. And all the time he was babbling, "Don't leave me, Rob, I'll fall, I'll fall, I know I will." I almost relented. Almost . . . But I just told him to sit tight until I returned and then I walked away until I couldn't hear him any more.'

'You left him?'

Rob had not heard my question. 'I sat down on a low stone wall a little distance away. I smoked a cigarette. I felt quite peaceful. I had enjoyed seeing him so vulnerable, but it had shaken me too. I began to see that the terror I'd seen in his face when he was looking up at me, that terror had been the key to Lucien all along. But I'd always been too much in awe of him to realise. Lucien was afraid. Underneath all the words and the tricks and the games, there was fear – though what he was afraid of, I've never known. That's why he had to keep everyone under his thumb. As soon as I understood that, I stopped feeling so angry. I almost began to feel sorry for him. I finished the cigarette and stood up to go back and help him. Just as I started walking towards the edge of the cliff, I heard a noise that sounded like a seagull screaming, but I knew at once it wasn't a gull. I was running. I remember stumbling over something, and when I reached the edge of the cliff, the ledge was empty.

'I couldn't take it in. I thought he might have climbed up the last couple of yards and that he was hiding somewhere just to give me a fright. Or that maybe he had worked his way along to a safer place. Or even that he'd found a way back down and was walking along the beach. And then I saw him. Saw that stripy jacket and my first reaction was: it's a broken deck chair. Somehow I couldn't absorb the fact that what I was looking at was Lucien. He was almost hidden because of the way the rocks rose up, that's why I hadn't seen him straightaway, and then . . . it was the angle, the way it looked all broken and wrong. It never occurred to me he might still be helped. I knew he was dead.'

'And?'

'I think I was sick.'

'Then?'

'I walked away, but I'm not sure. The moment I saw his body, everything was confused, as though there was too much oxygen or something and I had become light-headed. Up till then I can remember every single detail, but after that . . . it's just a fog. I do remember feeling as if I was floating away, not walking. And the same few words kept repeating themselves in my head, "This is too much," again and again, "This – is – too – much," very clear and slow. I had no idea what I was doing, only that I had to be somewhere else, far away, as soon as possible. It was panic, I understand that now, but panic so strong I didn't realise it at the time.'

'Was that what happened when you found Esme at the flat?'

'I guess it was similar.'

'You panic easily, don't you?'

'Maybe.'

'What time did you leave Lucien?'

'I looked at my watch when I was sitting on the stile. It was exactly ten past eleven.'

'And he wasn't found until nearly one o'clock. The doctors said that hour or two – they couldn't be sure because unlike you they didn't know the exact time of the accident – would have made all the difference.'

Rob looked directly into my eyes and his face was cleansed of all emotion. 'Do you honestly think I don't know that?'

'You killed him twice over.'

'Accidentally.'

'Accident nothing! You left him there deliberately. You knew Lucien had always been terrified of heights. It was your petty desire for revenge, your—'

'Go on, Jane. Anything you say I've told myself a thousand times.'

'I shouldn't count on that.'

'Believe me, I understand how you feel.'

'For Christ's sake, stop spewing out all those blithering clichés. And I sincerely hope your confession has made you feel about a hundred times worse.'

'No, in fact—'

'Well, it ought to. I think it's the most despicable, pathetic story I've ever heard. You're evil, Rob, and I hope you suffer for the rest of your life.'

To my amazement, he almost smiled. 'I'm sure I will, from time to time. The albatross – it will never go altogether. For the first year or two I thought about it constantly. Now I can sometimes go half a day without remembering. The past few days have been particularly bad. Knowing I might lose Esme. Seeing you again. You were right, Jane, I needed to talk. No one else would ever understand.'

I shuddered. He was implying that by listening I had made him some kind of gift of absolution. I felt he was trying to make me a part of his crime.

I reached for words but there were none to express my horror. Too late I comprehended Esme's howl of anguish in her journal: 'it feels like the most ghastly weight on top of me and I simply cannot think how to shift it.'

Suddenly I was so exhausted I could barely stand. It was almost five in the morning. Rob's confession had bound me to him more deeply than our lovemaking had done. I wondered if I would ever be able to break free.

He was still watching me as I dragged myself up the stairs towards my bedroom. I had some vague notion that it would still be possible to gather up my things and leave, but no sooner had I sat down on the edge of the little bed than I fell sideways and was instantly asleep.

13

Late morning, and Rob was once more facing me across the little table. I had slept until gone ten o'clock. When I awoke the house was silent and empty. At first I assumed that Rob had already left, but then I noticed a thin column of smoke rising from the far side of the orchard. On investigation I discovered him burning the heaps of wallpaper he had so industriously removed.

'It looks a lot better,' he commented cheerfully.

I returned to the house without a word.

Now he was saying, 'The question remains, Jane, can you be trusted?' His query was posed in a deceptively matter-of-fact manner. I resented the implication that I was the one who might be found faulty as a weak link.

'What will you do if I can't? Whack me over the head?'

He gave me a crooked smile. 'No, you're quite safe. I'm the only one in danger. If the truth about Lucien ever got out, I'd be finished.'

I wished my contempt was a missile which might blast him out of existence.

'Look at you now,' he said, 'hating me so. I can't say I blame you. And in a curious way it's almost a relief. Maybe that's why I told you. Everyone else sees Rob Hallam the do-gooder. You know different.'

'Why should I bother to keep it to myself?'

But even as I asked the question, I knew it was rhetorical. After all, who could I tell? Owen? We were hardly on speaking terms at the moment. Faith? I had no wish to inflict on my mother the pain I was now experiencing at the knowledge that Lucien's death had been caused by the malice of someone she had always regarded as a second son. The press, perhaps? However much I loathed Rob just now, I couldn't imagine feeding his squalid story to a newspaper.

Rob merely shrugged. 'That's up to you. Exposure is what I've always lived in fear of. I never used to mind much about other people's opinion. When Lucien was still alive I was always happy to be in his shadow. But when I came out of prison and began my public campaigns, I discovered what it was to be in the limelight. Inside, I knew I was still a shit, but on the outside there were all these people who admired me and listened to what I said. At first it was confusing, but slowly I became used to it. No, it was more than that: I began to depend on it. I keep thinking that if I can just make people respect me for long enough then the rotten me inside will fade away and there'll only be the public, respectable Rob Hallam left.'

I waited for a while, then said, 'What happened on the cliff was bad enough. But I'll never be able to forget the way you talked about Lucien last night. After all those years of friendship, and all you could remember was the negative side.'

He leaned back on his chair. 'I suppose,' he said, 'that if I could find a way not to love him, it would make it easier.'

'That's despicable.'

'Of course it is. But that doesn't stop what I said last night from being true, so far as it went. I just happened to omit the other side of the picture. There's always another side. Sometimes I think the real tragedy was that Luce never had the chance or the time to pull himself out of the mess he was in. All he had to do was come to terms with the fact that he was just an ordinary human being, not the boy wonder of all time, and then he might have begun to fulfil his potential. You and I are partly responsible: we made it harder for him.'

'You're not making much sense. How?'

'Because we *needed* him to be a hero. Just like Faith did. No one would ever allow him just to be a normal person. When Lucien stopped being the person I had decided he had to be, I couldn't forgive him. And you refused even to see the truth. I feel sorry for him now.'

'You're still not making sense.'

'Think it over. Will you tell Faith?'

'There's not much point.'

He nodded his approval. 'You're free to tell anyone, of course. I can't stop you and I have no right to ask for promises. But the moment the world discovers the truth about Rob Hallam, that's the moment I head for the river.'

'Is that supposed to be a threat?'

'Far from it. Merely stating facts. Would that make you a murderer too, do you think? No, of course not. It would be my responsibility entirely.'

'That's right.'

He half closed his eyes in a smile. 'But you'd feel like one, all the same.'

I stood up. 'Let's go,' I said.

There was frost in the air as our train journeyed towards London. The sky was tinged that smoky pink of a late autumn afternoon.

A London train had pulled out as we arrived at the station and we'd had a long wait for another. We hardly talked. Rob had bought three newspapers and had begun to read them from cover to cover. I had spent the last of my money on sandwiches, but eating them was difficult. All Rob had told me had left me with a feeling that was worse than sickness. I tried to puzzle it out, but a temporary overload had apparently caused all normal brain function to cease. I could formulate no plans and was quite unable to absorb the new vistas that were opening up. Random fragments of ideas and images popped up occasionally in my mind, then vanished completely. I saw Owen's fair hair brushing the collar of his overalls as he dropped the tiny lettuces on to the soil; I saw the stripy jacket Lucien had bought that last summer and which had indeed made him resemble a deck chair; I heard Lucien's voice, his piping boy's treble, asking, 'Do you think there are an infinite number of ways to murder someone? Why should that be?' And then I heard Laura's voice answering him in her most Billy-withering tones, 'It's obvious, stupid.' Laura, with her scorn, sounded exactly like Lucien. I wondered why I had never made that connection before and I supposed it must be because in appearance she was so similar to Owen. It struck me for the first time as tragic that Laura and Lucien would never meet; they would have enjoyed so much in common.

Yet Rob had said Lucien was scared. I could not dismiss this out of hand; my instinct told me it might be true. But why? His theory might have made more sense had there been any reason for Lucien to be afraid, but as there wasn't . . . the thought dissolved and vanished. I made a half-hearted attempt to retrieve it. But instead a painting began to form itself in my mind; it was a dark formless mass with bits of people emerging from the fog – here a foot which might have been Lucien's, there half a head and an upper arm which might have belonged to Rob – or maybe it was Owen. I wondered if I would ever have the courage to try to paint uncertainty and confusion. 'Paint what you see,' people always tell you. But what about what you can't see? Is it possible to paint secret half-spoken fears and the truths that are buried beneath a surface of lies?

Here a thought, there an unspoken terror, and there again a half-remembered dream. I longed for a great wind to gust through my life and blow away the darkness so I could see the picture clearly.

When we reached Paddington and I stood up, I found that my legs felt thin and watery, like overcooked spaghetti. Shock, I was learning, is a very physical experience. Rob flung down the last of the newspapers and beamed at me, then said, 'I expect you want to see Esme too. We may as well share a taxi.'

Since no alternative plan sprang to mind, I nodded my agreement. While I had been succumbing to confusion, Rob had apparently moved in the opposite direction and was filled with confidence. It was as though reading the newspapers had lifted him from his private nightmare and restored him to his place on the public stage. Once more he was brisk and efficient. As we walked towards the taxi rank, one or two people turned to look at him a second time, either because they recognised him or because he had assumed the mantle of a man of consequence. 'It's that actor, isn't it?' I heard one woman say to her companion. 'Incisive' was the word that described him now, like the Very Useful Person who pushes to the front of a crowd when there's been an accident. 'Make way, I'm a doctor. Don't panic, everything will be all right now I'm here.' But now who is here? I asked myself plaintively. How many Rob Hallams are there? I thought of the shrunken figure I had found hiding in the Rams; I thought of the guilt-haunted man who had talked of his dead friend in the protective darkness of the night. Once upon a time I believed I 'knew' Rob Hallam. Recently I had learned many facts about him, but I was beginning to understand that I did not know him at all.

'Are you all right?' Rob, in his new role of Mr All-Efficient, was looking at me with narrowed eyes that were warm with professional empathy. He took my arm.

I shook him off. 'I'm perfectly fine,' I told him, praying all the while that a taxi would scoop us up before my legs gave way entirely.

We were at the head of the queue. A taxi approached. Rob gave the name of the hospital and handed me into the cab. As if I was a damned geriatric, I thought bitterly.

As the taxi pulled away, Rob said, with deceptive casualness, 'Unless someone actually sees us arriving together, we might as well say we just bumped into each other on the way in. No point in telling anyone I've been at Glory Cottage. Okay with you?'

I nodded. That did leave me with the problem of the stripped wallpaper, but that would probably be easier to explain than Rob's secret presence for two days. Anyway, I thought, my life is a tissue of lies, why not throw in one more for good measure?

The phrase nagged at me: a tissue of lies. An odd expression, when you consider it. Why tissue, for heaven's sake? But certainly true, in our case at least. Rob's life could quite accurately be described as a lie. And if what he had told me was true, then much of Lucien's had been too. My marriage was a lie. And maybe there were other lies lurking beneath the surface. Maybe the whole world was a tissue of lies. That was it. A piece of Lucien's nonsense floated back to me, one of the earliest I can remember. He must have been about six or seven, and suffering from a heavy cold. 'Atishooh!' he sneezed. 'This cold is atishooh of lies. The truth is, Jane, I've broken my leg,' and he had sneezed again. It had taken me ages to understand the joke. That Christmas he had carefully wrapped all his presents in tissue paper on which he had written such bogus claims as 'Pet ferret, open with care', or 'Danger, poison'. He had explained that his gifts were wrapped in a tissue of lies.

Faith had been ecstatic, seeing this as further proof of his precocious genius. I remembered what Rob had said about Faith and me bearing our own share of responsibility for insisting that Lucien be remarkable. Perhaps the tissue of lies incident was nothing more than the playfulness of a bright child.

I wanted to talk of this to Rob, but was afraid that it might appear in the nature of an olive branch. As the taxi neared the hospital he turned to me and said, 'It feels like we're about to enter the real world. I'm terrified of seeing Esme. I've already lost her once . . .' He was silent for a moment or two before saying, 'I was beginning to think I was jinxed, that every time I let myself get close to someone, they suffered.' When I did not reply, he went on, 'I don't know how much we're going to see of each other from now on, Jane. I just want you to know one thing: I loved that damn brother of yours. My anger in those last few weeks was nothing in the long run, we would have resolved it, I'm sure. He gave me far far more than he ever took. I can't imagine what my life would have been without him. When I let him be destroyed, I also destroyed a part of my own self. I've almost learned to live with that. But I know I shall never stop missing him.'

'I know,' I said at last, and patted his arm before turning away to look out of the window.

Entering the side ward to which Esme had been moved was a bit like launching into the midst of some particularly ghoulish cocktail party. Like London buses, all her visitors had arrived at once. We had heard the first sounds from the corridor; there was a babble of animated voices and Faith's, I realised with a twinge of dread, was raised a few decibels above the rest.

At our entrance, all conversation ceased. At Rob's entrance, in fact, for no one did more than glance at me. All attention was at once focused on the imposing figure of the prodigal lover.

My mother's hand flew to her throat. 'Rob!' she gasped. She was wearing a pale grey dress of very fine wool, a jewel-bright scarf tied loosely at her throat and her dark eyes were magnified by a shock so intense it looked almost like fear.

Even Eric, who was standing a little to one side and looked as though he had been whiling away the time practising golf swings, registered acute surprise, an expression not often to be found on his blandly self-satisfied features. I heard him mutter, 'Better late than never, eh?' as he glanced anxiously towards Faith.

John Drummond was visibly shaken. He took a few steps forward and said, 'Rob, thank God you're here.' Two young men, both unseasonably bronzed, stood awkwardly behind him. It was a shock to realise that these must be Esme's twin brothers, recalled by the tragedy from their pre-university travels. One had the gaunt, heron-like attractiveness of their mother, Clare, while the other was shorter, but had Esme's lustrous brown eyes. They both had the dazed expression of people who remained mentally in a different place.

Owen and Angela had been standing together. Both looked ill-at-ease. A young red-haired nurse, and a man and a woman who must have been police officers, observed the whole scene with unfeigned curiosity.

Rob ignored them all. He ignored everything except the frail figure stretched on the bed. He stood for a few moments in the doorway while emotion flickered across his mouth and eyes. A low moan escaped him, and the next moment he was crouched beside the bed, ignoring the chair which the policewoman had left for him. He caught hold of Esme's hand and pressed it to his cheek, closing his eyes with an expression of intolerable pain.

'Oh, Esme!'

Having observed my mother in full flight on countless occasions, I considered myself a veteran of theatrical displays, but even so I experienced a wave of revulsion at seeing this particular charade. A small green thought edged its way into my brain. It told me to shatter the poignant tableau. Nothing would be easier: just announce what the stricken lover and I had been doing through the previous night.

My mother was dabbing at the corners of her eyes. I remained silent, too weak to challenge their illusions. Besides, I was fascinated by the drama that was unfolding and had no wish to interrupt it now.

As I felt the tears begin to tingle behind my eyes, I told myself that Rob was simply putting on a spellbinding performance. Maybe his affection for Esme was genuine, but still, what mattered to him most at this moment was the impression he was making on John and Faith, on the hospital staff and the police, on his wider public. Perhaps even on me.

And yet, as I watched him and despised him, and tried in vain to hate him, I was forced to admit that my cynicism was unfair. Rob was impersonating the person he wanted to be. I began to wonder if his public image wasn't as close to his true self as the haunted, self-loathing person I had come to know at Glory Cottage. He had accepted responsibility for his guilt where many might have claimed Lucien's death to be an accident pure and simple. He had tried to make amends. God knows, he had suffered. As I watched him grieving at Esme's bedside, I slowly understood that Rob was forced to put on a performance in order to discover the person he truly was.

My moment of insight was short-lived.

Faith put her hand on my shoulder. 'I can hardly take it in,' she breathed in my ear. 'Rob. After all these years.'

Instinctively I shrugged off her hand. I had no wish to take part in her Happy Family masquerade, but then I remembered my promise to Rob and I said, 'Extraordinary, isn't it? Heaven knows where he's been. We just bumped into each other on the stairs.'

Owen looked at me sideways. His expression, so cold and angry, made me feel as if something was keeling over inside me. How could he make me suffer confusion and guilt when all the time . . . ? And misery too, don't forget the misery.

All the people in the room were trying to give Rob at least the illusion of some privacy with Esme. They moved away from the bed and formed a little cluster round Faith and me by the doorway. I was introduced to the twins, and was too awe-struck by their unexpected size to mention that I remembered them as babies. I was introduced to the policeman, who was bald and shining with sweat, and to the policewoman, who had an abundance of brown hair but who was also suffering in the heat. I sympathised. The atmosphere in the side ward was that kind of cloying heat that makes one's clothes feel too tight, like hands placed around the throat. Even breathing had become an effort.

People chatted in a group while their attention was held by the sight of Rob with Esme. I tried to look at them as little as possible, but when I did the scene reminded me of one of those Victorian paintings that encapsulates an entire melodrama in a single moment. I imagined how it might be done: the pale November light, the ghostly face against the pillows, the face of the stricken lover, the white hands entwined on the white sheet. Only their brown hair and Rob's pleading dark eyes would provide the necessary contrast. And the title? I smiled as the obvious one sprang into my mind, 'Can she forgive him?'

Around me, various voices were filling in the spaces in my knowledge. I learned that Esme had regained consciousness earlier in the day, soon after Owen had arrived – of course, it would have been Owen – with the health-giving Snowy. At the sound of Owen's voice, or maybe it was the whiffle of the rabbit's whiskers, Esme had opened her eyes and tried to speak. The policewoman joined them at once, but despite their gentle promptings, Esme said little beyond the fact that her head hurt and she was thirsty. But she plainly recognised Owen which everyone agreed was a thoroughly good sign. She seemed to understand that there had been some kind of accident and that she was in hospital. But when the policewoman tried to probe how much she remembered of the incident, Esme said only that she was very tired. The general opinion, now shared by even the most cautious of the hospital staff, was that although recovery might be slow, it was sure to be complete.

Everyone was lavish in their praise for Owen and his unusual method of treatment. When she learned that I was married to the rabbit-handler, the policewoman subjected me to an all-too-familiar well-aren't-you-the-lucky-one-and-how-did-you-manage-that? scrutiny.

Meanwhile my mother was asking the twins about their interrupted travels and I could see that they were already falling under her spell, although her gaze continually slewed back to the figure of the man seated at Esme's bedside. John Drummond was glancing at her with some concern; once or twice I saw him touch her elbow in a gesture of reassurance. She leaned imperceptibly towards him, accepting his support. I had never seen such unspoken intimacy between her and Eric, whose emotional repertoire at times of crisis was a quick, 'There, there,' followed by speedy escape. All my childhood fantasies about a romance between John and my mother came back to me. I might have been wrong about the details, but my instinct had not been entirely unfounded.

Eric, aware that my mother was upset, turned his attention to me in the hope that we might enjoy a less emotionally charged exchange.

'And where did you disappear to, eh? Owen's been a bit cagey.'

'Glory Cottage.'

Faith was startled. 'What on earth for?'

'I needed some time alone. John very kindly said I could stay there. By the way, John, I left the key with Mrs Wicks.' I hesitated, wondering if I should mention the wallpaper removal, but procrastination won the day. 'Thank you very much, John,' I finished.

Faith's expression indicated that my disappearance at such a time of crisis had been in appalling bad taste, but she restricted herself to the comparatively innocuous, 'What a very peculiar child you are.'

I was glad I had omitted to mention the wallpaper.

Faith might have been tempted to expand on my oddness, but if so I was spared because at that moment all attention was diverted to the other side of the room where Esme had opened her eyes as though awaking refreshed after a long sleep. She began to talk.

Everyone moved across the room and formed a wall of bodies around the bed – everyone, that is, except Eric and me. Eric was sporting the glassy smile which indicated, I knew, that he was only there because he wanted to be seen as a thoroughly decent chap who could be relied upon to do the right thing. It was the expression he invariably adopted for school concerts, weddings and during any kind of family argument.

The tension that was being generated in the corner of the room where everyone was straining to hear Esme's faint words was overpowering. I began to move across to join them, but then I stopped. Suddenly I felt like an intruder. Or even worse. A wave of shame swept over me at having read her most intimate thoughts in her journal. At having betrayed her with Rob. I thought: I love you, Esme. We will be friends, I promise, even though we neither of us seem to know how to do it. We'll learn. And then I looked at Owen. He was standing at the foot of her bed, his fists clenched with determination that she recover, and his eyes held such tenderness and compassion that for one crazy moment I wished it was me lying there so fragile and loved.

The floor began to rock and sway. The policewoman was asking Esme about the accident. I was annoyed by her insistence that her first task should be to confirm what they already knew. I decided I'd had enough.

'Let's go to the canteen,' I whispered to Eric. 'They don't need us here.'

His face brightened at the prospect of escape but still, like some brainless mynah bird, he could not resist the chance to echo my mother's disapproval. 'Poor Jane,' he breezed, 'not really up to this sort of thing, are you?'

Even in the canteen it proved difficult to avoid drama. While Eric collected tea and biscuits, I chose a table as far as possible from an elderly lady in a mauve felt hat who was weeping quietly into her handkerchief while a stolid-looking woman who might have been her daughter munched thoughtfully on a Yo-Yo. Eric joined me.

'How are things?' he asked.

'Fine,' I told him.

His stepfatherly duty done, Eric lapsed into silence. We had never seen much reason to talk to each other in the past and just for the moment I felt quite incapable of conversation. I could have said, 'My marriage is collapsing and I think I may die,' or 'I'm about to have a total nervous breakdown,' but in this place of constant trauma, my own turmoil seemed insignificant.

I took a tentative sip of my tea, but there appeared to be some kind of obstruction in my throat and swallowing was difficult. I set down the cup and some of the tea slopped on the table. I put my hands in my lap and stared at them. They looked like pale and unfamiliar starfish. Nausea rippled through me in waves. My body had become totally unreliable and I did not see how I could get back home. I ached to be with my children. I did not want to have to wait until Owen decided he would drive me home. I wanted to go home on my own. But I had no money.

The obvious solution was to ask Eric for a loan, but that was impossibly difficult to do. For as long as I could remember, Lucien had always made it a point of honour never to ask a favour of Eric, thus maintaining the principle, which flew in the face of all the evidence, that Eric was surplus to family requirements and that Faith, Lucien and I could manage quite well without him. Besides, to ask Eric even for the temporary loan of a few pounds would be an admission of weakness which would be paid for many times over. ('Poor Jane, still as hopeless about money as ever, eh?') Still, the urge to escape was stronger than the threat of shame.

'Eric,' I began.

He glanced across at me, but then his gaze shifted slightly and he focused on a point some distance behind me. Turning, I saw Angela weaving her way towards us, her vast handbag clapped to her side like a surgical appliance.

'Jane,' she said breathlessly, 'I thought I'd probably find you here. Hello, Eric. Listen, Jane, I don't know what's going on, but your mother is anxious to see you right away.'

My response was automatic. 'Why? What have I done wrong?'

'I'm not sure you've done anything. But after Esme spoke to the police, Faith talked to them too, and then she said she wanted to talk to you, so I said I'd come down and see if you were here.'

I stared at Angela. Eric was watching her too, and even his expression was bewildered.

'Angela,' I said, 'you're not making much sense.'

She sighed, sat down on the edge of a plastic chair and began again. 'I'll tell you what I know and then maybe you can piece it together. Esme could remember what happened to her quite clearly, which is unusual, I'd have thought. I mean, you always hear about people being amnesiac after a blow to the head. But not Esme. Apparently she wasn't assaulted by that Hamish lad the police arrested at the hostel. She was adamant he wasn't the one.'

A splinter of something cold had lodged in the region of my heart. Rob, I thought. So it was Rob after all.

Angela rattled on. 'The police asked her several times. You could see they thought it was all a frightful nuisance because they had been so sure they'd arrested the right person. They were only asking her to confirm it. And now they were going to have to start again from scratch. Not pleased about that at all, but Esme was categorical. She gave them a detailed description of the man – well, as best she could, since obviously talking is still an effort. She said she'd never seen him before, though she had talked to him on the phone. About sixty, grey-haired, nothing special. She said he was on the thin side and had bad teeth. Then she remembered that he had a diagonal scar on his chin, quite a deep one, it must have been. She couldn't remember much else. Rob asked her why she had let him into the flat in the first place, but by then she was beginning to drift again and she couldn't tell him. The policeman was just beginning to look really teed off with the whole business when suddenly Faith grabbed him by the arm and said, "My God, then it's all my fault!" And then she asked if she could talk to him in private.'

Typical, I thought sourly. Trust Faith to steal the limelight. You have to admire her, really. Not many people would find a way to upstage Esme at a moment like that.

Angela continued, 'They went off into the corridor for a few minutes. By that time Esme was asleep again, or unconscious, I don't know how you tell the difference really, and then when they came back into the room, the policeman was saying, "Yes, Mrs Piper, I remember the case. Don't worry, we can put a warrant out straightaway. We're sure to pick him up soon." That was when Faith said – to John, I think – "You know what this means, don't you, John?" and he said, "Yes, you must tell Jane." And Faith said, "Do you really think so?" and he said, "Yes, I do." That was when we looked around and realised you'd gone. So I came to look for you.'

I turned to Eric. 'Do you know what all this is about?' I asked him.

He shifted uncomfortably. 'Well . . .' he muttered. 'You know how it is . . .'

'No,' I snapped, 'I don't bloody know. No one ever tells me a damn thing.'

'Then now's the time—' Angela began.

I stood up. 'I'm always the last to know! Damn secrets. I hate them!'

'Now then, no need to get hysterical.' Eric made hysteria sound like an antisocial disease.

'Why the hell shouldn't I get hysterical? I've every right to be! No one ever bothers to think . . .' Glancing quickly around the tables I saw that the lady in the mauve hat had stopped dripping tears into her handkerchief and was watching me with an expression of relief at the diversion. I lowered my voice. 'All right. Don't worry. I'm going.'

'Good girl,' said Eric. I think in that moment I truly hated him.

I walked stiffly through the canteen and into the main entrance hall. I was fully intending to climb the stairs to Esme's ward. Then I stopped. Behind me, Angela and Eric were deep in conversation. Inside my head Faith's voice was slopping around like dirty water. 'Jane, dearest, I know this is going to be difficult for us both but . . . now I want you to be very strong . . . you know you can always rely on me . . . only ever wanted the best . . .' Once again I was about to step on the stage and become a player in a drama where everyone but me knew the script. That haunting dream I so often had when sleeping was the same in my waking hours too. What is it? I had asked a hundred times. What does it all mean? Lies and smiles and silence. And now it was all going to begin again.

I gritted my teeth and told myself to get it over with. I was just about to start up the main stairs when I caught sight of Owen turning the corner to descend. There was a preoccupied expression on his face. First Angela, now Owen. Faith would be next. All the people in my life had become part of a huge net in which I was doomed to be for ever snared. Suddenly desperate to break free, but with no clear concept of how, or where to, I turned and hurried towards the main door.

The late afternoon air was cold on my cheeks. Cold and reviving. I began to walk briskly away from the hospital. It's only for a few minutes, I told myself. Just a few minutes while I gather myself together.

A small boy with fat cheeks was standing with doubtful pride next to a collapsing dummy.

'Penny for the guy,' he said.

'Sorry,' I told him, 'I don't have any money.'

He obviously didn't believe me.

There were guys everywhere suddenly. A little further down the road a particularly lifelike dummy had been left slumped in a doorway. Looking out from beneath the battered trilby hat were eyes that seemed to be fixed on me in particular.

As I hurried past, I could have sworn that the lifeless guy gathered itself together, stood up, and began to follow me.

14

About fifty yards down the street [illegible]

don't read the [illegible]

of panic. This was the [illegible]

I started [illegible]

through my [illegible]

[illegible]

And at the [illegible]

[illegible]. It [illegible]

would [illegible] [illegible]

the [illegible]

[illegible]

[illegible]

[illegible]

Shiela of [illegible]

[illegible]

[illegible]

[illegible] ready to [illegible]

And then [illegible] from inside my [illegible] without [illegible]

because there no longer seemed to be any difference. [illegible]

> Like one that on a lonesome road
> Doth walk in [illegible]
> And having once [illegible]
> And turns [illegible]
> Because he [illegible]
> Doth close [illegible]

14

About fifty yards down the street from the hospital, I began to panic. And I don't mean the nervous, fluttery feeling that we so often grace with the name of panic. This was the real thing.

It started as a current of fear in the pit of my stomach, then swept up through my lungs to my throat and head, a silent scream of primeval terror.

And all the while I could hear the footsteps behind me, keeping pace with my own. It was not yet dark, there were other people about, common sense would have told me there was no need to flee. I could go into a shop, return to the hospital, stop and confront him. But common sense had deserted me, undermined by the shocks of the past days and destroyed utterly by something elusive and yet terrifying in the face of the guy-man who had watched me pass and then stood up to follow.

Sheets of dirty newspaper flapped across the pavement in front of me and then wrapped themselves round a lamppost as though seeking protection. A cat screeched and leaped on to a low wall. Terror was pounding against my ribcage ready to burst out in a wordless howl.

And then, whether from inside my head or without, I could not be sure because there no longer seemed to be any difference, I heard Lucien's voice:

> Like one that on a lonesome road
> Doth walk in fear and dread,
> And having once turned round, walks on,
> And turns no more his head;
> Because he knows a frightful fiend
> Doth close behind him tread.

And the fiend too was both outside and yet within me. As if it was something I had been running from all my life. Some evil loathsome part of myself that followed me like the clanking of tin cans tied to a cat's tail. Above the noise of the traffic and the city I could hear a raw sobbing sound that came from my throat, from my own heart. A scorching pain burned against my ribs with every choking breath. I turned a corner.

Don't run, I told myself. Whatever happens, you mustn't run. You've lost completely if you run. I stumbled round a corner, half walking, half running, like a hobbled horse.

And the footsteps had drawn so close that they sounded like an echo of my own.

An elderly black man watched me pass.

'You in trouble?' His question trailed behind me like the smell of fear, but I had neither the breath nor the wit to answer.

At the corner of the street a woman manoeuvring a twin pushchair blocked my path, only for a moment, but it was long enough. I felt a hand clutching at my sleeve. There was a reek of stale tobacco and aftershave and an old sour smell that I couldn't identify, and a man's voice gasped, 'Jane, don't run away!'

The voice was all wrong. It didn't belong with the thin hand and the cast-off clothes. It was the voice of education and wealth.

'Don't!' my words escaped on a gasp of pain. 'Leave me alone!' Horror that he knew my name.

But no surprise.

Still he clutched at my sleeve. His face swung round so that I could no longer avoid looking at him. So that I was forced to see the thin lips and the bad teeth, the bony face and the watery eyes that I had never seen in my life before, yet which made me sick with recognition. A man who looked about seventy, thin and grey-haired. A man who, I could see now through the stubble that coloured the lower part of his face, had a diagonal scar on his chin.

The man who had tried to kill Esme.

Why? And why was he now following me?

He was still gripping my sleeve. His fingers were thin and yellow and the skin was flaking round the nails.

He too was breathless from running. 'Jane,' he gasped, 'listen to me!'

'No!' My denial was a furious shriek and I pounded my free hand down on his fingers, tearing my arm from his grasp as I did so. 'No, no, NO!'

Conscious only of the need to escape, I ran into the road. There was a howl of brakes, a rush of air as the gleaming metal wing of a car passed inches away from me and a scream of abuse from the driver. When I reached the far pavement, a youth in battle fatigues said, 'You want to watch yourself,' and then, as I started to fall, he said, 'Steady on,' and put a supporting hand under my elbow.

'I can't—' I began.

'Jane!' From across the road the man's voice was pursuing me. 'Jane, for God's sake listen to me, you bloody fool. You must listen to me, just give me a chance. I'm your—'

Father, I thought, watching him as he stepped into the road. His eyes were fixed on my face and he began to run in my direction.

Father. I finished the sentence for him as the pale blue saloon car nosed into his legs with the cosy familiarity of a cat nudging out affection, and spun him up into the air so that his final word was translated into a scream of shock and pain.

Father. I watched as the bundle of skin and bone inside the shabby coat plumped down on the tarmac and a few violent spasms convulsed it before it lay still, the only movement now a thin stream of blood that seeped out into the gutter.

Father. The whole sequence had been very brisk, efficient almost. Not slow motion like they say. In the distance I could hear the squeal of a police siren, while in the road a little group of people had gathered, some stooping over the man, some pausing to listen to the frantic driver of the pale blue car, a man who kept repeating, 'He just stepped out in front of me! There was nothing I could do!'

Father. My brain played the scene again. I saw the whole sequence: the gaunt figure, his eyes fixed on me, who stepped off the pavement; the pale blue car; the effortless leap of the man's body, like some modern copy of a Minoan bull dancer gambling with death and losing; the definitive thud as the body hit the ground. And then once more – the fatal step, the impact of metal on flesh, the curved arc of pain and then the deadening fall. I closed my eyes and saw it all again. I opened my eyes and the sequence repeated itself, only now a new ending had been added. This time there was a police car with blue light flashing and uniformed men clearing away the spectators.

Father. And I thought: I shall never stop seeing this moment. Now the sequence had a different conclusion. Now there was an ambulance arriving and the body, which seemed to be held together only by the shabby overcoat, was rolled on to a stretcher.

Father. I watched as they pulled a grey blanket over his head before lifting the stretcher into the ambulance.

Father.

Through the mingled voices asking me if I was all right, there appeared one which I recognised. John Drummond's face separated itself from the others. I watched as he approached and his whiskery, once handsome features were superimposed on the sequence of the accident which, it seemed, I was doomed to watch for ever.

'Jane,' he said, 'thank God you're safe.'

Safe? I didn't feel safe. I tried to speak but a violent shivering had taken possession of me, a shaking so intense that my bones ached yet I was powerless to stop. People were looking in my direction, their faces curious but distant. Blank eyes, blank faces.

'That man . . .' I croaked, 'he said . . .'

'I know.' John's voice reached me over a chasm of cold air. 'I know all about it. Don't try to talk now. You're in shock. I'll get you away from here.'

I nodded. I shook. In my brain the accident was still being repeated, but on the street in front of me the ambulance doors were closing and the vehicle pulled away slowly. One policeman was talking to the driver of the pale blue car. Another began to approach me, but John intercepted him. They spoke together in low voices for a few minutes and I saw the policeman glance at me and nod his head once or twice. Then John took a card from his inner pocket and wrote something down. The crowd was beginning to disperse. The young man in battle fatigues had vanished. Colour was fading from the sky and the sodium glow of street lights was spreading. And all the time I stood and shivered as if iced water was circulating through my veins.

John finished talking to the policeman who returned to his car and seemed to be talking into his fist. John came towards me.

He said, 'That's all settled, then. It's good to know a former QC can still pull rank occasionally. He's prepared to take a statement from you later. I exaggerated your present incoherence, I hope you don't mind. Can you walk a little way? My car is just round the corner and the flat's not far. We can talk there. Faith wants me to tell you.'

I nodded. John took my arm and we walked to his car which had been parked in a nearby side street. I sat down in his car and laid my shaking hands on my shaking knees. My spine ached. As we drove through the early evening traffic I managed to ask, 'How did you find me?'

'You found us,' he said. 'The police were just about to set off looking for you when they received the report of an accident behind the hospital.'

'I'd gone round in a circle?'

'Yes.'

Panic, I thought. It's the panic that does it.

Then I asked, 'Where are we going?'

'The flat. Unless you'd rather . . .'

'No. That's fine.'

In the minuscule fraction of my brain that was still unaffected by shock, I realised I was about to be allowed into John's London pied-à-terre, the place around which Lucien, years ago, had woven such extravagant fantasies, the place where Faith had once noticed the missing milk jug, the place Clare had never visited but which, indirectly, had brought our Glory Cottage summers to an end.

'Is . . .' I struggled to frame the question, '. . . is Faith going to be there?'

'No.' He frowned, assuming, I suppose, that in my state of near hysteria I was in need of a mother's tender loving care, though in fact nothing could have been further from the truth. 'She wanted me to tell you. The flat belongs to a friend.'

15

The block looked seedy enough from outside, but as soon as the front door closed behind us, all was deep carpets, polished brass and the smell of fresh paint. We took the lift to the second floor where John ushered me into the flat.

'Hello!' he called. 'There's been an accident. Rex was hit by a car. I've got Faith's daughter with me. She's had rather a shock.'

I looked around me. My first thought was how disappointed Lucien would have been. Far from being the ornate fin de siècle extravaganza of his imaginings, this apartment was a celebration of cool elegance, well-chosen but simple furnishings in soft shades of pale blue and buttermilk yellow.

'Here,' said John, as he led me into the sitting room. 'Why don't you sit down and make yourself comfortable.'

I sat, or rather sank, on a small sofa which was covered in some kind of wildly impractical silky material. I leaned my head back and closed my eyes and waited for the shaking to stop and for the events of the accident to cease their unending repetition behind my eyes. I could hear the murmur of low voices coming from the next room. A few words stood out: my own name, Esme . . . and Rex.

I knew that I ought to be pulling myself together, ought to be preparing myself for whatever it was that my mother had finally decided I was ready to be told, whatever it was that linked me to the stranger with the scar on his chin whose efforts to reach me had resulted in that horribly matter-of-fact collision between man and car. But all I really wanted to do was to turn my face towards the elegant cushions of the sofa, to sleep and not wake up.

'Jane, hello. I'm Oliver.'

A man of about my height was standing in front of me. He must have been in his sixties, but he had a pinkly scrubbed look that made him seem almost boyish. His hair was thinning into wisps and he carried a good deal too much middle for his height, but his eyes were wonderfully kind. And he was smiling.

'We've not met before,' he went on, 'at least, not properly. Though of course I've always known all about you.'

'Of course?'

'I daresay it sounds a bit odd, but you and I are related. Distantly, anyway. Don't worry, we'll explain everything. I always thought you should have been told years ago, but, of course, it wasn't up to me to say.'

Once again, that 'of course'. As if every detail was blindingly obvious to all the world but me.

'Now, first things first,' he beamed. 'You need a drop of the cup that cheers. Jonty has put the kettle on for some tea, but I thought you'd probably prefer something a little stronger. I do have some rather fine cognac. I suggest both together. Hot sweet tea *and* a glass of cognac. How does that sound?'

'Whatever,' I shrugged, which sounded horribly ungracious, but at that moment any choice was beyond me.

'Splendid.' Oliver's voice was somewhat too young for his body; he had a boy's enthusiastic breathlessness inside the body of a corpulent elderly man. In fact, I realised that his manner held echoes of Lucien's when he'd been reading too many old-fashioned adventure books for boys. He had said that we were related; I wondered if perhaps such quirks of speech could be genetic after all.

'Just sit there,' Oliver exhorted me. 'And don't you worry about a thing.'

I could have told him that I wasn't about to sprint off anywhere, but as for worrying, that seemed to be out of my control. But I merely nodded. Oliver bustled off and I heard him shooing John out of the kitchen and telling him that the dear child needed company, for heaven's sake. I don't think anyone had ever called me a dear child before, certainly not when I *was* a child. I began to warm to my unexpected relation.

Tea arrived in cups of almost transparent porcelain, and the cognac in wonderful balloons of glass poised on fragile stems. The tea soothed and the cognac revived, while Oliver fussed and bossed John into one chair and placed himself in another.

When we were all arranged, delicate teacups in hand, John cleared his throat.

'No need to rush her, Jonty,' Oliver scolded. 'She's just had the most beastly shock.'

'It's all right,' I mumbled, finding myself unable to meet John's eye when he had just been called 'Jonty'. 'Please tell me.'

John looked at his hands. 'I'll make it brief, then. I'd like to stay longer, but I ought to be back at the hospital as soon as possible and . . . well, Oliver here knows the story as well as I do. He can fill in the gaps later.'

Oliver beamed at me. 'You're welcome to stay here, my dear.' And he meant it.

'Thank you.' I turned to John. 'That man who was following me . . . ?'

'I believe you've guessed already. That was your father. Rex Turner. He and Oliver are first cousins.'

'On our mothers' side,' said Oliver.

'Oh,' I said. As if that mattered. 'And now he's dead?'

'I'm afraid so. He was killed outright. They don't think he can have suffered at all. It was much too sudden.'

This, I knew, was only said to comfort me, since no one could possibly have any idea what the helpless body inside the ill-fitting coat actually experienced during those last degrading seconds of life. Besides, the man who had gripped my sleeve on the corner of the street had had a lifetime's suffering etched into his face.

'Then why did I never meet him? Why did no one ever tell me? Why the lies and the secrets?'

'Faith always considered it was for the best.'

'Damn her! What right did she have to decide if I should know my father or not?'

'Wait, Jane. Don't judge until you've heard the whole story.'

'But now it's too late. Now he's dead. If I'd known, I could at least have seen him.'

'Not really, dear,' this time the soothing voice was Oliver's. 'You see, he's been in prison for over twenty-five years.'

'Prison?' So that explained the grey face and that indelible air of neglect. 'Why?'

'I was just coming to that,' said John.

But Oliver said, 'Murder.'

'Oh.'

One's reaction to impossible news is always curious. I was sitting very straight, very upright, hardly daring to move a muscle of my face for fear that I might suddenly burst out in hysterical screaming or hurl the delicate porcelain cup against the Japanese print on the wall behind John's head. But I didn't. I just sat there. And all I said was 'Oh.'

'I was going to break it to you more gently,' John darted an irritated glance at Oliver. 'But yes. Rex was sentenced to life imprisonment with a recommendation from the judge that he serve at least twenty-five years. Which he did. I had been hired as his defence counsel. Oliver had recommended me to his family. I built up as strong a case for him as I could, though the evidence against him was pretty damning. But once your mother took the witness stand, he didn't have a chance. That was how I first knew Faith. You were just a baby. Lucien must have been about three or four years old. Your mother was determined that your lives would not be ruined by your father's crime. She wanted you both to have a normal childhood. She was absolutely splendid about the whole business.'

Hearing people praise my mother always brings out the worst in me. 'A normal childhood?' I queried. 'With Eric?'

John sighed. 'I'd better start at the beginning.'

'Please.'

'It's difficult to know where to start. I only came on to the scene towards the end of the story, but people who knew him when he was younger say Rex Turner had considerable charm. When I met him I was impressed by something elusive and unusual in his character. Certainly I'd never met anyone like him in a remand wing in prison before. Your brother Lucien, I remember, possessed a similar kind of charm, although physically they were not in the least alike. But unlike Lucien, Rex Turner was prey to outbursts of uncontrollable rage. God knows what caused them. His family background appeared ordinary enough. His father was an army officer of the old school, a bit of a disciplinarian, by all accounts, and his mother, perhaps in order to compensate, spoiled the boy dreadfully. Let him get away with murder, as they say. But when Faith first knew him she saw only his charm and his brilliance. In those days there was little difference between him and a thousand other young men of our generation: he was good-looking and talented, sometimes he drank too much and he wasn't sure how he intended earning his living, but he was confident something would turn up. If theirs was not exactly a whirlwind romance, it was brisk. They were married six months after their first meeting. When Faith showed me the wedding pictures—'

'What pictures? She never showed me!' I interrupted him. Even to my own ears my voice sounded unbearably hurt.

'No, I don't suppose she did. They made a most attractive couple.'

John smiled at me apologetically. I realised that though this was difficult for me to listen to, it was not especially easy for him to recount. I said, 'I'm sorry. Please go on.'

'Faith told me that a couple of incidents before the wedding made her uneasy, but like so many young brides, she was confident that marriage would iron out their problems. Unfortunately the reverse happened. The first serious assault was only weeks after the wedding and she had absolutely no idea how to handle it. At that time, domestic violence was not a subject for discussion as it is now, and it was certainly not something that took place in "nice" families. There were no refuges for battered wives, the police at that date were loath to become involved and Faith was far too ashamed to turn to family or friends for help. Besides, after each outburst Rex would be overcome with remorse. He swore it would never happen again. Then she became pregnant. For a while they lived together in relative harmony, although money was always a problem. She had a difficult time with the first pregnancy and Rex looked after her well enough. He liked to be in control.'

John was silent for a few minutes, frowning. Then he went on, 'But a few months after Lucien's birth, Faith began working again.'

'As an actress?' I realised I had never properly believed in my mother's stage career; it had always appeared the mythic product of her own imaginings.

'Yes. You look surprised, but from what I've heard, she had considerable promise. And that was where the problems began. She got a small part in a new production which turned out to be an unexpected success and transferred to the West End. Rex became moody and difficult. She even considered abandoning her role just to keep the peace, but, quite apart from the pleasure it gave her, they needed the money. Your father was out of work most of the time. He found employment easily enough, but was too arrogant and quarrelsome to remain in any job for long. One night, when she returned home from the theatre, he was waiting up for her. He had been drinking heavily. They quarrelled. She ended up in hospital with a couple of broken ribs.'

'Did the police step in then?'

'They were informed, but Rex was not prosecuted. Such incidents were still classed as "domestics" and were rarely followed up. Besides, his family closed ranks to avoid scandal. His father took him back to Suffolk. Faith took Lucien away. Case closed. For the time being.'

'And she was already pregnant with me?'

For the first time I knew that John was deliberately avoiding my eye as he replied, 'No, that was . . . later.'

'Go on.'

'Faith went to ground for a year or so. I think that must have been when she began to move house frequently. She did not want Rex to be able to trace her. He had not wanted his marriage to end and he hated being parted from his son. But she wasn't taking any more risks. Then she heard from his family that he was living with someone else, a young singer called Dawn Lacey. His parents convinced Faith he only wanted contact with his child. She began to feel she was unfairly depriving both father and son. So she took Lucien to the family home in Suffolk a few times, though she was careful never to let Rex know where she was living. On each occasion Rex behaved impeccably. At about that time Faith was offered a small part in a pilot on television. After some agonising, she took it.'

While he was talking, John's voice had dropped to a bleak monotone, as though he hoped to leach all the poison from the story he was obliged to tell. 'Faith's part, perhaps unfortunately, was that of a young wife of somewhat lax morals. The psychiatrist who interviewed Rex in prison said he thought it possible that your father had difficulty distinguishing between fact and fiction. The pilot was a success and further programmes were planned. Rex found out where the rehearsals were taking place. One evening, when he was much the worse for drink, he followed Faith home and forced his way into her flat. A violent argument followed. And Rex . . . well, Faith is certain that if the neighbours had not heard her screams and broken down the door, he would have killed her.'

There was a silence. Beyond the windows of the flat, in the orange glow that passes for darkness in a London night, a few early fireworks burst and chattered above the rooftops. I was beginning to feel as if I had been listening to John's quiet telling of this terrible story all my life through.

I said, 'How?'

John glanced at Oliver, who nodded. John said, 'He picked up a knife and tried to slit her throat.'

'Yes,' I said woodenly, 'I see.' And I did. I had, many times. That scar just below Faith's ear, the one she had received in a 'car accident'.

'Incredible as it may seem with the benefit of hindsight, his family were once again able to shield him. He was packed off to an expensive American clinic for the delinquent sons of the wealthy. They found psychiatrists who were certain he would not repeat the offence. They promised Faith he would never try to get in touch with her again. And he didn't. But his next partner, the young singer, was less fortunate. Almost exactly a year to the day after the last time your mother saw him, Rex murdered Dawn Lacey.'

Even though it was what I had been waiting to hear, the information dropped into my consciousness like a package wrapped in warning signs. Don't open it, I told myself, don't look inside. Don't ask any more. But by now the unfolding of my history was unstoppable and I asked, 'Haven't you missed something? What about me? If my mother wasn't pregnant when they split up, did it happen on the evening when Rex tried to kill her?'

John's reply was barely audible. 'I suppose it must have.'

Suddenly it was difficult to endure the kindly gaze of the two men who were taking such pains to break this to me. Small wonder my mother had never told me herself. Small wonder that even now she preferred to leave the task to comparative strangers. A child had been conceived in violence and anger. At least Lucien's origins had taken place in a kind of harmony. My existence had begun with an act of outrage. Right from the very start, my brother had the advantage.

I swallowed. 'And that was when my mother testified against him?'

'Yes. This time, his family were helpless. Oliver recommended my services and I did what I could. Faith's evidence was particularly damning because of the similarities of the attacks and their motives. Dawn Lacey had just won third prize in a national competition for young musicians. Rex was once again consumed with jealousy. He had been drinking too much and he picked up the first thing that came to hand. It happened to be a cast-iron lamp base. I'm afraid that when Faith took the witness stand I was obliged to make it as difficult for her as I could. Rex's only hope of acquittal lay in discrediting her evidence. But she was magnificent. She refused to concede an inch. She told her story with tremendous dignity and conviction. Above all, with courage.'

'Yes. I can imagine.' And for once the usual edge of sarcasm was missing as I praised my mother.

'Inevitably the court case attracted huge attention in the press. All the necessary ingredients were there: the two beautiful young women, the young man of good family who had gone to the bad, passion, jealousy and violence. It made the front pages for days. After it was over, your mother suddenly found herself in demand as an actress – but of course it was for all the wrong reasons. She realised then she would never be free of the notoriety of the court case. She had been dubbed "Star of Stage, Screen and Old Bailey" and no matter how brilliantly her career developed, she would always be known first and foremost as the wife of a murderer. Even if she considered it a price worth paying in order to continue the profession she adored, she knew that you and Lucien stood absolutely no chance at all of any kind of normal life. It was several months before she could bring herself to sever all links, but eventually she could see no alternative. She told me that was the hardest decision she ever made. But she stuck to it. She changed her name – and yours too – by deed poll, to make sure she'd never be subject to one of those "where are they now?" enquiries. Eric had been in the background for some time and she decided to throw in her fortunes with him. She said that what she valued above all else in Eric was his wonderful predictability.'

Inwardly, I groaned. Oh, Lucien, why aren't you hearing this with me? You were right about Eric all along. It was his status as the most boring man in southern England that made him Faith's Mr Right.

I said, 'But why should Rex . . . I mean, my father . . . why should he want to hurt Esme?'

'We've been trying to piece that together. It seems that he wanted to get hold of you. When Lucien died, Rex wasn't even allowed out of prison for the funeral. Your mother sent some photographs of Lucien – via his parents, of course – as a substitute for memories, I suppose. Among them she thinks there may have been one or two taken at Glory Cottage when you were children. And another with Rob and Esme at Oxford. Once Rob became a public figure, it wouldn't have been difficult for Rex to put two and two together, especially as Esme has been mentioned in some of the articles about Branden House.'

'Yes, a recent one even said that she was your daughter.'

'It was probably the only lead he had in his search for you. Perhaps he was motivated by paternal feeling, though Faith thought it more likely that he wanted to get money from you. He had phoned Esme several times, but Faith had warned her not to say anything. She did not tell Esme who he was. Presumably Rex became increasingly frustrated. He went to the hostel to confront her. He had been drinking. He must have picked up the nearest object to threaten her with – and then once more he lost control and . . . well, there's no need to spell it out.'

Indeed not. A great deal had been spelled out already, rather more than I could absorb all at once. So many secrets uncovered. If a few gaps remained, I had no doubt they would be filled in time.

There was a long silence. John and Oliver were both observing me as if I was a patient who had just been administered a kill-or-cure medicine and they were waiting to see the outcome.

John's story was at an end and some kind of response was expected from me. I said, 'I suppose we should be thankful that it was an alabaster bowl he picked up and not a knife.'

John winced. 'Yes,' he said, 'I suppose you could say Esme has been lucky.'

16

With the outline of his story told, John departed for the hospital once again, leaving me to what he affectionately described as Oliver's 'tender care'. And so it was.

Oliver stood by, a rotund and solicitous sentinel, while a couple of police officers came and took down a statement. They were nothing if not thorough. Several sides of paper were covered in the policewoman's untidy writing before they were satisfied that all the details had been included and it was handed to me for signature. I had been dreading the prospect of having to relive the events of the accident with strangers, but discovered the exercise to be oddly therapeutic. The sequence no longer repeated itself continuously in my mind. I still saw an occasional image – the body cartwheeling in midair or a frail hand clawing the tarmac – but not the complete cycle. It was a kind of progress.

After the police had gone, Oliver suggested that I might try a relaxing bath and, since we were nearly the same height, he lent me some clothes to change into for the evening. When I saw his chosen offerings I was glad to accept: a pale silk shirt, heavy linen trousers and, since I was a good deal thinner than he was, a very necessary belt. I was beginning to enjoy being told what to do by this kindly relative and, as I lay in the tastefully pale bathroom and watched the tasteful prints on the wall gradually become obscured with steam, I debated whether I could ask Oliver to direct his sympathetic bossiness towards my private life. A change of tack in almost any direction could only be an improvement. It occurred to me that while the past – my past – was becoming clear for the very first time, the present and the future were beginning to look distinctly murky.

An odd little debate was taking place inside my head. There was a voice which said: that man on the street corner was nothing at all to do with you. Eric might be boring and embarrassing and generally infuriating, but he is at least an ordinary human being, not some homicidal freak of nature. Oh God, I promise I'll never complain about Eric again. But then another, equally persistent voice said: you fool, that man was your *father*. Isn't that what you've wanted ever since you can remember? Didn't you realise that half of what you are has come from him? Didn't you know that as soon as you saw his face? His eyes? You see a version of that same face every time you look in the mirror. And there were echoes of Lucien, too. Then the first voice chipped in again: that means nothing . . .

I was worn out, tired in a way I've never been before or since. It was simpler, somehow, to concentrate on such details as the luxurious feel of the warm towel in which I wrapped myself when I stepped out of the bath, to relish the smooth touch of silk and linen against my skin. And the final effect wasn't so bad at all. I surveyed myself in the mirror and was surprised to see a fairly appealing face rising above the high collar. Perhaps the secret that had eluded me for so long was that I should always dress in too-large and extremely expensive men's clothes. Some chance.

Oliver did interfere in my private life to the extent of suggesting that I ring Owen.

'He'll want to know where you are,' he reasoned.

'I don't suppose he cares.'

Oliver raised his eyebrows. 'As bad as that?'

'Worse.'

'All the more reason.'

It was the children I most wanted to talk to. Although I had not been particularly aware of missing them, there was an ache inside me each time I thought of them. This early evening time was set aside for baths and stories. I imagined their bedtime faces, damp hair clinging to their foreheads, cheeks flushed from the steam, dressing gowns and slippers and their endless night-delaying chatter. But supposing Dinah answered the phone, what then? I was still debating whether or not to dial when the phone rang.

'It's for you.' Oliver handed me the receiver.

Owen's voice sounded strained and irritable. 'I'm calling from the hospital,' he said.

'How did you know where I was?'

'John told me. I'm just leaving for home. I can come round and pick you up in about twenty minutes.'

I considered this. I marvelled at the insouciant way Owen uttered the word 'home'. I imagined having to sit next to him in the ramshackle van all the way through south London and debated whether talking or silence would be worst. Either seemed unbearable. Perhaps if I delayed long enough, a miracle would happen. Besides, I did not want to relinquish my borrowed clothes.

I said, 'I think I'll stay here tonight. I'll come down on the train tomorrow.'

There was a silence. Owen must be in the phone booth at the end of the ward. I could picture his face, taut with suppressed disapproval.

'Are you sure that's what you want to do?'

I sighed, leaned back in my chair and dangled the phone around my neck. 'Well, obviously. I wouldn't say so otherwise, would I?'

'What was that?'

I spoke with perfect enunciation. 'I shall return home tomorrow.'

'Jane—' he began, and then, 'Oh, hell—' as the line went dead.

I hovered by the phone for a minute or two in case he tried to ring again, but it remained resolutely silent. Now I pictured him picking up the receiver again to tell Dinah that the coast was clear for one more night and I began to shake with jealousy and rage.

A loud buzzing sent me flying to pick up the receiver, but Oliver said, 'That one's the front door. I'll get it.' He went to the entry phone and said, 'Hello! Yes, Faith, of course. I've been expecting you. It's on the second floor. Come on up.'

My customary dread at the approach of my mother gave way to a hesitant curiosity. The landscape we shared had altered for ever with John's revelations, and I thought – though barely dared to hope – that some of the discord between us might be erased. Was it possible even that we might begin to like each other?

I observed her carefully as she entered the flat. It was easy to imagine a younger version of the dark-haired woman who was letting her coat slip off into Oliver's hands, easy to imagine her standing in the courtroom and speaking the words that would send the man she had once loved to prison for over twenty-five years. Possible also to imagine her sacrificing her chosen career to safeguard the privacy of her children. I had always seen her as a woman who had once been beautiful. Now, conscious for the first time of the pain she had endured, I began to see how she might look when she grew old.

It should not have been a shock when she and Oliver greeted each other like old friends. I ought to have realised by now that the whole cast of characters in this drama had known each other for years. Only I had been excluded.

Oliver fetched her a large whisky and asked if she wanted to stay for supper. She thanked him graciously but said that since 'poor' Eric was waiting outside in the car, she'd be as brief as possible. Her brisk manner at once raised my defences.

I said, 'John's already told me the story. You needn't have bothered to come since you're in such a hurry.'

To her credit, she launched in without hesitation. 'I suppose you're annoyed because you feel you should have known years ago,' she said as she sat down on a small chair and crossed her shapely legs. Oliver murmured something about leaving us to talk in private and retreated to the kitchen. She went on smoothly, 'Well, as it happens, I did wonder whether to tell you once or twice, but somehow it was always too much effort. There are some things one tries to forget. Anyway, now you know.'

'Yes.'

'But not quite everything. I expect you've been wondering why that man – Rex – was so anxious to find you that he'd even batter poor Esme when she refused to help him.'

'I assumed he wanted to meet me.'

'He was after your money.'

For the first time in what felt like ages, I burst out laughing.

'My money?'

'Yes.'

'Like what, for instance? My family allowance? What made him think I had money?'

'But you do have, or you will once the legalities are sorted out. It's not a huge amount, so don't go raising your hopes, but still, I have no doubt he'd have managed to wheedle a good chunk of it. His mother died a couple of months ago, you see. She had always doted on Rex – more fool her – and she wouldn't let a mere murder conviction change that. Her husband, your grandfather, who died about ten years ago, had tied up all his money so she couldn't tamper with it. Most of it went to his nephew, though there was a small amount for you.'

'Was that the money you gave me when Owen and I were married?'

'Yes. I thought it was simpler to tell you it was an insurance policy. I thought that would be the end of it, but it turns out that Rex's mother did have a small sum of capital she was able to dispose of as she wished.'

'How do you know all this?'

'I've always kept in touch, if you can call it that, through their solicitors. They paid Lucien's school fees and in return I sent them occasional progress reports, though I never let them know where he was. That was the deal. They never knew of your existence. I only told them, again through the solicitors, after Lucien died. I suppose I must have felt sorry for the poor woman and it seemed cruel not to let her know she had another grandchild still living. She obviously decided to leave her own money to you.'

'When did you know about the money?'

Until now my mother had spoken in the efficient and unemotional manner she might have employed when dealing with an accountant. Now, for the first time, she appeared uncomfortable. She said vaguely, 'I can't remember the exact date. Probably a couple of months ago.' I knew she was trying to minimise the delay and I mentally doubled the time. She said, 'I was going to tell you sooner but—'

'But what? Why didn't you?'

She drained her glass of whisky and recrossed her legs, then looked across at me with an expression I had never seen before, one that was almost defiant. 'To be perfectly honest, Jane, I was waiting for you and Owen to see sense about that ridiculous plant-growing business of yours. You'd already sunk the money your grandfather had left you. I thought that if you had the prospect of another windfall, you'd fritter that away too.'

'We did not sink that money, we invested it, for God's sake. And all this time you've just been sitting there, waiting for us to go bankrupt. Christ, I can hardly believe it!'

'Don't be outrageous, Jane. I've always supported you and Owen one hundred per cent of the way, no one could argue with that. But it would not have been responsible of me to encourage an enterprise that was clearly doomed from the outset.'

The familiar demon of rage began leaping up and down inside me, but I managed to say, with heroic self-restraint, 'Are you implying that you knew better than either Owen or me how we should live our lives?'

'Jane, I know you've had an upsetting day, but this is ridiculous. Never have I been guilty of interfering in your marriage.'

'So keeping the money secret wasn't interfering?'

'I had no intention of keeping it secret. Honestly, you make it sound as if I wasn't going to tell you. I only hope to goodness you use it wisely.'

'How much?'

'As I said, it's not a vast amount. And there's death duties, of course.'

'How much?'

'When all the deductions have been made, there should be about twenty-five thousand.'

I felt the blood rush to my face, but not with pleasure. With fury. My guess was that Faith had known about the money some time in the early summer, which was just when our own fortunes had taken a severe downward turn following the bankruptcy of our main customer. I did some quick calculations. Twenty-five thousand pounds would be enough to get the bank off our backs, buy a van that worked – perhaps even one with some fancy lettering on the side. We could have a brochure printed and think seriously about mail order. We could install heating in the main greenhouse and expand our range. We could halve the mortgage. We could . . . And now it was too late. Now the money would come in useful, certainly – but only to help me and Owen to separate. Now it would be possible to buy my way out of the dream we had once shared.

I stared at Faith. 'You should have told me as soon as you knew.'

'Well, I'm telling you now. You know what lawyers are like. And I fail to see what difference a couple of months makes. I would have expected you to be pleased, Jane. Instead of which, God help me, you're obviously more angry than ever. You really are impossible.'

'No,' I said, speaking with painful clarity, 'I am not impossible. It's only that I've been blundering around in the dark for so long that this sudden illumination is bound to be dazzling. But I am beginning to see more clearly.'

Faith looked doubtful. 'I'm delighted to hear it,' she said.

'I look like him, don't I?'

She looked away swiftly. 'He was your father, dear. There are always similarities.'

'That's not what I meant. This went deeper.'

'I don't see—'

'I remind you of him, don't I, even now?'

She was absolutely still. Her face was still turned away from mine, but I could see her eyes rapidly scanning the titles of the books in the corner of the room, as though seeking either inspiration or escape. I willed her to turn towards me and help me begin to take down the wall that had always existed between us.

She said, 'I have always been a conscientious mother.'

'Yes, I know, but—'

She set her glass down on a side table. Her decision was made. 'We really ought to discuss this properly one day, but this is neither the time nor the place. We've both had the most appalling day, and poor Eric must be languishing out there in the car.'

I sank back exhausted on the sofa. There wouldn't be any other times, I saw that now. Yes, she had been a conscientious mother. As far as possible she had even been a loving mother to me, but it had never been easy for her. Not easy in the way that loving Lucien had been easy. The scar below her ear had made sure of that. Memento of my violent conception. Even now, as she stood up, I could see the relief that our separation would bring. My new-found clarity brought fresh pain as well as welcome understanding.

I said, 'Just one thing, Faith. Did Lucien ever know about the murder?'

'We did talk about it, but only once.'

'When?'

'He came home from Oxford one weekend. Eric was away and the two of us spent the evening getting sozzled. He had guessed, somehow, and so I told him.'

'But you don't think he knew when we were younger? In the Glory Cottage days?'

'Certainly not.' She was indignant. 'I dedicated the best part of my life to protecting you both from the legacy of that man.'

'Luce did know, though. I'm sure he did.'

'Impossible. He would have said something to me about it. Luce always told me what was on his mind. Not like you, dear. Now, I'd better go and rescue poor Eric.'

For once I was so convinced that Faith was wrong that I felt almost fond of her. I remembered Lucien's strange persistence that summer. I remembered his constant questions: how many ways were there of killing someone? Were murderers different from other people, or was murder something that anyone could do if they were pushed beyond their limits? I remembered his fascination with heredity – were people born murderers or did they grow that way because of what happened to them? He had found a Victorian book on phrenology and had spent a couple of days making us feel our scalps for 'murder bumps'. I remembered too Rob's belief that beneath all the bravado Lucien was afraid, though of what precisely, Rob never discovered. I remembered Lucien's fury when I made up the secret of our father's heroic death. Had my father's story been Lucien's fifth secret all along? I would never know for sure. And I could have howled my rage and despair that Lucien had suffered our shameful secret alone. If only we had been able to share the torment of our heredity . . . but that 'if only' would be with me for ever.

Faith was putting on her coat. Oliver had emerged from his discreet preoccupation with kitchen details and was watching us as we said our goodbyes.

'Well, thank heavens that's all settled.' Faith was smiling with relief as if talking to me had been on a par with unblocking a drain. 'Oliver, dear, it's so good of you to take Jane in like this. Don't let her be a nuisance.'

I half expected her to remind me to help with the washing up, but she contented herself with a cheek-to-cheek embrace before departing.

Oliver and I stood alone in the hall.

'A remarkable woman,' he said at last.

'Amazing,' I agreed.

'But perhaps not the easiest of mothers.'

I could have hugged him.

The shocks I had endured during the previous twenty-four hours had not succeeded in diminishing my appetite. Oliver had 'thrown together' some chilled avocado soup, scrambled eggs with anchovies, followed by a selection of cheeses and fruit. And the bottle of white wine was one of which even the fastidious Rob would have approved.

While quartering a ripe fig, I asked, 'Did you know my brother Lucien at all?'

'At second hand, through Jonty. The only time I met him – met all of you, in fact – was just after the twins were born. You were all staying at the cottage.'

'Glory Cottage. What did you think of him?'

'A remarkable boy. Very quick and alert, the sort of child you look at and think: that one will make his mark. Full of zest and mischief. And yet—'

He broke off and began peeling a tiny grape.

'And yet?'

'It's hard to put one's finger on it exactly. I have a very clear memory of coming back to London and mulling it all over in my mind. Lucien was such a confident child, and it was obvious that the five of you were blissfully happy in your little kingdom, but still . . .' he paused again and peeled another, even smaller grape, '. . . for all his exuberance, one gained an impression of something that was *missing*. Perhaps it would be putting it too strongly to say that he seemed lost, but . . . I mentioned this once to Jonty and he said he'd noticed the same thing. In fact he said he thought it applied, one way or another, to all of you. He was aware that Esme's home life was far from ideal. Rob and Owen had no home life of any kind, so far as one could tell. While you and Lucien had a father, but he had become a "non-person", like the victim of some totalitarian purge.'

I said, 'I think Lucien knew.'

'About Rex? Why?'

'Lots of little things that never added up at the time. Remarks that only make sense if he was struggling to come to terms with the knowledge that his father was a murderer.'

'You could be right. But you'll probably never know for certain.'

I pondered. 'It's odd that we seemed lost at Glory Cottage, of all places. I think those summers were the only occasions when we ever had a sense of belonging.'

'Fleeting pleasures often have a kind of desperation about them.'

'Very profound.' I grinned at him. Since he had brought up the subject of Esme's far from ideal home life, I felt I was able to ask, 'And was this the flat that John came to during the week? Was it because of you that Esme and Clare never visited?'

'Yes. It was my flat, as it happens, and I was not overly fond of his family.'

'Did Clare know? About you, I mean?'

He frowned slightly. 'I think she chose not to know. So long as Jonty remained publicly loyal, she turned a blind eye.'

'Lucien used to make up wonderful fantasies about John's London pied-à-terre. The secrecy fascinated him. He imagined a place of baroque splendour, all gilt chairs and red velvet furnishings. An endless cornucopia of sensuous delights. And lots of buxom women lounging everywhere.'

'Not too many buxom women.'

'So Clare was only there to protect his reputation?'

'A barrister must be above reproach.'

'Isn't that incredibly hypocritical?'

'Of course. Don't blame him, though. Blame society for insisting on the pretence. Besides, now that the unfortunate lady is deceased, I can hazard a guess that Jonty was always quite fond of her. In his way.'

Later on, John dropped by once again. I was afraid I might have to give up the second bedroom and spend the night on the couch, but he said he was on his way back to Martin's Court with the twins. He had come to warn us that there was likely to be an item on the evening news about Rex's death and the release of the lad who had been wrongly charged with the attack on Esme. He was anxious that I might be upset if I saw it without warning.

'Thanks,' I said, before adding with some hesitation, 'I know you're in a hurry, but there's just one thing. Is there any way Lucien could have known about Rex Turner while he was still a child?'

John paused. His eyes were very penetrating. 'Oh yes. Your brother always knew. He was four years old at the time of the trial, and very bright. He quickly learned that he must never mention it to Faith, but he absorbed a great deal of information. It made no sense to him at the time, but he stored it away in his memory for later.'

'What makes you so sure?'

'He visited me once. It was just after the quarrel between Faith and Clare, so he must have been about fifteen. I guessed immediately why he had come so I was able to make it as painless as possible for him. He was extremely agitated. He had been going through old newspapers for the year of the trial which had confirmed what he already guessed. All I did was add a few missing details. I felt enormously sorry for him, but pity was the last thing he wanted. I remember being hugely impressed by his dignity and courage. He requested that I never mention our conversation to Faith. He commented that this gave a whole new poignancy to the nature/nurture debate. When he left I was aware that he felt he had to find some way to face down the stigma.'

Poor Lucien, I thought, no wonder the pressure to succeed and make amends was so intolerable that you cracked up.

When John had departed, Oliver and I declared we had no intention of watching television at such a time, but in the end our curiosity got the upper hand and we switched it on. There was a brief mention of the accidental death of Rex Turner, who had recently been released from prison after serving a long sentence for the notorious Dawn Lacey murder. This information was accompanied by a photograph of a youngish man who bore hardly any resemblance to the man who had gripped my arm on the street corner, apart from that diagonal scar on the chin. But in his nose and eyes, in the shape of the cheekbones and the jaw, I saw a good deal of myself.

Before I had a chance to take this in, the newsreader changed tack and began talking about the release from custody of the young resident of Branden House, as a result of information received concerning the attempted murder of Esme Drummond. And then – I should have been expecting it, so I don't know why it came as such a shock – there was Rob, handsome and confident as ever, expressing his concern that yet another miscarriage of justice had been so narrowly avoided. The sight of him stirred up a whole gamut of emotions. I wanted so desperately to hate him. By leaving Lucien on that ledge he had contributed to his death – but did that make him my brother's murderer? When I dashed out into the traffic rather than face up to my own father I had led him to his death, but did that mean I too was guilty of murder? No sane person would say yes. If Faith had warned Esme properly she would not have let Rex into the flat . . . so many ifs. One could go mad blaming oneself for everything, just as Rob had so nearly done. Or one could get on with the problems of the present, as Rob was once again attempting to do. I wanted to throw something hard and sharp at the smug face on the screen; I wanted to cheer his courage.

Just before leaving to drive his sons back to Berkshire, John had handed me an envelope the corners of which had been rubbed into an aged furriness.

He said, 'You were asking about your brother. I found this at Rob's flat when we were going through Esme's possessions looking for clues about her attacker. I'm sure she won't mind if you read it. Leave it with Oliver, and I'll see that Rob replaces it before she goes home.'

I saved it for later, when I was revelling in the luxury, for the first time in what felt like ages, of sheets and a warm bed.

The envelope was addressed, in Lucien's minute handwriting, to Esme. He must have posted it the day before he met Rob for their Dorset hike. He began by explaining, fairly briskly, that he thought their affair should end, and that he planned to tell Rob of his decision when he came down from London the following day. The last paragraph read:

> During that row on Tuesday you said, with more insight than you

> knew, dear Esme, that you thought the problem was that I was always so discontented. That I didn't know how to relax and enjoy life. Let me affirm that you were never the cause of my discontent, only myself. You asked me if I'd ever been happy and over the past couple of days I've asked myself the same question, and the answer is a resounding, an unhesitating 'Yes'. I only have to think back to those summers at your father's cottage. How complete and satisfying the world was then, and what an anticlimax all the rest has been since. It's a cliché to talk of lost Edens, but sometimes it feels damn close. Perhaps when you have forgiven me for the past few months, we can recapture some of the magic that once was.

I read it many times before finally switching off the light. I could hear Lucien's voice saying the words, but though it was his own voice, it was subtly altered from the one I remembered. He was speaking from the heart, a heart he had always struggled to keep hidden, even from me. While he remained alive I had always believed that we were close, and yet I had not known him at all. And now that he was dead, and memories were beginning to fade, I felt I was getting closer than ever to the heart of him. And this contradiction was more than I could understand.

17

The train swayed and chattered in the morning sunlight. I had come to relish the in-between feeling of travel, that unique sense of not belonging to anywhere in particular. I needed time, more time than this brief journey offered, to come to terms with the huge changes and discoveries of these days. I felt a bit like a snake that has grown too large for its original skin and must shed it somehow and wriggle away in its shiny bright new one. It would have been more flattering to imagine myself a butterfly struggling to free myself from the imprisoning chrysalis. But reason told me that a larger, wiser snake – one of Lucien's thousand thousand slimy things from our *Ancient Mariner* days – was, after all, the best I could hope for.

Everyone I knew, everyone I had ever known, had been touched by these changes. No one would ever look quite the same again. Faith and I would never be close, but I could at least respect her for what she had done. Later I might come to wonder if her decision to shield us from the truth had been the right one. But there was no doubting the extent of her sacrifice. Perhaps there was a clue here as to why she had always undermined my own creativity: perhaps it was hard for her to see me enjoying what she had been denied. I was beginning to see that everyone connected with a murderer is in some way punished as a result of his crime.

I had a father. Given the choice, I would have opted for kindly John Drummond, or even the mythical racing car hero whose creation had so enraged Lucien – but since I definitely had not been given the choice, I would have to find some way of coming to terms with reality.

As the view of densely packed houses gave way to fields and suburban towns, I allowed myself to dwell on this new map that was forming of the past. Disturbing though it was in many ways, it was a good deal more reassuring than the contemplation of what lay ahead.

Bolstered by the knowledge of my looming wealth, I had borrowed thirty pounds from Oliver and so I was able to take a taxi from the station to the nursery, an unprecedented and wholly enjoyable luxury. The sun was still shining as we drove up towards the gate, and I asked the driver to drop me at the entrance. My growing apprehension tempted me to delay.

I walked slowly past the rows of pots towards the little house. For a moment, with the sun shining from a clear blue sky, I was able to see the walled garden with the same vision that I had had when we saw it first, when it still had that strange, wistful beauty that only derelict gardens possess. And then I remembered the other garden I had seen in those days, the one that only existed in my mind's eye, the place that Owen and I planned to create together. It would have a pool fringed with primulas and irises and marsh marigolds, a shady area where the woodland species could be displayed and there would be tropical exotics in the restored Victorian glasshouse. And I wondered what had happened to that dream.

As I pushed open the back door I was startled by the unaccustomed stillness of the place. No children, no Owen, no note on the kitchen table to explain. Even the cat had vanished. I looked outside and saw that the van was missing from its usual place.

Hysteria began to rise inside me. This was worse even than I had expected. I had anticipated rows, the horrendous negotiation of separate lives even. But never in my worst nightmares had I imagined Owen would simply decamp with the children and leave me – leave me with nothing at all.

Dinah would know. Of course. Bloody Dinah. No sooner had I vowed to myself that I'd sooner die before I crawled to her for information about my husband and children, than I realised I had no other option.

Then I heard the sound of a pane of glass breaking.

Rage gave me speed as I raced round to the lane behind the garden wall. After all the anger and pain of Owen's defection, it would be pure pleasure to release a few hundred thunderbolts around the heads of our young persecutors.

But the lane was empty.

I swore. This time, however, I had no intention of returning meekly to the nursery to await their next attack: I had a shrewd suspicion which youngsters were responsible and I would go and tell them and their parents exactly what I thought . . .

The sound of breaking glass again.

A chill shivered through me. Had they realised that the place was empty and climbed over the wall to gratify their craving for destruction? Calmer now, but no less angry, I returned to the garden and approached the main glasshouse.

What I saw, as I stood in the open doorway, was so shocking that for a moment or two I could neither speak nor move.

Owen was standing with his back to me in the centre of the glasshouse, cohorts of tiny lettuces stretching away from him in green dotted lines. He held something in his hand. Then, very slowly and with great deliberation, he drew back his arm and hurled the stone with all his strength to smash a pane of glass at the far end.

At the sound of the shattering glass, he gave a little grunt of satisfaction and began to hunt through the earth for another suitable stone, kicking aside plants in his eagerness. It was only when his search made him turn slightly that I saw his face. His expression was savage. His eyes were dark with bitterness and rage and his cheeks were flushed. He caught sight of me and his mouth twisted with an uncharacteristic sneer.

'So,' his voice resonated with hate, 'you've decided to come back at last.'

I took a step forward. 'Owen, what the hell are you doing?'

'I'd have thought that was obvious.'

'Owen, don't!'

'Why not?' Another pane of glass smashed.

'Stop it, Owen! What's the matter with you? Have you gone mad?'

'Probably.'

'Where are Laura and Billy?'

'At Dinah's.'

'Why?'

'Because that's where they wanted to be. No one likes it here, hadn't you noticed? Besides, one of the kids from the new estate lobbed half a brick over the wall this morning and Laura was hit on the cheek by a piece of flying glass. Oh, no need to be upset,' he added, as if my concern was faked anyway, 'it was only a scratch. I took her to the surgery just in case.'

'God, how awful.'

'Not really. At least the police sat up and took notice at last. They've warned the families. Luckily Dinah spotted the culprits as they ran off. Good old Dinah. Laura and Billy were shaken more than anything, so Dinah offered to have them for the morning. I had business in town, anyway.'

I was about to be angry with Dinah for being the one to help my children when they had clearly needed me, but I checked myself in time: it was my fault, not hers.

'Poor Laura.'

Owen contemplated me scornfully. 'A shame you missed it all, I'm sure you'd have enjoyed the fun.'

I couldn't think of anything to say. My heart was racing and I had not the first idea how to approach this changed Owen.

At length I said, 'Thank God the police have acted at last.'

He grunted. He was tossing a stone from one hand to the other. He said, 'Almost too late, though. God, why the hell does nothing ever get done until after someone has been hurt? Laura might have been killed.'

I shuddered. 'Is that why you're wrecking the place.'

'Why not?' He ground half-a-dozen plants into the soil with the heel of his boot. Watching him destroy his recent labour was obscene, like seeing someone attack their own child. A wave of revulsion washed through me. He said, 'It's pointless, anyway. We won't be around to harvest this lot.' He threw the stone, but without his former vigour and it fell harmlessly into the soil. '*Requiescat in pace*, OJ Nursery – it's all been a bloody pointless waste of time.'

'It could still work out.'

'No chance. It's too late. Anyway, what's the point? You hate it, you said so. And now it's just too late.'

'Why?'

'Another little drama that you missed. It's just as well you chose not to come back with me last night. The van packed up on the way home. The garage says it's not worth repairing. No point throwing good money after bad, they said. Not that we've got any, good or bad. I phoned the bank just now and they said there was absolutely no chance of letting us have anything towards a new one. They said we were overstretched already.'

'The bastards.'

'They're right, though. If it hadn't been the van, it would have been something else. I realised a couple of days ago we were going to have an uphill struggle to survive until the cash starts coming in the spring.'

'Is that why you were so tight-lipped when Angela gave us her blessing yesterday?'

He nodded. 'The irony should have been amusing but somehow I failed to see the humour of it. Which reminds me. I had the oddest letter from Armand Baer this morning. He suggests I try to get a psychiatric opinion of Angela's condition. I can't think why.'

I too was baffled until I remembered that Angela had invented a drug problem and a radical lesbian commune in order to cut herself free for ever from the danger of domestic bliss. Owen barely listened as I explained, so sunk in gloom was he at the imminent collapse of the OJ Nursery.

'I thought when the end came there might be some relief,' he said, 'but I couldn't have been more wrong.'

I said lamely, 'Maybe things will still work out.' I almost wanted to mention my grandmother's legacy, but I didn't dare.

Owen was not to be consoled. 'We haven't stood a chance since those swines went bankrupt on us, but I've been too bogged down in work to see what was right in front of my eyes. More fool me. I don't see what you're looking so bloody miserable about. I thought you'd be glad. If we can get back what we paid for this place we shouldn't come out of it too badly. You've wanted this for ages, haven't you?'

Had I? I wondered. I had loathed the anxiety and the cold and the sense of slipping backwards all the time, but I was quite certain I had never wanted this.

'What happens now?'

'God knows.' He had found another stone.

As much to stop him from throwing it as for any other reason, I said, 'Did anyone tell you what happened yesterday?'

He half turned towards me. 'I was there, Jane, or didn't you even notice that? I spoke to Esme. And Rob.' He raised his arm.

'But apart from that. Didn't anyone tell you about my father? That he was a murderer?'

The stone fell from his hand. 'Eric?'

I had to fight down a surge of wholly inappropriate laughter. 'His name was Rex Turner. He had served over twenty-five years in prison for murdering a woman called Dawn Lacey. He once tried to murder Faith. He was the man who made the phone calls. He was trying to find me. He wanted to speak to me. He followed me from the hospital. Then a pale blue car came round the corner and hit him, and he was flung up in the air. By the time the ambulance came it was too late and he was dead.'

'Jesus.' The rage and savagery were draining from Owen's face and he was suddenly very pale. He moved half a step towards me, as though propelled by some old habit of consolation, then turned away and sat down on a pile of polystyrene trays. 'Are you sure?'

'John told me.' I had begun shivering violently, not with cold, but with accumulated shock. At the back of my mind was the memory of all those times after Lucien's death when Owen had taken me in his arms and comforted me like a child, and I thought: now that we are both hurting so much, it's too late. There's nothing we can do to help each other any more. And I knew that this was the black hole I had feared all my life, and I was tumbling into its depths, and I talked on to drown out the terror of the darkness. 'It's all very complicated, but I think I'm beginning to understand. John was my father's defence lawyer – he and Faith only became friends later on. It was her evidence that clinched the trial. John said she was magnificent. She changed her name. She gave up her stage career. She wanted us to have a normal childhood. She tried to love me. But I think I always reminded her of him.'

Owen had been staring at the earth between his feet while I spoke, so I was unable to see his face properly. 'So that's what all the whispering was about yesterday. Everyone kept slipping off in pairs to have little private conversations. I assumed it was to do with Esme and Rob.'

'Well, so it was, in a way. Rex Turner, my father, was the man who attacked Esme. She wouldn't tell him where I was and he wanted to know . . .' I remembered what Esme had said in her journal about learning to say no. The lesson had nearly cost her her life.

Still without looking at me, Owen stood up and, thrusting his hands deep into his pockets, he crossed to the side of the glasshouse and stared out over the rows of thousands of tiny little pots of plants that were waiting for the spring. 'I'd always guessed there was a mystery.'

'So had I, though I never imagined a murderer. But Lucien knew. I think that's why he was always so determined to prove himself. Why he was always so desperately afraid he'd fail.'

'Maybe.'

Owen was silent for a little while, then he said thoughtfully, 'But we were all afraid, in our different ways. Rob and Esme and you and me, as well as Lucien. I don't think any of us really believed that we belonged anywhere.

That's why we all needed Glory Cottage. When we were there, we could create our own world and put ourselves slap bang in the centre. And I suppose I've been trying to do the same thing here. All the time when I was growing up I vowed it would be different for my own children. I was determined they would always have a real home. They'd never be made to feel they were guests who had overstayed their welcome in someone else's home. Laura and Billy would have something better than that. But of course I botched it up along with everything else.'

'Don't say that.'

He ignored me. 'I thought all you had to do was stay in the same house, work hard, try not to argue. Above all, don't argue. It was always when Angela started her arguments that we were turned out and had to begin again.' He clenched his fists. 'I swore that would never happen here.'

I thought of all those occasions when his self-control had aroused my rage, and I wondered why it is that this kind of insight always comes too late. Owen stood gazing bleakly over all the products of our work. The space between us was too vast ever to be bridged. And what made it all so much harder was knowing that this black separation had been unnecessary. I remembered Esme's words in her journal: 'Owen has always loved Jane, but she was too stupid and angry to notice.' Was that really true? Was it possible to be so blind? Since I had always been so wrong about everyone else, it was perfectly likely that I had always been wrong about Owen too. And in my blindness, I had chipped away at his affections until there was nothing left.

And if I had been blind and stupid before, was it not also possible I was being blind and stupid now?

Perhaps for the last time, I heard Lucien's piping schoolboy voice, clear and insistent, and a sudden vivid image of him standing in the punt came into my mind. His magical dark eyes were vibrant with a combination of anxiety and fun. A clever, vulnerable boy who laboured for much of his life under the shadow of a great burden, a burden he had been condemned to shoulder alone, a burden that had driven him to the edge of the abyss, a burden that had now been passed to me.

> The selfsame moment I could pray;
> And from my neck so free
> The Albatross fell off, and sank
> Like lead into the sea.

Well, I wasn't praying, exactly, or not what I had always thought of as praying. Unless listening to a too-long-ignored inner voice could be called prayer.

Ever since that summer at Glory Cottage I had always thought that knowing Lucien's secret would be the equivalent of finding the charmed thread which alone would be able to guide me through the maze. As though this secret alone could show me how to cope with the baffling business of life in the adult world. But in spite of all that I had learned – far far more than I had ever expected – I was no nearer to finding the key to it at all.

Or maybe the truth was that the key had been so close to hand that I had overlooked it all this time.

I examined Owen carefully: his precisely chiselled profile, the stubborn set of his mouth, the streaky fair hair swept back from his forehead. For years I had been so obsessed with my own needs and failings I had been blind to his.

I said, 'Owen, how important is Dinah?'

He glanced at me nastily, then looked away again. 'That depends,' he said. 'She's in no hurry to end it. She and Aidan have always had an open marriage, apparently. The only problem was that what with Duncan and one thing and another, all the openness so far has been on Aidan's side. She's glad to even up the score. And Rob? You were with Rob, weren't you?'

I nodded. Owen said, 'I was afraid of that. It's odd, isn't it, when your worst fears are realised? There was always the doubt in my mind that Rob had been your first choice. That I just filled an empty space.'

I stared at him in amazement, before saying, 'No. Whatever existed between me and Rob ended ten years ago. I only had to finish it.'

'It hardly matters, now.'

His words were so bleak and final, they sounded like a sentence of execution. I could feel the familiar comforting anger rising up inside me, but I struggled to control it. The darkness was all around and I had only words with which to fight it.

'Was there ever a time when you loved me, Owen? I mean, really loved me?'

His face was cold. 'What's all this about, Jane? It's too late for games now.'

A week ago I would have heard only the hostility in his voice; now, behind all that, I heard the pain and despair.

'It's not a game. It's important. We're going to have to decide . . . I need to know, Owen. Did you just feel sorry for me? Was it only because of Lucien?'

'Lucien? What the hell did Lucien have to do with anything?'

'Because I thought . . . you see, I'd always assumed that . . . I always thought you'd only married me to be kind.'

There was no doubting the look of absolute disbelief that he turned on me now. 'Kind? Why the hell would I want to be kind? Don't be daft, Jane.'

'Yes, stupid, that's what Esme said.'

'Esme?'

'It doesn't matter. So why did you marry me?'

'Christ, Jane, you do choose your moments. I suppose there must have been a reason. Maybe I just thought I loved you.'

'Why?'

'I agree that just at present it does seem an unlikely and illogical sensation, but at that time I suppose it must have made some kind of sense.' He examined me closely, then said, 'You really do want to know, don't you? Why, Jane? So that you can leave here with your vanity satisfied?'

'No—'

He turned away again with a bitter laugh. 'Yes, I do remember now. Ridiculous though it may sound, I rather believe it was your energy I loved. Your energy and your anger. Next to you, the rest of the world always seemed torpid. Torpid and dull. But recently I've found myself longing for a little dullness—'

'Owen, stop.' I could see that I had driven him to suffer from the Eric syndrome, and I was desperate not to let him say anything that would carry us past the point of no return. 'Owen, look, I think I may have got things wrong. I mean – oh, hell, I'm not very good at this . . .' An understatement if ever there was one. This was the point at which I was supposed to apologise for about a thousand different failings and misunderstandings, but despite my determination to make amends, I wasn't yet ready for that. 'I think maybe we're giving up too easily. I don't see why it all has to end just because we've made some mistakes. We can make a success of the nursery, I know we can. And so do you. You've said so a hundred times. All we have to do is want it enough. We can learn from our mistakes.'

'We've certainly made plenty.'

'But if I really helped.'

Still he wasn't looking at me. He ran a finger along one of the wooden struts of the glasshouse. 'And what about us?' his voice was tight with suppressed feeling.

I took a deep breath. 'I think we should try again. I want it to work.'

'I see.'

From across the garden came the sound of children's voices. Billy, cheeks glowing with health, his woolly hat askew, was running ahead. Laura had the white rabbit in her arms and was following more sedately at Dinah's side. Dinah, trim in her waxed jacket and jaunty cap, appeared to be carrying a tray of something that had been covered with a chequered cloth.

'Oh God,' Owen groaned. 'Another bloody freezer dinner.'

I began to see a glimmer of hope.

I said, 'I'm sure we can make it work.'

'Why the sudden change? Is it because of the children?'

I considered this as I watched them pause briefly in their erratic progress across the garden. Billy had squatted down to pick up and examine a spent rocket that must have fallen there the previous evening. The love I felt for our two children was so strong it had become a kind of hurting. It would have been so easy to shelter behind the alibi of family life.

'No,' I said at last, 'I want it to work because of me. Because of us.'

He turned to face me at last, but his face was still shadowed with a frown. 'Why?' he asked.

'Because . . .' I was floundering desperately. 'Because it's important, of course. Because I don't want it to fail. We've known each other for so long and been through such a lot and it would be the most terrible waste to end it now and . . . oh, hell. Because I bloody love you, Owen. I always have done, deep down, I just haven't been very good at showing it, that's all. And even if it's all spoiled and it's too late then I still want you to know, because I love you.'

Ha, I thought. Take that, black hole and smothering darkness.

My eyes filled with tears. I could almost imagine that Lucien might have applauded my sudden, unexpected burst of courage. I wondered then if perhaps this was my own fifth secret. Perhaps everyone has one, I thought. Lucien carried the secret of our father, Faith had closed the door on her earlier self, John, Esme . . . no one was exempt. Maybe even Mrs Wicks hid a mystery more profound than the possibility of webbed feet, though that relatively trivial puzzle had ultimately proved the only one still unsolved. But that did not concern me now. All that mattered now was my own secret, the knowledge that I wanted above all else to stay with this man who had once offered me his love.

So I said it again, 'I love you, Owen.'

The children burst into the glasshouse on a wave of excitement. Laura was clinging to the rabbit who struggled valiantly to escape. Billy was waving the spent rocket in triumph. At the sight of me, my face red and streaked with unaccustomed tears, they stopped suddenly. Billy accidentally poked the rabbit with his rocket stick and Snowy-ten made a huge effort and lunged for freedom.

Owen barely noticed the interruption. 'Are you sure about this, Jane? It isn't just a reaction to finding out about your father? Some kind of delayed shock?'

'I'm absolutely certain. You don't think it's too late, do you?'

Dinah, who was now within earshot, was listening with a wholly satisfying expression of disappointment souring her amiable face. Laura and Billy were watching us intently, perhaps understanding the significance, though not the details, of what we were saying.

Owen frowned. 'I don't know,' he said at length. He ran his fingers through his hair so that it stood up in peaks. His shoulders were still hunched and tense, but there was the trace of a smile around his eyes as he examined my face, as though he was about to begin a journey back from a great distance away. 'We'll just have to find out.'

He raised his arms slightly, in a tentative gesture of welcome.